ROBERT RADCLIFFE

FREEFALL

HEAD of ZEUS

9 7 5 3 1 2 4 6 8

A catalogue record for this book is available
from the British Library.

ISBN (PB) 9781784973889
ISBN (E) 9781784973858

Typeset by Ben Cracknell Studios

Printed and bound by CPI Group (UK) Ltd,
Croydon, CR0 4YY

Head of Zeus Ltd
First Floor East
5–8 Hardwick Street
London EC1R 4RG

WWW.HEADOFZEUS.COM

FREEFALL

Robert Radcliffe was born and educated in London.
A journalist and advertising copywriter, he also
spent ten years flying as a commercial pilot.

His first novel, *A Ship Called Hope*, was published
in 1994. In 1997 he sold his house and business and
moved to a cottage in France to write. The result
was *The Lazarus Child*, a book that sold more than
a million copies worldwide.

In 2002 he published *Under an English Heaven*
which was a *Sunday Times* top ten bestseller. This
was followed by *Upon Dark Waters* (2004), *Across
the Blood-Red Skies* (2009), *Dambuster* (2011),
Beneath Another Sun (2012) and *Airborne* (2017).
Other works include theatre drama and a BBC radio
play. *Freefall* (2018) is his ninth novel.

Robert and his wife Kate, a teacher,
live in Suffolk.

For my brother, John, and my sisters, Judith and Deborah

CHAPTER 1

At 6 p.m. Lieutenant Charteris appeared round the door of the hut. 'It's on, boys,' he said breathlessly, 'get your stuff together.'

Heads shook knowingly; wry smiles were exchanged.

'Aye aye, sir,' someone sighed, 'soon as I finish my newspaper.'

'Yes and I've darned my socks.'

'I mean it!' Charteris protested, 'it's really happening. Tonight!'

'That's what they said last night.'

'And the night before, and the one before that.'

'Yes, but this time it's true. Listen!' He opened the door wider. Beyond it the moonlit field lay motionless.

'Listen to what? I cannae hear a thing!'

Charteris grinned. 'Precisely!'

'So...'

'The wind.' Theo sat forward. 'It's gone.'

'So it has.'

'Christ, boys, it's on!'

Fifteen minutes later the 120 Scotsmen of C Company, the 2nd Parachute Battalion, were crammed aboard army buses, singing lustily as they lurched along narrow Wiltshire roads to the aerodrome at Thruxton. There they disembarked to find twelve black-painted Whitley bombers dispersed around the perimeter being prepared for flight. Fuel bowsers hurried to

1

and fro, engineers kicked tyres and screwed down cowlings, flight crews checked maps, radios, signal flares and code books, while gunners loaded and tested their weapons. Meanwhile, beneath each bomber, ground crews carefully manhandled equipment canisters into the Whitleys' bomb bays, and attached their parachute lines ready for release over the target.

A wan-looking airman in an RAF greatcoat was watching proceedings to one side.

Theo rubbed his hands against the cold. 'All right, Charlie?' he asked him, although it came out as *a-reet*.

'Yes, thanks. Looks like we're really going, doesn't it?'

'It does rather.'

'Can't quite believe it. All that running around on cliffs and messing about in boats, I think I persuaded myself it wasn't actually, you know, real.'

'I know what you mean.'

'Now I'm scared stiff I'll mess everything up. For everyone.'

'You won't, you'll be fine.' Theo regarded the airman. Inserted late into the team as a 'technical expert', Charlie Cox was the typical boffin, intense, nervy, bespectacled – and slight, child-like in size compared to the huge Scotsmen noisily disembarking from the buses around them. Theo had been told to stay close to Cox. A few minutes later he finally learned why.

'Well, good evening, everyone!' Major Frost, standing on a chair, grinned broadly at his men, ranged in an attentive semi-circle before him. They were assembled in one of Thruxton's cavernous hangars; no one outside C Company had been allowed in, and Company Sergeant Major Strachan had locked the door shut behind them. Up to that moment, only Frost and his officers knew details of the assignment they were tasked with; now it was time to tell the men who would carry it out.

2

'Thank you for your patience this week. I know how difficult it has been, especially having trained so hard.' Frost checked his watch. 'But in two hours from now we will have embarked upon a mission of great importance. Its code name is Operation Biting, and its aim is to seize a radar facility belonging to the enemy. This facility sits on a cliff on the coast of Normandy; our job is to secure it and the area around it, so that our RAF radio technician, Sergeant Cox here, can dismantle it and bring key components back home for analysis.' A hundred pairs of eyes turned on Cox who forced a wan grin. 'Now, we need not trouble ourselves with the technicalities, our role is to deal with the enemy, but let me assure you that success will save thousands of Allied lives. Also may I remind you this is the first operation ever assigned to our battalion, and therefore a great honour and responsibility.'

Theo glanced at the men around him, listening to their leader in rapt silence. Almost all were Scotsmen, many still wearing their Highland insignia, in defiance of regulation: bobble hats, Glengarry caps, tam-o'-shanters, some displaying the coloured 'hackles' of their regiment – he saw Black Watch, Seaforths, Camerons, Argylls, Gordons, and was reminded of an insane attack against tanks in France, four boys charging down a lane to their deaths, and an entire division desperately fighting for its life. At home in Scotland these men would squabble like feral cats, but in battle he'd seen them die gladly for one another. It's what made them so special.

'... we go in by RAF and we come out by Royal Navy,' Frost was saying. 'We operate in four groups, exactly as trained, and deploy according to known enemy disposition.' He stepped off the chair to pull a sheet from a blackboard, revealing a chalk-drawn map. 'This is our target, the radar unit, close to the cliff edge here. It's manned by Luftwaffe technicians who may be armed. Lieutenant

Vernon's team, which includes Sergeant Cox and our German speaker Trickey, will take it. Oh, and there's a three-hundred-foot drop over the edge so watch your step! A quarter-mile north is the radar-receiving building and guardhouse, which is where the main enemy concentration is expected, so Lieutenant Timothy and his group will deploy there to stop anyone approaching. Leading south from the radar unit is our exit route, which is a steep footpath down to the beach area. Intelligence suggests this is guarded by a second enemy detachment located in this blockhouse down on the shore, with more enemy garrisoned in the village of Bruneval just inland from the blockhouse. So Captain Ross and Lieutenant Charteris will bring their teams there and secure the beach for the navy landing craft to pick us up. Meanwhile, my team will oversee operations, help with the radar unit and mop up as required. The DZ is a quarter-mile inland from the radar station, here behind these trees. After the drop we all assemble there, then take up our positions as stealthily as possible. The signal to commence attack will be four blasts on my whistle. We must be off the beach by oh three hundred hours latest, our drop time is midnight, so we emplane at twenty-one hundred.'

Frost concluded with a goodwill message from their divisional commander, General Browning; then everyone was told to disperse to their groups for more detailed instructions. Theo waited with Cox until they were summoned forward.

'All set, Sergeant?' Frost asked Cox.

'Yes, sir, I… I think so.'

'Trolley ready, tool kit packed?'

'Yes, sir. Checked everything myself.'

'Good man.' Frost glanced at Cox's uniform, a lone patch of blue amid a sea of khaki. 'I'm sorry we couldn't fix you up as a temporary Para, Cox. I tried, you know, but it's RAF regulations apparently.'

4

'It's all right, sir, I don't mind.'

Frost dismissed him and then turned to Theo. 'Will he be all right, Trickey? He looks like a rabbit caught in headlights.'

'It's just nerves, sir. I think he'll be fine.'

'He'd better. Everything depends on him.'

'It's the jump. That and the responsibility. He'll be better once he lands and starts work.'

'Let's hope so. Now listen. Stick to him like glue. Your interpreting services will be needed at the radar unit, sorting out the Jerry technicians and so on – ideally we'd like to nab a couple if possible. But I can't emphasize enough the importance of speed, for we must get off that cliff before they call up reinforcements. Boffin types like Cox get bogged down at the slightest thing, so just make sure he gets the guts out of the blasted apparatus quickly, then get it and him down to the beach, you got that?'

'Yes, sir.'

'Good.' Frost passed a hand over his face. His eyes were bloodshot, his face fatigued; he looked weary and old beyond his twenty-nine years. Five consecutive days and nights this ordeal had been going on. And many weeks of training before that. To cap it all the final dress rehearsal, which had involved scrambling over a Dorset cliff in pitch darkness to be picked up by navy landing craft, had been absolute chaos, with men getting lost in the dark, several falling and injuring themselves, and the navy landing at the wrong beach. Now this. Five times the mission had been set and then cancelled, five days of careful preparation and nail-biting anticipation, only to receive the 'cancelled-due-weather' phone call at the last moment. Then today he'd been told the window had finally closed, that the February tides were now wrong and the moon too weak to mount the operation. After all the effort it was heartbreaking, and yet secretly a relief, and he'd begun preparing to stand everyone down, even allowing himself the notion of a weekend's quiet leave to recover. Then suddenly a higher authority intervened, possibly Churchill himself; the telephone rang and he was told one final go might be attempted, *if* the weather cleared. All afternoon he had waited, and slowly, impossibly, the winter clouds parted, the mist melted and the wind dropped to a zephyr. 'Fancy a crack at it, Johnny?' General Browning had quipped over the phone at teatime. 'Good luck, and make sure you're home for breakfast!'

'The RAF uniform, Theo,' Frost was saying, 'I wanted Cox added as an extra, you know, with false name and Para uniform and everything. In case it all went wrong and we got captured. At least he'd have a chance if he looked like one of us.'

'Yes, sir.'

'But the point is, if it does all go wrong, the War Office is adamant.'

'About what, sir?'

'He has too much technical knowledge. About our radar, our countermeasures, our research and development.'

'Sir?'

'So he can't be taken alive, Theo. Under any circumstances. Do you understand?'

As part of HQ section, he and Cox rode in Frost's Whitley. Cumbersome and heavy in their jumping gear, they queued to board while C Company's bagpipe player, Piper Ewing, strode back and forth playing Highland marches for the Scotsmen; then they struggled inside and settled themselves near the front, sprawling on to the freezing metal of the fuselage floor. There they waited with the rest of the stick, while their leader fussed between aircraft making last-minute checks. Finally all was ready and Frost boarded, the door was sealed shut, and a minute later the engines thundered to life.

'Everybody OK?' Frost called cheerfully. Nods and thumbs up were exchanged as, bulky in his jumping smock and harness, Frost clambered forward and took his position behind the pilot. Now that the mission was actually under way he, like everyone, felt immeasurably better.

He had first learned of Operation Biting eight weeks earlier, shortly after Christmas 1941. First Parachute Brigade was barely formed, he was a lowly captain and hadn't even completed his jump training, when suddenly he was promoted to Major and given command of 2nd Battalion's C Company – a post he greatly coveted. The only problem was his friend Philip Teichman was commanding C Company, but got moved to B Company, which put a strain on their friendship. Then came rumours of a mission. Everyone assumed 1st Battalion would be assigned – after all, 1st Battalion had formed first, it held the original paratroops from 2 Commando, it had mounted Operation Colossus, it was proven, ready and able. But for some reason the mission went to 2nd Battalion and Frost's Scottish C Company. Frost was astonished, 1st Battalion insulted, and Philip so angry that he demanded they see the brigadier. *He* should command the Jocks, he insisted to Brigadier Gale, he knew them, had worked and trained with them, and brought them to readiness.

'Yes,' Frost conceded, 'but I formed C Company, I interviewed and chose them, and in the short time I've led them have earned their trust and loyalty. In any case,' he added carefully, 'like it or not, I am now their commander.'

'But, Johnny' – Philip then played his ace – 'you're not even qualified to jump.'

Gale compromised. C Company would go to Wiltshire to start training for the mission. Philip would go with it. Frost, still not fully recovered from his balloon-jumping injury, was given one week to complete his training. If he succeeded the mission was his, if not it would go to Teichman. Frost packed his bags and headed for Ringway. It was midwinter, the weather foul, and for four days he sat around seething with impatience, praying for it to clear. On the fifth day it did clear, but a backlog of jumpers filled the queue ahead of him. Mysteriously he was pulled out and sent to the front, and over the next twenty-four hours he threw himself from the Whitley five times, qualified, grabbed his parachute wings and caught the train to Wiltshire. Teichman handed him command of C Company with barely a word.

The flight from Thruxton was noisy, smooth but cold. Having formed up, the twelve aircraft set course over the black waters of the Channel, Theo's stick huddling down in the fuselage wrapped in blankets for warmth. Some had brought flasks or newspapers, a few dozed, most lay in contemplative silence. Cox, wide-eyed, sat nervously hugging his knees.

'Why do they call you tricky?' he asked Theo.

'Well, it's my name, Charlie.'

'Oh. Where are you from?'

'It's um, it's called South Tyrol. In the Alps. And you?'

'Stevenage.'

An hour passed. Frost busied himself checking his maps and consulting the pilots. After a while he came back to sit beside Theo and grinned. 'Was it like this on Colossus?'

Theo thought back. The long climb out from Malta, the sea crossing to Sicily, then up Italy's west coast, the icy Apennines glinting white in the moonlight. Exactly a year ago. 'Colder, sir. And longer.'

'Let's hope we have better luck getting away.'

Another thirty minutes passed, then came a shout from the pilot: 'Coast ahead!' At the same moment bright flashes burst outside as flak started up, light and inaccurate, but enough to jostle the Whitley and rouse the men. They unbolted the hatch from the floor; the icy gale whirled, below slid white surf, a strip of pale beach, a chalky cliff, then fields and heathland dusted with snow. The red light came on; they shuffled down the fuselage, clipping on static lines, fastening helmets, checking weapons. Frost was to go first, Theo last, immediately behind Cox, who turned to him wide-eyed with apprehension.

'Theo?'

'Arms tucked, Charlie. Knees bent like we practised. Everything'll be fine.'

Suddenly the green light flashed and they were going, vanishing from sight like dropped toys. Frost went, then seven more in quick succession, Cox and Theo shuffling down the fuselage after them. Cox reached the hole, swung his legs over, stared into the abyss and froze.

'Go, Charlie!' Theo shoved him, two-handed, over the edge, then leaped after, catching his shoulder a glancing blow and tumbling badly, gasping in the cold, until the familiar jerk righted him and he was floating serenely earthwards. Overhead more Whitleys rumbled, pouring jumpers. He looked down for his stick: Charlie was below and to his left, the others beyond in a neat receding line. Beneath lay the snowy cliff top, the line of trees, the DZ, the guardhouse, and the little circle marking the radar itself, all exactly as on the blackboard at Thruxton. The black shadow of the trees slid by, then the ground was rushing up; he braced, tucked and rolled. The impact winded him but swiftly he was up, the parachute released and he was hurrying to help Cox.

'We made it!' Charlie was struggling with his harness.

'Yes, come on, let's find your tools.'

They helped gather the weapons and equipment, then Sergeant

Major Strachan formed them up, his voice unusually muted in the moonlight. Incredibly, now the Whitleys were gone, there was no sound, no sirens or alarms, no shouts or barking dogs, and no gunfire. But there was a problem.

'Charteris's stick didn't make it,' Frost told them. 'Missed the drop or something. They were to neutralize the village and help Ross secure the beach, but we'll just have to manage without them. You all know what to do. Keep quiet until you hear my signal. Let's get on with it.'

They edged their way through the trees towards the sound of distant surf. The sky was clear, the moon still bright. Reaching open heathland they saw the main guardhouse amid farm buildings to their right, and a second villa-style house straight ahead. Beyond that, housed in a bunker close to the cliff edge, the ten-foot curve of the radar dish rose against the skyline, while to their left the terrain sloped steeply down towards the village and beach. The parties split up: Timothy's made for the guardhouse, Frost the villa, Ross for the beach, while Theo and Cox followed Vernon's group to the radar, awkwardly pushing a folding trolley loaded with Cox's tools and equipment. At thirty yards Vernon gestured everyone down and they knelt in the snow to wait. A minute later Frost's whistle pierced the night; instantly shooting and shouts broke out in several directions.

'Come on!' Brandishing his revolver, Vernon charged the bunker, seven bellowing Scotsmen in his wake. As they drew near two figures emerged. One froze, arms raised high, while the second, stumbling backwards in panic, vanished from sight with a strangled cry.

'Christ, he's gone over!'

'Leave it! Right, everyone, defensive positions round the bunker. Sing out if you see anything. Cox, you get to work.

10

McHugh, search this Jerry. Trickey, check the cliff for the other one.'

Theo crept forward, probing the cliff top with his boot, the night air smelling of gorse and sea-kelp. Bursts of gunfire rose from the guardhouse to his right, which meant Lieutenant Timothy's group was engaging the enemy, while behind came the crack of a grenade from Frost's party. Sinking to his knees, he reached the brink and peered giddily over. Surf seethed far below; he glimpsed a necklace of white breakers, a gull eyeing him from a ledge, and a figure clinging to a bush, not ten feet away.

'*Hilf mir!*' it whimpered.

'Can you climb up?' he asked, in German.

'*Nein!*'

'Yes you can. Use the bush, there, then reach up for my hand.'

Two minutes later he was back at the bunker. 'His name's Denkmann,' he told Vernon, 'he's a radio technician from Stuttgart.'

'The other's a techie too. Ask them about the garrison, and troops down in the village.'

Theo asked. 'They don't know, they were only posted here last week. Denkmann thinks there may be fifty in the village and another fifty or so in the guardhouse.'

'Christ, then it's going to get busy up here. And where the hell's Charteris when you need him.' As if on cue a rapid burst of shooting came from their right. 'That'll be Ross trying for the beach, we must hurry while—'

A flash lit the night, then a second, blinding white, bathing the whole dish like a floodlight.

'What the... Trickey, get down there and tell him to stop!'

Cox was behind a thin curtain, sitting on a stool before a control console, camera in hand. 'Hello, Theo, just look at this!

Marvellous stuff, Telefunken, top quality. Still warm too – they must have only just switched it off.'

'That's good, Charlie, but—'

'I'll just take a few more snaps then we'll start dismantling.'

Theo grabbed the camera. 'No, Charlie! The flashes.'

'Can you see them?'

'Every German for miles can see them!'

'But, Theo—'

Fresh gunfire rattled nearby, more sustained, closer and louder as bullets ricocheted from the dish. Scottish oaths followed, then thunderous shooting overhead as Vernon's party returned fire.

'Let's get on with it, Charlie.'

'Yes. Right. Pass me that long-handled screwdriver.'

They worked for several minutes, Charlie dismantling while Theo passed tools and held the torch. A collection of smaller components gradually accumulated in the trolley, but the main prize, a large oblong box Charlie called the pulse gear, together with the control console and transmitter, remained stubbornly fixed. And all the while the sounds of warfare grew louder and more intense. Bullets impacted the bunker, more shouting was heard, then John Frost himself appeared at the curtain, Sten gun in hand.

'How's it going, Cox?'

'Rather slowly, sir, I'm afraid. It's modular, you see, which is clever engineering, but taking it apart is proving—'

'Use a bloody crowbar then!' Frost panted. 'Or an axe if you have to. We're outnumbered, taking casualties, and Jerry's bringing in reinforcements. So we're getting off this cliff in five minutes, and not a minute more. You got that?'

And he was gone. Theo allowed Charlie a further minute with screwdriver and spanner but then, seeing he was getting nowhere, grabbed a crowbar from the trolley and wrenched the offending module from its base by force.

'Theo, no!'

'Sorry, Charlie, no time. What's next?'

'Oh, well, the transmitter unit, I suppose, but do be careful with—'

Five minutes later they were hauling the heavily laden trolley up into the moonlight.

'About bloody time!' Vernon greeted them. 'Up here quick. Jerry's advancing from the guardhouse; we're to fall back to the footpath and cover Timothy's withdrawal. Trickey, tell the prisoners to behave; they're coming too.'

They set off, dragging and pushing the trolley over the tussocked ground while Vernon's men returned fire on the advancing Germans. Soon they were descending, then dropping into cover behind a ridge where they met Sergeant Major Strachan and his men. 'Over here, lads!' A defensive position soon formed; more Highlanders appeared, running in from Timothy's group, and Frost's, some injured among them. Lastly Frost himself.

'Where's Ross? Is the beach secured?'

'We don't know,' Strachan replied. 'I cannae raise anyone on the radio. It's all to pot down there.'

As if to confirm it, a furious exchange of shooting rose from below, rifle fire, the stutter of Stens, then heavier German machine guns and the crack and crump of grenades. A lull followed, then a hoarse shout.

'Don't come down!' Ross cried. 'Beach not secure!'

Frost cupped his hands. 'What about the boats?'

A poignant pause.

'No boats.'

Timothy appeared, hurrying over the ridge with the last of his men. 'Sir, a lorryload of Jerrys arrived at the guardhouse. One section made for the villa – we held them off best we could... McIntyre's dead.'

'All right.' For a second, two seconds, Frost's expression in the moonlight was indecisive, and close to despair. Then he was striding towards Theo. 'All right. We've one chance. Everyone to me. We're attacking.'

'Attacking upward?' Timothy grinned. 'Or downward?'

'Up. We must buy time for Ross to secure the beach, so we charge the villa with everything we've got. With luck we'll catch Jerry on the hop and push him back to the guardhouse. Get ready. Wait for my signal.' He drew his service revolver and handed it to Theo. 'Stay here with Cox and the prisoners,' he murmured. 'This is for, in case, you know...'

Nodding blankly, Theo dropped the pistol in the pocket of his smock, then watched as Frost, armed with Sten gun and flanked by Highlanders, crept up the side of the ridge, his whistle ready in his mouth.

Just then they all heard it: a yell, from far up the valley beyond the village. More the echo of a yell, followed by others, primal, blood-chilling, like distant wild animals. Or Scotsmen charging tanks.

'My God, that's Seaforths!' Strachan exclaimed. 'That's Charteris!'

'And not a moment too soon.' Frost peered up the valley. 'Come on. He'll need time to link up with Ross – we charge the villa, push Jerry back, then head down to join them.' With that he blew his whistle and scrambled over the ridge.

Twenty minutes later C Company was assembled on the beach below the cliffs. Charteris's stick had been dropped in the wrong valley, his pilot thrown by the flak, so they'd had to tramp a mile across unknown countryside to reach Bruneval, where they ousted the small garrison before linking up with Ross's team to neutralize the blockhouse. Frost's feint on the villa also succeeded, with the Germans falling back to the guardhouse to regroup. Now everyone was together on the beach, the village and shoreline were secure, pickets guarded the perimeter, the injured were attended to, and Charlie Cox and his precious cargo were safely secreted beneath the cliff.

But the Scotsmen's problems were far from over. Headlights had been seen heading towards Bruneval, reinforcements for the garrison busy regrouping in the village. And three hundred feet above, Germans were massing along the cliff edge, trying to snipe at them with their rifles. Rocks and boulders were being hurled down, soon followed by the first grenades. Worst of all, despite repeated urgent radio calls and the firing of emergency signal flares, there was no sign of the Royal Navy.

'Where the bloody hell are they?' Frost stood at the water's edge, one foot on an upturned rowing boat. Clouds were now obscuring the moon, and fine mist wafted over the water like smoke. 'Bastards should've been in twenty minutes ago.'

'Aye,' Strachan said, 'and in another twenty it'll be too late.'

A thump came from the direction of the blockhouse. They both turned: a moment later a shell exploded not twenty yards away, flinging sand and shingle high into the air.

'That's mortar. Now we're for it!'

'Yes and we can't stay here. Fan the men out, Sarnt Major, and prepare to assault that blockhouse. We've got to get off this beach!'

'Aye, sir, only—'

Shots rang out from a machine gun above, sparks flew at their feet, then Strachan reeled, his hands at his belly, and slumped at Frost's feet.

'Medic! Medic over here, quick! And get back, everyone, under cover of the cliffs!'

But there was little cover under the cliffs, and with rifle fire and grenades raining down on them from above, and the flash of gunfire now visible in both directions along the beach, and mortar shells added to the mix, chances of a successful break-out were now zero. All they could do was form a defensive ring around their injured and shoot back as best they could.

Frost approached Theo. He was on one knee, sighting his rifle along the beach. Behind him Cox and his trolley were pushed flat against the cliff.

'Pistol, Trickey.'

Theo hesitated. 'Sir, couldn't we—'

'It's all right. I'll do it. Give me the pistol.'

'That old rowing boat there, sir. Maybe we could get Charlie and his gear aboard it. With a strong rower or two...'

'Give me the damn pistol, Private!'

'BOATS!'

Everyone turned.

'Boats! Look in the mist there!'

'It is too! It's the landing craft!'

'Thank Christ!'

'Tardy bloody Sassenachs!'

'God bless the ruddy navy!'

Their extraction was a disorderly rout. The landing craft were supposed to approach the beach in a rehearsed sequence, but in their haste came storming ashore all at once. Chaos ensued. Armed sailors aboard the landing craft to provide covering fire began shooting at anything that moved, including fleeing Scotsmen. The Paras failed to adhere to embarkation orders, but simply dropped everything and ran for the nearest boat. Vernon's team grabbed Cox and his trolley and threw him aboard one landing craft, the badly injured Strachan, roaring incoherently, was manhandled into another, Theo found himself escorting the two German technicians through chest-deep seas to a third, while Frost's boat became stranded on rocks, so he had to jump out and help push it off. Everyone was muddled up, there was shouting and confusion, but with the tide falling and Germans advancing from all directions there was no time for orders, or even a proper roll call. With a final anxious scan of the beach and bullets whining overhead, Frost gave the word, the coxswains threw their engines into reverse, backed away the boats, and turned for home.

Operation Biting was over.

CHAPTER 2

Dawn found them in mid-Channel, transferred aboard motor patrol boats for the journey to Portsmouth. The sea was rough, the boats overcrowded, the exhausted Scotsmen hunched into whatever spaces they could find and trying to rest. But the freezing cold and rolling motion denied them sleep, and many were sick – including Theo's hapless Germans, who, crouching dog-like on the gratings, moaned and vomited in misery. With the coming of daylight the threat of aerial retaliation also became a worry and sure enough alarm spread suddenly when a klaxon went off and shouts of 'Aircraft!' were heard from above. Then the shouts turned to cheers and word went round that a squadron of Spitfires had appeared, circling overhead for protection. And as the day wore on their little flotilla began to grow, joined firstly by a destroyer and escort, then a pod of motor torpedo boats which sped round them waving and cheering, then the troop carrier *Prins Albert*, until by the time they finally docked at Portsmouth late in the afternoon they had amassed a minor armada of supporters. Wearily they stumbled ashore to assemble on the dockside; then Frost and his officers were led off for debriefings, the Germans taken into custody, and Charlie Cox whisked away, together with his precious cargo. Theo and the rest of C Company meanwhile clumped aboard navy buses to be driven back to their Wiltshire barracks and the cramped huts they'd left just twenty-four hours earlier, there to collapse into bed.

He was awoken late the following morning by Lieutenant Charteris bursting through the door brandishing newspapers.

'Look, chaps, we're famous!'

'Leave us alone.'

'I'm still a-sleeping.'

'Anyone got a ciggie?'

'No, it's front-page national news, there's photos and everything. Trickey, look!'

Theo struggled to bleary wakefulness, the *Sunday Express* thrust before him. 'Um, yes, so it is. That's Major Frost, isn't it?'

'Yes and there's more!' Charteris sat on Theo's bed reading out the details, which focused entirely on the success of the mission, and omitting any hint of its near disaster. Churchill was quoted praising their courage and daring, Charlie Cox's booty was already yielding vital information, Germany had been *humbled and humiliated*, while all Britain cheered. That six men had failed to make the boats and been left stranded, seven were injured, while two, Privates Scott and McIntyre, had been killed, was not mentioned. Much weaponry and equipment had been abandoned too, Charteris murmured, including the radios, which were new and secret. 'And Brigade isn't happy about that!'

'What about the boats?' Theo asked. 'Why were they so late picking us up?'

'Jerry patrol boat sniffing about offshore apparently. Navy boys couldn't come near until it cleared off.'

'But another few minutes...'

'And we wouldn't have made it.'

'No.'

Charteris lowered his voice. 'And Charlie Cox would be dead.'

Theo said nothing.

'Could you have done it, Trickey?' Charteris whispered. 'I know what your orders were. Could you? Actually shoot him dead in cold blood?'

'It's... I find it unthinkable.'

'Me too. Thank God it wasn't my problem.'

'No.' He glanced at Charteris, at twenty the youngest officer on the raid. He'd had a difficult night too – yet come through well. 'It was a great relief, I must say, up on the cliff, when we heard you coming at last.'

'It was a relief to get there! But you know I did a damn stupid thing.'

'Oh?'

'Charging down the lane from the village with my section, I came upon this hut. Without thinking I just kicked open the door and stormed in. Six Jerries, fully armed, sitting there wide-eyed with surprise, staring at me, a lone Tommy with a pistol. Bloody idiot. Fortunately the others arrived before they could gather their wits.'

C Company celebrated, long and hard as only Scotsmen can. Firstly around their Wiltshire training base, then back at Hardwick and its environs. And everywhere they went they were fêted, for suddenly the Paras were famous. This unknown corps of oddities, men the public knew little of and regular soldiers looked on as outlandish, were now respected and admired as heroes, symbolizing Britishness itself, grit and daring and defiance in the face of overwhelming odds. It did not matter if you had actually taken part in Operation Biting or not: parachute wings on your uniform guaranteed you handshakes in the street, back-slaps on the bus, and free drinks in the pub.

Heady stuff. And inevitably the Jocks over-indulged. Trained warriors at peak fitness swiftly grow troublesome with enforced inaction, especially Scottish ones, and before long rumours of fighting and drunkenness were circulating, then petty larceny, damage to property and trouble with the local constabulary. Soon the Hardwick guardhouse was filling and the Military Police closing in. Rein in these men, came the warning from above, or arrests will follow. So with no new operations in the pipeline and nothing to train for, C Company was stood down and sent on leave.

Theo's first day of holiday was not as imagined. He had intended to head straight for Kingston and the boarding house where his mother lived, but at the last minute decided on a diversion to Wandsworth, the location of Britain's largest prison. He went there on impulse, arriving at the fortress-like entrance in time for visiting, but with no prior arrangement. 'Who are you and why are you here?' the guards asked, studying their lists. I don't know, he wanted to say, maybe it's to do with a scientist, and a moonlit beach, and a pistol in my pocket. 'No matter,' they said, winking at his insignia, 'dump your kitbag and we'll sort something.' So he waited, standing amid jostling crowds of relatives, mostly women, who cracked jokes and teased him cheekily.

'Saw you parachute lads in the paper,' one told him, 'bloomin' gorgeous!'

'You can drop in on me any time!' said another. At her side a small boy stared in awe.

'Thank you,' Theo replied shyly.

After processing they were admitted to a cavernous hall smelling of cabbage, and set out with tables and chairs. Around him the womenfolk settled themselves with accustomed ease, extracting newspapers, cigarettes and knitting from their bags while their children ran about playing. He took a seat, watching them, and trying to ignore the knot of tension in his stomach. Minutes passed, then doors opened and guards entered, followed by men in prison garb who made their unhurried way between the tables towards their loved ones. Among them, short and spare, with watchful eyes and slicked-back hair, was his father, Victor Trickey.

'Fancy this,' Victor said, pulling out a chair, 'hail the conquering hero. Didn't expect to be seeing you.'

'No, well, after last time...'

'Had to come back and tidy up some loose ends?'

'Something like that.'

'Thought so. Better be quick, mind you, can't stay long.'

Theo watched as Victor seated himself, took out a tin and began rolling a cigarette. His air was proprietorial, his relaxed gaze wandering the room, noting the guards, nodding at other prisoners, lingering on their wives and girlfriends. In his late forties, slight of stature with pallid complexion and nicotine-stained fingers, he did not embody the imagined hero of Theo's childhood. If that person ever existed.

He'd first heard of Victor's existence from Captain Grant, his special ops handler at Baker Street. Returning from his Italian adventures the previous autumn he'd been summoned for a debrief on Operation Colossus and his contact with the Action Party partisans in Italy. During the interview, which was long and exhaustive, he learned firstly that his mother Carla had been freed from internment, and secondly that his father was not dead, but alive and well and living barely five miles from Kingston. Albeit in prison. This revelation left him shocked and bewildered and for some weeks he did nothing with it, not even telling Carla. Eventually though, unable to suppress his curiosity, he visited Victor, only to find he felt no connection with the louche stranger sitting before him, no bond, no kindred spirit, not the slightest sense of shared lineage. They didn't even look alike. Victor too seemed unmoved by the reunion, smirking and smoking in bemusement, so after a few minutes and with a chasm of silence yawning between them, Theo fled, leaving his many questions unasked.

Victor blew smoke, glancing at a large wall clock. 'Snout?'

'I'm sorry?'

'To-bac-co.'

'No, um, no, thank you, I don't.'

'I *meant*, did you bring me any!'

'Oh, no I didn't, sorry.'

'Typical.'

'Ah. I wonder, could I ask—'

'No. Me first,' Victor interrupted, and then gestured at Theo's uniform. 'So you were in on that raid then? The one to France we all read about.'

'I'm not allowed to say.'

'I'll take that as a yes.' He blew another plume. 'I told the lads you were. Properly impressed they were. That's my son, I told them, chip off the old block.'

'No I'm not. Because you were never in the army.'

'That's a lie.'

'Not in the East Surreys, not as an officer. They checked.'

'That's as maybe. I was in the Territorials. Till they chucked me out.'

'For what?'

Victor shrugged. 'Insubordination. Some trumped-up thieving charge. Going absent, what they called desertion.'

'Did you desert?'

'Course not! It was the skiing, you know, the winter sports and that. I got the chance to go to Austria with an army team, fetching and carrying, orderly work and so on. They let me have a go with the skis. After that I was hooked. I got a bit delayed coming back, that's all.'

'Why are you in prison?'

The eyes flickered. 'The beak said it was fraud. Not true. An investment went bad, corners got cut, maybe a couple of dodgy cheques. These things happen in business.'

'Is this your first time?' Theo ploughed on, needing to know.

'Hardly.'

'Then...'

'Blimey, what is this? All right, it's the fourth, since you ask.'

'Did you actually serve in the First War?'

'Christ, you ask a lot of questions!'

'That's because I thought you were dead. Did you?'

'Restricted to home duties. On account of flat feet. Then I got discharged.'

'But after the war you went back to Austria, dressed up as an officer, and seduced my mother.'

'No, damn you!' A flash of anger. Heads turned; a guard glanced over. Across the hall a gaggle of late visitors began wandering in. 'That is *not* what happened!'

'It's what I grew up believing.'

'Well, it's wrong, and you can shut up about it!' He crossed his arms, turning sideways on his chair, a scowl on his face. Silence fell between them; instinctively Theo waited. Eventually Victor glanced up.

'Look, Theodora, or Andrew, or whatever your bloody name is, your mother was very, you know, strong-willed. Very persuasive. Liked to get her way. She's as much to blame for all this as me.'

'Is that what you think?'

'Yes. And now, frankly, I'm not caring for your tone, so I think you should leave.'

'You haven't asked about her.'

'You what?'

25

'Not one question. Not even if she's alive.'

A sigh, a shake of the head, a glance at the door. 'It's too late for that.'

'Don't you care?'

'Course. Only...'

Theo swallowed. 'Not enough to come back for us.'

'I was going to! It was all planned. But business got in the way, then I got delayed, then had some trouble with the law, then everything got complicated...'

'So you faked your death and abandoned us instead.'

'Fuck you!' Victor glared. But no more words came. And in that moment, holding his gaze, Theo saw his own reflection, and recognized a young man in a photograph, standing with a youthful Carla at a family baptism in Bolzano twenty years ago, and he glimpsed something across the years, like regret.

Seconds passed, the clock clicked, the buzz of chatting families filled the air. Then Victor slumped back. 'What do you want from me?'

'I...' But he didn't know, and couldn't think. His head reeled, his throat felt tight, his hands were trembling in his lap. He'd never imagined anything like this: the father he'd worshipped through childhood, the war hero, Olympic sportsman, officer and gentleman, not killed on a mountain but alive, living in a grimy London prison, exposed as a liar, cheat and a fraud. He struggled to absorb it, to digest and comprehend it, bitterness welling in him like bile. Anger too, and worse – grief, for the loss of his idol, and of his own heritage. He looked away, struggling for sense, sightlessly watching as an anxious-looking woman led a little girl gingerly through the throng, like a mare leading her foal.

Victor's gaze was still down. 'You should go.'

'Is that what you want?'

'Yes.'

'Why?'

A pause. 'Because of them.'

'Who?'

'Them.' His chair scraped back. 'Hello, Vi.'

'Hello, Vic. Who's this bloke then?'

'This is Anders, um, Thea... an army acquaintance, from the old regiment.'

The woman's eyes were wary. 'How d'you do.'

'Andrew. This is Violet. Trickey, that is. My wife. And my daughter Nancy.'

Theo staggered out, mind numb, on to rain-splashed streets, then on a whim kept going, route-marching another six miles, kitbag on shoulder, until he finally arrived back at the Kingston boarding house. Where his welcome was predictably more fulsome.

'Here 'e is at last, the clever clog!'

'Hello, Eleni, how are you?'

'All the better. Come 'ere. Give us kiss. Blimey, bad boy, you soaking or what?'

Relieved of bag and greatcoat he followed her to the front room where, to his astonishment, a dozen or more people stood up and erupted into applause. In their midst, clutching a file of papers and with a pencil tucked behind one ear, was Carla.

'Welcome home.' She smiled, embracing him. 'Everyone is so proud.'

He found himself hugging her back, fervently, like a child. 'Mama.'

She laughed. 'Goodness, what is this?'

I've found him, he yearned to say. He's alive and a few miles away. You are so close, barely a valley apart, yet the gulf between you is fathomless; he disowns us and he blames you, he even has another family. I'm so sorry.

'Theo? Are you unwell?'

He broke away, conscious of watching eyes. 'I am fine. Just tired. Um, who are all these people?'

Partito Popolare Sudtirolese, it transpired, the South Tyrol People's Party, a fledgling political pressure group campaigning for South Tyrol's independence. And nothing whatever to do with his homecoming. He stayed for a while, out of politeness; she introduced him to its members, who enquired uncomprehendingly about his mission, then swiftly changed the subject: 'And where does the British army stand on the South Tyrol question, Theodor?' Then she showed him their leaflets and posters, their agendas and manifestos, their files, letters and programmes of protests, and suddenly he was transported back fifteen years to a Bolzano print shop, the clacking of mimeograph machines and the smell of turpentine, Carla and her father Josef, their faces smudged with ink as they toiled, secretly churning out their handbills and pamphlets like Russian revolutionaries.

'Look, Theo, these go to everyone. Politicians, clergymen, diplomats, newspaper owners, the Pope, you name it, even fascist dictators like Hitler, look.'

'You've written to Hitler?'

'Yes, well, his Foreign Minister, von Ribbentrop. Why not? He has influence. Mussolini also – see, Theo – we have written directly to Il Duce demanding recognition!'

'Yes, but, Mama, I mean, isn't this the kind of thing that got you interned?'

'Pah! The British know we are on their side. We both want only to overthrow the fat pig. And look at this too, Theo.' She handed him a clipping. 'It's beginning to work – see, the undertaker Tolomei has resigned! We have undercover friends in Italy now, and partisans fighting our cause!'

Theo scanned the clipping. Taken from Italy's Fascist newspaper and several months old, it reported the hated governor's retirement following death threats and an arson attack on his property. Much embellished, it even printed one of the resignation letters Theo had made him sign, then went on to talk of *seditious foreign infiltrators*, and the need to stamp out *traitorous insurrectionists like Partito d'Azione*.

'Have you heard from Grandpa?' he asked, anxious suddenly for his grandfather. Carla knew he had visited Josef in prison in Rome, but nothing more – at Captain Grant's insistence.

'A letter came from Regina Coeli' – she waved vaguely – 'some weeks ago. He seems much the same.'

After a while he retreated from front-room politics to the aromatic sanctuary of the kitchen, where he found Eleni preparing tea and ravani cake for everyone.

''S no good, Teo,' she fretted, 'this damn war no good!'

'It does seem to be getting worse.'

'You telling me! Semolina I can find, maybe half a lemon, but flour and eggs? Damn ration nonsense, how a hell I make proper ravani?'

'Ah.' He looked round the kitchen, and its familiar air of organized disorder. This was her battleground, he realized, the place she fought her war. Dignity, self-respect, national pride, the ability to feed family and guests. To proud, hard-working people like Eleni, these things mattered more than guns and tanks.

'You go out tonight?' she asked. 'You look worry when you come in earlier.'

'Worried? No. Just... It's nothing.'

'Hmm, I don' think so.'

'I was hoping to spend time talking with Mama tonight, but she has a meeting.'

'Ha! You mean she has pub with Foreign Office chappy with no chin.'

'Really? Is this a new, um, person?'

'You know your mama, if he can *do* favour then he *get* favour! Listen, Teo, you go out, that nice Price girl, wha's her name, Susanna, she been round asking 'bout you.'

So he went. After an hour on his bed, fruitlessly pondering the reunion with Victor, he rose suddenly, washed and shaved, donned civilian clothes he hadn't worn in months, and stepped into the cold March night.

'Theodorable!' Susanna greeted him at her door, flinging arms round him like a lost brother. 'My God, it is you. I heard you were back. Come in out of the blackout!' Then she was ushering him in, taking his coat and standing him back for inspection. Her family was out, she said, gone to the pictures, a Western film she didn't fancy, so she was waiting at home with the wireless. Waiting? Theo wondered, sensing a Greek hand. He followed her into a snug parlour with dark curtains and a hissing gas fire. Music played on the Home Service; a cat stirred on a chair; a magazine lay open on the sofa.

'I have beer,' she said, 'a bottle of stout. Don't tell my dad!'

'I won't.' He watched as carefully she opened and poured the beer, then sat, patting the sofa beside her.

'You're the talk of the town.' She sipped. 'That raid to France.'

'It's supposed to be secret. Who actually went on it, I mean.'

'Your landlady told me. She seems to know everything.'

'Yes she does.' The sofa was small. Their bodies touched, hers smelled of scent and he saw her lips were rouged. He recalled the youthful red-haired Juliet kissing his tongue-tied Mercutio backstage at school. Four years ago, and another lifetime. Her hair was darker now.

'All sounded very exciting in the papers. Were you scared?'

'A little. Everything seemed to happen rather fast.'

Her arm slipped through his. 'What was it like?'

Thrilling, terrifying, a muddle, a panic. Storming the radar bunker amid roaring Scotsmen. Dragging a heavy trolley through snow. Stumbling down a cliff path, bullets whining overhead. Cowering before an empty ocean, dread in his heart from the pistol in his pocket. The menacing blast of mortar shells creeping nearer. The blessed relief of salvation.

'Things went wrong, you know. They often seem to on these operations. But Major Frost, our commanding officer, he was terrific. He just kept dealing with the problems, kept attacking the enemy, kept everyone's minds on the mission, kept us together and moving.'

'He sounds a good man.'

'Yes he is. It gives you great confidence, a leader like that, makes you believe anything's possible, that you're, you know, better than you think. He'd have fought it out to the end, I'm sure, if we'd had to.'

'I don't like the sound of that!'

'No. Well, it was a near thing.'

He'd asked for a report, he remembered. Major Frost had. A few days after the raid. 'You're an intelligence chap, Theo,' he said, 'write me one of your reports, from the perspective of the bunker team. Just the facts, best as you remember them.' Theo had been alarmed, then honoured, then perplexed. Should he include hauling Denkmann up from the cliff? Or being told to use an axe on the radar? Or the order to shoot Charlie?

'There was this RAF scientist, you see. A bit of a boffin.'

31

'On the raid?' Susanna's cheek was on his shoulder.

'Yes. My job was to look after him...'

She raised her head. 'What happened?'

'Well... Nothing. I probably shouldn't talk about it.'

'Would you like to kiss me instead?'

'Can I?'

'I jolly well hope so.'

Her eyes closed as she leaned towards him, and when they kissed her lips parted, and felt soft and moist. They lingered, withdrew, then joined again, more firmly this time, and with the tip of her tongue touching his. He tasted hops and barley, and when he looked, her eyes were open and gleaming.

Then came a sharp rapping on the window.

'You in there! Thadeus or whatever your name is!'

She broke away. 'Who's that?'

'I have no idea. Sounds like a woman.'

More rapping. 'Open up! I want a word with you!'

'I'd better go. The neighbours...'

He heard the front door open, then muffled raised voices, and a moment later Susanna returned, face confused, followed by Violet Trickey and her daughter.

'That's him!' Violet pointed. 'Thadeus whatever it is.'

'Um, Theodor.' He rose to his feet. 'Can I help you?'

'I'll say! You can stay away from Vic. He's ours, see, and don't want nothing to do with you!'

'Oh, I see. Well, yes, he told me. And I'm sorry, only...'

'Theo, who is this lady?'

'She's, well, this is Mrs Trickey. My father's wife. Second wife, that is, although—'

'His *only* bloomin' wife, if you don't mind!'

'But I thought your father was dead? Killed when you were little.'

32

'So did I. Only... Excuse me, Mrs Trickey, how did you know where—'

'They had your address at the guardroom. Then that Turkish woman at your lodgings said you was here. We been walking for hours.'

'Eleni, Greek, yes. But—'

'Then you must be very tired,' Susanna said firmly. 'And cold. Won't you sit by the fire a moment?'

'You what?'

'And your shoes, look, they're soaking wet. So are your little girl's. You could dry them a bit.'

'Eh? Oh, yes, well, s'pose there's no harm. Just for a minute.'

'And I expect she could do with a drink.'

'Pardon?'

'Your little girl. We've got squash.'

'Nancy? Want a drink?'

But Nancy was studying Theo. She was eight or nine, he guessed, long-limbed and scrawny, with thin legs and straggly fair hair. Her clothing was poor and grimy. She had the small mouth and nose of her mother, but her eyes were larger, steady, bright and blue, and as she stared at him, for the second time that day he glimpsed himself in their reflection. And felt an unexpected surge of longing.

'Are you my brother?' she asked.

He stayed three weeks. He and Susanna walked out often; Theo enjoyed the companionship, the novelty, and the new-found intimacy, but fretted about the commitment. 'Perhaps we shouldn't get serious,' he would say, 'I'm sure to get posted and I'd hate you to worry.' 'Who's worrying?' she'd reply breezily. They went to the pictures, the river, the dance hall; once or twice they travelled into the West End, wandering the sights arm in arm like tourists. London was emerging from winter at last and the Blitz was largely over, but with the war news gloomy and rationing biting hard, shops were thinly stocked and many cafés and restaurants closed. Londoners themselves, they noticed, seem to go about their business in a mood of grim resignation.

'Look at this.' Theo picked up a discarded newspaper. 'We've lost Benghazi.'

'Ben who?'

'Benghazi. Libya's second city. We won it from the Italians last year. Now we've lost it again.'

'Oh.'

Theo studied the paper. 'To Rommel.'

'Who's Rommel?'

Days passed. The boarding house was busy and he soon found himself reprising his juvenile role as Eleni's home-help: serving breakfast, running to the shops, coaxing wet laundry through the mangle in the yard. Meanwhile Carla was equally busy managing Partito Popolare Sudtirolese. Most days she went out to 'meetings'; most evenings were spent writing letters, stuffing envelopes or lobbying contacts on Eleni's telephone. When she did find time for Theo they spoke mostly of South Tyrolean matters, local gossip or the war. Once she quizzed him about his Italian activities following the aqueduct mission, Operation Colossus, but, instinctively reticent, and mindful of Grant's warnings about secrecy, he dissembled. 'Just lying low mostly.' Similarly he decided not to broach the subject of Victor with her, convincing himself that the matter was best left closed for the moment. He did probe Eleni about it, however. 'What he was like?' he ventured casually one evening. 'You know, in the days when he lived here?' Eleni's face hardened. 'He gone,

Teo, he never no bloody good, an' you bes' forget him. For your sake an' your mother.'

Finally one day he returned from an errand to find a telegram on the hall table. *URGENT TO PTE TV TRICKEY STOP REPORT IMMEDIATE 2 PARA HQ HARDWICK HALL MANSFIELD STOP SIGNED GOFTON-SALMOND LT/ COL 2BN STOP.* A thrill of expectancy ran through him as he read and reread the message. It could mean only one thing, and a surreptitious phone call to the adjutant at Hardwick confirmed it. 'It's an op, Trickey, hush-hush and urgent, so get your arse back here at the double!' Scrawling notes to Carla and Susanna, he left that afternoon, and by dusk was home with the Paras.

The op, not urgent it transpired, nor very hush-hush, was a demonstration jump for the King and Queen, arranged at an RAF aerodrome in Yorkshire. His Majesty had specifically expressed interest in seeing men from the Bruneval raid, so urgent messages had gone out to C Company, most of whom were still living it up in Scotland. Few received the summons in time so A Company had to make up the numbers. The day of the drop dawned overcast and blustery. Six sticks were to jump from the Whitleys while John Frost would provide commentary for the royals on the ground. The appointed hour arrived and the bombers duly droned overhead and commenced circling, but an hour later they were still circling with the monarch yet to appear. Finally the cortège pulled up and with fuel running low the Whitleys were hastily signalled to commence their run. At that moment the King decided to wander indoors and shake hands with office staff; by the time he emerged ten minutes later all but the final stick were already on the ground. Watching the last few men sink to earth he declared the enterprise remarkable, climbed back into his car and was driven off.

With only a short period of leave remaining, and encouraged by Frost, who hinted at impending deployment, Theo stayed on at Hardwick Hall. Sure enough in May the entire 1st Parachute Brigade decamped to Salisbury Plain where for the first time in its history all three battalions were to train together. 2nd Battalion was billeted at Bulford, with Frost promoted to second-in-command under Colonel Gofton-Salmond. His friend Philip Teichman, still technically senior, might have expected this promotion but was left in charge of B Company, while Frost's Scottish C Company was given to Bruneval stalwart John Ross, and A Company to East Surrey regular Dick Ashford. Theo went to Frost's HQ Company as runner and interpreter.

Brigadier Gale remained in overall charge of the three battalions and by midsummer training was in full swing, with special emphasis on physical fitness and stamina. Every man in the brigade, he decreed, must be able to march a minimum fifty miles in twenty-four hours – with full packs. Little did he know how valuable this endurance training, soon a hallmark of the regiment, would become in forthcoming months. Competition between battalions was fierce and some epic marches were recorded. On one occasion 2nd Battalion was sent to Exmoor on manoeuvres. Colonel Gofton-Salmond was ill so Frost led it. Having successfully completed the exercise he then marched it back to Bulford in full battalion order, a distance of some eighty miles. Not to be outdone, 1st Battalion then night marched seventy miles to Oxford and back.

Apart from field training, the Paras once again took to the air, this time finally in what would become their operational workhorse: the Douglas DC3 Dakota. These American-built cargo aeroplanes were newly arrived in Britain and few in number, thus eagerly anticipated by the waiting Paras. But when they finally got to clamber over them for themselves their reactions were mixed. Spacious certainly, big and powerful, with a cabin wide enough to carry twenty jumpers instead of the Whitley's ten, the 'Dak' also had a huge removable side door enabling a swift and safe exit compared to plummeting down the Whitley's hated 'tube'. But unlike the Whitley the Dakota was not armed at all, nor did it carry armour plating as protection against gunfire and flak. Basically a civilian cargo plane, it was also mostly flown by American civilian pilots, who had little training in combat flying, modest experience flying in cloud and none at all flying at night. And their preferred technique for dropping parachutists also raised eyebrows. This entailed running in at top speed and ground level to avoid flak, followed by a violent pull up to seven hundred feet, cutting the engines and throwing out the jumpers, before diving to the ground once more to escape. Notwithstanding these antics and the Dak's military shortcomings, men and machines gradually bonded.

Summer waned, the Wiltshire crops were harvested, the men trained, the war ground on. Then the rumour started. 1st Para Brigade was going into action. More small raids like the one to Bruneval, someone said. No, a battalion was going to Malta; then it was a different one going to Greece, then Norway, then suddenly everyone was destined for Burma. As one of HQ Company's runners, Theo theoretically had better access to 'gen' than most, but he learned nothing and even Frost didn't seem to know. Then one day in September his boss took him aside.

'It's embarkation orders, Trickey, and soon.'

'Embarkation for where, sir?'

'Can't say. Take a few days' leave, report back in a week.'

'Thank you, sir, but I don't really need—'

'Take it. Report to Baker Street while you're there. Be back in a week.'

He went, passing restless days at the boarding house, where Eleni was tearful, Carla distracted and Susanna stoic. 'It'll be fine, Theo,' she said, patting his hand. 'Don't worry about me, write when you can but don't if you can't.' On their last evening together they went to the bench by the Thames where they'd first sat when he returned from France two years earlier. There they talked and kissed and held each other, watching the passing river traffic until dawn. Later that day he reported to Captain Grant at Baker Street, and finally learned where the Paras were destined.

'Tunisia, Theo, and your old friend Erwin Rommel.'

'But I thought he was—'

'In Libya, yes he is, hundreds of miles to the east. But the point is we're going to squeeze him and his blasted Afrika Korps to buggery. He's already got 8th Army in front of him in Egypt; we're going to land another army behind him in Tunisia.'

'I see. Who is?'

'Us, the Yanks – God knows, even the bloody French if they can organize themselves. It'll doubtless be a bugger's muddle to begin with, cock-ups galore, everyone at sixes and sevens.' He lit another cigarette, glancing at Theo. 'Intelligence will be a nightmare.'

'Yes, sir.' Theo looked around. Grant had moved to a new office, in another building near the old one; this one was bigger, although just as cluttered. Special Operations Executive, as it was now known, was evidently growing. Grant soon confirmed it.

'We've already got a section running in Cairo, and they'll be starting one up in Algiers, which is where you'll report. If required, that is. Algiers office code name is Massingham, and your contact there' – he shuffled papers – 'is a Major Yale, like the key. Think you can remember that?'

'Yes.'

'Good. Don't write it down, and don't breathe a word of this to anyone.'

'I won't. Um, when do we go? 1st Para Brigade, I mean.'

'Soon. The next few weeks. Some of you by air, the rest by sea.' He ground out his cigarette and immediately reached for another. His uniform tie was loose, as usual, but his eyes, less usually, seemed round with worry. 'Listen, Theo. It's going to be messy out there. Supplies, organization, logistics, the whole command structure: it'll be a lash-up, at least at first. As will be the way troops like you parachute lads get deployed. And Rommel's no fool, we both know that. He'll hit back hard, and it'll get bloody. Do you understand me?'

'Yes, sir.'

'So just take care of yourself.'

The house was identical to all the others, one of dozens in a scruffy-looking terrace stretching a mile in either direction. Somewhere in the East End, it was, not far from London's docklands; rubble piles, fenced-off craters and buildings shrouded in scaffolding showed it had suffered badly in the Blitz. Checking the address Grant had supplied him, he set off along the numbers, until he came to the door and knocked.

'And what the bloody hell do *you* want!'

'I'm sorry, Mrs Trickey, it's me, um, Theo. Trickey, that is. As well.'

'I know *who* you are, I asked what you want!'

'Nothing. Well...' He produced a crumpled package. 'I brought you some tea, you see, and some biscuits. Susanna made them. And also something, a toy – a doll actually – it's nothing really, for your daughter.'

As if by summons, Nancy appeared from behind her mother.

She was wearing the same dress and shoes as in March, though her hair was longer and her skin less pale. Something green, like crayon, was smeared across one cheek.

She smiled. 'Hello.'

'Hello, Nancy. I, um, I've brought you something.' He glanced at Violet, who rolled her eyes; then he stooped, opening the package to reveal a doll dressed in Tyrolean folk costume: white blouse, red waistcoat and skirt, hair braided in plaits. 'Do you like her?'

'Ooh!' Nancy's eyes widened. 'Why's her mouth round?'

'Because she's singing. She's from South... From the mountains, where I was born. Little girls love to sing there. She's got blond hair like yours, see?'

'Yes!' Nancy hugged the doll to her cheek. 'Thank you.'

Violet was tapping her foot. 'Anything else?'

'What? Oh, um, no, that's all.'

'We'll take the tea and biscuits thanks.'

'Of course. It must be difficult, what with Vic—'

'We manage.'

'Yes. Well, then...'

Nancy's hand reached out. 'Are you going?'

'Yes, I've got to.'

'Where?'

'Well, it's rather a long way.'

'Are you coming back?'

But before he could answer, Violet led her back inside, and the last he saw of her was a little wave as the door closed.

CHAPTER 3

Despite Padre Pettifer's best efforts, Christmas 1944 is without doubt the most dismal on record, at least for those remnants of 1st Airborne Division living in Stammlager XIB, Osterheide, Bad Fallingbostel, Lower Saxony, Germany. The only crumb of comfort is it's just as dismal for folk living outside the camp, for as well as enduring the hardships of war – shortages, sickness, starvation, misery, cold, bereavement and the rest – they also have their enemy to contend with, i.e. getting bombed and being invaded, whereas for us inside the wire, as our guards keep reminding us: 'For you the war is *kaputt*.'

We know Stalag XIB's address because we've been allowed to send out Red Cross cards notifying loved ones of our status and location. Although we've had no mail ourselves yet, receiving news of us will come as a relief to our relatives, many of whom, following the chaos of Operation Market Garden three months ago, still have no idea if we're alive, dead, wounded, in captivity or on the run. It's also a comfort for us to know we're putting their minds at rest, particularly at Christmastime when everyone's thoughts are of family. The process is oddly poignant. One snowy evening we're huddled in our huts playing draughts or rereading dog-eared paperbacks when the commandant Major Möglich's men come round with the cards. A flurry of excitement ensues as they're handed out, everyone talks at once, we medical officers

41

even boldly discuss encoding secret messages in them, but soon the chatter fades to silence as we reflect on the significance of the cards to us individually – and also ponder what to write. In the end I address mine to my parents, dutifully reassuring them I'm in the best of health and heart (no point in saying otherwise), Pip Smith and the others do the same and we all hand them in. Then, because there's nothing else to do, we gather round the stove, sing a rather lacklustre 'Silent Night', chew solemnly on our black bread 'Christmas cake', and settle down to await whatever fate has in store for us in 1945.

There are few signs of obvious change at XIB following my holiday at Stalag 357, but there are some subtle ones. With the exception of serious cases, many of our patients are now back on their feet, which means the workload for us medics is gradually slackening. Many are getting transferred to other camps too, further easing numbers, but the huts are still crowded and unsanitary, resulting in chest and stomach infections, which aren't helped by the cold, damp and poor diet. Rations of food, heating coal and medical supplies are still short, but a trickle of Red Cross parcels is getting through so we're able to distribute tea, tobacco and other precious luxuries which the men seize upon like starving waifs. It's all a far cry from our triumphant jump into Holland, I reflect, watching them trudge round the compound like bent old tramps, shadows of the proud warriors they once were. I can only wonder at the change in them. The change in us all. From heroes to zeros, as someone puts it.

Nor can I exclude myself from this decline. Healthy enough physically (albeit thinner), this interlude finds me in the lowest of spirits. I'm not sure why. Obviously imprisonment, the camp, the weather and the dismal day-to-day existence here don't help, but it's as though, with more time on my hands, my mind is suddenly free to ruminate on what's happened these last months, and *keep* ruminating on it over and over until I'm exhausted and close to despair: Arnhem, the killing and maiming, the Schoonoord, the horror of the shelling, the blood-spattered storeroom, Apeldoorn, the train, poor Cliff Poutney. And other images like the dreadful internment camp Inge Brandt showed me, Private Jenkins's anguished face, the guard's rifle at my head, and the chilling encounter with the Gestapo at Fallingbostel Station. And then my ridiculous escape attempt, which weighs heaviest of all. Ill considered and unrealistic perhaps, I nevertheless attached great significance to it, because it signalled a vital change in my mind-set, like throwing a switch from passive to active, from victim to protagonist, from a leaf adrift in a stream to master of my own destiny. Now it's gone and I'm drifting again, feeling beaten and worthless.

And it's getting me down – I know enough psychology to recognize the symptoms. I keep myself apart, socialize less, show little interest in my work or in news and gossip, or eating the revolting slop they call food here. I don't bother keeping up appearances, my clothes are dirty, my hair too long and I've stopped shaving. Worst of all I don't sleep, just pass my nights staring up at the hut's mildewed ceiling, my mind plodding through the darkness like a slow goods train, while Pip and the others snore on like babies.

'OK, Dan?' Pip enquires one day, perceptive as ever. 'You seem a little sotto voce these days.'

'It's nothing.' We're outside, walking the wire, which is camp slang for traipsing round the perimeter. I've been back here a month. The weather's grey and oppressive; an icy wind cuts through my French greatcoat. 'It's just...'

'This place, eh?'

'Yes. Among other things. This whole existence really. It's so... debasing. So inhuman. It's getting to me rather.'

'Write it down.'

'Write what down?'

'All of it. Like a memoir or something. Call it occupational therapy. It may be a debasing existence, but it's a unique one. So record it. Your thoughts, feelings, impressions, the whole experience. The people too.'

'It'll make pretty tedious reading.'

'Doesn't matter, it's just therapy. Anyway, it won't be for long, will it?'

'How do you mean?'

'Spring!' He gestures at the sky.

'But it's December.'

'A new year, new offensive, a final push, a few weeks and it'll all be over.'

'You really think Jerry will give up that easily?'

'Absolutely.'

'That's not my reading, having seen them in action.'

'No, but thinking negatively gets you nowhere.' He nudges me. 'As a doctor you should know that.'

Irrepressible, Pip is. I don't know how he does it: cheerful, positive, optimistic – it's enough to drive you mad. Or even more cussed.

'Negatively, or realistically?' I bleat. 'They thrashed us at Arnhem, remember. And since arriving in Germany I don't get the impression they're throwing in the towel.'

'Maybe not. But the point is, *we* mustn't give that impression either.'

'Ah. Stiff upper lip and all that.'

'Yes, Dan, all that. It's vital they sense we're confident. All of us.'

'Hmm.' We slog on in silence. I tug up the collar of my greatcoat; litter blows across the compound while the mud squelches from our boots. I can guess what's coming next, and would rather it didn't.

'How's your boy?'

And there it is. The rub, the nub, the nexus of my discontent. Theodor Victor Trickey, still here, still alive, still haunting me. He's not my boy! I want to shout, I don't know him, wish I'd never heard of him, so leave me alone!

'Stable. So I believe.'

'You haven't seen him?'

'Not for a day or two.' Five, in fact.

'I hear he's awake. Taking nourishment.'

'Not really.' The eyes open, the patient swallows when force-fed. But no words come, no recognition, no awareness. 'Catatonic. Or something like it.'

'You should see him. Spend time with him.'

But I don't want to spend time with him. He's a curse, a millstone round my neck like that bloody albatross. But for him I'd be enjoying Christmas at Stalag 357, or even at home after escaping. Instead he's dragged me back to rot in this dump. And for what? He doesn't speak or cry out or make faces or do anything; he's a living corpse and has been since we found him at the Schoonoord. 'Remember the Chinese proverb,' Colonel Alford cautioned me, back at Apeldoorn, 'if you save a man's life you're responsible for it for ever.' How I laughed it off back then. Not now.

'Orderlies will call me if there's any change.'

'That's not the point.' Pip stops suddenly. 'You should spend time with him because he's leaving.'

I'm shocked; it's no use pretending otherwise. 'Leaving where?'

'Down south. Some place called Ulm. Orders from the Medical Directorate.'

Moving again. Mysterious orders again. That sense of unknown forces at work. Again. 'But when?'

'Soon. And there's more. Möglich says they've requested a medic too, a qualified doctor. To make up the numbers down there.'

'I don't want it. Send someone else.'

'Gladly. Every doctor here would kill for this posting. Myself included. Anything to get away from this place.'

'Then—'

'But he's your patient, Dan' – he rests a hand on my arm – 'so you get first refusal. And I think you should go, for your wellbeing as well as his.'

And everyone else's too, I sense.

'Sleep on it? Will you?'

'Yes, but...'

'Good. Let me know.' He turns to go. 'You should write about him as well! He's got a tale to tell for sure.' He plods away through the mud. 'And go see him. That's an order!'

4/5 April 1941

Dearest Lu,

I have no idea if the date is right. We've been attacking for days now in the endless desert and I have lost all idea of space or time, nor have I slept these past nights. Things are going well, our main force is forward after a 220-mile march over the sand and rock. We've been attacking since the 31st. There's alarm among my superiors in Tripoli and Rome, probably in Berlin too. But I took the risk against orders because the opportunity was too favourable to miss. We've already reached our first objectives; next I

must push on east then tackle Tobruk. The British are
falling over themselves to get away, while our casualties
are small. Though tired I am well; you need not worry. I
send loving best wishes to you and Manfred.
  Erwin

Unknown to him, the bustling Libyan port of Tobruk would
come to dominate Erwin Rommel's Africa campaign. Occupied
by a sizeable Allied garrison, and strategically placed midway
between Tunisia and Egypt, Tobruk was heavily fortified with
walled defences, anti-tank ditches, minefields and pillboxes,
plus natural cliffs and escarpments providing extra protection
to landward. Being a peninsula enabled resupply from sea and
also favoured the defender. Attacking it would be no trivial
matter, Rommel knew, but to achieve his goal of taking Libya,
and seizing Egypt with its ports of Alexandria, Said and the
vital Suez Canal, taking Tobruk was imperative.

Arriving in Tripoli soon after Operation Colossus in February
1941 he immediately set about the task. Hastening eastwards
through Libya he surprised the British, who, weakened by the
transfer of troops to Greece, duly retreated, almost to Benghazi,
three hundred miles west of Tobruk. There he was supposed to
pause and regroup, but eager to maintain momentum he urged his
Italian superior General Gariboldi to press on. Gariboldi refused
and an angry exchange took place. At its height a signalman
entered and handed Rommel a message from Berlin. It reminded
him to use tact and discretion in his dealings with the Italians.
Knowing Gariboldi could read no German he waved the message:
'Discretion, you see, *Generale*?' He pointed. 'The Führer leaves
it to my discretion!'

He resumed the advance, retaking Benghazi, Derna and then
Gazala, steadily forcing the British eastwards. They seemed

disorganized and nervous, he noted, over-estimating his strength and repeatedly withdrawing rather than risking defeat. They often replaced their generals too, a sure sign of disarray. When they did offer resistance the fighting could be hard and the desert conditions merciless. Tanks overheated and broke down, artillery jammed, convoys became mired in sand, and his men, roasting by day, freezing by night, constantly short of fuel, water, food and ammunition, were soon close to exhaustion. But Rommel kept driving them on and ultimately his long-honed methods – move fast, strike hard, don't stop – prevailed yet again.

Within two months of arriving in Africa he'd driven the British out of Libya and back into Egypt. Given the paucity of resources, unfamiliarity with conditions, and general lack of support, this was a remarkable achievement, the product of tactical mastery and sheer force of personality. And as before, with victory in his pocket his critics were silenced, the recriminations shelved, and the flouted orders conveniently forgotten. Hitler wrote congratulating him, Mussolini too, Germany rejoiced, Britain lamented, even General Gariboldi was grudgingly mollified.

Up to a point. For there remained just one blot on the newly drawn landscape, like a boil on an otherwise smooth cheek. Tobruk, which was still stubbornly in Allied hands. And no minor blot either; with its deep-water harbour, formidable defences and 36,000-strong garrison, Rommel knew Tobruk held the key to the conquest of North Africa, and must be taken. His instincts, as always, told him to take it now, before the enemy could regroup. But after weeks of gruelling campaigning, his Afrika Korps was in depleted condition, thinly stretched, under-equipped and badly in need of rest. Prudence dictated he wait, and rearm, and recover strength. Yet each night the Allies shipped more supplies into Tobruk: more tanks and artillery, more ammunition and food, and more men, so the longer he delayed the harder the task ahead. Expedience told him to strike.

So he struck, committing the full might of the Afrika Korps in an all-out assault. For several days and nights the battle raged, fighting was fierce and casualties ran high. The defenders, mainly British, Australian and Indian, showed grit and determination, while his German boys fought bravely too. But their Italian counterparts, so vital in making up the numbers, were unreliable and weak, fleeing or surrendering at the first sign of trouble, and in the end this swung the pendulum against him. After six days the attack failed and he was forced to withdraw. Rommel was shocked. For the first time in a major confrontation he'd got it wrong, misjudged the situation and received a bloody nose for it. He fell back along the coast to regroup. Probing raids continued, artillery barrages and air attacks too, but to little avail; days turned to weeks and what began as an assault developed into a siege. Running short of supplies, he begged Berlin for more – more tanks, more aircraft, more guns and more men – but with the invasion of Russia looming nobody had time for his African sideshow. Instead they sent a general, Friedrich Paulus, to reason with him and calm the situation. Paulus arrived to find Rommel in high agitation, busily preparing another attack. 'Tobruk is unassailable,' Paulus said, studying the plans, 'we should seal it off, blockade it, and wait for improved circumstances.' But Rommel wasn't listening. 'We can take it,' he assured Paulus, 'a hard strike, a concerted effort, proper support from the Italians and all will be well.'

Reluctantly Paulus conceded. The second attack went ahead, and it failed like the first. Suddenly Tobruk stopped being a sideshow and began taking on global significance. Paulus was recalled to Berlin to explain, German High Command banned further action against the port; Churchill, meanwhile, sensing opportunity, ordered his latest general, Archibald Wavell, to seize the initiative, advance west from Egypt and catch Rommel on the hop. Wavell tentatively complied; Rommel hurried east to confront him, weeks of bitter fighting followed and he drove the British back again. Wavell was duly sacked and replaced by a new general, Auchinleck, while Rommel, by now ill and exhausted, withdrew to regroup. A few weeks' welcome rest then befell both sides; the summer of 1941 was marked by sporadic fighting and structural reorganization. Auchinleck fashioned the Western Desert Force into a new army, 8th Army, under the command of yet another general called Cunningham, while Rommel was promoted to lead a larger force, Panzergruppe Afrika, and finally sent the reinforcements he'd begged for. Recuperating at his seaside headquarters, the British secure on the Egyptian border and his Panzergruppe growing daily in strength, his thoughts inevitably returned to the coming season's campaign, the push into Egypt and on to Suez. And to achieve this, he must first settle the Tobruk matter, once and for all.

That evening, and only because Pip Smith ordered it, I visit Theo Trickey. Approaching the infirmary in the gathering dusk it's no use denying the dread I feel, for Theo has come to represent the utter misery of this war, and my miserable role in it, a role which has been going steadily downhill ever since I jumped from a Dakota fifteen weeks ago. As though in that moment my life changed and I became some other being, some existential anomaly like that poor ancient mariner, doomed for eternity. As Coleridge puts it:

I moved, and could not feel my limbs:
I was so light – almost
I thought that I had died in sleep,
And was a blessèd ghost.

My ghost lies in a room for the most seriously ill, of which there are now very few. Swaddled in blankets against the cold, in effect he's been in this state, unconscious and unresponsive, for over three months. The orderlies turn him to avoid bed sores and efforts are made to massage and exercise his limbs, but these are futile gestures, and basically he's wasting to a husk before our eyes. I crouch beside him, studying the sunken cheeks, the pale pursed lips, the Slavonic slant to his closed eyes and wonder, seriously, whether I did right to save him, or whether I was just prolonging his suffering for my own vain ends. Because Anna asked me to and I wanted to impress her. It's a sobering notion. First do no harm, the doctor's oath decrees, *first do no harm.* How much harm have I done by insisting his lifeless body keep breathing? I reach out, brushing the hair from his brow, and recall the night we found him in the garden among the dead. There were others during that battle, I know, carried out while still alive because their injuries were too severe to treat. Some were even conscious. 'Am I dying, Doc?' was a question we too frequently heard. Try answering it. A shared cigarette, a shot of morphia, a squeeze of the hand, and they were soon slipping away. *Try and save him,* Anna had said, yet never said why. Perhaps I should write, as promised, and ask her. I glance around, sniffing at the disinfectant odour of the sick. The room is dim and silent, only two other beds occupied, shadowy humps deeply asleep from sedatives. Outside all is quiet save the sigh of winter wind and the distant barking of a dog. Soon the guards will come for lock-up, and I will return to Pip and the others for another sleepless night on the slats. Alive yet dead, like Theo and those others. I close my eyes, kneeling now, barely aware my hand is moving from his brow to touch his nose and lips. 'I'm sorry,' I whisper. His breaths are warm and shallow on my fingers. My thumb and forefinger close over his nose, my palm pressing more firmly on his mouth.

'I'm sorry.'

I press harder.

His eyes open.

A creak comes from behind.

The eyes stare up at me, tar-black and gleaming.

'Doc?'

'I... What?'

'Thought I might find you here.'

'Sergeant Bowyer?'

'Saying goodbye...'

'What?' I snatch my hand back. 'Er, no, nothing...'

'Not you.' He chuckles. 'Me.'

I shake my head. 'I don't understand...'

He drops to a squat beside me. I smell tobacco and carbolic soap. His boots are polished, his face clean-shaven. 'I'm off. Come to say goodbye.'

'What – you mean, transferred?'

'No.' He glances at the door. '*Off*. As in getting out of it.'

The penny drops. 'Christ, you mean escaping!'

'Yes but you could keep your bloody voice down.'

He's going under the wire, he explains. Rumours are circulating about orderlies being moved to POW camps far to the east, in Poland. These camps are large, purpose-built and allegedly escape-proof. Patrolling guards, dogs, machine-gun towers, searchlights, the lot, he says. Hundreds of miles from friendly borders too, so once there the likelihood is you're there for good. Stalag XIB may be a hellhole, he goes on, but it has advantages, namely its location in western Europe, its proximity to the North Sea and the Baltic, and its wire that is vulnerable. 'North corner ain't dug in properly. Five minutes' digging, couple of snips, and we're out. Tonight.'

I'm astounded, and impressed, and oddly forlorn. Jack

Bowyer, the man I jumped into Arnhem with, worked through the carnage of the Schoonoord with, performed surgery on a train with, lived, slept and ate with, cheerfully insolent Jack, always ready with a jibe, a cigarette and a joke, is leaving.

'Well, my God, that's... marvellous,' I stammer. 'Who?'

'Me and George Stebbings. Loose floorboard in the hut washroom: we can squeeze through. There's bikes at the railway station. Plan is to pinch a couple, pedal to Bremerhaven by night and jump a ship.'

'Sounds good. What can I do? Do you need anything?' I recall my own escape kit: map, compass, food, blanket, money – so painstakingly assembled, so quickly superfluous.

'Thanks, Doc, but we're all set.'

Shouting from afar, the banging of shutters. 'We'd better get back.'

'Too right.' We rise; he hesitates. 'Wish me luck?'

'God, yes, Jack, all the very best of luck, to you both.'

'You too.' He shakes my hand, grinning in the half-light. 'Goodbye, Dan. You're a pretty useless soldier, you know.'

'Ah, well, yes I do.'

'But a damn fine doc.' He nods at Theo. 'He's the living proof.'

Erwin Rommel's third assault on Tobruk was set for November 1941, a full six months after the second, so humiliatingly overseen by General Paulus. This time he was determined to succeed. His build-up was slow and measured, his planning meticulous, his Panzergruppe Afrika strong, hungry for action and carefully deployed. Even the Italians were ready, properly organized and eager for the fray. Air cover was not ideal, and keeping his forces supplied was always a challenge, but these matters would be overcome. Overall he was satisfied, and confident. This time there would be no failures and no mistakes; everyone knew exactly what to do, when to do it, and how.

Including Winston Churchill unfortunately, for, unknown to Rommel, British codebreakers had been successfully decrypting German radio signals for months, including those detailing his plans for Tobruk. Churchill therefore instructed his latest Africa chief Claude Auchinleck to make plans of his own, and just one week before Rommel's assault, he unleashed them in Operation Crusader, a bold scheme to relieve Tobruk using the new 8th Army. Splitting this force in two, Auchinleck ordered General Cunningham to advance west from Egypt, the aim being to encircle Panzergruppe Afrika and then link up with Tobruk's defenders as they broke out of the city. Crusader launched on 18 November; Rommel responded, cancelling his own offensive and wheeling to confront this new threat. Days of fighting followed with artillery barrages, air strikes and fast-moving battles between tanks and armoured columns. Keeping abreast of events became difficult: soon the situation was fragmented and confused; nobody knew where the front line was or who held which objective. Rommel as usual was everywhere at once, charging across the desert in his staff car or flying his own spotter plane over the field of battle. One day he landed it and made for a makeshift HQ, only to realize that the tents there were British. Another day his car was strafed and he was thrown out, badly bruising his chest and abdomen. On another he drove to a town to visit his wounded, strode into the hospital and found it full of injured New Zealanders. 'Do you need anything?' he asked their medics, without batting an eye. Bemused, they gave him a list and he left, promising to return.

The fighting went on, losses mounted, yet he sensed Cunningham's advance was faltering. Furthermore, pleasingly, the Italians were repelling the break-out from Tobruk. It looked like Crusader was failing. He telephoned Berlin. 'Now is the moment to attack,' he urged, 'detach two Panzer divisions, drive towards Egypt, circle behind the enemy and cut off the entire 8th Army.' The idea was spectacularly ambitious, even by Rommel's standards, and fraught with risk. Berlin was sceptical, Rome too, and even his own officers voiced doubts. 'Nobody knows the British situation,' they said, 'their advance might have slowed but they're not beaten. Nor is Tobruk fully secure. Anyway there aren't supplies enough to sustain such an excursion – especially fuel.' But Rommel was adamant, and compelling, and the possibility of annihilating the British too tempting a prize for Berlin to refuse. The counter-attack was approved.

As always he led from the front, the tip of the spear, driving between columns harrying and chivvying, or flying his plane from one hotspot to another, landing, conferring, then taking off again. Time and speed as ever were crucial; if they were to succeed the Panzers must stop for nothing. Overflying a column one evening, he found it making camp for the night, hastily scrawled a note and threw it through the window: 'Two hours' daylight yet! Get moving!'

The plan was working. General Cunningham, alarmed, requested an urgent retreat of the 8th back towards Egypt, but was refused by Auchinleck, who replaced him with yet another general, Neil Ritchie. Ritchie held his nerve, sensed Rommel was over-reaching himself and renewed the offensive towards Tobruk, succeeding after several days in linking up with the garrison there. Suddenly a corridor lay open and Tobruk was relieved. Meanwhile Rommel's Panzers were becoming strung out, taking heavy casualties from air attacks and running out of fuel. A column stopped mid-desert when it ran dry. Furious, Rommel ordered its trucks back thirty miles to a fuel cache, only to find it blown up by the RAF. On their return they passed within a mile of a huge Allied fuel dump – enough petrol to last a month – but never knew it.

His luck was changing, his great counter-attack was foundering, and worse still it was becoming irrelevant now that the main prize, Tobruk, had been lost. Hastily he sent more forces back to attack the corridor, but orders became confused and the Panzers held back. The British now turned on the offensive, inflicting fatal damage. By December Rommel was in retreat, dragging his battered expedition back to Gazala, west of Tobruk. Still the British came at him, especially the RAF, which wrought havoc to his stricken ground forces. Further retreat was inevitable; by Christmas he was back at Benghazi, by January 1942 all the way back to El Agheila – his starting point the previous March.

It was a disaster. Tobruk was gone, Panzergruppe Afrika in shreds. Yet Rommel was unflustered and unrepentant. He was a career soldier, and a pragmatist; to him retreat was a necessary part of warfare, and when all looked hopeless a leader's duty was to save his forces, not squander them, withdraw to good defensive positions and regroup. This strategy earned him few plaudits. Hitler believed only in 'stand or die' and Mussolini, humiliated, was openly contemptuous. But to Rommel it was all perfectly logical. El Agheila might be where he started from, but it had advantages. An Axis stronghold, beyond reach of the British, it was easily defended and readily resupplied. Barely had he set up HQ there than he was shipping in reinforcements, rebuilding Panzergruppe Afrika, and planning a new offensive.

And launching it sooner than anyone believed possible. Brushing aside Pearl Harbor and America's entry into the war, by February he was back on the advance, surprising the British and retaking Benghazi before moving forward into the desert south of Gazala and digging in. There a climactic confrontation took place between the forces of the Allies under Claude Auchinleck, and Rommel's Panzerarmee Afrika. Covering an area of desert more than three hundred miles square and involving two hundred thousand men, thousands of tanks and hundreds of aircraft, the battle, which lasted through the spring, showed Rommel at his most masterful, employing feints, surprise attacks, fast outflanking manoeuvres and a final drive that split the defence in two, threatening to cut off the entire 8th Army. Auchinleck ordered Ritchie to form a new defence line but that too was quickly over-run and before he knew it Ritchie was retreating towards Egypt, leaving Tobruk to its own devices. Rommel then threw everything at the besieged town, bludgeoning it into submission, and a few days later finally drove inside to accept its surrender, together with more than thirty thousand Allied troops and vast stores of supplies. It was the greatest victory of his career, a glorious triumph of willpower and mastery. The news spread round the globe; his sunburned face stared out from every front page. Yet again his critics were silenced, while his supporters crowed, and Hitler promoted him to Field Marshal.

Yet typically he didn't rest on his laurels, and leaving newly captured Tobruk he set off in pursuit of the retreating British. Desperate to stop the rot, Auchinleck sacked Ritchie and took command of 8th Army himself, withdrawing deep into Egypt before finally turning to confront Rommel barely sixty miles from Alexandria. The place he chose was a railway halt of no significance, but strategically located in a natural bottleneck formed by the Mediterranean to the north and a giant depression in the desert to the south. Its name was El Alamein, and there he finally checked Rommel's advance. Churchill immediately pressed him to counter-attack but Auchinleck baulked – he wanted 8th Army to rest and regroup. So Auchinleck was replaced by a new chief, Harold Alexander, who installed a tough First War veteran called William Gott to lead the 8th. But flying in to take up his command Gott's plane was attacked and he was killed. Frantically Churchill and Alexander scoured the lists for yet another replacement, finally settling on an abrasive and outspoken vicar's son from Donegal called Bernard Montgomery.

'It's been a pretty easy war up to now,' Monty told an aide when he arrived in Cairo, 'but it's about to get a lot tougher.'

'It'll be all right, sir, don't you worry,' replied the aide.

'Not me, you idiot! I'm talking about Rommel!'

The next morning something feels different. Quite what is hard to define at first. I can't say my gloom suddenly evaporates like the mist, or the weather unaccountably perks up, or that life at XIB takes a miraculous turn for the better. Far from it – the next few days are as bad as any. But for me there's a sense of change, of recalibration, and of pages turning, both literally and figuratively. Several factors may account for this: Pip Smith's pep talk certainly strikes a chord; as does the news I'm being moved again. And last night's 'encounter' with Theo is significant to say the least. Undeniably though, the main catalyst for change is the news that two of our men have escaped.

The story breaks at morning roll call, or *Appell*. We're roused as usual by the window shutters banging open and coarse shouts of '*Aufstehen!*' and '*Heraus!*' from the guards. Normally I'm long since wide awake at this, but today I am soundly asleep, unusually, and have to be bullied from bed by the others who clump about the hut wrapping themselves in everything they possess before shuffling out into the meagre dawn light. I descend reluctantly from the bunk, pull on damp clothes, beret and French army greatcoat and follow. Outside low cloud blankets the scene; the light is a pewter colour, heavy with the threat of snow, while around the compound sleepy men are gathering, their breaths misting the air as they form up for counting. The French are still the largest group and take up one side of the square; we Brits stand opposite while smaller groups of Poles, Czechs and Dutch make up the rest. There's even a contingent of Americans, captured bomber crews, who slouch about in their leather flying jackets and baseball caps. Regarded curiously by us and with hostility by the guards, they soon get moved on to bigger camps further east.

At first, in my bleariness, I completely forget about Jack Bowyer and George Stebbings, and just stand there shivering, willing the guards to hurry up so we can get back to the huts for breakfast. But as they begin passing along the lines, chopping their hands down as they count, I suddenly remember and, craning my neck, see that the NCOs' section is more restive than usual, the men nudging and jostling each other, talking and murmuring in low voices when they're supposed to be standing silently at attention. Such sloppy behaviour would normally attract a reprimand from the CO, but Pip, I note, standing out front as Senior British Officer, is also watching them intently. Clearly he's in on the plan, and also awaiting news. It soon comes, and as the NCOs are counted by the clipboard-wielding guards, then counted again, their restlessness becomes more boisterous, and by the time Möglich wanders over to see what's going on, ribald laughter and general tomfoolery is breaking out. Möglich consults his men; there's a baffled rechecking of clipboards, and yet another count, then suddenly the penny drops.

'*Ruhe!*' Möglich bellows, 'Silence!' but to no avail for the news is rapidly spreading: 'Bowyer, Stebbings, out last night!' Excitement mounts, Möglich barks orders, the guards form up, rifles raised, but still the NCOs keep it up, the laughs become cheers and then there's a cry of *Waho Mohammed* and suddenly the entire British contingent, myself included, are in uproar, shouting and whistling in unrestrained celebration. It's silly, and provocative, and decidedly reckless, but the release from pent-up frustration feels marvellous, and for a moment we are the dominant party again, in charge, invincible, proud and victorious. The war cry swells, caps and berets fly, jeers and insults too. The Czechs and Poles join in for fun, the French watch in bafflement, while the Germans look increasingly rattled. Pip's right, I realize, they are losing this war and they know it. They *will* be defeated, and it's our job to keep reminding them. And reminding ourselves.

But we must do it cannily, because Möglich, though puce with fury, is nevertheless keeping his head, to his credit, and just as a riot seems inevitable he snaps his fingers at a watchtower and a burst of machine-gun fire tears into the muddy compound. This quietens us rather, as does the sight of three men, heavily laden, sprinting from the guardhouse to set up a second machine gun right before us. An uneasy hush descends. Both sides are overwrought and edgy, the danger is palpable and very present. Paras are an unruly bunch at the best of times, bloodthirsty and primed for recklessness. One false move and anything could happen.

Möglich beckons Pip forward.

'Major Schmitt,' he says loudly, and in English for the first time in my hearing. 'You will bring your men to order. Or there will be blood. Which will be *your* responsibility.'

Angry muttering continues in the ranks, someone shouts 'Bollocks!' but the moment has passed and Pip knows it.

'Parade!' he shouts, holding a hand up for quiet. 'Parade, a-ten-shun!'

The heart-warming thump of boots as we all stamp to attention. The Poles and Czechs join in too, bless 'em, while the French look on snootily.

'Last night,' he goes on, 'two of our men escaped from here, and are now, even as we speak, hopefully making their way home to their loved ones.'

Sombre murmurs of approval.

'Home with our loved ones, is where we all belong...' He turns pointedly to Möglich: '*Wir alle gehören dahin*... And where, God willing, we soon shall be. So with that happy thought in our hearts, let us now return to our huts, give thanks for our deliverance, and remember those who will never return home.'

Fine words, perfectly pitched, and we all dutifully troop back to the huts. Whether Möglich is moved or not is another matter, but either way the sanctions inevitably follow. Locked in all day, no exercise or fresh air, stoppage of all privileges, no mail or Red Cross parcels, worse slop than usual to eat, and so on. It's petty and tedious and we just have to lump it. Stuck in our huts, some retreat to their bunks to catch up on sleep, others read books or magazines, a few play chess or cards. I, meanwhile, both stirred and perplexed by it all, scrounge paper and pencil and attempt, as Pip suggested, to make sense of it in written form, thus beginning the first pages of what will eventually grow into a sizeable tome. Later, desperate for the outside, and only because medics are allowed to attend their patients in the lazaret, I visit Theo once more.

He's where I left him the night before. On his back, head angled to the window's fading light. He's been turned, fed, bathed and changed, I note, checking his chart, otherwise nothing's different. Except perhaps my attitude.

'Hello, Private,' I announce briskly. 'And how are we this evening?'

No response; none expected. But if we're ever to establish a rapport, at least one of us must start making an effort.

'It's been quite a day, let me tell you...' and I proceed to fill him in on camp gossip, including the news of Jack Bowyer's escape. 'Splendid chap, Bowyer, if a little forthright. And, er, hasty. He was all for sticking you full of morphine months ago, you know. Yes, well, anyway...'

I then get on to the business of our forthcoming move. Which is when it finally happens. '... Elm, I think Pip said, or was it Olm? God knows, I've never heard of it, and quite why we're going there is also a complete mystery. Anyway, down in the south somewhere, which will hopefully make a pleasant change. Anything's got to be better than this dump, eh? Hopefully warmer too. No, no, it wasn't Elm, it was Ulm! That's the place, Ulm!'

A pause while we digest this. Over at the guard hut furious barking tells me the dogs are preparing to come out for the night. The guards will be locking up again too, extra vigilantly no doubt.

'I must get back.'

A sigh. Like a whisper. Nothing more. A tiny sibilant sound like '*sim*'.

'Trickey?' I'm not sure I hear it, not sure even if it's him or a draught at the window. I bend lower. His eyes are slits, his face white and waxy in the last of the light. 'Trickey, did you say something?'

The sound comes again, another whispered exhalation: '*sim*'.

Then I realize it's not just a sound. I realize he's saying something.

'*It's him.*'

Following 8th Army's first encounters with Panzerarmee Afrika at El Alamein, by the end of August 1942 a period of stalemate had set in, with both sides dug in along a front stretching from the town to the great Qattara depression forty miles south. Rommel's force was dangerously deep inside Egypt, barely sixty miles from Alexandria, but Montgomery knew it lay at the end of a long supply line and needed time to re-equip. This in turn gave him the time he wanted to prepare 8th Army for a fresh offensive. Back in London Churchill fumed at the delay, but both Monty and his boss Harold Alexander held firm; 8th Army would not move until it was ready and that was that. This suited Rommel, who also needed time, although not just to reinforce his positions and resupply his men. He needed time because he was a physical wreck. By now he'd been in post eighteen months without respite and the strain was killing him. Headaches, nausea, fainting, low blood pressure, a liver infection, exhaustion, the chest and abdominal injuries from the car crash: the list went on and his doctors were aghast. 'Rest,' they insisted, 'the Generalfeldmarschall needs complete rest from the rigours of command – and from Africa.' Wearily Rommel concurred, even Hitler agreed, and in September he at last flew home to Lucie in Neustadt. 'At the rate we've been using up generals,' he wrote to her before leaving, 'that's five in eighteen months, it's no wonder I too need an overhaul!' Six weeks, the doctors told him, before a return to duty could be contemplated, six weeks minimum.

He barely got four. One morning in October the Führer himself telephoned with news that Montgomery had launched a massive new offensive against Panzerarmee Afrika at El Alamein. The suspicion was he'd done it because he knew Rommel was away. Worse still, General Stumme, the man flown in to replace Rommel, had apparently dropped dead of a heart attack on the first day. Hitler was ordering Rommel's immediate return to Africa to repel the attack. 'I'll need the troops and supplies I requested in August,' Rommel said. 'You shall have them,' Hitler replied. But that night Rommel flew to Rome where he discovered the extra troops promised by Mussolini had been diverted to Tripoli; next he went on to Crete where he learned the British had sunk his vitally needed fuel supplies, and then finally to Africa, arriving at his HQ only to find the Panzerarmee was already short of fuel and ammunition, and the extra tanks and artillery Hitler promised had been diverted to Russia.

He would lose at El Alamein and he knew it: it was simply a matter of numbers. And even as battle was joined, his strategy became less about beating the British and more about saving his beloved Afrika Korps. At first the omens were good; 8th Army made little progress and by mounting a ferocious defence Rommel all but halted its advance. He even began to counter-attack, but after eight days of bitter fighting, the Allies began breaking through, and with barely a hundred serviceable tanks against Montgomery's eight hundred the tide inexorably turned. Worse still, Monty had reserves enough to replace lost equipment, whereas Rommel had none, nor did he have the fuel to mount counter-attacks. By the tenth day he was being outflanked and in danger of encirclement, so he signalled High Command requesting a strategic withdrawal. Hitler's reply was unequivocal: You will stand and fight to the last man. Shocked at this madness Rommel initially complied, then disobeyed and began pulling his men back. Then followed a long fighting retreat of many weeks and over twelve hundred miles, back through Egypt, across the entirety of Libya, past Tobruk, Benghazi beyond even his first starting point of El Agheila. Beyond ultimately Tripoli itself. There the arid desert landscape began to change into the wooded hills, rivers and grasslands of eastern Tunisia. Here lay the Mareth Line, a fortified narrowing of the route where Rommel might turn, assemble the remnants of his force and mount a last-ditch defence against the advancing 8th.

But then worrying rumours began. Landings were happening, far to the west in Morocco and Algeria, an armada of ships was amassing off Gibraltar, and swarms of aircraft filled the skies above them. Soon the rumours were confirmed and the awful truth dawned. A massive new army of British and American forces had landed and was heading east into Tunisia, opening up a new front behind him and cutting off any chance of retreat. Rommel read the reports with dismay, but his soldier's instincts told him what to do. Save Panzerarmee. Africa was finished, and in any case irrelevant now for ultimately the war would be won or lost in Europe. Common sense dictated Germany evacuate Panzerarmee to Italy, or Spain, or even southern France, regroup and prepare to meet the Allies head-on. He put the proposal to High Command, but they refused to discuss it, or even meet with him. Reinforcements were being shipped to Tunis to confront the new threat, they would repel this Yank/Tommy army, while Rommel's duty was to destroy Montgomery's 8th Army advancing from the east. Defeat was unthinkable, evacuation out of the question, and any talk of surrender would be considered treason. Panzerarmee would fight to the last.

Rommel was appalled, yet unsurprised. Hitherto a loyal supporter of Hitler and his expansionist aims, his experiences in Africa caused him to see his leader in a new light: irrational, dishonest, deluded, disastrous for the future of Germany. Yet Rommel was a career soldier, and orders were orders. So he would stand and fight as told. And of one thing he was certain. Afrika Korps would not go down easily.

My dear Manfred,

I send you warmest congratulations on your 14ᵗʰ birthday! How swiftly time passes these days. I only hope this doesn't come too late. The war is hard and it is doubtful whether I will be permitted to return to you. You must realize the seriousness of the situation and study as much as you can. I'm displeased the Hitlerjugend makes such demands on you when you should be at school. Times may become very hard, dear Manfred, so be guided by your mother and know that you are always in my thoughts. Be brave, young man!

Your loving father

CHAPTER 4

The three battalions of the 1st Parachute Brigade arrived in Algiers in November 1942. Part of the new 1st Army under the American general Dwight Eisenhower, 1st Army's task was to take and secure Tunisia, especially the vital port of Tunis, before advancing to annihilate Rommel. 2nd Battalion arrived last, clumping down the gangplank in bemusement like tourists on a cruise. None had experienced North Africa before; few had even travelled abroad. Imposing waterfront colonnades lined the port, while jostling houses with sun-bleached faces crowded the hills above. The wide harbour was busy with shipping; the air was filled with blaring horns, revving motors and the guttural shouts of Algerian dockers, while the smell was of engine fumes, oily water and sewage. And everywhere was the accumulating paraphernalia of war. Cranes swung overhead bearing stores, vehicles and weaponry. Supplies and equipment lay stockpiled along the docks. Tanks, trucks and armoured vehicles filled the quays, troops marched, Jeeps sped in and out, and Hurricanes thundered overhead.

The Paras formed up, their baggy jumping smocks and rakish red berets drawing curious glances. Two passing infantry officers scowled with disapproval, watching sailors smirked, and Algerian labourers pointed and laughed. In a while Colonel Frost appeared and stepped up on a crate, and everyone waited to hear his first words to the battalion. But instead of the stock lecture about tidiness and good behaviour, he instead produced a little brass hunting horn and blew a ragged fanfare. 'We've a job to do!' he shouted. 'You're ready, so let's get on with it!' And with that he jumped down. Glances were exchanged, wry murmurs heard; 'Well, well, Johnny,' muttered a Scotsman. Then the NCOs were barking their orders, and with that the five hundred men of 2nd Battalion stamped to attention, turned smartly about and marched off to war.

Frost was at their head, sniffing vaguely at the foetid air and wondering at the events that placed him there. After the success of Operation Biting, he had been promoted from C Company to the role of second-in-command of the whole battalion, under its leader Colonel Gofton-Salmond. He then spent an enjoyable and undemanding summer on a Bruneval lecture tour, catching up on leave, and training with the men down in Dorset. Then in October came news of an overseas deployment and Salmond put him to work preparing for departure. Finally, amid much excitement, 2nd Battalion was ordered to entrain for Scotland. But on the very night it embarked the troopship at Greenock, Salmond suddenly fell ill and had to be taken off. Within an hour Frost was standing before Brigadier Gale.

'You'll have to lead the battalion, Johnny.'

'What! But for how long?'

'God knows. Gofton's seriously ill. It could be permanent.'

'What about Philip?' Philip Teichman, still technically senior to Frost, might reasonably expect this promotion.

'He may not like it, but I want you. He'll be your second-in-command. Don't worry, I'll handle it, you just see to your men.'

The Algiers weather was mild; the rain-splashed streets smelled rank and exotic and, climbing up from the harbour, everyone marching in step behind him, Frost felt a sudden surge of pride. 2nd Battalion really was his! Soon they were swinging along elegant tree-lined boulevards where French colonials waved and doffed their hats. Then they were entering poorer quarters crammed with ramshackle dwellings of rough stucco. Children in Arab dress ran alongside, women in black watched from doorways and dogs nipped at their heels. Above them a domed basilica brooded portentously. They marched on, their boots ringing on cobbles, then crunching on dirt as urban areas gave way to tracks and brown fields. Palm trees, olive groves and eucalyptus began appearing, and after an hour they reached a suburb called Maison Carrée. Frost checked his instructions, continued past a military airfield, and then turned between wrought-iron gates into the former girls' college where 2nd Battalion was to be billeted. The buildings looked careworn but functional; a floral mural decorated one wall, a dusty sports field stood to one side. 'Any lassies still here?' someone quipped. Frost handed over to the NCOs and went exploring, commandeering the headmistress's office for his own, then spending the rest of the day attacking the bottomless catalogue of chores commanding officers must cope with at a new barracks: messing, washing and catering arrangements, transport, signals, and communications, weapons and ammunition supplies, standing orders and duty rosters: the list went on and on. Still technically a major and with barely a fortnight's experience leading a battalion – all of it in the bowels of a troopship – by midnight he was exhausted and demoralized. To cap it all a knock then sounded on his door and Philip Teichman appeared.

'Heard about 3rd Battalion?' he said, his eyes scanning Frost's desk.

'What about it?'

'Dropped into Tunisia three days ago.'

'So?'

'Some town called Bône, barely a hundred and fifty miles from Tunis.'

'Really,' Frost replied testily. He did know 3rd Battalion had been deployed, as had 1st Battalion. Both had arrived in Algeria before 2nd Battalion, and both were now busy making names for themselves, 1st Battalion going great guns 'harassing and disrupting' the enemy inside Tunisian lines, and now this Bône thing with 3rd Battalion. Apparently the men were laying bets on which battalion would be *primus in Carthago* – first into Tunis. 2nd Battalion was the long-odds outsider.

Frost picked up his pen. 'What of it?'

'Well, evidently they arrived in Bône to find it unoccupied by Jerry, see, but crawling with subversives and spies – you know, dodgy French colonials and untrustworthy locals.'

'Philip, I am rather busy...'

'So their CO marched the whole battalion right through the centre of town, you know, as a show of force.'

'Really.'

'Twice.'

'What?'

'Once with their tin hats on, then a second time ten minutes later wearing their red berets. So word will get back to Jerry there are two battalions occupying Bône, not just one! Brilliant, no?'

It was, Frost conceded, and typical Para brio. But with inter-battalion rivalry fierce, and 2nd Battalion lounging around a girls' school hundreds of miles from the action, it didn't make him feel any better.

Teichman gestured at his desk. 'How's it going?'

'Fine, thank you.'

'Doesn't look like it.'

'I *beg* your pardon?'

'I'll do it.'

'What?'

'I'll do it, you go and get some rest.'

'I couldn't possibly allow that!'

'Yes you could.' Teichman smiled. 'I'm a lawyer, remember. We love paperwork.'

'Yes, but—'

'Listen, Johnny. We have to make this work, you and I. For the sake of the regiment. And we will. So here's what I propose. Leave the admin to me, that's what I'm good at. You get some sleep, then tomorrow go and find 1st Army HQ and get us a job. That's what you're good at.'

The forty-four Dakotas began taking off at 11.30 a.m. Already late due to last-minute plan changes, confusion over loading and a waterlogged airfield, it took another hour to get them all airborne and formed up. Finally, three hours later than scheduled, the formation turned east and set out on the four-hundred-mile trip to Tunis.

Theo rode in Lieutenant Charteris's aircraft. After Bruneval the youthful Charteris had been promoted to intelligence officer for the battalion, reporting directly to Colonel Frost. Theo had been transferred to his section, where, as well as combat duties, he was to assist Charteris 'as required'. Albeit without any promotion.

'I'm sorry, Theo,' Colonel Frost told him before they left England. 'I put in the paperwork, but the East Surreys are being tiresome, and it seems there's a problem with your OCTU. You'll have to do it all again and that'll take months. You can if you wish, but you'll miss the deployment...'

'OCTU can wait, sir.'

An hour later the Dakotas crossed into Tunisia, at which the pilots dived to low level to avoid enemy detection. The ride, already bumpy, now became violent and within minutes hardened Paras were turning pale. Just as the first man jerked forward to vomit, Charteris caught Theo's eye and beckoned him over.

'How's your Arabic coming along?' he asked.

'Not too good, sir. I'm still studying the phrasebook you gave me on the ship, but it's hard going.'

'Keep studying. I've a feeling we'll need it.' Charteris steadied himself against a jolt. 'Plan's changed again.'

'Oh.' Theo knew nothing of the operation they were embarked on, except it had been repeatedly changed or cancelled.

'Yes and Colonel Frost's not pleased. We're now dropping to knock out a different airfield, before hiking fifteen miles to a second, which we're also to knock out before hiking another fifteen miles to meet up with 1st Army, although God knows how.'

'Sounds like a lot of hiking.'

'All of it behind enemy lines, with no protection and no transport. And apparently there's a Panzer division lurking in the vicinity, although nobody really knows. Anyway, our job is to liaise with the locals, gather information about the enemy and barter for transport.'

'Barter?'

'Buy or rent trucks and so on from farmers and villagers, so HQ says; failing that horse carts will do, mules, barrows, anything to carry the heavy weapons and equipment. We've plenty of cash at least, but if necessary we'll commandeer the stuff. So keep that phrasebook handy and stay close when we land.'

Theo nodded, recalling a German Panzer division glimpsed through binoculars in France. Tanks, half-tracks, motorized infantry, heavy artillery, speeding fearlessly down the road. Against one battalion using horse carts?

'Um, are we expecting opposition at the drop zone?'

Charteris grimaced. 'Haven't a clue.'

Another nauseating hour passed; then, through the open doorway, harsh rocky terrain gave way to a flat brown plain and the ride became smoother. Minutes later the dispatcher appeared from the cockpit and signalled to make ready.

Charteris took first position by the door. 'No time to recce the DZ!' he shouted to the nineteen men queuing behind him. 'So when the CO goes, we all go, right?'

'And pray Jerry ain't waiting,' muttered the man behind Theo.

Jerry wasn't waiting; no one was. Theo exited cleanly, felt the familiar jerk and sway, and was safely down in seconds. Rising to one knee, he released his harness and shouldered his rifle, instinctively scanning for trouble. But all was quiet save the drone of receding engines and distant toot of Colonel Frost's hunting horn. Taking stock, he saw that the ground was of rough plough, gently undulating with hills further off, wide open with little cover, and dotted with Paras far and wide. Bundling up his parachute he went in search of Charteris.

An hour later 2nd Battalion was deployed in a defensive perimeter around the drop zone, ready to move off towards their first objective, which was an airfield a mile away called Depienne. Not a shot had been fired, no enemy had been seen, although several locals were visible watching from a distance, with some helping themselves to equipment containers and discarded parachutes. Of potential motorized transport there was no evidence. Charteris left for an officers' meeting with Frost, while Theo waited with the others of HQ Company. Smaller than a regular company, it consisted of signals staff, the medical section, admin and clerical, and the padre. Theo didn't know them; they seemed friendly enough if rather unnervingly cheery, completely lacking that instinctive wariness many older hands had. He sensed few had been in combat before. There was a 'protective' section attached, armed with mortars and Bren guns, but they too appeared unconcerned, brewing tea and cracking jokes nearby.

He wandered to one side and took out his new binoculars. They were German-made; he'd bought them at a market stall in Algiers, not asking how they came to be there. He searched the horizon, noting how rapidly both the light and temperature fell with the setting sun, but seeing no sign of the enemy. Then a familiar sound drifted to him and with it a pang of longing. C Company, his Scottish friends: he could see them now, half a mile away across the plain, making ready for the attack on the airfield. He knew they'd be busy loading up with weapons and ammunition, stuffing pockets with grenades, sheathing knives, checking rifles and Stens. Major Ross was their leader now, the man who'd led the charge against the pillbox at Bruneval. The sound came again, a plaintive wail, and he smiled. Piper Ewing was among them evidently, complete with bagpipes.

Charteris returned. 'Airfield's deserted!' he reported breathlessly. 'Recce patrol just got back. They say there's no aircraft, no vehicles and no Jerry. Not so much as a wind-sock on a stick!'

'So what's the plan?' the padre asked.

'Lie low till midnight then move out towards the second target. Meantime we eat and rest.'

'Rather chilly for camping al fresco.'

'It's just for a few hours, Padre. Right, Theo, you're with me.'

They set off in search of transport. But the locals seemed to evaporate with the dusk, and in two hours they found only tumbledown farms, some Roman ruins and a few deserted barns. 'Careful, sir,' Theo cautioned, as Charteris shouldered his way into one, but it too was empty. The nearest they came to motor transport was a rusting motorcycle in a ditch, and reporting to Colonel Frost later could only list wheelbarrows, bicycles, mule and hand carts, and about a dozen ponies and donkeys among their purchases.

'Can't say I'm surprised.' Frost was squatting beside a radio operator. 'No transport, no support, no extraction plan: this whole operation's a mess.'

'Rather seems so, sir.'

'To top it all the radios don't work.' He glanced up. 'What about the enemy?'

'They were here,' Charteris reported, 'but now they aren't. Locals say they've seen aircraft, vehicles and, er, tanks too, though they were vague about numbers.'

'Vague?'

'Yes, sir. To be honest we – Theo and I, that is – formed the impression they weren't entirely frank with us.'

'Probably reporting to Jerry as we speak.' Frost checked his watch. 'All right, rejoin your men. We move out on my signal.'

At midnight the hunting horn sounded and 2nd Battalion moved off. No one complained, as with freezing temperatures and only jumping smocks for protection, sleep was impossible. They walked all night, picking their way across the alien landscape like Bedouins across a desert. The terrain was harsh and exposed; the order was to proceed in silence, so the only sounds were boots on rock, muttered oaths as someone stumbled, the clatter of cartwheels and occasional clopping of hooves. Theo walked in mid-column, near Charteris who was mounted on a pony, his helmet at the saddle bow, his water canteen clanking against a stirrup. His section followed, and with their weapons slung across their backs like crossbows, and the jerkin look of their belted smocks, Theo was struck by the timelessness of the scene: the officer on horseback, foot soldiers trudging behind, the moonlit landscape, just like the Carthaginians of old. To further add to the impression, small fires were occasionally glimpsed on the tops of hills, warnings to their enemy, he presumed, of their approach.

They stopped before dawn. As they did so, flopping to the ground for tea and cigarettes, faint flashes could be seen over the horizon to the north. 'Tunis!' Charteris exclaimed, checking his map. 'My goodness, chaps, that's anti-aircraft fire at Tunis. We're barely a dozen miles away!'

'Maybe we'll be *primus* after all,' the padre said wearily.

After a breakfast of bully beef and biscuit, they advanced down a shallow valley towards their second objective: an airfield outside the small town of Oudna. Having seen no sign of the enemy since dropping, Frost sent them forward in open formation, led by C Company, who set off to a jaunty tune from Piper Ewing. Rather like a field day exercise, Theo felt. Drawing nearer the target the Scotsmen became more guarded, but upon investigation, this second objective, save empty hangars and one burned-out Messerschmitt, also appeared deserted. Perplexed and wary now, Frost called a halt. Beyond the airfield lay a railway station and then the town of Oudna itself. Both would need checking. 'Proceed with caution,' he signalled C Company. 'I'm coming down. Everyone else wait here.'

Theo watched through his glasses as Frost's detachment descended. All remained quiet. A gentle breeze sighed through the grass; a train whistled in the distance; a buzzard circled high overhead.

The padre sauntered up. 'Everything all right, old chap?'

'I hope so, Padre.'

'Splendid.'

At that moment he glimpsed smoke puffs coming from one of the hangars, closely followed by a distant popping sound. Grabbing the padre, he dived for the ground.

'I say, what's—'

'Down!'

A deafening crash. Mortars, exploding all round, flinging earth and stone high in the air, closely followed by a spattering noise as machine-gun bullets struck rock. In seconds the scene was transformed from order to chaos, with blinding flashes, thunderous explosions and choking smoke filling the air. Theo lay prone, one arm over the padre while the mortars crashed and bullets pecked the ground all round. A minute passed, two; the bombardment went on, the ground shuddering beneath him, the explosions deafening in his ears, the debris showering his body. He kept his arm over the padre, who recoiled with shock at each blast. Then a pause came and he risked a glance, saw smoke, and men moving, and casualties falling, one writhing from a bullet, another with bloody chest gaping, a third cut down as he ran. Faint shouts rose above the din; he glimpsed Charteris, on his feet and gesturing towards an outcrop. He hauled the padre up and forced him into a run; others too were running, bent low, hands on helmets, some dragging wounded, others pausing to shoot back.

A minute later HQ Company was in partial cover behind boulders. Several men had been wounded, and the medics were already at work scurrying between them. More casualties lay in the open, some unmoving. The company's own mortars were shooting back, furiously lobbing shells at the unseen enemy, while everyone let fly with rifles and Stens. But rifles and Stens were useless at this range, Theo knew, even if they could see anything to shoot at. What they needed was heavy weapons, and a better position, or the Germans would bombard them to pieces like the Highland Division in France. The starter before the main course. We should move, he fretted, fumbling his binoculars, we should find better cover and move. Smoke obscured much of his view, but B Company was visible in meagre cover away to his left, while A Company was spreading itself along a ditch halfway down. Of C Company he could see nothing. Far to the right, perhaps a mile away, the ground rose to a craggy hill. He trained his glasses down again and saw shelling was coming from the railway station now as well as the airfield. Then he saw something else, movement, and with a shock he glimpsed familiar dark shapes creeping from the town.

'Tanks! Lieutenant Charteris! Tanks inbound!'

Charteris appeared. 'My God, you're right. And Colonel Frost can't see them, he's too low.'

'We should warn him.'

Another shell crashed in and they both ducked. 'Signals! Anything on the net?'

'Still trying, sir!'

'For God's sake!'

'Sir.' Theo struggled for calm. 'C Company's down there.'

'I know that! But with no radio what can we do?'

'Send a runner. Warn Colonel Frost. He can recall them. Before it's too late.'

'But we're under bombardment!'

'Then I'll be fast.'

'No, wait...'

But Theo was already unbuckling his webbing. Another salvo exploded, and another, the barrage intensifying as the Germans found range. Charteris squinted through the glasses. 'Christ, there's infantry too, scores of them. It's a whole armoured column.'

Theo unslung his rifle and helmet. 'Sir, I must go. Now.'

'No!' Charteris stared through the glasses. 'All right, yes! Tell Frost this: enemy armour advancing in force towards station from town, infantry in heavy support.'

'Right.'

'And for God's sake be quick!'

He ran, arms flailing, legs pumping, sprinting headlong down the slope of loose shale and tussocked scrub. Mortars burst, bullets zipped, choking smoke stung his eyes and lungs; soon he was gasping, breathless and disoriented. He kept going until he felt the ground levelling beneath his feet. Through the smoke he glimpsed running men, motionless bodies, a section manning a Vickers, then the rest of A Company, hastily digging in along their ditch.

'Tanks!' he yelled without stopping. 'Got to find the colonel!'

'Down and left!' someone replied.

He jinked left, ran on, stumbled and recovered; a clump of trees appeared, then a track leading to a fence, then a water tower and suddenly he was at the airfield. The fence led him left again; he came to a wrecked car, a pile of empty fuel drums, a hut, and more crouching Paras.

'Blimey, who are you?'

'Trickey, HQ Company. You?'

'Recce party, B Company.'

'Where's C Company?'

'Fuck knows. Halfway to Tunis probably.'

'Where's Colonel Frost?'

'Trying to stop them.'

He pushed on, legs numb now, lungs gasping for air, skirting the airfield in the direction of the station. The smoke cleared. Soon he came to rail tracks and began following them, using bushes to one side for cover. He slowed, moving more cautiously;

gunfire was sporadic behind him now, though mortars thumped on. Ahead he could make out new sounds: the crack of grenades, the stutter of alien machine guns, and something else, distantly familiar – the grinding squeal of tank tracks.

'Get down, you bloody idiot!' A hissed shout from the bushes. 'In here, quick!'

He ducked under bushes and found himself amid more squatting Paras. At their head was an officer he recognized: Major Teichman, battalion second-in-command.

'Who the blazes are you?'

'Trickey. Runner from HQ Company. Lieutenant Charteris sent me to warn—'

'There's a tank, yes we know.'

'Not just one sir, several, with heavy infantry support.'

'Christ. 10th Panzer. Looks like we found them.'

'Or they us,' someone muttered.

'Back!' Running feet from the railway. 'Everybody back. NOW!'

Colonel Frost appeared, followed by his protection section, two of them supporting a man with a bloody leg.

'Armour,' Frost gasped, 'coming our way. Everyone back to the ridge. Right now.'

'What about C Company?'

'They're holding them off.'

Teichman gaped. 'Alone?'

'It'll buy us time.'

'But we can't just leave them. Let me stay.'

'No. Ross is handling it. They're to rejoin us when they can.'

'But—'

'Philip, I've *ordered* them to rejoin us.'

An hour later three of 2nd Battalion's four companies were back on the rise overlooking Oudna airfield. It offered poor cover but did afford a view, and as the day wore on, while they were digging in on the unyielding ground, hacking at it with bayonets and piling rocks around them, they were able to witness the steady encroachment of the enemy. Shelling continued, sometimes intense, sometimes sporadic, indiscriminately lethal, but then the sniping began and Paras began falling from bullets. One moment a man was busy digging, the next he was dead on the ground. Casualties rose steadily, the cries of the injured mingling with the barrage, while a distant crackle of grenades and small arms signalled C Company's struggle for survival.

Even as his battalion was savaged around him, Frost strove to save it, never resting, always moving despite the risk, visiting the injured, repositioning his forces, checking dwindling food and ammunition supplies, roving from position to position offering advice and encouragement.

'All set here, Corporal?'

'Yes, sir. We're using our jumping smocks for camouflage, see?'

'Good thinking, you're barely visible at all. Need anything?'

'Sausage and chips wouldn't go amiss.'

'See what I can do. Meanwhile don't go shooting that rifle unless you have to.'

Their situation was desperate and he knew it. Outnumbered, outgunned, weakly positioned, one determined assault by the enemy and they'd be wiped out. But the afternoon crawled by and no assault came, and at dusk the miracle happened and the barrage withered to silence. Once sure the lull was lasting, he sent out messages calling his company commanders together.

'What's going on?' they asked, their voices hoarse in the sudden calm.

'Knocking off for Schnapps and sandwiches?'

'Maybe they're giving up.'

'You wish! They're just getting started.'

'What do you think, sir?'

'My guess is they're rearming,' Frost told them. 'And repositioning, moving infantry up, distributing food and ammo, redeploying, getting everything ready.'

'For what?'

'An all-out attack. Most likely at dawn. Which means we've got to be long gone before then.'

'Gone where?'

The hill, Charteris explained to HQ Company later, pointing to the hill Theo spotted earlier in the day. Its name was Sidi Bou, he said, and Frost's plan was to evacuate the whole battalion there under cover of darkness, take up defensive positions and hold out until relieved.

'And how long's that likely to be?' the padre asked.

'1ˢᵗ Army knows we're here. And they said they were coming. So they will. Won't they?'

'Not if present performance is anything to go by.'

'No, well, we don't have much choice frankly.'

'That hill looks bloody steep,' someone else said.

'Which is why the colonel chose it,' Charteris insisted doggedly. 'He says we don't have the strength to attack the enemy head on, but we can easily hold out there. He says it's unassailable.'

'But what about the casualties?' a medic asked. 'They'll never make it.'

Theo watched as Charteris struggled. Just twenty-one, with Bruneval his sole experience of war, he was learning leadership the hard way.

'I know,' Charteris sighed. 'We're taking the walking wounded with us, but the seriously injured, and the dead, we're leaving behind, together with a contingent of orderlies. There's no other choice.'

The hunting horn sounded a muffled withdrawal at midnight. Heavy rain added extra hazard to their departure, but also helped mask their movements, and three hours later, bedraggled, weary, and down in strength by over a third, 2nd Battalion was digging in on Sidi Bou's steep slopes. The remainder of the night passed in rain-drenched misery. Even Frost was beaten, sinking into gloomy torpor, back to back with Teichman in a waterlogged furrow. This is not what Paras are for, he kept telling himself, not what we do. He'd told his superiors too, repeatedly, at HQ; we carry no protective clothing, he'd said, no tents or blankets or waterproof capes, just light weapons and minimal rations. That's our modus operandi, he'd said, our whole *raison d'être*. We drop in, do the job, then we leave. 'How marvellous,' they said, and took no notice.

Theo spent the night wedged in a crevice on the hill's flank. Draping his smock over his head, he could protect himself from the worst of the weather, but was still soaked to the bone. He was too cold for sleep, so allowed himself food: army biscuit supplemented with a mix of nuts, dates and honey he'd bought at the market. Shutting his mind to discomfort as his great-grandfather had taught him, he passed the rain-drenched hours of darkness practising his Arabic, trying not to reflect on the day's setbacks, and dreaming dozily of the quilted warmth of his grandmother Ellie's bed in Bolzano. A while before dawn, he awoke from reverie to hear Charteris calling his name.

'Theo? Ah, there you are, been looking for you.'

'Sir?'

'C Company's back. Lieutenant Spender brought them in twenty minutes ago.'

'Thank heavens. What about Major Ross?'

'With the medics, injured in the arm. They've suffered terrible losses, but they're back now and that's the thing. Colonel Frost has them guarding the rear of the hill, so now we're all together again. Thought you'd be glad to know.'

'I am. Thank you, sir.'

'Call me Euan.'

'Euan. Um, would you like some nut mix? It's a bit sticky.'

They munched in silence. Then:

'I mean, you were on Operation Colossus, weren't you, Theo?'

'Yes.'

'And Biting, of course.'

'And Ambassador.'

'What was Ambassador?'

'A bit of a muddle actually. It didn't go well.'

'Oh. *And* you saw action in France, Dunkirk and so on, isn't that right?'

'I... Yes.'

'My God, then I should be calling *you* sir.'

'I've never felt, you know, like an officer.'

'Me neither.'

'Although I am an acting officer cadet. In theory.'

'Really? How come?'

'It's rather a long story.'

'Oh.' Charteris turned his head to the sky. 'Rain's stopping.'

'That's good. It'll start warming up soon too.'

'Yes. Do you think 1st Army will come today?'

'Hopefully.'

'Yes. Only the thing is, I have a rather bad feeling.'

Theo stopped in mid-chew. 'What?'

'Even though Battalion's back together, and we're in a strong defensive position, and the weather's getting better, and 1st Army is coming. I just do. Stupid, isn't it?'

By mid-morning the clouds had cleared, the sun was bright and the temperature climbing. The enemy, having let slip its quarry during the night, was now actively reacquiring it, albeit at a cautious pace. Recce parties initially, they arrived at the base of Sidi Bou, sniffed about like dogs at a post, then left. Eventually one troop ventured on to a lower slope and began a tentative climb, whereupon it was sent scurrying by a fusillade of grenades, rocks and verbal abuse from the Paras. Knowing the Germans would now return in strength, Frost deployed the battalion to cover all approaches, with A and B Companies on the front and flanks, and HQ and the remains of C Company protecting the rear. This direction overlooked a wide plain to the south from where, it was hoped, advance elements of 1st Army would appear. With the enemy steadily assembling below, anxious eyes kept close watch on this sector, and sure enough, around eleven o'clock, triumphant shouts were raised when a dust cloud appeared in the distance. At the same time the battalion radio finally crackled to life and Frost was hastily summoned to receive a message. Maybe, the Paras dared believe, the nightmare was coming to an end.

But they were cruelly mistaken. As the dust cloud neared, it wasn't 1st Army that materialized from it, but mechanized enemy reinforcements, including self-propelled guns, tanks and artillery. And Frost's radio message – the only one he received in the entire mission – was to inform him that 1st Army's advance had been called off. The nearest 'friendlies', it went on, were at a town called Medjez, which may or may not be in American hands. Rereading the message in disbelief, Frost picked up his map. Medjez was over thirty miles away. It might as well be three hundred.

'What's the word, Johnny?' Teichman asked.

'That we're on our own,' Frost replied stonily.

Half an hour later the barrage began.

Surviving it was a lottery. Well dug in, with rocks and boulders for protection, the odds were reasonable, except for a direct hit which no one could survive. But the intensity and ferocity of the bombardment was unlike anything previously encountered. Artillery, tanks, mortars and heavy machine guns poured shells on to the hill's slopes. The noise was a thunderous hell, the smoke and din all-enveloping, such that normal thought or action was impossible. Solid trunks of dirt and rock erupted outwards like trees, their limbs hanging starkly until subsiding to dust. Where one sank, ten more sprouted, until the whole hill was like a forest in motion. Within it men cowered in their holes like trapped rats. Movement was suicide, shooting back pointless, all anyone could do was grit their teeth and pray. Helmet tightly strapped, fists gripping his rifle and binoculars, Theo hunched deeper into his crevice and watched the horror unfold. An entire Vickers section was blasted to fragments before his eyes, men flung through the air like dolls, others vanishing into red smoke. And the secondary effects of exploding rock: a man with his arm severed as if by axe, another with a stone shard protruding from his back, a third staggering, holding his face which had been sliced from his head. Wincing at a nearer blast he felt a tug at his sleeve, and saw a rent appear in his smock. At his feet lay the lump of red-hot shrapnel, while not ten yards away gaped a steaming hole where the mortar had exploded. It was the worst barrage he'd ever experienced. His orders, like everyone's, were to lie low and wait, but waiting, and watching, and not flinching, and not throwing his weapon aside and fleeing, was diabolical torture. Too diabolical for some, he saw, as a man nearby leaped up and ran, only to be felled by a blast.

Then it ended, thunderous hell faltering to an eerie silence. For a minute nobody moved, too stunned to react, yet alone think or speak. Then as the smoke cleared, heads began appearing from foxholes, voices sounded in ringing ears, cigarettes were lit and cramped limbs stretched, while medics hurried to aid the injured. Soon machine guns and mortars were setting up, with shouts and whistles echoing round the hill as everyone made ready. The shelling was to soften them up, Colonel Frost had said. When it finished the main assault would begin, and *that* was when they would hit back. Theo trained his binoculars, searching for signs. His position was on the rear of the hill, immediately above C Company's. Minutes ticked by, nothing happened, but then he saw movement, and a lone figure labouring up towards them. It was Major Ross, C Company's CO, with his arm in a bloody sling.

'Hello, Trickey,' Ross panted. 'Nice to see you're still with us.'

'You too, sir. But, um, you're injured.'

'It's nothing.' Ross glanced at his arm. 'Listen, run and fetch Colonel Frost, would you? I've got a Jerry wants to parley.'

Frost was at his command post atop the hill. He and Major Teichman exchanged glances at the news, before following him down.

'Interesting development, John,' Frost said to Ross. 'Who is it?'

'Some artillery commander. A captain, name of Hecht. Says he's from 10th Panzer. Strolled up to our position waving a white handkerchief.'

'What does he want?'

'Our surrender. Says it's hopeless, we're surrounded, needless waste of lives, all that twaddle.'

'I see.' Frost gazed around, scratching absently at his moustache. Face stubbled, cheeks grimy, his jumping smock darkly stained with someone's blood, he seemed to have aged ten years in three days. 'Philip?'

'Well. We are in a pickle and no question.'

'Think we should call it quits?'

'Absolutely not. I'm just thinking of the injured. It could be their best chance.'

'Indeed. John?'

'Fuck surrender, I say.'

'What's C Company got left?'

Ross shrugged. 'Mortar, grenades, a few Gammons, one Vickers.'

'Ammo?'

'A handful for each.'

'Men?'

'Maybe fifty, plus the two subalterns, Ken Morrison and Dickie Spender.'

'Hmm.'

'Let them come, Colonel, they'll no' find it easy.'

'I agree. Give Captain Hecht his answer.'

Though the slope was against them, the Germans were fresh, fit and organized. They were also numerically superior and plentifully armed. Delivered by vehicle around the hill, they hurried on to the lower slopes and swiftly set up firing positions, shooting, moving, covering each other, shooting again, ever forward, ever upward. Their weapons, mostly mortars and machine guns, were accurate and quick to reload. Assisted by smoke shells and artillery from below, they mounted Sidi Bou en masse, aiming to overwhelm the Paras by sheer numbers. Soon the sounds of small-arms fire was heard as pockets of fighting broke out. Theo, Charteris and the others of HQ Company made ready, closely watching the slopes below. In a while they glimpsed grey figures ascending, zigzagging painstakingly upward, seemingly unchallenged. Theo sighted his rifle over a boulder. It held eight bullets, with one magazine of ten left in his bag, together with two grenades. After that there was nothing. A single shot rang out. 'Hold your fire!' Charteris shouted. But it was a signal, and as they watched, men in smocks leaped from C Company's positions and with blood-curdling yells fell on the enemy like animals. Furious fighting broke out, close quarters, hand-to-hand, with Scotsmen wielding clubs and daggers as well as rifles and bayonets, stabbing, bludgeoning, battering the attackers like men possessed. In seconds the Germans were wavering before the onslaught, then turning downhill to escape it. Moments more and they were in full flight, hotly pursued by screaming men hurling rocks and grenades.

The last Theo saw of the attack was a Scotsman flinging a spear. Then it was over, the Germans repulsed. Shooting died away around the hill, to be replaced by whistles and cheers, the triumphant hoot of the hunting horn, and the sight of red berets flying. Yet reprieve was temporary, all knew, and hard won, with many new casualties and the ammunition all but gone. Frost wasted no time, hurrying from position to position, redeploying his exhausted men and exhorting them to hold firm. C Company, despite its heroic stand, was virtually spent, B Company too was battered, and elsewhere on Sidi Bou Frost's defences were weak. Many men he visited were out of ammunition, many more, crucially, out of water and suffering desperate thirst in the noon heat. Frost could do little but urge them to hold on.

The next assault came after an hour. This one was slower and more methodical in its build-up. Advancing behind a creeping artillery barrage and supported by heavy ground fire, the Germans stole upwards like a foul tide. Soon fighting was breaking out once more. Theo listened as it neared, trying to gauge direction. A flanking attack to avoid C Company seemed probable, he sensed. Ahead the ground sloped to a ridge, before dropping steeply away, offering cover to the attacker. Nearby Charteris watched through binoculars, while around him HQ Company waited, squinting nervously over their sights. Shots rang closer now. Theo breathed out, feeling a familiar stillness draw over him. Then he glimpsed movement, and a grey helmet appeared on the ridge; he sighted, the rifle kicked and the helmet vanished. More figures appeared, running in from the left, still more scrambling over the ridge, and suddenly HQ Company was under siege. Wild shooting broke out: grenades cracked, mortars thumped, a machine gun rattled. Figures in grey charged through the smoke. He found himself standing, shooting his rifle left and right. A German fell, then a second, shells burst, bullets slammed, grenades were falling everywhere. One clattered at his feet; he stooped and flung it back. Close-quarters fighting broke out, grey and khaki mingling, bayonets stabbing, rifles swinging like clubs, and still the enemy came, some running, some kneeling to shoot, some throwing grenades, two setting up a machine gun not twenty yards away. Charteris leaped up to charge it, shouting and waving his pistol, then stumbled suddenly sideways.

'Euan!' Theo scrambled after him.

'I'm all right! Help me up!' He staggered to his feet. 'HQ Company forward!' and they all charged. Chaos followed, everyone running, everyone yelling, Charteris, the medics, even the padre was charging. Theo too. His gun was empty; he threw his grenades, the air was exploding with noise and confusion. But the mad charge worked: the Germans became separated, began losing direction and momentum. They faltered, and drew back in confusion, while the men in smocks leaped after them, screaming with fury. A minute more and the attackers were turning, then fleeing headlong back down the hill to safety.

The third and final assault came at sunset. Following the second, the Germans held off, as though unsure how to proceed. But no one doubted they would try. An hour went by, two; the Paras licked their wounds, tended their injured, redistributed the last of their ammunition, food and water, and waited for the end to come. Nothing happened. The sun sank, the heat abated, still the Germans hesitated.

'What are they waiting for?'

Charteris stared through his glasses. Gashed leg bandaged, he surveyed the hillside, now pockmarked with craters and littered with bodies and the wreckage of battle. Somewhere below was the remnants of C Company, although no word of them had been heard. Elsewhere the story was similar, with only A Company under Major Ashford reportedly intact. HQ had suffered losses, several killed and many injured, including the medical officer and the padre, his shoulder smashed by a bullet. Now he sat among the wounded, talking, comforting, patiently waiting his turn for medics with no water to clean his wounds, no disinfectant to treat them, and nothing to bind them with but bloody rags.

'Plain as day,' Charteris was saying. 'All formed up and ready for the off. So what are they waiting for?'

Theo followed his gaze. 'Sunset, do you think? More favourable light?'

Charteris grunted. 'It'll be dark before they know it.'

Theo shook his water canteen, then turned to study the clouds. 'Maybe it'll rain again,' he mused. 'We could certainly do with the water.'

'I'd rather it rained 303 ammunition!'

'What's that noise?' someone asked.

'Tanks?'

'No, too far.'

'I don't get it. What *are* they waiting for?'

Theo froze, still staring at the clouds. 'Them! Stukas!'

They appeared from nowhere, six dive-bombers, falling from the sky like hawks, engines roaring, sirens screaming, plunging vertically; at the last moment they pulled up, levelled, and released their deadly loads.

On the wrong positions. Explosions lit the dusk, the sound rolling away like distant thunder, not on the hill but far below it. The Paras raised their heads, only to witness the impossible. Far beneath them, toy-like aeroplanes were banking round, climbing, circling, then diving again, pouring bombs and bullets on to the German positions. A third pass they made, then to complete the devastation four Messerschmitt fighters arrived and began a series of murderous strafing runs using machine guns and cannon. The noise made a crackling sound and their gun ports twinkled with sparks; the Paras could see tracer bullets arcing into the enemy, the Messerschmitts racing in at high speed and low level to kill their own people. Then suddenly it was over, and the planes were flitting away into the sunset like swifts to the eaves. Silence descended, smoke and dust drifted, and through it flaming vehicles, wrecked tanks and scattered bodies appeared. Explosions still echoed over the valley as burning ammunition blew up, while thick coils of dark smoke rose, staining the evening sky with black.

A while later runners began moving among the Paras.

'Jerry's withdrawn,' they repeated. 'We descend in an hour, pull out through A Company and rendezvous at the Roman ruins one mile west. Silent order, light weapons only, the injured stay behind.'

And so 2nd Battalion came down from Sidi Bou. If German pickets saw or heard them, they gave no sign, nor made any attempt to stop them. As though the failed assaults and the final devastating attack from their own air force had knocked the stuffing from them. As though they couldn't face any more fighting that day. So, section by section, the Paras descended through A Company's positions and made their way to the rendezvous. HQ Company was last to leave, and before departing Theo paid a final visit to the padre, who had chosen to stay behind with the wounded.

'Goodbye, sir, take care of that arm.'

'Goodbye, old chap, and thanks for, you know... during the shelling.'

'Yes.' Theo peered round the darkened summit. About fifty casualties sat or lay there, shadowy humps like the boulders around them, while, poignantly to one side, the many dead were stretched out in unmoving silence.

'Was it in vain, Trickey?' The padre followed his gaze. 'Is that what you're wondering? Their sacrifice?'

'I'm not sure it's what they volunteered for.'

He and Euan Charteris waited until the last HQ stragglers had gone, then descended. Navigating by moonlight, and with Euan leaning on a stick, they made slow but steady progress, and were among the last to reach the rendezvous. There they reported to Colonel Frost, whom they found in heated discussion with Major Teichman.

'How can they not be here?' Teichman was saying. 'Didn't they get the order?'

'As far as we know.'

'What does that mean?'

'It means as far as we know!'

'Then where are they?'

'Perhaps they were held up. Or took a different route.'

'Or never got the order!'

'Ross knows what he's doing, he'll work it out.'

'No. I'm going back.'

'You can't...'

'I'm not leaving them.'

'Philip, listen...'

'No! *They were mine before they were yours.*'

A while later Frost called the remaining officers together. 'Major Teichman has gone back to find C Company,' he told them in a voice that invited no comment. He then went on to explain that rather than make for Medjez as a single column, which would be glaringly obvious to the enemy, he proposed splitting into smaller units, each making its own way and aiming to rendezvous at night. All agreed it was a sound plan.

'Furthermore,' he continued, 'I want to send someone ahead to make contact with 1st Army, with a view to bringing armed support and transportation.'

Euan's hand shot up. 'I'll do it!'

'But your leg's injured.'

'It's nothing, a scratch, won't slow us a bit, will it, Theo?'

And Theo found himself volunteering too, an offer Frost gratefully accepted, especially when Euan said Theo spoke Arabic. So with little further discussion, nor much planning it seemed, he and Euan loaded up with whatever food, water and ammunition they could find, hoisted it on to their backs and set off into the darkness.

They walked all night, slogging up hills and down vales, through sodden fields of plough criss-crossed with water-filled wadis and steep dykes. In no time they were soaked and exhausted, their boots huge with mud and their clothes rain-drenched. Furthermore, Euan's leg grew troublesome, so Theo had to help him. Their navigation was not sound either: with a ragged overcast obscuring the stars, Euan kept turning them in different directions. Towards dawn, after an estimated ten miles' trudging, they could go no further and began seeking shelter, eventually stumbling upon an abandoned farm.

'That hut, look!' Euan pointed. 'Maybe there's food, or straw for bedding and whatnot.'

'No, Euan, wait!'

But he was hobbling to the door and pushing it open. And in a flash of white light the booby trap exploded, blowing the door off its hinge and flinging him ten feet backwards into the dirt. A wave of smoke and dust rolled over him. For a moment he just lay there, staring down at his shattered body, his blackened face a mask of surprise, then with an amazed laugh he fell back.

Theo rushed up. 'Euan, can you hear me?'

His eyes were still wide. 'Oops.'

'Hold on. It'll be all right.'

'Did it again, didn't I?'

'Don't talk. We're fixing you up and getting out of here.'

He tried, but the damage was devastating, the front of Euan's body torn open as though by a wild animal, the flesh shredded, the bones smashed. Theo mopped and dabbed as best he could, bathing his face, dribbling water between his lips, but with no field dressings, no sulphanilamide or morphia, and nothing to stem the bleeding, he could do little but hold him and murmur encouragement.

An hour passed. 'Remember Bruneval?' Euan whispered at one point.

'Of course. You were terrific.'

'Scared to bits. But it was a marvellous do, no?'

Theo nodded. 'Yes it was.' He'd managed to drag Euan into some bushes, but their position was precarious, and he'd been hearing the enemy: patrolling aircraft, a passing lorry, the rumble of distant artillery. Discovery was a matter of time. 'A near thing, though, waiting for those boats.'

'Better than this. For us Paras, I mean.'

'Much better.'

Later Euan became restless, crying out in pain until Theo had to shush him like a baby. Then he complained of the cold, so Theo wrapped his own smock about him, watching helplessly as Euan's blood soaked it through. At one point he heard a motorized column passing, and drew branches over them for camouflage. Finally, around noon, Euan's eyes opened, and stared up at Theo with an expression of curious calm. Then he nodded and went limp. Theo sat with him a few minutes more; then, pulling him deeper into the undergrowth, he covered him with leaves and branches, collected his discs and emptied his pockets. As an afterthought he removed the leaves from Euan's face, cleaned it again and laid his red beret over it. Then he rose and hurried away.

CHAPTER 5

Major Yale lowered the report, his expression sombre. For a minute or more he said nothing, eyeing the youth before him, one finger tapping his desk.

'Quite a story.'

'Yes, sir.'

'And you spent the next five days on the run, until being picked up by an American patrol, somewhere outside Quballat.'

'Yes, sir.'

'And how long were you there?'

'A week. Then they put me on a lorry back to their lines.'

'At Oran.'

'Yes.'

He flicked pages. 'Where you had to wait a fortnight for transport back here.'

'Yes.'

'So you've been gone four weeks, give or take.'

'Yes.'

'And haven't been back to Maison Carrée.'

'I was told to report straight here.'

'Quite right.'

'But I'd like to get back to my battalion—'

'In good time.' Yale saw the youth's shoulders sag. Beyond him the guttural chatter of Algerian tradesmen floated through the open window, together with the sounds of motor traffic, clopping carts and raucous children. The smell of cooking smoke and engine fumes wafted, while somewhere, incongruously, a radiogram played Christmas carols. It was January 1943, a month after the Depienne operation, and upon Yale's desk lay two files, one on the operation, one on the youth. As he read the latter, he stole dubious glances at him. Delicate and pale, staring at the ceiling and nervously fingering his beret, this slightly built twenty-year-old did not match his paper profile. Smooth-skinned cheeks dusted with grime, hair tousled, wearing a badly soiled battledress with faded yellow lanyard, and that oversize smock thing with the dangling tail that the paratroops wore, he looked more like a schoolboy cadet than the Mediterranean bruiser he'd imagined. *Unquestionably resourceful,* Grant said in his notes, *and something of a loner, Trickey's loyalty appears beyond doubt. And as an asset to the Executive he is unique. But his motivation may never be understood, for it is as contradictory as the South Tyrol question itself.* Indeed, Yale reflected, and how confusing. Even his name made no sense, Andreas Giuseppe Vittorio something, while Grant referred to him simply as Trickey. Which seemed apt. Yet the boy's operational record was astonishing: 51st Highland Division in France, then 3 Commando, then 11 SAS, now 2 Para, mentioned in dispatches twice and no fewer than three special ops including the German radar raid in Normandy last year. And before that apparently he'd been training partisans in Italy. Not to mention surviving this Depienne débâcle. He swapped files and read again.

'And Teichman actually said that to Frost?' he asked. '*They were mine before they were yours.*'

'Yes, sir.'

'What did he mean, d'you think?'

The boy shifted uneasily. 'I, um, well, Major Teichman commanded C Company before Colonel Frost did. Before the Bruneval raid.'

'So he felt responsible for it?'

'I... suppose so.'

'Was there friction between them about it?'

'I don't know. Not that I was aware of.'

Yale held the youth's gaze, which seemed wary, and conflicted, haunted even. He should probe further, he sensed, but not now; other matters were pressing. Outside his street-level office two Algerians were beginning a noisy argument, while the baleful blare of ships' horns signalled new arrivals in the harbour. Still reading, he wandered to the window and latched it shut.

'I'm going to need you here for a while.'

'Sir?'

'No doubt Grant filled you in back in London. This is a new office; we've a great deal to do, mostly, at this stage, relating to the processing of prisoners.'

'Processing?'

'Translating, you know, interpreting and so on when we question them. We're collecting quite a few, Italian and German – I gather you're fluent in both.'

'Yes, but...'

'We'll retrieve your belongings, fix you a billet, fresh uniform and so on.'

'What about 2nd Battalion?'

'You're being detached here.'

'But with respect, sir, my duty's with them.'

'Not for now it isn't. It's here interpreting for us.'

'But 2nd Battalion—'

'Has gone!' Yale leaned forward. 'Ceased to exist. Don't you get it?'

'Ceased...'

'The 2nd Parachute Battalion is not currently a functioning unit. It's been stood down. Frost too. He's lodged complaints, and there's an investigation ongoing.'

'But...'

'But nothing. That's all you need to know. Except that you have been detached here for the foreseeable future.' Yale tapped the file. 'Do you understand?'

Trickey's eyes bored into him suddenly. 'Where's Major Teichman?'

Yale sighed. 'Teichman's dead. He was killed trying to lead C Company survivors through enemy lines.'

Yale showed him to an adjoining office and handed him over to an orderly. The orderly, an overbearing corporal named Bryce, gave him money, a chit for a fresh uniform, and directions to his billet, which was in a requisitioned boarding house two streets away. Take the weekend off, Bryce instructed, and report for work first thing Monday. More instructions followed. Stay away from Maison Carrée. Make no attempt to contact 2nd Battalion. Keep clear of the harbour at night – unless you want your throat cut. Watch out on the streets, Algiers is crawling with spies, double agents, fifth columnists, deserters, thieves and prostitutes. Trust no one and don't mix with the locals, especially the French. Curfew's at 2200 hours; be indoors or else. And keep away from the casbah, it's banned to all servicemen.

'Why?'

'Because it's a hotbed of crime and depravity. In fact, my advice is stay in the billet and go nowhere at all. Sign here.'

Theo signed. 'Anything else?'

'Yes.' Bryce grimaced. 'Take a bath, for God's sake. And while you're at it put that ghastly smock thing in there too, it smells like a backstreet butcher's.'

He found the billet, ate a stale sandwich in the mess, bathed and changed, then went to his room, which was a cramped garret on the top floor with flaking walls, furnished with two army cots, chairs and a table. Personal effects littered one cot, so he selected the other, stretched out and tried to sleep.

Though his statement to Yale was accurate, including his summary of the Depienne operation, he wished he'd left out the part about Teichman and Frost arguing. Because it felt disloyal. 2nd Battalion stood down, Yale had said, an investigation ongoing, but what did that mean? Was Colonel Frost in trouble? Yet he'd only done everything possible to save the situation. He tossed and turned on the cot, reliving the nightmare. The carnage and slaughter, the shelling and the sniping, the night marches and the rain, the cold, thirst and hunger. The desperate last-ditch defence of Sidi Bou. And the final night, wandering the hills with Euan searching for help. He regretted reporting that too. How he had failed to stop Euan entering the hut. The shocking flash and bang of the booby trap. Holding him in his arms afterwards. Trying to calm him when he cried out. The look in his eyes when he passed, and the dreadful loneliness after. These things were not for sharing.

The rest was as he'd reported it. After finally leaving Euan, he'd made his way slowly south, keeping away from roads, avoiding towns and villages, travelling mostly by night. He lived off the last of his rations, a rabbit he snared and stolen fruit when he could find it. For two days he had to hide beneath an embankment when a German motorized patrol stopped and made camp. At night he could hear them talking around their campfires. Finally they moved on and he set off once more. On the fifth morning, exhausted and starving, he spotted a well at a crossroads and descended in search of water. As he was filling his bottle a half-track roared round the corner bristling with infantrymen. But they weren't German, they were American, a recce patrol, and once satisfied he was not a 'kraut saboteur' they made him welcome, gave him food, and drove him back to their base, which was a huddle of tents outside Quballat. No, they said, in answer to his repeated questions, they knew nothing of a missing Brit unit, but they'd seen plenty of Jerry and been hearing their artillery for days. After a week at Quballat they gradually started shunting him rearwards, before flying him to Algiers from Oran this morning.

He awoke with a start to the drumming of feet on stairs. A moment later a dark man in a suit burst through the door.

''Ello, 'ello! Is mus' be my new bed fellow.'

Theo sat up. '*Was ist los?*'

'*Keine Panik, Junge.* I am Antoine. We share this room, no?'

'What?' He shook his head.

'Is true. An' you are?'

'Um, sorry, I'm Theo Trickey.'

'Theotricia.'

'No, that's *Theo*.'

'Tadzio.'

'No, it's... I'm sorry, who did you say you were?'

'Antoine. Sharif.' He bowed. 'Of the French army intelligence. Linguistics section, don' you know.'

'You're French?'

'French, Algerian, Arabic – you choose. Some English also. Call me Tony!'

'Tony? But—'

'Enough questionings, Tadzio, come. We go eat now, hup hup!'

Ten minutes later, wearing ill-fitting civilian clothes forced on him by Antoine, he was hurrying along cobbled alleyways that twisted up through the town like creepers up a tree. Darkness had fallen. The alleys were poorly lit, shadowy images passing like pictures in a book; men playing cards, old women talking, children squabbling, someone smoking a hookah. In one doorway he glimpsed a chicken being strangled.

'Where are we?' he puffed.

'Away from riff-raff, away from military, Randon quarter.'

'In the casbah?'

'Of course, is best food here. You bring money? Quick. Along this!'

They turned a corner, ducked through an archway and emerged on to a narrow lane crammed with shops, stalls and cafés. Vendors sat on the cobbles touting goods by lantern light – ornately worked copper, fruit, spices, army equipment, smuggled cigarettes. It was like the market he'd bought his binoculars at, but quieter and more furtive. People seemed wary as they approached, until Antoine greeted them with laughs and handshakes. Halfway along, he grabbed Theo and dragged him into a tiny café. Embracing the patron, he collected a carafe and glasses.

'Muscatel! Good stuff too, not slop they give GIs. Drink, Tadzio!'

Theo tasted musky sweetness. 'Very nice.' He gazed around. 'Um, isn't there a blackout?'

'Pah! Nobody give damn. Anyway Luftwaffe only bomb ships in harbour and never French quarter. I learn this from prisoner.'

A while later their food arrived. 'Ah – *chakhchoukha*!' Antoine rubbed his hands. 'Is local specialty.'

Theo chewed. 'What kind of meat is this?'

'Lamb, *idéalement*.' Antoine considered. 'But this horse.'

He was about thirty, Theo guessed, short and wiry, of Middle Eastern complexion with dark eyes and curly hair. His suit was linen and too tight; he wore a tiny bow tie at his throat, like a waiter. His shoes looked expensive.

'Who did you say you worked for, Tony?'

'For you boys! *Alors non*: BCRA, is Bureau Central de Renseignements et d'Action, except no, Action Militaire they call it now. Is bloody mess, name changes every damn week.'

'But you're in the French army.'

'Yes, yes. *Sergent-chef*, don' you know. But 'ow you say, *détaché* now, to your Massingham chappies here in Algiers.'

'Linguistics section.'

'Yes, yes, French, Arabic, Inglés, prisoners and deserters mos'ly but plenty other bad boy traitors and spies in glasshouse here, you know. *Et toi*?'

'Italian and German. And I'm trying to learn Arabic.'

'An' I want speak better English! We can help each other, no? *Excellent!*' He patted his pockets. 'Tadzio, you bring money?'

After the meal, Antoine led him to a succession of bars and clubs, each one seedier than the last. Muscatel flowed, crowds swirled, rain fell, Theo's head began to throb. Finally they arrived at a larger building with colonnaded entrance and two uniformed heavies at the door, which was wooden and ornately carved. Above it hung a sign: 'Starlight Club'.

''Ello, boys!' Antoine greeted the doormen. 'Is me, Tony!' Then he spoke rapidly in Arabic, money changed hands, and they were ushered in.

A haze of smoke filled a large salon. The air was hot and foetid, heavy with the scent of perfume, incense, sweat and tobacco. Furnished in Moorish style, the space featured rugs and carpets scattered with divans and cushions, upon which lounged middle-aged men in suits. The centre of the room was bare, like a stage; a bar lined one wall, a reception desk another, and stairs led to a balcony with numbered doors leading off, like in a hotel. Leaning over the balcony, smiling and waving, flimsily dressed and heavily rouged, were several young women, some European-looking, others Algerian, one ebony-black. More girls circulated among the men downstairs, serving drinks and lighting their cigarettes. An older woman appeared, small and business-like and smartly dressed in a Parisian suit. She spoke briefly with Antoine in French, took their money and led them to a sofa beside the stage.

'Tony,' Theo began uneasily, 'Listen, I am rather tired, and there's something—'

'This very old place, you know.' Antoine gestured at the ceiling, 'Ottoman, *seizième siècle*, is once gathering hall for Barbary corsairs. Pirates and that.'

'Yes, but—'

'Watch now. Best floorshow in casbah.'

Lights dimmed, a hush fell, French accordion music began on a gramophone. Two of the girls from the balcony appeared on the floor, and immediately began kissing and fondling each other. Their clothes – thin shifts and wispy chemises – were quickly discarded, then they knelt, naked, and the kissing became more ardent, and the fondling more intimate. Before he knew it they were lying on the floor, barely yards from his feet, their arms and legs tightly entwined, groaning and sighing and caressing each other, including between their legs. He swallowed, shocked yet transfixed; all around him the men on the cushions sat as though frozen, eyes wide, faces glistening with perspiration. The girls' movements became more rhythmic, and more urgent; they rolled aside, and opened their thighs so the men could watch as they rubbed one another. A minute more and they were gasping, their bodies thrashing and jerking as though in spasm, before, in a climactic torrent of shouts they went rigid, then subsided, and fell apart, arms and legs splayed, into breathless silence. Then they picked up their clothes and left the stage.

It took him an hour to locate Yale's office. He had no memory of the route Antoine had taken to the Starlight Club, let alone the café where they'd eaten, only that it had been endlessly uphill, so by heading downward he reasoned he would find a way out of the labyrinth. Leaving Antoine and the club behind he hurried away through fresh rain. By now the curfew was in force, yet the alleys still bustled. A few red-capped Military Police prowled, and he hid in doorways when he saw them. Finally he emerged on to a street he recognized; from there he located his billet, then it was a short walk to the administrative quarter. He found the window in the lane where he'd heard the Algerians arguing. As he'd hoped, it was latched shut, as Yale had left it, but not locked. A minute's probing with a bent wire and he was in.

The Depienne dossier consisted of a dozen mimeographed documents, reports, statements, letters and memoranda covering the six days of the operation. The longest was Frost's official record, which was factual, unembellished, and seemingly without emotion. Yet between the lines Theo could detect his frustration at the poor planning, the bad intelligence, lack of support, transport and radio communication. And especially the absence of an extraction plan, compounded by the 'we're not coming' radio message from 1st Army. Appended to the report was Frost's covering letter to his new superior, Brigadier Flavell. Here his tone was unrestrained, angrily despairing at 'the disgraceful way 2nd Battalion was thrown to the wolves'. He went on to request a formal investigation: 'to establish how on earth HQ could ever have sanctioned such a pointless and poorly thought-out operation'. And his final sentence was a shock. 'We dropped into Depienne as a battalion of 540 men. Six days later we crawled into Medjez with less than 170. And for what?'

The next document was Flavell's reply, which sympathized with Frost and assured him the matter was being investigated. 'Plainly the planners at HQ have no grasp of the purpose and value of a force like ours,' he wrote, adding ominously, 'I hear they are proposing no more airborne ops for us, but some kind of infantry role. All three battalions have been withdrawn accordingly.'

The other documents were reports from the individual company commanders and officers who survived. From these he was able to piece together 2nd Battalion's final hours. HQ and A Companies had fared best, struggling into Medjez more or less intact. But coming down from Sidi Bou, B Company became separated from the main body. At dawn next day they stumbled into an enemy ambush and found themselves surrounded. Desperate fighting followed during which many in B Company were killed, including its commander Major Cleaver. The rest were captured. Only a few made it to Medjez, including one lieutenant, Crawley, who walked for two days led by the hand having been blinded by a shell.

John Ross staggered in later the same day, together with one subaltern, Spender, and six other C Company survivors. The rest, Frost's beloved Highlanders, the wild men of Sidi Bou, the raucous heroes of Bruneval, had vanished. Theo read on in disbelief: Berryman, Duncan, Falconer, Fletcher, the casualty list was bottomless. C Company gone, B Company gone, 370 men killed or captured. The heart had been torn from the battalion. Even if replacements were found and trained, it would never be the same. 2nd Battalion, as he knew and loved it, had ceased to exist. Exactly as Yale had said.

A sheet slipped from the file. He picked it up. It was a poem, handwritten by Ross's subaltern, Richard Spender. Theo didn't know him well; 'Dickie' Spender had joined C Company after Bruneval. But he'd quickly established a reputation as a quirky and flamboyant lieutenant of the Royal Ulsters, who wore a huge green hackle on his regimental bonnet, carried a blackthorn stick, and marched his men to a piccolo he kept in his pocket. Few knew that he was also a writer of poetry.

> *Perhaps some God looking down*
> *With dull, cold eyes, by the near stars, will see*
> *One lonely grim battalion cut its way*
> *Through agony and death to fame's high crown...*

Returning the sheet to the file, he tidied Yale's desk, turned off the light, and slipped through the window to the street.

On the Monday morning he reported for work. 'Major Yale is in meetings,' Bryce told him brusquely, 'in any case you report to me, not Yale, as he's busy with more important matters.'

'Yes, Corporal.'

'Right, here's your list, and here's your pro forma. You know what to do.'

'Yes, Corporal. Although, um, actually no, Corporal.'

'What?'

'I don't know what to do.'

'But you've done this before.'

'Done what, Corporal?'

Bryce rolled his eyes. 'Question prisoners, you ass!'

A girl in FANY uniform was typing at a desk. Though her eyes were on her work, her mouth stifled a smile.

'Well, no, Corporal.'

'No?'

'Although I have done it the other way round. Once or twice.'

'What are you babbling about?'

'Well, I have been questioned, as a prisoner, as it were, by other people. But I've never actually done the, um, questioning. As a questioner.'

The girl's shoulders were now shaking.

'Are you taking the mickey, Private?'

'No, Corporal!'

'You'd better bloody not, or I'll have you on a fizzer fast as flash!'

'But—' The girl made a tiny shake of her head. 'Yes, Corporal. Sorry.'

'Right. Well, you just watch it, that's all.'

The list, Bryce explained slowly, as though to a deaf pensioner, contained the names of the prisoners Theo was to question that day. The pro forma contained the questions he was to ask them. He was to fill in one form for each prisoner, like a questionnaire, then at the end of the day return to the office and put the completed forms into Driver Taylor's basket for typing.

'Now, have you got all that?'

'Driver, um...'

'That's me.' The girl smiled. 'Clare Taylor. Hello.'

'Oh, right. Hello. Yes, Corporal, I've got it now.'

'Thank Christ. Right, off you go, and don't hang about, you've a lot to do.'

'Yes, Corporal.' He strode to the door. 'One thing, Corporal.'

'What now, for pity's sake?'

'Where am I going?'

It was a transit camp on the western edge of town. Red beret on head, a leather satchel under one arm, it took him an hour to march there, finally rounding a bend to find a ramshackle cluster of tents and huts parked beside a railway line. Smoke rose from fires, limp laundry fluttered, inmates stood around aimlessly; in the desultory January drizzle it reminded him of the Kempton camp where his mother had been. He found the gate, presented his papers and was directed to a wooden side-office. Ten minutes later the first prisoner was ushered in.

Eight hours after that the last one left. Throughout that time Theo was offered no refreshments, no food, no rest breaks, not so much as a glass of water. Nobody enquired after him, or checked on him, or showed the slightest curiosity in his task; they merely brought prisoners, then took them away again. That another odd sod from Intelligence wanted to question them was clearly of no interest to anyone.

The prisoners themselves were all Italian, and also of no importance. Lowly of rank, often young, poor and ill educated, inadequately clothed in the coarse tunic of the foot soldier, most had been captured – or surrendered – during the early stages of Operation Torch. Few had seen any fighting, several were deserters, all just wanted to go home. Leading them through his questionnaire, Theo found them willing to talk, but ignorant of matters military, and when he got to their homes and families, they often broke down and wept. Some pleaded with him to contact loved ones; several muttered darkly of Mussolini and the evil that had brought them to this predicament. None showed conviction in the war, and just one, an older man from Milan, queried Theo's loyalty.

'You speak like a northerner. Why aren't you in our army? Are you a Bolshevik?'

'No. It's because I believe in South Tyrol's independence.'

'Oh.' The man sniffed. 'One of *them*.'

He trudged back to the office with his forms. Bryce was gone, Yale also absent, only Clare the FANY clerk was still there, typing up her reports.

'Oh dear,' she said. 'Bad day?'

'Not quite as I imagined.'

'What did you imagine?'

'I don't know. Some, um, defiance, I suppose. Pride in their cause. You know, fighting spirit, or something.'

'Ah. You need to go up the ladder for that. These boys are bottom rung, the lowliest of the low, just humble draftees who've been away from home too long. You want fighting spirit you need regulars, preferably officers.'

'I didn't seen any officers.'

'Nor would you – they're housed elsewhere.' She rose from her desk. 'Don't worry, it's just Bryce throwing his weight about. It'll get more interesting.'

'You think so?'

'My guess is Major Yale's saving you up for something.' She shrugged on a greatcoat. 'There's a NAAFI nearby. Fancy a cup of tea? Looks like you could do with it.'

A pattern evolved. Each morning he reported to Bryce and collected his instructions and satchel. Using a bike bought at the market, and provisioned with his own food and drink, he then pedalled to one of several transit camps in the Algiers area, and spent the day interviewing prisoners, before returning at dusk to hand the forms to Clare. Twice, contrary to orders, he cycled via the girls' school at Maison Carrée to glean news of 2nd Battalion. The first occasion he found it empty and boarded shut, and the second it was occupied by a battalion of South Staffordshires. '2 Para?' the guard on the gate shrugged. 'Never 'eard of 'em.'

His evenings he spent with Antoine, who mainly worked at the Barberousse civilian prison, occasionally with Clare at a film or ENSA show, or alone, reading in his digs or out wandering the streets. This last soon lost its allure, as the popular venues were invariably packed with servicemen, usually drunk and often quarrelsome. Street crime was rife, thieves and pickpockets proliferated, fights broke out, the Redcaps were in frequent attendance. Disheartened by this seamy aspect of service life, he soon stopped going. Once or twice he donned Antoine's civilian clothes and ventured into the casbah, captivated by its hidden mysteries, its winding lanes and alleys, tiled walls, cobbles and keyhole-shaped doors. However, he never went back to the Starlight Club.

One day, six weeks after arriving in Algeria, he returned to the office to find a packet of mail waiting. In it were five letters, all from women. Two were from Eleni Popodopoulos, who gushed and fretted like a doting aunt. One was from Carla and read like a manifesto for Partito Popolare Sudtirolese, and the fourth was from Susanna Price. Decorated with loops and curls and floral embellishments she wrote warmly of remembered hugs and kisses, Kingston gossip and the wonderful news that Kenny Rollings was safe and well in a German POW camp. Though he was glad to hear from her, and especially the news about Kenny, her words seemed so removed from reality. So far away.

'Missive from the sweetheart?' Clare enquired innocently.

'Oh, yes. Well, no.'

'Which.'

'Actually, I don't know.'

She stopped typing. 'You don't know.'

'Well, yes, I know who it's from. Obviously. I'm just not sure if she's, that is, if we're, you know...'

Clare rolled her eyes. 'Don't you think you *should* know?'

'Should I?'

'I'd say so. For her sake if not yours.'

The final letter, astonishingly, was from his cousin Renata in Rome. Dated the previous year, and badly dog-eared after months of travel, it spoke in unusually subdued tones of the deteriorating situation in Italy, the strife and suffering, the disenchantment with Mussolini and the war, the political infighting, and the plight of the poor and starving. She made passing mention of her parents, and his grandmother now living in a sanatorium, concluding that she wished him well, and thought of him with affection. He lowered the page, recalling their evening in Rome two years earlier. Walking through the streets arm in arm, singing to Tyrolean folk music, the chance meeting with Rommel. The coolness of her body beside his.

That evening he asked Clare on a date. Wearing his clean uniform and with boots and beret brushed, they met at her digs and then walked to the colonial quarter, eventually selecting a bar off Rue Saint-Augustin called Café de Paris.

'Looks civilized enough,' she said, peering through the window. 'Quiet too.'

'That's because it's officers only.' He pointed to a sign.

'Stuff and nonsense! Chin up, hold my arm and act like you own the place.'

'But—'

'No buts!' With that she pushed through the door and strode in. Heads turned, conversations stopped, a waiter pounced, she disarmed him in fluent French, gesturing haughtily to a table by the window.

'*Ça va pour toi, Théodore?*'

'Oh, um, *oui, tout à fait.*'

'Shall I order wine?'

'Not Muscatel.'

'Rosé then please, waiter.'

Two years at the Sorbonne, she explained, when he complimented her French. That and finishing school in Switzerland. 'Hideous place.' She shuddered. 'All starched clothes and frozen lavatories.'

'Where?'

'Gstaad. The Alps. Your neck of the woods.'

'I'm from the other side, the Italian side, a town—'

'Bolzano. In the southern Tyrol. Yes I know.'

'You do? How?'

She smiled. 'Because I do.'

He sipped wine, studying her anew. Dark hair cut regulation short, smart khaki uniform, she had an oval face with teasing eyes and a tiny scar by her mouth. They saw each other daily, and spoke often, and went to occasional films, or the NAAFI, yet how little he knew of her, he realized. And how much she knew of him. Which didn't seem fair.

'What is FANY? Is it a women's branch of the army?'

'Not likely. First Aid Nursing Yeomanry. We were formed in the First War, to do nursing, and drive ambulances, that sort of thing. These days it's more, sort of, administrative.'

'Driver Taylor, Bryce calls you, yet you're not a driver.'

'I am, actually. A jolly good one. But no, it's my rank, not my job.'

'So your job...'

She shook her head. 'My turn. Why do you use the name Theodor, when your first name's Andreas? Which is a beautiful name.'

'That's rather a long story.'

She smiled again. 'I have all evening.'

So he told her. Of growing up above the Bolzano print shop, with its smell of ink and turpentine. Of living with his volatile

114

grandfather Josef, anxious grandmother Ellie, and beautiful but headstrong mother Carla. Of winter hikes in the mountains with his great-grandfather, and summer camping with school friends. Of political indoctrination, ethnic strife, family arguments and riots in the street. Of the undertaker Tolomei toppling statues in the square, and of Hitler, Mussolini and the humiliation of the Option Agreement.

'And you never signed?'

'Some in the family did. That caused a lot of tension. And my grandmother wanted us to; she worries a great deal. But my grandfather refused. Mother too. That's why we left.'

'And why he's in prison.'

He looked up. 'I never said that.'

'Sorry.' Her hand touched his. 'I hope I'm not intruding.'

'How do you know?'

'I must've heard it somewhere. Bryce perhaps. But do go on, please, I want to hear about London, joining the army, forming the paratroops and that.'

'No.' He held her gaze. 'My turn now. What is your job?'

'You know that.' She looked away. 'Same as yours.'

'But doing what?'

'I'm sorry, but I can't tell you.'

'Oh. Well then.' He made to rise.

'Wait!' She grabbed his hand. 'Please stay. I... I do want to tell you. Something that I shouldn't.'

He hesitated. 'Like what?'

'Sit down.' She squeezed his hand. 'Please?'

He sat. 'Tell me, Clare.'

'Yes, yes I will. But it's *things*, actually. Three things. In fact, no, four.' She glanced round the room. 'Firstly. And I *definitely* shouldn't be telling you this. But your work is about to get a lot more interesting.'

'Really? How d'you—'

'Secondly. Be careful with Antoine. I'm not certain he's entirely trustworthy.'

'Ah.'

'Thirdly.' She paused. 'Yes, I read your file, and I apologize for that. But, well, it's because I like you, and want to know about you. Sorry, but there it is.'

'Oh.' He sat back. 'And fourthly?'

'There are two men in the corner. Army officers. One of them is staring at you.'

He checked. 'So we're about to be thrown out.'

'Yes and he's coming over now.'

'Right, let's—'

'Trickey? Private Trickey, is that you?'

He stood, and stared, and his mind reeled back, and he recalled a tall figure waving a pistol in the moonlight, on the cliff top at Bruneval. Attacking upward? He'd grinned at Frost. Or attacking downward?

'Lieutenant Timothy. It's good to see you.'

'You too!' Timothy pumped his hand. 'I thought it was you. What on earth are you doing in Algiers?'

He glanced at Clare. 'Oh, I'm on temporary detachment. Helping out with translating and so on. What about you? I heard you went to America after Bruneval.'

'I did. Liaison officer with the first American airborne units. Marvellous time, taught them a thing or two. But now I'm back and rejoining Battalion.'

'That's wonderful news. At Maison Carrée?'

'Maison... No, they're in Tunisia, didn't you know? A town called Beja. Busy working up to strength there. Loads of new faces apparently. Frost's recruiting like mad, you know Johnny!'

'He's rebuilding 2nd Battalion.'

'You bet. And he's made me a platoon commander in A Company, reckless bugger! I join them tomorrow.'

They stayed for one drink, then Clare had to get back to her digs. On the way she took his arm.

'It's very special to you, isn't it? Your battalion.'

'I feel I belong there.'

'I had a nice evening, Theo.'

'Me too. A little unusual, but nice.'

'Very funny.'

They reached her digs.

'I'd ask you inside, but...'

'I understand.'

'No, I want to, but it's utterly forbidden. And I share with two other girls. Both fusspots, of course.'

'Don't worry. It's been quite an evening.'

'Yes.' She rested a hand on his chest. 'Busy day tomorrow too.'

'So I hear.'

She leaned up and kissed him. 'Promise me you'll be careful.'

'Ever heard of the LRDG?'

'No, sir.'

'Long Range Desert Group. They've been doing recce work for Monty in Libya.'

'I see.'

'No you don't. Long-haired irregulars in beards and turbans, charging round the desert in souped-up Jeeps, answerable to no one. Bloody liability, if you ask me.'

'Yes, sir.'

'It's no way to run a war.'

'No.'

'Yes, well, anyway...' Yale, scowling, shook open a map. 'Like

117

I say, they've been scouting ahead of 8th Army, and actually probing round behind Jerry, who as you know is retreating towards us.'

'Yes, sir.'

'But retreating where, is the question, and that's what LRDG is trying to find out.' He jabbed at the map. 'Best guess at the moment is this natural bottleneck here on the coast between Libya and Tunisia. Town called Gabès, malaria-ridden fleapit of a place. There's a line of disused fortifications the French built there, called the Mareth Line. Monty thinks they'll dig in there. However our 1st Army HQ bods aren't so sure. And want it looked into.'

Theo felt a thrill of anticipation. Clare was right; this was more interesting. Yet what followed was not as expected.

'Now then. Two days ago, whilst scouting south of Gabès, an LRDG patrol stumbled on a lone German vehicle and captured it.'

'What kind of vehicle?'

'Unarmed, one of those Jeep-type things...'

'*Kubelwagen*?'

'That's the one. Anyway, in it is just the driver, who turns out to be an officer, and a staff officer to boot. But he flatly refuses to talk to anyone, either that or he speaks no English – and these LRDG boys speak little German. They were all for passing him back to 8th Army for processing, but fortunately checked his papers, which show he's from 10th Panzer.'

Theo touched the map. 'Which is based up here. In our sector.'

'Two hundred miles north of Gabès.'

Teichman: *It looks like we've found 10th Panzer.* 'We fought them. At Oudna.'

'Indeed. So technically he's our prisoner, not Monty's. And now HQ's wondering what a staff officer from 10th Panzer is doing two hundred miles away in Gabès.'

'Arranging a link-up between German forces?'

'Maybe, or maybe it's just coincidence. But the long and short of it is we need better information, so I'm sending you and Sharif to get it.'

'Antoine.'

'Yes. He knows the area and can blend in like a local. He can also negotiate with the French and pump the Arabs for gossip. Meanwhile you're to link up with the LRDG, and interview the prisoner.'

'But he refuses to talk.'

'Then make him! We need to know what the wily fox is up to.'

'The prisoner.'

'No, Rommel of course! What we want to know, what the whole world wants to know – including German High Command apparently – is will he stand and mount a defence against Monty. Or will he turn and attack us here in Tunisia.'

Theo stared at the map. 'Both, probably.'

Yale waited. 'Go on.'

'We learned that in France. He likes to surprise people. General Fortune—'

'You knew Victor Fortune?'

'A little. We learned Rommel prefers to keep people guessing: you know, do one thing while everyone thinks he's doing another. It was a tactic he developed in the First War, when he was a junior officer.'

'Is that so.'

'That and always moving quickly. My grandfather served with him in Austria.'

Yale began folding the map. 'So it's true. You and he have history.'

'We, um, we've met. On a few occasions.'

'So I gather.' He produced a note. 'Now, there's one more thing, Trickey, as if things weren't complicated enough.'

'Sir?'

'A colonel. Name of Stirling. Another beardy bloody irregular. He commands something called 1st SAS, who do special ops in Libya: blowing up fuel dumps, sabotaging airfields, that sort of thing. Mad as a hatter apparently. Anyway, he's been travelling the area with the LRDG, with a view to mounting an operation there.'

'What sort of operation?'

'A capture-or-kill operation.'

'On who?'

'On Rommel. Only the problem is he's gone missing.'

Less than twenty-four hours later Theo was ten thousand feet above the snow-capped Atlas Mountains aboard a small, twin-engined aeroplane called a Bisley. Noisy, cold and smelling strongly of petrol, the Bisley featured a cramped cockpit for the pilot, behind whom Theo sat wedged in a dickie seat. Out of view below and forward of the pilot lay Antoine, reclining on a bomb-aimer's couch, and by peering past the pilot Theo could just make out his feet. Somewhere down at the back of the Bisley, sealed into his capsule like a chick in an egg, was the gunner, who was asleep. Although unsettling, this was understandable, as they'd all been airborne since long before the dawn, which only now was throwing misty shadows into the valleys ahead, like pointing fingers, while draping the mountains with pink.

'*Mes couilles sont gelées!*' Antoine's pained tones came over the intercom.

'What's that, old sport?' the pilot queried.

'His, um, testicles are frozen.'

'Nasty. But don't worry, you'll be roasting them when you land.'

'Yes! 'Ow bloody long now, God's sake?'

'Not too long. We'll be descending to the plain soon, then another hour or so. What about some more coffee, to warm up?'

'Don' mention bloody coffee! I bloody bursting already!'

Theo too was uncomfortable. His seat was too small, and his parachute too big. It was completely unfamiliar to him, a Type B5, as issued to bomber crews for use in emergencies. It had no static line and didn't open automatically, the user was required to leap from his stricken aircraft, wait a few seconds to get clear, then pull a metal ring on his chest to open the chute. Theo had never done this, nor even simulated it in training. 'But you're a paratrooper, ain't you?' the quartermaster at the airfield had scoffed. 'One two three pull! Should be a doddle.'

Ninety minutes later he was doing it for real. But baling out of a Bisley was no simple matter. Having squeezed past the pilot, he and Antoine then had to squash together on the cockpit floor, prise open an escape hatch, then somehow arrange themselves to jump through it.

'Fack me, Tadzio, you do this many time?'

Theo examined the opening, which was small and square. Wriggling through it in a bulky parachute would be tight, and he wondered how people managed in real emergencies. He peered downward, the slipstream buffeting his head. A thousand feet below the desert rolled by, smooth and boundless in the morning sunlight like an ocean. 'Never like this.'

''Ow we gonna do it?'

'Coordinates coming up!' the pilot shouted.

'Head first, I suppose.'

'Fack me.'

'Stand by!'

'I'll go first.' Theo squirmed forward until poised over the opening. The wind roared like thunder in his head now, and

121

the desert looked dizzyingly near. Suddenly he glimpsed tents off to one side, tyre tracks in the sand and smoke from a signal fire. Then he heard a distant shout, felt a thump on his back and thrust himself two-handed through the hole. He fell clear, body tumbling, and waited for the familiar jerk and snap. But none came, just an accelerating warm hurricane and the spiralling ground. The ring! His hand flew to his chest, scrabbling furiously. Seconds passed, the fumbling went on, the wind roared, the desert rushed, then his fingers found metal, seized it and pulled frantically outward.

'You left that pretty late, man.'

He blinked up at a pearl-grey sky. 'I... What?'

'Then I suppose you paratroop lads train for it, don't you?'

He lifted his head from the sand. 'Where's Antoine? My, um, colleague.'

'Over there. Taking a piss.'

Five minutes later they were sitting in a tent drinking tea. Around them lounged six New Zealanders, tanned, hairy and bearded as Yale had described, wearing desert fatigues and boots, and assorted headgear including bush hats, pith helmets and keffiyehs. Several more were busy loading trucks parked in the heat outside. The trucks were American, Chevrolets, yellow-painted and laden to the axles with weapons and equipment: jerry cans of fuel and water, sand mats, pierced steel planks, ropes and shovels – and bristling with weaponry including anti-tank rifles and twin machine guns. Painted on the nose of each truck was a bizarre talisman like a gargoyle. 'Maori,' explained one of the New Zealanders when Theo asked. '*Hei Tiki*, bringer of luck.' Pleasantries were exchanged, footwear admired, sandwiches circulated and war news swapped. Despite their outlandish clothing, blunt manner and strange accent, the New Zealanders seemed friendly, if no-nonsense – and impatient.

'So what's the plan, boys?' their leader asked. 'We need to clear out of here pronto.'

'Is dangerous?' Antoine asked.

'Too right. Dangerous to stay in the open anyhow. Whole area's crawling. Forward units, recce and observation patrols and so on – Jerry could come blundering round the corner any time. Air activity too. Spotter planes everywhere. Sooner we pack up and move on the better.'

'I mus' go Gabès, speak with town elders for information. My frien' Tadzio here is for interview Jerry prisoner.'

'Good luck with that, mate!' someone quipped. 'He's tighter than a Scotchman's wallet.'

'Um, where is he?'

He was in the tent next door. Theo lifted the flap to be confronted by an armed New Zealander in full Arab garb. Apologizing politely, he asked if he could see the prisoner alone.

'No skin off my nose,' the guard replied and ducked outside.

This tent was smaller than the first, more gloomily lit, hot, stuffy and humming with mosquitoes. The German was seated at a camping table, reading from a leather pocketbook. About thirty-five, handsome, dark-haired, wearing the uniform of a colonel, his bearing was superior and unconcerned. Glancing only momentarily at Theo's uniform and insignia, he returned his attention to his book, where it remained throughout their preamble.

'Good morning, sir,' Theo began in German. 'Would you like some tea?'

'A German speaker at last. No tea.'

'Very well. Um, do you mind if I sit?'

'Be my guest. Your accent is Austrian.'

'South Tyrolean.'

'Then we are neighbours. I am from southern Bavaria, near Augsburg.'

'I competed in the Hitlerjugend games near there in thirty-six.'

Flinty eyes flickered. Then the page was turning. 'And you are a separatist therefore, to be wearing a British uniform.'

'Yes, sir. I left two years later. For London. My father was, is, English. I went to school there.'

'So much information. Then you'll be familiar with this.' He held up the book. *A Tale of Two Cities*, the title read, in English.

'I have read some Dickens, yes. And you speak English. Obviously.'

'Fluently. But not to these Kiwi scoundrels.'

'So...'

'Your uniform, *Junge*. This is not 8th Army.'

'No.' Theo took out a notebook. 'Sir. My name is Theodor Trickey. I am an interpreter for 1st Army in Algiers, here to—'

'You're not from Montgomery?'

'No. My base of operations is in Tunisia.' He hesitated. 'Like yours.'

The man looked up at last. 'You have seen action there.'

'Um, yes. In fact my unit met with elements of yours. Not far from Tunis.'

'When?'

'In November.'

'Ah. Before my time. I only arrived last month.'

'I see.' Theo swallowed. This was not going well. He seemed to be telling the German far more than he was learning. But at least they were conversing.

'One moment.' Pocketing the Dickens, the German sat forward. 'Your beret. Yes, you're from that new British *Fallschirmjäger* brigade. You're a paratrooper.'

'Yes, sir. 2nd Battalion.'

'I did hear of you. Our men said you fought bravely.'

'Thank you.'

'Although suffered grave losses.'

'Yes. Now, I'm sorry, but I must ask—'

'No notebook.'

'What?'

'Tell me, Theodor Trickey. When you left your homeland in Italy, and settled in another country, then found yourself at war with your homeland: how easy was it for you to decide which side to fight on?'

Theo felt his whole body twitch, as though electrified, and an icy chill prickling his neck. 'I beg your pardon?'

'Did you not hear me?'

'I... Yes, of course. I just...' *You must decide,* Rommel said, and kept saying, in Bavaria at the games, in France on the beach, and endlessly in his dreams. *You must decide which side you are on.* Now once again, through this man.

'It's complicated isn't it, Theodor? Because we fight for a cause, not an ideology. We fight for our beliefs, not someone's dogma. And we fight for a people, not one person. So when our beliefs match the ideology and the person and the dogma, then all is well. But when we find our beliefs betrayed by the person, then everything becomes much harder. Until, like you separatists, we are left with just one thing.'

'Sir?'

'Which is?'

'Conscience?'

'Precisely. War is a failure of reason, Theodor. But you can't reason with fanaticism, and that's the unfortunate paradox of war. So ultimately it is necessary to act solely according to conscience. Which is why I'm sitting here with you. I have a message. It is important, and I share it because I hope you might understand. You will pass it to your superiors, and they will not believe you – that is their concern. But you may not write it down. And I need your personal word on that.'

Bargain with him, Yale had said. Agree to nothing without obtaining something in return. So he asked, and obtained more than was imaginable.

'Tell me your name, sir, at least.'

'My name is Claus von Stauffenberg.'

CHAPTER 6

These are the facts as now known. Early in 1943, British Intelligence, through Ultra decrypts, learns that Rommel has been ordered to stop 8th Army's advance at the Mareth Line – or annihilate himself in the attempt. Rommel, exhausted, demoralized, pitifully short of men and arms, considers this plan insane and says so. Which goes down badly with the Führer. He does agree, however, to go to Gabès and inspect the Mareth Line for himself. This too is known to the British, including the dates, which is where David Stirling's madcap plan to capture or kill him comes in. Acting alone, Stirling hitches a ride to Gabès with the LRDG, and hides out among the fortifications. But unfortunately a six-foot-four Englishman with fair skin pretending to be an Arab sticks out like a sore thumb, and he's soon picked up.

Von Stauffenberg meanwhile also arrives in Gabès to meet with Rommel, albeit for very different reasons. A member of Germany's aristocratic elite, he belongs to a secret sect dedicated to the overthrow of National Socialism and the restoration of a society governed by a benevolent nobility. He's also a devout Catholic and finds much Nazi ideology abhorrent. Knowing his movement needs the support of senior officers to have any credibility, and hearing that the people's hero Rommel is losing faith with Hitler and Nazism, he arranges a meeting.

What comes next is less straightforward. Gabès is swirling with irregulars, undercover agents, secret police and spies of all persuasions, and it's little surprise von Stauffenberg and Stirling are captured. Within days, however, both have 'escaped' – or more probably been released, possibly in a prisoner exchange (both are colonels). Von Stauffenberg returns to his unit, where two months later he's critically injured in a strafing incident near Mezzouna. This leaves him politically radicalized as well as physically disabled, and his thoughts shift from overthrow to assassination. Meantime Stirling, who seems accident-prone, heads back towards Tripoli but gets apprehended a second time, this time by the Italians who delight in embarrassing their German allies over his recapture. Duly humiliated, the Germans pack him off to the infamous Colditz POW camp where he spends the rest of the war. Rommel meanwhile visits the Mareth Line, and writes a scathing report on its unsuitability. A short time later he's recalled to Germany from Africa on 'sick leave'. And never returns.

'He said so,' Theo whispers from his hospital bed. Since arriving in Ulm he has showed small signs of recovery, and is even saying a few words, albeit randomly.

'Who did?'

'He did.'

'Rommel?'

'Yes. No. The other one.'

'Von Stauffenberg.'

'No. A major. Um, Brundt. In Salo.'

'Where?'

'I don't know. Major Howard said... '

'What?'

'I'm sorry. I'm very tired.'

A typical exchange of the day – which was two years after

the event. And with much yet to happen in between, getting to the bottom of it all would be a lengthy business. Especially when I had matters of my own to contend with.

The picturesque little walled city of Ulm lies on the River Danube in southern Germany between Stuttgart and Munich. Surrounded by hills and forests, it is just sixty miles from the Alps, with decidedly Bavarian influences evident in its culture and architecture. Ulm rose to prominence during the Middle Ages as a trading centre, particularly in textiles. Later it became more industrialized, with mills and factories springing up beyond its walls and across the river. Although of no great strategic importance, during the 1940s several factories supplying military hardware were located there, plus a sizeable barracks. Much of the surrounding land is under the plough, intensively cultivated to support the war effort. The labour for this, and for the factories, is mostly supplied by POWs.

My base of operations is Ulm's POW hospital, situated in a former town house a stone's throw from the minster and its famous spire. More a villa, externally it's something of a Gothic horror with steep roofs, exaggerated gables and pepper-pot towers, but it's solidly built with thick walls, a stout cellar against air raids, balconies and tall shuttered windows. It's also quite well equipped, and once inside rather reminiscent of an English cottage hospital. Downstairs the living rooms are divided into 'wards', each with tiered bunks for the patients. Another room is for examinations and sick parades, and there's an orderly room for the Germans, with kitchens at the back. On the first floor is a bed-sitting room for us doctors; it has French windows opening on to a balcony and a serviceable bathroom next door. Across the landing is the surgery, a dispensary and a storeroom, while the top floor houses two more wards. Our staff comprise two doctors, myself and a genial Dutch army medic called Erik Henning. Although theoretically my subordinate, Erik has been here much longer, knows the ropes and speaks excellent German as well as English and Dutch, so I defer to his wisdom in most things. He's also good company and a terrific doctor. We have two British orderlies, a Scot called Pugh, and Fenton who's a Londoner. Our wardens are a moody German *Gefreiter* (corporal) called Prien, three privates, and an elderly *Sanitäter* (orderly).

In charge of the whole outfit, and indeed all of Ulm it often seems, is our collective *bête noire*, Oberstabsarzt Wilhelm Vorst, who lives in a billet away from the hospital, thankfully. A medical major, fifty, portly, bespectacled, Vorst is a vain and quarrelsome stickler, whose one aim is to make life unpleasant for everyone – including his own countrymen. Erik cautions me about him on day one, and the *Gefreiter* Prien too, repeatedly pleading with me to avoid confrontation. But as time goes on, this becomes progressively harder.

Our days are long. Apart from the sixty or so in-patients at the hospital, or *Revier* as it is properly known, there are several smaller clinics to visit in the environs. So we rise early, usually five thirty, washing and dressing in bleary silence – and swiftly too because the weather's freezing and the *Revier* poorly heated. Breakfast is ersatz coffee, black bread, marge and hoarded Red Cross jam. Erik and I then complete a ward round, treating and dispensing as necessary, updating records, and trying to vacate beds for the day's inevitable admissions. Then at eight we hold the first sick parade. We're awake and alert now, and need to be, because sick parade is unlike any medical procedure ever. 'Like walking a tightrope with someone shaking the wire,' as Erik puts it.

Waiting outside in the snow are queues of POWs from nearby *Lager*. British, French, American, Dutch: these are the

130

labourers who pass their days in the city's streets, sweeping up debris, clearing roads, mending sewers, filling in craters and so on. Repairing the damage, in other words, caused by our bombing raids. This is hard manual work in harsh conditions, so unsurprisingly sickness and injury are common. As is malingering, which brings us to the tightrope.

As a doctor I hate malingerers; they waste time and resources, and offend my professionalism by trying to trick me. Also there's something odious about bunking off work by pretending to be ill, especially as someone else – a colleague presumably – will have to do it for you. On the other hand, the POW workforce in Ulm is being used to aid our enemy. And that goes against the grain, because we should be doing everything to make their lives miserable, including shirking off work, so as to show defiance, lower their morale, tie up their own labour force, and thus end the war sooner.

A typical sick parade consists of a hundred or so patients. Erik and I tackle them in two lines, aided by Fenton and Pugh. We do it standing because it's quicker, and speed is everything, for *Gefreiter* Prien is sitting behind us timing our consultations and noting our findings. At first I find this intolerable.

'*Zwei minuten*?' I protest early on. '*Two minutes* per patient?'

'You haven't heard the half of it,' Erik quips cheerfully.

The half of it he's referring to is the 'quota', for it turns out that no matter the numbers of sick and injured, or their seriousness, or any other medical consideration, the '*nicht arbeitsfähig*' or 'off work' list may comprise only 10 per cent of the parade. Maximum. Vorst's orders. If we go over that figure, he simply cancels sick parade and orders everyone to work – then sets about punishing us all including the POWs. Indeed my predecessor Collinson is now MO of a notoriously harsh camp in Poland, just for exceeding the quota. So what we have to do, clandestinely and at ridiculous speed, is sort out the malingerers from the genuinely sick, deal with the latter as best we can, all the while juggling the numbers so we keep up to, but not over, the 10 per cent. After much initial chaos, and several severe tellings-off, I gradually evolve a system.

'Hello, chum, what's up?'

'Terrible backache, Doc.'

'Really?'

'Well...'

'Sorry, quota's full, try again tomorrow. Next!'

Conversely: 'Hello, chum, what's up?'

'Terrible backache, Doc.'

'Sounds nasty, take two days off. Next!'

And so on. To further speed things up, I send Pugh along the line to sift the genuines from the malingerers, and also undress whatever part of their anatomy is ailing them, thus ensuring best use of the allotted two minutes. The result is a queue of half-naked Tommies shuffling round the room like a conga gone wrong. But at least the system works. Usually. For at some point in the proceedings Vorst appears. A frisson of tension always heralds his arrival, because everyone fears the man, and the power he holds over us. Power to send a sick prisoner to shovel snow all day, power to send a sloppy guard to the Russian Front, and power to contradict and humiliate a doctor.

'What is wrong with this man?' he demands angrily in German. Vorst will only converse in his own tongue, which I am having to study fast.

'*Gastroenteritis, Herr Oberstabsarzt,*' I stammer back.

'Preposterous! Show me.'

'Yes, *Herr Oberstabsarzt*, he has fever see, suffers cramps, the abdomen is tender, he makes multiple visits to the latrine.'

'To shirk his duties. Send him to work!'

'But, *Herr Oberstabsarzt*—'

'Do as I order!'

After a second ward round and a pause to catch up on paperwork, there's just time for lunch. Today as usual it's watery cabbage soup and potatoes with more black bread. Erik and I also share a tin of fruit from our dwindling Red Cross stocks, followed by powdered coffee and a smoke of precious pipe tobacco.

'We're getting very low,' he comments, checking the cupboard. With the RAF pounding Germany's infrastructure to pieces, Red Cross parcels now get through only intermittently. But it's no better for the civilians.

'Maybe Fenton's buck will come through again.'

'Let us hope.' He glances my way. 'What happened with Vorst today?'

'The usual. Hateful bastard.'

'You allow him to enrage you, Dan. It's a mistake.'

'I know, but what can I do?'

'Try flattery.'

'God, must I?'

'It works, believe me.'

At 1 p.m. we leave the refuge of our bedsit and head down to the *Gefreiter*'s office. Prien issues us with our afternoon lists and money for the trams; then, bundled up in coats and scarves, we step out into the cold. After a brief conference: 'I'm going west so will do the drop-in,' we split up and go our separate ways.

As always at this moment my spirits lift. Despite busy clinics to visit, insufficient time to visit them, and strict orders to return by dusk on pain of death, I am now gloriously alone and at large in an attractive city. As though in some small way I'm master of my own destiny again, which of course I'm not. Checking my list, I see I have three clinics, all on the eastern side of town, which is even better, so setting my beret at a jaunty angle, I strike out along the street.

It's two weeks since my summons to Lucie Rommel, and nearly a month since I arrived here. Little has changed in the intervening period. The war drags on, as does the winter, with no end in sight to either. Food, medicine, coal, good news are all in short supply, and as always it's the needy who suffer the most. But the crushing depression I felt at Stalag XIB is receding, largely because I've regained a measure of control over my life. And purpose, and choice even. Soon after my arrival here, Erik told me about a secret drop-in centre he and Collinson set up in a poorer part of town. Once a week, one of us goes there to dispense whatever medical aid we can to the sick and destitute. Vorst would instantly shut it down if he knew, and probably send us to prison, but he doesn't know, and that makes it all the better, for as well as providing succour to the needy, it's another small gesture of defiance against the oppressor.

The streets are still icy, pocked with slush-filled craters and mounds of snow-dusted rubble, and as I walk I pass many wrecked buildings. Ulm is not a prime target, I've learned, but still gets regularly bombed, supposedly because of its factories, although I have doubts about that. As usual I proceed via the minster, relieved to find its flying buttresses, parapets and towering spire undamaged, even though other buildings in Münsterplatz have been flattened. Work parties are out in force; one or two feature British POWs who whistle when they spot my beret. Further on I pass another party, slow-moving, silent, unmistakably Russian. Housed in squalor, fed scraps and clothed in rags, these pitiful wretches are appallingly treated, and with their stick-like limbs and hollow faces look barely human. Yet they are regarded with fear by the civilians. Which is the whole point, Erik says. 'Support the struggle against the Bolshevik,' the Nazis are telling their people. 'Or end up like this.'

At a crossroads I join a queue for the tram to Böfingen and the ball-bearing factory which is my first port of call. The queue is busy with civilians: women who talk in low voices, pensioners who stare, and a few curious children. No one in uniform today, thankfully. Sparks from the overhead cable herald an arriving tram, and I board the outside platform, which is where undesirables like POW doctors must ride. Wiping grime from the window I glimpse a female clippie inside checking tickets, but it's not the one I'm hoping for. I check my watch. Despite bombings, power cuts, manpower shortages and the rest, Ulm trams run with amazing punctuality, helped no doubt by the track-clearing parties. So I must be early. The rather matronly clippie duly appears, sells me a ticket and departs, leaving me out in the cold. I don't mind; it enhances the sensation of freedom, and saves me being gawped at by passengers. Leaning against the rail, I watch the battered city trundle by. After a while it begins to snow.

Each factory has an infirmary, and twice weekly Erik and I must visit them all. The Böfingen plant is large and the list of patients long. The POWs here are mostly French, ordinary *soldats* too long in captivity, rather like McKenzie and the others at Stalag 357. Their attitude is resigned, institutionalized even, and they suffer a range of ailments attributable to poor diet, damp conditions, insufficient exercise and lack of fresh air. Chest complaints top the list, some of which are serious, but once again I'm dancing the tightrope two-step, juggling the seriously sick against the less so, with one eye always on the 10 per cent. Though Vorst rarely visits these outlying *Lager*, he ruthlessly checks the figures each week, and woe betide any fiddling of the quota. After an hour I'm at the limit and starting to turn away sick patients. A man down the queue doubles over with coughing, then shows me his handkerchief which is flecked with blood. His brow is burning and his lungs rattle like old machinery, but there's nothing I can do. '*Pardonnez-moi*,' I say helplessly, 'try and hold on till next week.'

I visit two more clinics, in thickening snow and growing haste as time is pressing. The last is for women farm labourers shipped in from Germany's eastern conquests: Poles, Czechs, Romanians, Lithuanians; while their menfolk work in weapons factories on the Ruhr, these tough ladies toil on the land. Little food grows here in midwinter except a few stunted turnips; nevertheless they're out in all weathers hacking at the frozen tilth ready for spring. And remarkably robust for it, although weakened by lack of proper nutrition or clothing. Chest complaints thrive as usual, although I also see back and limb strains, a broken finger and one case of incipient trench foot. Language is problematic. They have a female *Sanitäter* who translates into rough German; the rest we manage with nods and gestures. Sick parade is in a bare wooden hut; as anticipated the numbers are safely within quota and I'm soon packing up for the tram back to town.

Then something unexpected happens. A younger girl, perhaps eighteen, slight, dark, somewhat hunched, is ushered forward by the other women. She says nothing, makes no sign or gesture, just stands there staring at the boards. '*Ja, junge Dame?*' I offer, which yields only a shaking head. '*Was ist los?*' I ask again, but still get nothing. Then the *Sanitäter* shuffles up, mutters the one word '*schwanger*' and I know we're in trouble.

The girl is three months gone. She doesn't speak, but the story from the women is that Dita, which is short for Ditunka, became separated from her Czech husband in the autumn. He was sent to a factory in Norway while she came to work in Ulm, and only when she got here did she realize she was pregnant. I'm not sure I believe this – the women recount it too earnestly – but any other explanation is unthinkable. A slave labourer falling pregnant to a German would have deadly implications for both.

Obstetrics is not my field but I make a perfunctory examination, learning via the women that this is Dita's first pregnancy, and apart from malnourishment and back pain she's healthy. The big question, of course, is what's to be done, and they soon make that clear. But I can't, even if I could, or would. I don't have the knowledge, skills, facilities – or the authority; and if Vorst learned of it we'd both be for the chop. There's a hospital in town but largely for the military, and slave workers certainly have no access to it. Some sort of 'backstreet' arrangement might doubtless be procured, but quite how I have no idea, nor could I ever condone such a thing. All in all it's a grim outlook for mother and child. East Europeans like Dita are the lowest of the low as far as the Nazis go; '*Untermenschen*' or 'sub-people', they call them. There are *Konzentrationslager* camps in the region similar to the one Inge Brandt showed me in Bergen. Dita and her baby, if they survive the birth, will most likely end up in one, only to die there of disease and starvation.

Suddenly it's all too much. I need to get out, need air, and space to think.

'I will consult with my colleague.' I make to rise.

'*Hilf mir!*' She grabs my arm. '*Hilf mir!*'

Her dark eyes are wide with fear. I pat her hand, and gently prise it loose. 'I will try, I promise.'

Outside the light is failing and the snow heavy, thick coils of it swirling through the streets in icy blasts. I'm late, and by the time I board my tram I'm also plastered white and shuddering with cold. Clutching the handrail, I watch curtains of snow spiralling from the black sky, dully despairing at the misery this endless war wreaks, when the door opens and a hand draws me inside.

'*Komm*. Sit in here, no one will mind.'

It is Trudi, the clippie I was hoping to see earlier. I know her name because we have spoken three times. I also know she is twenty-four, unmarried, and lives with her widowed mother.

'Are you sure? I don't want to be any trouble.'

'Of course. We are not inhuman, you know.'

I take a seat in the warm, nodding warily at the few other passengers. To my surprise they nod back, and one or two even smile.

'*Englischer Doktor*,' Trudi explains, to more nods and smiles. An old man mutters something, pointing.

'Your coat,' she goes on. 'He's asking about it.'

'Ah, well, it is French army. A friend gave it to me. A while ago.'

'*Das ist gut*. Friends are very important these days.'

She punches my ticket and turns away.

'If she has that baby, they're both done for.'

'I am aware of that, Erik.'

'So what will you do?'

'I don't bloody know!'

'Sorry.'

'No.' I rub my neck, which aches damnably. It's evening; we're back in the bedsit, following the usual featureless supper and a final ward round. The windows are blacked out, the room dimly lit, I'm still feeling cold which has given me neuralgia, there's the Dita business to contend with, Prien's reporting me to Vorst for returning late, and now I've offended Erik. I glance at him: short and fair, with thin sandy hair and youthful eyes, he's wearing an affronted frown. 'No. *I'm* sorry, Erik, it's not your fault. It's been a long day. And now this...'

'On top of everything.'

'Exactly. Here.' I pass him the tobacco tin. 'Have a fill.'

'Sure? It's nearly empty.'

'Finish it. And tell me your news. You've word of your brother, I hear.'

'Ah yes.' Erik brightens. 'Well, from our father, who has received a card.'

'That's marvellous. You must be relieved.' Erik's older brother, Pieter Henning, another doctor, is a prisoner of the Japanese, in Burma or thereabouts. But the family has heard nothing in years. 'What does the card say?'

'It's printed with three boxes.' Erik strikes a match to his pipe. 'One says *I am fit and well*, another says *I am working for pay*, and a third says *I have been ill but am recovered*. Pieter ticked the first one.'

'Nothing else – no other message?'

'According to the Red Cross, POWs are forbidden to write anything else or their cards are torn up.'

'But at least he's alive and well.'

'Yes.' Erik puffs. 'Although the card could be a year or more old, apparently. And the rumours of bad treatment by the Japanese... I can't help worrying.'

'Take comfort from the card, it's proof Pieter's alive.'

'Or was, at least.' He smiles. 'Thanks, Dan.'

'Sorry I snapped at you.'

'It's all right. How's Trickey?'

Making slow progress, is the answer. Sitting up, taking nourishment, walking a few wobbly steps, sleeping a lot, talking, sort of. Tonight I mentioned my clippie friend, something I haven't told anyone. 'Her name's Trudi,' I tell him, 'short for Gertrud.' 'Oh,' he says, 'like his daughter.' 'Whose daughter?' I ask, but he drops off to sleep.

'A little stronger every day,' I reply. 'How was drop-in?'

'Growing. At least thirty. We need more medicines.'

'Hmm.'

We fall into contemplative silence. Beyond the blackout curtains the snow has stopped, and the sky has cleared, which is good news for the street sweepers, but less good news in terms of air raids.

'You'd be saving her life, Dan,' he murmurs eventually.

'I suppose so.'

'Dilatation and curettage. It's quick and safe.'

'But I've never... the procedure, the instruments – I have no idea...'

'We'll read up on it. Prepare you, step by step. So you're completely ready.'

'Christ.'

'I know.'

A few minutes later the air-raid sirens sound and we all troop down to the cellar.

Next morning, halfway through sick parade, Vorst appears and immediately heads my way. I'm startled and nervous, but have my plan ready to forestall him. Hastily grabbing the patient waiting behind me, I come smartly to attention, even clicking my heels as he strides up.

'Good morning, *Herr Oberstabsarzt*,' I greet him, before he can speak. 'I wonder, could I trouble you for your professional expertise?'

'You were late back yesterday! You know the penalty for this?'

'Yes, my apologies, *Herr Oberstabsarzt*, the tram broke down in the blizzard.'

'That is no excuse!' He glares angrily, his cheeks dotted with pink. But his eyes are darting to the patient. 'What is this?'

'An interesting case, *Herr Oberstabsarzt*, but I confess I am at a loss. The prisoner's heart, you see. Knowing your expertise in this field, I wondered if you could honour me with an opinion.'

Vorst's eyes narrow behind his spectacles, but I can tell he's intrigued. A hospital doctor by trade, his speciality is cardiology. 'What is wrong with his heart?'

Nothing. The prisoner's heart is fine, except for a childhood murmur. I detected it down the stethoscope in seconds, a twanging sound called Still's Murmur. Rarely found in adults, Still's is completely harmless.

'I cannot tell, *Herr Oberstabsarzt*,' I say, offering him the stethoscope. 'Perhaps you could advise me?'

He stoops to listen, his bald brow furrowed in concentration. I glance at Erik, busy with another patient, and he winks. Eventually Vorst straightens.

'My diagnosis is complete!' he announces loudly, and the room falls to an attentive hush. 'The patient has Still's Murmur. Have you not heard of this, Captain Garland?'

'Still's... No, I... Goodness, *Herr Oberstabsarzt*. How marvellous. Is it dangerous?'

'Not at all. It is a benign condition, the patient need have no fear.'

The patient looks bemused. 'But I came for my piles...'

'... And can safely go out to work.'

And there's more good news when we return from lunch. Fenton and Pugh are waiting in the bedsit, hands behind backs.

'What is it?'

With a conjuror's flourish each produces a dead rabbit. 'Ta-da!'

'Hurrah! Well done, Fenton!'

'Stew tonight, anyone?'

'And well done, Roger!'

Roger is Fenton's pet buck, his name aptly describing legendary prowess in the fatherhood department. Many townsfolk breed rabbits, as a cheap and flavoursome source of much-needed protein. Roger is lent out to them as required; payment, a few weeks later, is in kind.

'Outstanding work, chaps, very well done.'

'And Pugh traded four bottles of beer with the *Gefreiter*!'

That evening we feast like royalty on rabbit stew and *Schwarzbier*. And a restful night follows with no trips to the cellar. The next morning I descend to the *Gefreiter*'s office to find an envelope waiting. Prien hands it over without a glance. Inside is a second summons from Lucie Rommel.

We have to do Dita's procedure in the hut. The women have roll call three times a day; she cannot miss even one. I arrive with the instruments in my bag, and lead in my heart. I step inside and the women are waiting, about twelve of them, with Dita in their midst. She's wearing a short shift and nothing else. Her feet are bare, she's shivering with cold, and in her terror she looks small and very young. Through the *Sanitäter* I explain what's to be done, and how. But even before she translates, the others begin preparing, as if they already know. A rough table is dragged out, a piece of cloth smoothed over it, and a cushion for Dita's head. There's also a bowl of water and tiny sliver of soap for me. I scrub up, trying to hide that my hands are shaking. Dita climbs nervously on to the table. There are no stirrups, but two women step forward to support her legs in the lithotomic position. Two more are at her head, stroking her temples and hair, while the rest surround her in a protective ring. Now gloved, I apply a few drops of ether to the mask and bring it to her. As I do so, her eyes widen in fear. I bend to her, murmuring, '*Nebojte se,*' which is the one Czech phrase I have learned. Don't be afraid. She blinks tears, and nods bravely. I apply the mask, she struggles, but the women soothe her and she relaxes into unconsciousness.

Then we begin. The winter light is poor, but I have a torch which one woman holds. I also have Lysol for disinfecting and am cleaning the perineal area when another woman gestures that she will do it. I nod and turn to the dish of instruments. Utter silence has descended. I can feel my heart pounding in my chest. Suddenly I'm on a train, surrounded by shocked onlookers as I force a hand drill into a man's skull. Panic grips me. I can't do this, shouldn't even try, I'm not qualified, and not worthy. A distant humming sound is starting in my head, like an incantation. '*Nebojte se,*' someone says, '*Nebojte se, britský doktore,*' and a steadying hand touches my arm. I swallow, turn back to the dish, and pick up an instrument. I have no tenaculum, so must use ordinary forceps to steady the cervix, then insert the Hegar dilators Erik obtained. I turn to the task, but the table height is wrong and I can't see. I stoop down, panic rising again, but squatting's too low, and there's no chair. The humming grows louder, like a spell being cast. 'I'm sorry' – I gesture helplessly – 'this isn't...' But they understand, and the hand grips my arm again, another cushion appears and I'm lowered to my knees. 'Good?' someone murmurs in English. My eyeline is correct suddenly, my posture steady. 'Yes, yes, good, thank you.' And kneeling before my patient, I turn and pick up the curette. And as I do so the humming breaks into song. A soft melodic chant taken up by all the women. A lament for a lost child.

Only much, much later, am I able to track down the words.

Out of the day and out of the night
My dear little joy has taken flight.
Spring and summer and winter hoar
My heart moves with grief, and delights no more.
Oh never more.

CHAPTER 7

'Fucking mines everywhere, son. Sappers clear 'em best they can during the day; Jerry buries a load more every night. That's why afternoon's safest for driving. Don't for fuck's sake drive anywhere first thing in the morning.'

'I won't, Sergeant.'

'You a driver then, son?'

'No, I'm, well, I'm a runner.'

'Well, don't run anywhere in the morning!'

'No, Sergeant.'

'What unit?'

'2nd Parachute Battalion.'

'Fucking nutters. I seen 'em in action. That screaming they do, wahoo something, what's that about?'

'*Waho Mohammed*?'

'That's the one. What's it mean?'

'It, um, well, it doesn't mean anything. It's a sort of battle cry.'

'Fucking weird one if you ask me.'

'We did a lot of walking. On our last op. The local people would watch us from the hilltops and shout messages to each other. It sounded like "Waho Mohammed". Our men copied it and—'

'FUCK!' The sergeant wrenched at the wheel, skidding the ambulance to a halt. 'There, look at that!'

Rubbing his eyes, Theo peered through the windscreen. The road stretched ahead, the dirt rusty red, a muddy river ran alongside, while thick woodland rose steeply to either side. Overhead misty clouds filled the slash of sky visible between the trees. 'Sorry, I...'

'There! Where the dirt's been disturbed!'

A slight discoloration, as though a damp patch had been smoothed over. Nothing more. 'Yes, I see it now.'

'That's a fucking mine! See and remember, son, if you want to stay alive.'

Cursing volubly, the sergeant eased the ambulance into gear and manoeuvred carefully around. 'Fucking mines. Worse than fucking Stukas.' He glanced at Theo. 'Ashford. He one of yours? A major, I think.'

'Major Ashford? Yes, he's our A Company commander.'

'Killed by a mine last week. Another one, a captain. Moore?'

'I don't...'

'Killed by a mine last week. Stephenson, or was it Stephens, can't remember...'

The list went on. Theo sat in the cab, his mind a bleary daze. Major Ashford. Another stalwart. Gone. After all he'd done to save A Company at Sidi Bou: it didn't seem possible. The lorry lurched and the sergeant cursed. He was from 16th (Parachute) Field Ambulance, which was positioned close to 2nd Battalion, on a road near a town called Sedjenane. That's all Theo knew, except that Sedjenane was in the north of Tunisia, near the sea and somewhere east of Beja. Where he'd arrived only yesterday after two days on the road with no sleep and a bad headache. It was early March, two weeks after his trip to Gabès and the interview with von Stauffenberg. Major Yale wanted him to stay on in Algiers: 'You've the makings of a useful operative, Trickey.' But 2nd Battalion was back in the thick of it, and he wanted to rejoin it. So did Colonel Frost. A tussle ensued. Frost won.

Rounding a bend they arrived at the huddle of tents which was 16th Field Ambulance. Red Cross flags fluttered, medics in aprons moved purposefully, walking wounded stood about smoking, while more seriously injured lay on stretchers, some of them unmoving. To one side, a row of humps in freshly turned soil signified graves. As he jumped wearily from the cab, Theo could hear the sound of gunfire echoing around the valley.

'Up to the right, son.' The sergeant pointed. 'Follow that yellow tape through the trees and it'll bring you to your lads. But keep your head down, plenty of Jerry about.'

'Yes, Sergeant.'

'And watch out for fucking mines!'

'I will. And thanks for the lift.'

Hefting his rifle and rucksack he set off, following the tape and the noise of shooting which grew louder as he went. Ten minutes further and he was back with his battalion. Not that he knew it from the welcome.

'Who's this one then, all clean and shiny!'

'Another wet-behind-the-ears straight from Ringway.'

'Does Mother know you're out, dearie?'

'Hold on, lads. That's Trickey, ain't it?'

'Who?'

'Trickey, you pillock, he's practically a legend.'

'Never 'eard of him.'

'Watch out, here comes the colonel!'

A familiar figure appeared, tall, mustachioed, striding towards him across the clearing. Theo dropped his pack and saluted.

'Hello, sir.'

Frost's hand was outstretched. 'Good to have you back.'

Another ten dizzying minutes later and he was sitting at Battalion HQ being briefed. Frost's command post was beside the road, in thick woodland at the bottom of a steep hill. It consisted of a tent, with table for maps and radios, an armed protection unit, his new adjutant Willoughby, and about a dozen signallers, radio operators and clerks. Adjacent to the road was a railway, beyond that the river, beyond that rose another hill. As Frost spoke, the gunfire sounds, including mortars and machine guns, could be heard in all directions.

'Because we're *all* here, Theo,' he explained. 'All three battalions, first time ever in the brigade's history. How about that?'

'Rather, um, momentous, sir?'

'Too true.'

And their mission, he went on, was equally momentous. 'Repulse the enemy, and that's it.' He pointed down the road. 'They're bottled up around Tunis and desperate to break out. This road is their only route west, and we're to stop them using it. If we succeed, and with Monty due to link up with 1st Army down south, then it's pretty much stumps for Jerry in Africa. So we've got 1st and 2nd Battalions here on this side of the road, and 3rd Battalion dug in opposite. Jerry's got at least a division in Sedjenane, crack troops too, including our old friends from 10th Panzer. Plus they've got mobile armour, heavy artillery, air cover, the lot. And tanks, the usual Panzers, and these new Tiger monsters. They've been softening us up with probing raids for a couple of days; we're expecting a concerted effort any time. Probably tomorrow. Got all that?'

'Got it, sir.'

'Good. Now, I want you back in your old job. These trees provide good cover but I can't see anything – especially what's going on up the hill. Radios are working, more or less, but we don't have many, and the brigadier wants constant updates, so you're my eyes and ears on the ground: liaison, communications, situation reports, enemy movements, casualties and so on.

Translating too, we've local muleteers for transport, and we're already collecting prisoners, so make sure you question them and report any gen.'

'Yes, sir. Um, who am I reporting it to?'

'To me. We've a lot of new faces here, as you've probably gathered, and many of them are pretty green.' He smiled. 'I need people I can depend on.'

Theo spent a restless night in a hip-scrape in the trees. Sleep eluded him, his headache nagged, and the bombardment went on late, enlivened by a lone Stuka attack and a half-hearted attack on 3rd Battalion, which was vigorously repelled. Eventually all fell quiet, save for the popping of star shells, punctuating the night like a clock counting down the hours.

At eight the following morning, duly washed and breakfasted, he was at the command post meeting new staff, when a deafening shriek split the air, followed by the ground-shaking thunder of explosions up the hill. Seconds more and the artillery barrage was in full swing. 'Positions!' Frost shouted, and everyone scattered to their units. Steel helmet strapped tight, Theo waited at the CP, crouching on one knee and listening as the bombardment unfolded. It was heavy, yet removed, and he soon sensed the main target wasn't the hill, but its eastern flank. There the enemy's infantry would be assembling, ready to follow the barrage as it crept slowly upward. Sure enough garbled messages were soon arriving from A Company, which was defending that flank, reporting that they were under attack. 'But don't worry,' John Lane, their new CO radioed, 'we're quite all right.' Two hours later he radioed again to say A Company was surrounded. Then contact was lost.

'Get up there.' Frost scribbled notes. 'C Company's above them, see if Ross can help. And take an ammunition mule with you: they'll be running low.'

The mules were corralled in a railway culvert, their drivers visibly recoiling as Theo ran up. He selected one at random, summoning him forward in Arabic. As they ascended through the trees the noise of gunfire drew nearer, familiar Bren and Vickers sounds mixed with the thump of mortar and distant rattle of German machine guns. Tree-limbs occasionally splintered overhead, showering them with twigs and leaves, while tendrils of smoke drifted eerily through the trees. Then with a crash an oak tree jumped and fell sideways ten yards away; he ducked, only to glimpse the mule driver fleeing downhill, leaving his startled animal behind. Grabbing the rein he began dragging it upwards. A few minutes later he stumbled into a clearing.

'Who the fuck are you?'

A foxhole lay at his feet, two Paras concealed within.

'Trickey, CP runner,' he panted, glancing round. Now he could see them: camouflaged figures prone in the dirt, crouching behind trees or lying in dug-outs. 'Are you C Company?'

'Bloody right. Hold on.' The man raised his rifle, squinted along the sights, then fired a single round. 'Missed, fuck it.'

The mule flinched, jerking Theo's arm. 'The enemy's coming up here already?'

'Not if I can help it.'

'Hello there.' An officer sauntered up. Theo recognized him from Oudna, the night of Sidi Bou. Lieutenant Spender, the surviving platoon commander from C Company. 'Trickey, isn't it? I see you've brought ammo, you splendid chap.'

'Oh, um, yes. It's for A Company. They're hard pressed.'

'Is that so?' Spender smiled. He produced a cigarette case and lit up. His beret was askew, his piccolo poked from a breast pocket, a sprig of heather adorned his lapel and, save for the dagger on his thigh, he was completely unarmed. 'Ciggie?'

'No thank you.'

Spender examined the case. 'My sister gave it to me, before we left for Greenock. Charming, no?'

'Very nice. Sir, could I—'

'Do you have sisters?'

A fleeting image came, unbidden, of a little girl on a Stepney doorstep, her cheek smudged with green. *Are you coming back?*

'Well, yes I do. A half-sister.'

'How delightful. What's her name?'

'Nancy.' The mule tugged his arm. 'Um, is Major Ross here?'

'He's down there, trying—'

'DOWN!' The deafening crash of a mortar shell, then several more in quick succession, erupting round the clearing like geysers. Earth spurted, trees split, dirt and rocks flew high, to fall pattering to the ground like rain. Theo crouched down, still holding the mule, which strained and bucked in panic. Then a hand joined his on the rein; he glanced up and saw Spender calmly steadying the animal, as though a donkey at the seaside. Then the shelling stopped, and the Paras were scrambling to their feet, and shooting furiously back.

'That'll do!' Spender waved. 'Cease fire, chaps, save the ammunition.' The shooting petered out. 'Well done, everyone. Any hurt?'

Heads were counted, limbs checked and weapons reloaded. Spender brushed dirt from his beret. 'Right, back under cover, all you chaps. Trickey, you come with me.'

They set off downhill, pulling the mule behind. Soon the trees were thinning, and then they came to a ridge; beyond it the view was wide open, down and across the valley far below. Overhead the sky churned with rain clouds; beneath it, more than a mile away, tiny figures crept across the skyline. Still gripping the mule, Theo fumbled for his binoculars.

'Panzer Grenadiers,' Spender murmured. 'Formidable chaps.'

151

'Where's Major Ross?'

'Down here to the left.' He pointed. 'And A Company's just below him, along the ridge in that copse, see?'

'Yes, I see. I must get this mule to him.' He tugged on the rein.

Spender grabbed his arm. 'Admirable intention, old thing, but not really practicable. Jerry everywhere, you see. Worming round behind A Company, creeping through trees, lurking in the bushes, not many but enough to give us trouble – as you've just witnessed. They've also been plastering A Company pretty hard. Wander out there in the open and you'd not get ten yards.'

'But—'

'It's all right – I'll see Ross gets the ammo. Meantime you should report to the colonel. Now, see that peak, about three miles distant? The one with all the smoke.'

'Yes.'

'1st Battalion. They're catching it too.'

'And the enemy's trying to get between them and us?'

'Precisely, so be sure to let him know. Although that's the brigadier's problem. Ours is holding this hill. So tell Frost we're doing what we can for A Company. Tell him Jerry's getting in among our positions but we're not budging. Tell him we're fine but could do with more ammo.'

'Yes. I will.'

'And be sure to give him my compliments.'

Theo descended to the CP, but was soon on his way up again, this time to B Company, which Frost wanted to move east. On the next trip he successfully coaxed two ammunition mules up to the summit, where a machine-gun position overlooked the ridge held by the German grenadiers. As he watched, panting and dizzy, the gunners reloaded their weapons, then opened fire at maximum range. Seconds later they observed dust puffs where their shots fell, followed by a scattering of the men on the ridge, like confused ants. 'That should shut 'em up for a bit!' the gunner quipped. On the way down he collected a stretcher party and several walking wounded whom he led to the dressing station. There he observed many new casualties, including four killed. He also interviewed two enemy prisoners, infantrymen, both lightly injured.

'May I know your unit?' he asked in German.

'27th Schützen, of course,' one retorted. 'Attached to 10th Panzer, who will destroy you this day.'

The second prisoner, bloody head bandaged, seemed less assured. 'We weren't told we'd be fighting you,' he muttered.

'Fighting who?'

'*Die roten Teufel.*'

The red devils. He'd never heard the expression, noted it down, took a few more details and headed back to the CP. Parched and perspiring, he gratefully accepted tea from an orderly, but before he could drink, a throaty roar turned everyone's heads. A moment later two Messerschmitts appeared, thundering up the road towards them, guns blazing. Bullets smacked into rock, dirt spurted, splinters flew, and everyone dived for cover. Weapons were grabbed; snatching up his rifle Theo glimpsed Frost, standing in the open, calmly shooting his service pistol at the aircraft. Seconds later they were gone and uneasy silence descended once more.

The day dragged on; he toiled up and down, pain and fever spreading through his body like poison. And with every passing hour the plague of enemy encroachment also spread. Fighting continued, mostly on the hill's eastern flank where A and C Companies bore the brunt, yet increasingly elsewhere too, often in penny packets, with individuals leaping on each other from behind rocks, or springing from bushes, daggers and bayonets flashing. 2nd Battalion dug in and held on. Repeatedly the Germans probed forward; repeatedly they were repulsed. After each clash came a pause to withdraw and lick wounds. And get messages to HQ: 'Still here, still holding.' 'Losses heavy but manageable.' 'Enemy attacking on all sides.' Their fighting was dogged, their defence heroic, but with an armoured division against an infantry brigade, defeat inevitably loomed, and steadily the Paras lost ground. Down at the CP Frost and his team struggled to keep track. Quite apart from Frost's own situation, news from the other two battalions was equally ominous, with 3rd under pressure, and 1st completely encircled. Yet he was impotent to help, and had emergencies of his own.

Returning from a sortie, Theo slumped dizzily to the ground. But ammunition was still needed up the hill so Frost's adjutant, Willoughby, desperate to do something, loaded a mule and set off. Within minutes he was lost, stumbled into the enemy and was shot dead. Only the muleteer returned to recount the tale.

'Jesus.' Frost shook his head. Oudna, Sidi Bou, the piecemeal destruction of his battalion: the nightmare was repeating itself.

Theo struggled to his feet once more. 'I'll go.'

Frost stared into the trees. 'I so hate being stuck down here.'

'They need the ammunition.'

Still Frost hesitated. 'All right, yes, but listen. Tell Lane, tell Ross, they've just got to hang on until dusk. If they can do that, then there's a chance. Tell them I'm speaking to the brigadier right now.'

Wearily Theo set off once more, following now familiar paths up through the trees, two mules in tow. After twenty minutes and with daylight fading, he reached the clearing Spender's platoon had held earlier. But although shooting was audible down the slope, the clearing itself was deserted. Then a coppery glint caught his eye, and looking down he saw a trip-wire inches from his boot. For seconds he could only stare in groggy fascination, then he stepped gingerly back. Immediately a burst of gunfire erupted from across the clearing.

'*Halt!*' an angry voice demanded. '*Wer ist es?*'

'I... *Nicht schiessen*, um, *verdammt!*'

'Who is it?' the voice insisted in German.

'27th Schützen,' Theo shouted back. 'Of course. Who else?'

'*Gott, Mann.* You nearly got your arse shot off.'

'Well... Be more careful next time!'

A finger to his lips, he reversed the muleteers from the clearing, carefully retraced his steps and found another route down, following the sounds of shooting, now more sporadic in the gathering dusk. Finally he heard the murmur of voices, and, recognizing them as English, emerged through bushes to find a group of Paras clustered behind a rock. Standing in their midst, stuffing his pockets with grenades, was Lieutenant John Timothy.

'Ah, Trickey, good to see you. Just in time.'

'I... What?'

'You've got .303 ammo, I hope. Christ, you're as white as a sheet.'

'It's nothing, um, yes, on the second mule.'

The men fell on his supplies. They were stripped of their packs and webbing, he noted, each wearing only battledress and smock, and a beret instead of a helmet. Their bayonets were fixed to their weapons. 'What's happening?'

'Jerry machine-gun nest.' Timothy pointed through the trees. 'MG34s. Behind those rocks down there. Moved in half an hour ago, been a blasted nuisance since.'

'You're going to attack it?'

'No choice. It's got half of A Company pinned down.'

Theo peered, briefly glimpsing a helmet moving behind rocks.

'The aim is to surprise the buggers,' Timothy murmured. 'Care to join us?'

'I, well, of course, if you want.'

'Only joking. Stay here and keep your head down, this shouldn't take long.' He cocked his Sten gun. 'All right, lads? Let's get it done!'

And with that six men leaped from cover and hurled themselves down the hill. Theo watched in horror. A frontal assault, on machine guns, like Scottish boys in a French lane. Seconds later confused shouts and frenzied shooting broke out, including the crump of grenades and deadly clatter of the MG34s. Then screams could be heard rising above the gunfire, tortured, high-pitched, and he closed his eyes. A few seconds more and the screaming was fading to silence.

Back at the CP he recounted the facts to Frost. 'Four killed. Four taken prisoner. Two MG34s captured, brand-new and undamaged, with ammunition and tripods. A Company is already using them.'

'Good grief. And not a man lost?'

'No, sir. The, um, buggers were surprised.'

'I'll bet they were. Where are the prisoners?'

'I took them to the dressing station. We've quite a number there now.'

'Yes, and rumour is they're not all crack troops, which is encouraging.' He glanced at Theo. 'You OK?'

'Me?'

'Look a bit pasty. Caught something in Algiers maybe?'

Clare had seen him off. It seemed an aeon ago. *Stay safe, Theo.*

'It's nothing. Flu or something. I'm fine.'

'Good. Feel up to one more job?'

He didn't. And even as Frost requested, and he accepted, and the rain began to fall, something solid settled in his stomach. Like resignation.

It was back up the hill. To C Company, who were to launch

an attack right away. An enemy detachment had occupied the road between 1st and 2nd Battalions, cutting them off. Holding the road was the brigade's main objective, and the brigadier wanted it back, fast, before the enemy could establish itself. One company each from 2nd and 3rd Battalions was to carry this out, simultaneously from opposite sides of the road. Frost was in radio contact with his old rival Stephen Terrell in 3rd Battalion, but not with John Ross. Theo must ascend the hill and brief him on the plan. As quickly as possible.

Frost looked at his watch. 'It's nineteen hundred now. I'll radio Terrell and fix the attack for twenty hundred. Does that give you enough time?'

'Yes, sir.' Theo rubbed his neck. 'Maybe not with mules.'

'No mules, no supplies, no weapons. Travel light and fast. Here, take this.'

Theo looked down. Frost was holding out his pistol. 'Sir?'

'It's an old favourite of mine. Just in case. Remember Bruneval?'

Theo hefted the pistol, which felt cold and heavy in his hand. The same gun he'd been ordered to kill Charlie Cox with. 'I remember.'

The rainstorm started in earnest as he was setting out, thrashing the trees into wild motion and hissing like surf, erasing routes, confusing paths and deceiving his senses. In minutes he was off track and panicking, his clothes drenched and his boots huge with mud. He couldn't see, couldn't hear, couldn't navigate, each step felt clumsy and threatening, as though every bush hid a trip-wire, every rock a German. He paused, gasping, searching blindly and gripped by child-like terror. Like fleeing the tanks in France. Or in the blizzard with his great-grandfather. *It is fear and inaction that kills, Theodor.* He struggled on, scrabbling at rocks and roots, hauling up through the mud only to slither back down again. Thirty minutes passed, forty, he couldn't tell, he knew only that men's lives depended on him. His chest heaved, he felt giddy, his limbs heavy and useless like lead. *Horatio, what do we do?* He pressed on, gradually making ground; he breasted a rise, traversed a ridge, then tripped and stumbled headlong into a gulley. Its sides were steep, and he tumbled helplessly, rolling over and over like a corpse, until crashing to the bottom. There to rest in a stream, stunned and winded, feeling the icy water trickle over him like oil. 'I can't, Great-grandfather,' he gasped, 'I can't do it.' Fever gripped his head, every limb ached, he tasted blood on his tongue. He rolled sideways, hauling himself to the bank, to lie and rest in the mud. For ever. And there, staring up at the hissing canopy of leaves, his gaze fell upon the tape.

Either of the other two battalions – green for 1st or red for 3rd – and he would never have seen it. *Why yellow?* he'd asked Frost. Because it stands out better! And there it was, a ghostly strip of hope in the darkness, like a thrown lifeline, snaking up the side of the gulley. Clutching it tightly he hauled himself to his feet and began climbing one final time. In a while the tape led him around the hillside and up towards Spender's old position, from where he was able to reorientate himself. Five minutes after that he staggered into C Company.

Of the following hour he remembered only fragments. Like images at a picture show.

Beginning with a rain-drenched scene with Ross:

'Thank you, Trickey. You'd best get back to the CP. Colonel Frost will—'

'No.'

'I'm sorry?'

'They were mine before they were yours.'

'What did you say?'

'C Company. I joined them a long time... right at the beginning.'

'Trickey...'

'I'm coming too. You won't stop me.'

Then a long slithering descent, mesmerized by the back of the man ahead. Squelching mud and the click of kit. Down on all fours, creeping to a road. Lying in a ditch, waiting for the off. *'You laddie, know how to arm a Gammon?'* A nudge, someone pointing, shadows moving. The rumble of nearby motors. Star shells bursting suddenly, blue and red, fizzing as they fall. The signal! Scrambling up, everyone together, everyone screaming. *Waho Mohammed!* Flashes and thunder, gunfire and grenades. Grey figures running, Frost's pistol kicking in his hand. Sten guns crackling, bayonets flashing. Dazzling yellow as the Gammons burst. A Para on the ground, his hands at someone's throat. Rivers of fire as fuel tanks blow. Whistles and cheers as the grey men flee. A figure on fire, writhing at his feet. *Hilf mir!*

One more kick of the pistol.

'It's malaria all right,' the MO told Frost later. 'We've got him on quinine and hydrates. Let's just hope it's the PV strain and nothing more deadly.'

He spent forty-eight hours unconscious on a 16th Field Ambulance cot, deliriously unaware of the brigade's struggle for survival on the hills around him. He missed how time and again the three battalions were attacked, yet prevailed, how they lost ground by day, only to steal it back by night, how the rain never stopped, driving them to the brink of despair yet bringing mudslides and misery on to an enemy forced always to fight uphill. How valour became routine: 3rd Battalion clearing the road every night; 2nd Battalion capturing a hundred prisoners in a day; 1st Battalion's cooks and clerks grabbing weapons to fight off an assault; 16th Field Ambulance refusing to move from the field of battle, the better to help its victims. How they held out far longer than anyone could have asked or expected, yet still it wasn't enough. And how, with casualties at unsustainable levels, supplies running out and reinforcement impossible, the order was finally given to pull everyone out.

Almost everyone.

'Sorry, lads, he stays here with the too-sick-to-move.'

'The fuck he does, he's coming with us, ain't you, Trickey boy?'

Gradually he became aware of an argument. He was suspended, head lolling, between the arms of two burly Paras smelling of mud and cigarettes. Barring their way was a medical officer in surgical hat and apron.

'No. He stays. He'll be well looked after. By tomorrow, God willing, he'll be in a proper hospital.'

'A Jerry hospital though, Doc, and we can't have that. Nor would he want it.'

'But—'

'What d'you say, Trickey boy? Do you want to tag along with us or stay here with the too-fucked-to-move?'

'I... please... tag...'

'There you go, Doc, all settled.'

'Yes, but—'

The brigade pulled out at dusk, each battalion making its own way to a rendezvous twelve miles west on high ground near the town of Nefza. 2nd Battalion's escape route was along the river using the rain and darkness for cover, but barely had they set off than the Germans sensed the retreat and began shelling from behind. The river too was deeper than anticipated and swollen with rain, so the Paras found themselves wading chest-high in fast-flowing water thick with mud and branches. Struggling for footing, several lost balance and were washed away, still more became separated, blundering through the darkness never to be seen again, while many, particularly those at the rear, were caught by shellfire. Theo found himself among this rear cohort, half swimming, half drifting, dragged and carried along by a succession of C Company Paras while bullets stung the water and exploding shells flung surreal pillars of white high into the air. Leading them was Dickie Spender, who kept everyone together and moving with a commentary of jokes and rhymes.

'This river's called Oued el Madene, did you know?' he called out cheerily. 'Which of course is Arabic for Shit Creek.' And when a shell smacked into the muddy bank nearby but failed to detonate: 'Thud. In the mud. Another dud. Thank Gud!'

The long night dragged on. The battalion made slow progress, strung out along the river in a snake-like procession, rifles above heads. At dawn Frost, anxious to make better time, led them from the water to continue along the railway. The rain stopped, a steaming sun rose, the temperature soared and the Paras were soon pouring sweat. And all the while the sounds of pursuit were never far behind. Men dropping too far back fell from sniper fire, and artillery and mortar shells continued to explode all round; meanwhile Theo became mesmerized by the wooden railway sleepers, convinced he was ascending a long ladder towards distant mountains of green. Sure enough by noon these dream-like peaks had crystallized into reality: three pointed hills Dickie christened the Pimples.

'Our new home sweet home, chaps.'

'And what happens there?' someone asked wearily.

'We turn and stop the enemy!'

'Oh. Yes. Of course.'

They arrived at dusk and began to dig in. Another cold night passed beneath the stars, then next morning they were roused early, only to be told to pack up again.

'What's going on?' Unfamiliar faces began appearing among them. 'And who the hell are you buggers?'

'We're Leicesters, of course! Here to relieve you, so sod off!'

Another six-mile march rearwards brought them to their billet, an abandoned tin mine outside Nefza. The place was deserted and eerily silent, furnished only with rusting machinery and running with rats, but, too weary to care, the Paras flopped down along the dusty corridors and fell into exhausted slumber. When they awoke it was to the miraculous rumble of NAAFI lorries outside bringing hot food and drink, cigarettes, fruit, chocolate, blankets, clean uniforms, fresh weapons and ammunition. There was even a mobile shower unit, and medics, too, to tend their many sick and injured. Safely concealed within the mine and with the sounds of battle reassuringly distant, for three days they rested and fed and bathed and fed some more. Theo's malaria slowly abated; he began taking nourishment and an interest in his surroundings and situation. A hundred and fifty from 2nd Battalion, he learned, had been lost killed or captured, a third of their strength.

'How do you feel?' Colonel Frost asked on the third morning.

'A little groggy, sir, but I'm fine. What's the gen?'

'We're supposed to be pulling back to Algiers for some much-needed leave.' Frost sighed. 'But the Leicesters are taking a pounding. And can't hold out much longer.'

'So when do we go back in the line?'

'Tomorrow. Leave will have to wait. Again. Think we can handle it?'

'I'm sure of it.'

The next day 2nd Battalion rejoined the rest of the brigade on the Pimples for the last phase of what was the Battle of Tamera. Well concealed on a wide wooded ridge a mile ahead of them was a formidable enemy force heavily supported by tanks on the ground, fighters in the air and heavy artillery hidden among rocky outcrops to either side.

'Their position gives them complete command of the coast road west.' Frost briefed his officers. 'If they control that they control northern Tunisia and we can't have that. Eisenhower himself says they've got to be driven off.'

'Do we know who "they" are?' John Ross asked.

'Panzer Grenadiers, apparently,' Frost replied warily. 'Among others. Crack lads, Witzig Regiment so I'm told.'

'Sheep-shaggers then.'

'I thought it was bears. You know, for the hats.'

'Bearskins aren't made from real bears, you knob!'

'They jolly well *are*! I've a chum in the Grens.'

'Well, don't let him near your sheep.'

'Bunch of girls, the lot of 'em!'

At ten o'clock that night they crossed the start line. 1st Parachute Brigade led the attack backed by an infantry brigade on either flank, a battalion of Moroccan Goumières for good measure and an entire division of artillery in support. Climbing up through the darkness behind a creeping artillery barrage was a new experience for most and it both impressed and awed them. The non-stop shriek of shells overhead, the retina-scalding flashes, the concussion and the thunder, the thick rolling smoke. Gradually they ascended, the going slow and painstaking: tapes had to be laid to guide followers, mines had to be marked and skirted, pockets of resistance dealt with, and soon the battalion was becoming strung out and fragmented; worse still the barrage was creeping too far ahead, leaving them exposed and vulnerable. Frost tried to maintain contact by radio but as the barrage passed clear of the enemy positions the Germans sprang to life, and fighting broke out in all directions. They began taking casualties, and capturing prisoners too, further slowing progress. He was unsure of his own position, let alone those of his forward units. Elements of A Company entered a clearing only to find themselves amid enemy positions. Wild shooting erupted, grenades flew, fighters ran shouting in all directions before, badly outnumbered, the Paras hastily doubled back into cover. Elsewhere B Company blundered into a minefield and became stuck. Theo was sent forward to help guide them back out. Then towards dawn Frost reached what he believed was their objective for the night, a narrow plateau atop a hill with the enemy ridge right ahead. The position had been vacated by Germans, so already featured dug-outs, foxholes and even some abandoned weapons. Reassembling his battalion around him, he ordered them to dig in and make ready.

But as the grey dawn strengthened into daylight, he realized he was gravely mistaken. The plateau was not atop the hill but far beneath it, and still a considerable distance from the enemy ridge. And though the terrain dropped away on three sides, favouring the defender, dense woodland surrounded it, providing cover to the attacker. Furthermore, the clearing was much smaller than he'd realized in the darkness, and his battalion too closely bunched, offering an easy target to mortars and artillery. Nor, it turned out, was it completely unoccupied by the enemy, and even as he surveyed the situation in dismay, several sleepy infantrymen in grey crept from their foxholes yawning and stretching, only to find themselves staring down the barrel of a British rifle.

Their position was dire, the only option to attack, right away, uphill through the woods. Swiftly the order went round: Battalion will advance in battalion formation. All round the clearing Paras made ready, loading weapons, pocketing grenades, adjusting packs, fixing helmets. Theo stood alongside his commander, sweating and giddy, his rifle like lead in his hands, but ready, and when Frost finally took out his hunting horn and blew the charge, he felt the adrenalin surge in his veins like fire and stepped eagerly forward with the others. C Company led, Ross and his men sprinting forward and upwards into the trees. B Company lit out to the right while A and HQ Companies followed through left and centre. Soon they were deep in the woods and making good progress up the hill; then the sounds of battle being joined broke out ahead. Theo instantly recognized the heavy rattle of MG42s above the crack of British weapons, mixed with light machine guns and rifle fire. This was no haphazard or panicked defence by the Germans, this was disciplined and methodical shooting from a strong force moving purposefully down towards them. Suddenly Witzig men began appearing through the trees: advancing, kneeling, shooting, advancing again, unhurried and systematic. C Company caught the brunt, diving for cover, returning fire as best they could, but was quickly overwhelmed by sheer numbers and firepower. Machine guns, machine pistols, rifles, grenade launchers, mortar, even a flame-thrower appeared flinging a giant tongue of molten fire through the trees. Theo felt the heat of it and dived behind a boulder, while nearby foliage crackled to cinders. He smelled petrol and smoke, then risked a glance round his boulder, rifle raised. The flame-thrower was moving on but the forest ahead was now thick with flitting figures in grey. He glimpsed one, aimed, fired and it vanished; he saw another, a man with a grenade launcher, and fired again. Nearby he saw a Para blown apart by a mortar shell, another lying dead, his battledress black and smouldering, and a third spinning to the ground as he was struck. Many others were scurrying for cover. One rose to throw a grenade but a machine gun cut him down. Then he heard the trill of a piccolo and saw Spender's section jump to their feet and charge into the trees. A Bren-carrying Para stepped from cover and fired a burst, but a moment later he too was crumpling to earth. Theo leaped out, grabbed him under the arms and hauled him into cover, while bullets zipped through the trees and a blizzard of leaves and branches fell from overhead. B Company joined the fray from the right, but the Witzigs were everywhere now and still coming on. Soon close-combat fighting was breaking out, men shooting at point-blank range, knives and daggers flashing, boots kicking and rifle butts bludgeoning, all accompanied by animal yelling and the blood-chilling screams of the injured. Theo fired his last round at a Witzig throwing a grenade, then saw another crouching over a Para, his hands at his throat. Reversing his rifle he leaped forward and swung it at the German's head, feeling the stock splinter as the man's neck snapped. The German slumped, the Para beneath him squirmed free, then simultaneously two cries began rising above the melee: '*Zurück!*' from the Germans and 'Back!' from Frost, followed by blasts on his hunting horn. They were drawing apart, he realized, both sides were falling back to regroup, separately and simultaneously, as if on a signal.

An eerie calm descended as the fighting petered out and the Witzigs melted back into the trees. 'Take that, you bastards!' someone shouted as they went. 'Go fuck a sheep!' shouted another. Theo slumped against his boulder. Beneath it the Bren-carrying Para he'd helped lay groaning, his shoulder smashed and bloody. 'Get me up, lad!' he hissed through gritted teeth. 'Get me up, I ain't done yet.' Theo swung his broken rifle over his shoulder, stooped to the man and helped him to his feet.

Ten minutes later they were staggering back into the clearing they'd started from.

A lull. 'We can't do this alone!' Frost was pleading on the radio. 'Where are the Goumières? Who's protecting our flank? Hello? Hello? Oh, for God's sake!' He threw down the microphone. All around the clearing Paras lay about the ground, tending wounds, reloading weapons, draining water bottles and lighting cigarettes. Some even had little stoves of tea brewing. Elsewhere on the Pimples the sounds of battle echoed. 1st Battalion was apparently making steady progress, Frost reported, while 3rd Battalion's situation was unknown. 'The two supporting brigades and the Moroccans are tied up *elsewhere*,' he added disparagingly. 'Brigade is trying to send help but makes no promises. Meanwhile we're to hold the enemy as best we can.'

'And what does that mean?' someone asked.

'It means—'

A shot rang out, then a shout: 'They're coming! In the trees – look!'

'Take cover, everyone!'

A succession of mortar shells exploded around the clearing, throwing columns of dirt and sand into the air. Then followed bursts of machine-gun fire from several directions. 2nd Battalion was trapped, bullets and shells coming at them from three sides as the Witzigs drew near. Soon they were barely a hundred yards away at the forest's edge. Where they stopped. Content, it seemed, to wait, and pick off the Paras one by one. Like fish trapped in a net.

'Come on then, you buggers!'

'What are they doing?'

'Calling up reinforcements probably.'

'Or a fucking air strike!'

Frost watched through binoculars, hunched into his dug-out.

'Why aren't they advancing?' his adjutant murmured. 'One determined push and it's all over for us.'

'God knows.' Frost lowered his glasses. 'But it could be a mistake.'

'So what do we do?'

'What we always do. And if we go down, so be it, but we go down fighting.'

He sent Theo to pass the word, scurrying head down from one dug-out to the next. Frost's orders were to fix bayonets and wait for the hunting horn. The effect was electrifying, he noted, grins and cheers as the steel blades came out, and the sounds of battle cries rising all round.

The horn went, they sprang up as one and charged, fanning out left and right and spraying the trees with gunfire as they ran. The Witzigs responded, stepping from cover to greet them. Close-quarters fighting quickly broke out, bloody and merciless; the enemy had superior firepower and more men, but the Paras had speed and aggression. And they'd surprised the Germans, and while Vickers teams poured bullets into the trees, a mortar section rained shells into the German's rear, sowing panic and confusion among those following. Using the distraction, B Company sprinted unseen through the forest in a flanking move. Meanwhile Theo ran forward with the others of HQ Company, firing his damaged rifle at anything grey. He lost his helmet and his gun was soon empty, so he threw it aside, pulling a grenade from his pocket with one hand and his dagger from his hip with the other. Through the trees a young German was kneeling, wrenching at the jammed breech of his rifle. Theo leaped forward, dagger raised, then the youth saw him and stood to shoot. Immediately a bullet snapped his head back and he fell. Theo turned and saw Frost waving, pistol in hand; then a mortar erupted close by and flung Theo to the ground.

As his senses returned, he knew they were losing. The fighting was still furious, the shouting, the smoke and the gunfire as intense, but it was more desperate, and more concentrated, as if the Germans were pressing in on all sides. Those Paras still on their feet were backing into each other, forming a steadily shrinking perimeter. The mortar shelling had stopped, and the heavy machine guns, the sounds now were of small arms and the occasional grenade, gasped breaths and shouted German orders.

'Surrender, Tommies!' came a guttural yell. 'Surrender. You know it's over!'

'Fuck off!'

'One last push, boys!' Frost called. 'Drive uphill and split them in two!'

The Paras charged, bellowing like madmen. '*Waho Mohammed!*' someone yelled and the cry was swiftly taken up. Then Theo heard it repeated up ahead and a moment later B Company appeared, charging down on the enemy from behind. The Witzigs turned to confront them, and at the same moment a mass of new Paras began bursting through the trees to the left. '3rd Battalion forward!' someone cried and suddenly the Germans were under assault from three sides, and breaking in confusion, and turning before the onslaught and fleeing for cover.

In barely minutes they'd gone.

Learning of 2nd Battalion's predicament, 3rd Battalion's commander, Colonel Bill Yeldham, had immediately detached one of his companies to come to Frost's aid. These extra men and the surprise attack by B Company were enough to save the day. More was to follow. After a respite to rearm and regroup the whole brigade advanced on the enemy ridge, only to find it abandoned. The Germans were in retreat. Two more days of fighting pursuit and the Paras were astride the road at Sedjenane once more. That night they advanced over their old positions, only to find them abandoned too. Frost stood at his old CP by the road sounding his hunting horn in triumph. The Germans had gone, falling back to Tunis and defeat. Within six weeks, though no one knew it yet, the survivors would surrender, and the war in Africa be ended.

Not that 1st Parachute Brigade would be there to witness the victory. After five months of fighting, and more than a third of its strength gone, it was in dire need of rest. Following the Battle of Tamera, its battered remnants began pulling back in easy stages to Algiers, Theo among them. On the final stage they rode in a train, following a meandering route through cork woods and olive plantations, with the sea glinting in spring sunshine to their right. Rounding a bend they came to a wired-off compound and saw it was a huge POW camp full of captured Germans. Paras leaned from the windows, waving; the prisoners saw their berets, and before anyone knew it, began surging to the wire, cheering and throwing their caps in the air.

'Blimey, look at that!'

'There's a turn-up for the books.'

'What are they shouting?'

'No idea. Sounds German.'

Theo sat watching through the glass.

'*Roten Teufel!*' they were cheering. '*Roten Teufel! Roten Teufel! Roten Teufel!*'

CHAPTER 8

The brigade was sent to Boufarik, a peaceful country town thirty miles south of Algiers, to rest and regroup. Food was plentiful, the weather spring-like, the countryside was of vineyards and orange groves, in all a welcome and much-needed contrast to the mud and carnage of Sedjenane and Tamera. Individual sections were billeted in surrounding French farms, there to recover in peace and comfort. Little soldiering went on: some light training, kit replacement, talks and lectures, much paperwork and admin, but mainly it was a time for relaxing, catching up on news from home, and reflecting on the past five months of war. VIPs visited, including a new brigadier, Gerald Lathbury, General Browning, who was head of the airborne division, and, amid much excitement, General Eisenhower himself, supreme commander of Allied forces in Africa, who charmed everyone with his wit and humour, and spoke gratefully of the brigade's achievements and sacrifices. Theo stood with the others of 2nd Battalion as he addressed them. Still pale and weak after the malaria, he couldn't help noticing how depleted the battalion looked. Quite apart from countless dead and captured, scores were still missing, and many more lay in hospitals, where apparently they refused to remove their berets, even in the operating theatre.

A day after Eisenhower's visit, he was called to see Colonel Frost.

'And how are you feeling?'

'Much better, sir, thank you.'

'Good. You're due some leave. You should go to Algiers. Visit friends.'

'Friends?'

'People outside the battalion. They do exist, you know!' He sat back. 'And you should probably check in with your SOE-handler chap.'

'Has he been asking?'

'Someone from his department has. I expect it's getting busy there.'

'But what about Brigade?'

'Brigade's in no fit state for anything. In any case the war here is all but wrapped up. My guess is the next step will be an invasion of southern Europe, but not for some time.' He smiled. 'We can spare you for a while.'

'Yes, sir.'

'Meanwhile my job's to get 2nd Battalion back up to strength, men and officers, most especially officers. Which brings me to this.' He produced a sheet. 'There's an OCTU being set up in Cairo under the Middle East Command. I've applied to send you there to complete your officer training.'

'I... Well, thank you, sir.'

'Don't thank me; you've earned it. Unfortunately there's a waiting list, so God knows when you'll be summoned. In the meantime I've had a word with the brigadier and he's in agreement.' Frost waved the paper. 'Field commission. Acting second lieutenant. Immediate effect.' He leaned over and shook Theo's hand. 'Congratulations.'

'Field...? Um, well, thank you, sir. Again.'

'Think nothing of it, we'll be needing you, and you'll be worked hard.' Frost began describing the job of the subaltern:

his lowly status among officers, the merciless teasing, the monotonous duties. Theo half listened, his gaze drifting to the window, and the cloudless blue beyond, questioning for the thousandth time his fitness for leadership.

Frost too became pensive. '… far too many,' he murmured. 'Willoughby, Moore, Cleaver, Charteris. Dick Ashford of course, Dickie Spender, Geoff Rotheray. Not forgetting poor Philip…'

'I was sorry to hear about him. Lieutenant Spender, I mean.'

Frost sighed. 'Charged an enemy position with no thought for his own safety. Typical Dickie. Saved countless lives sacrificing his own.'

'I, um, read his poem. About Oudna.'

'Hmm.' Frost looked up. 'He spoke of you, you know. That's partly why you're here. He said you showed great pluck. John Ross too, despite you shouting and waving my pistol at him!'

'I don't remember much of that night.'

'I'm not surprised.' He shuffled papers. 'It was a young lady, by the way.'

'Sir?'

'Asking about you. From SOE. A young lady named Taylor.'

They met a week later at Yale's office. Yale was there, curt and harassed, Bryce too, as officious as ever, and several new faces, more interrogators, he assumed, and more clerks busily typing, filing and answering the phone. Yale briefed him with updates and instructions, Bryce lectured him on security, someone issued him with identity cards and passes, all the while he yearned only to speak with Clare. Because the moment he walked in, and they saw each other, he knew something fundamental had changed.

'Café de Paris?' he whispered when a moment finally arose.

'Yes please!' She grinned, and pointed to his shoulder. 'And you'll be legal!'

He waited at the same window table, sipping the same rosé wine and anxiously scouring the drifting seas of khaki for her arrival. Something else had changed, he noted, apart from the number of servicemen on the streets. People's attitudes. Simply because he wore a pip on his shoulder. Second lieutenant might be the lowliest of the low, but shopkeepers now fawned, waiters bowed, ordinary soldiers eyed him warily, girls smiled, and a young navy rating in the street even jumped up and saluted. It was a heady cocktail of caution, regard and respect, as if he'd married royalty suddenly, or won an election. He wondered what his grandfather would think.

'Hello, Theo.' He turned, his chair scraped, he stood, they embraced. Tightly and for a long time.

'Goodness!' she gasped. 'I wasn't expecting that.'

'No. Although I was hoping.'

'Me too.'

They walked along packed streets smelling of damp pavements and hair lotion, jostled by freshly cleaned servicemen, badgered by street vendors, and skirting the rougher quarters in search of calm and privacy. Finally they arrived at the botanical gardens, a favoured venue for couples, and settled on a bench beneath a giant palm. An awkward silence grew. They watched roosting starlings flock to the trees, children playing with a hoop, and tried not to notice nearby lovers embracing. At her prompting, he began to talk of his month since they parted. His journey to Beja, the lorry ride with the sergeant, the hill, the road and rejoining the battalion. The fighting at Sedjenane and Nefza, his malaria, the return journey and recuperation at Boufarik. The losses.

'Ghastly.' She shook her head. 'The fighting, I mean, it sounds so... *desperate*.'

'It was. Although I don't remember it well.'

'Perhaps that's for the best.'

'Yes.'

Another silence. His hand found hers. 'And what about you? The office seems very busy.'

'Insanely.' She snorted. 'And it's all Intelligence Corps stuff, you know, processing prisoners and that. I mean, it's important work and someone's got to do it, but still...'

'It's not what you joined the FANY for.'

'Precisely.'

'Which is?'

She nudged him. 'Watch out. Yale's got you earmarked for a ton of work.'

'But I've got leave owed.'

'Me too. But don't expect to take it.'

He hesitated. 'How's Antoine?'

'He's... the same. He was gone a while after you went to Gabès. He works with the Free French a lot. We don't see much of him.'

Then he was kissing her. Clasping her hand, eyes closed, he tasted lipstick and rosé, felt the urgency of her mouth, the arousal in her breathing, and the tightness of her hand squeezing his. As though time itself was short.

The next day he reported for work. Which was much as before except for subtle if significant changes. Firstly, as an officer he was now entitled both to transportation and refreshment during his working day, so he travelled between camps by taxi whilst eating sandwiches bought from petty cash. He had a better billet too, in a building for officers where he also dined in starched formality. Furthermore, he was no longer filling in questionnaires with hapless Italian conscripts, but using judgement to tease information from seasoned regulars, many of them German – including officers. He was afforded a modicum of respect by camp staff, and also by the prisoners, many of whom visibly flinched at the sight of his beret and insignia. Why red devils, he began asking them, as a matter of routine. Why do you call us *Die Roten Teufel*? Their answers varied. Because you're always caked in that red mud. Because of that tail hanging down from your *Kampfbluse*. Because of the hellish way you fight. Because of your red hats. Because of all the bloodshed.

May came, and with it Germany's surrender in Africa. While the Allies celebrated, the numbers of POWs soared. Most were quickly processed, cursorily questioned and moved on, destined for camps in Wales or Scotland or Canada. But a few marked themselves out for closer scrutiny. Among these were engineering officers, especially those with a scientific background. Certain key locations were also of interest.

'Neustadt?' Theo asked one man. 'Do you mean Bad Neustadt. In Bavaria?'

'*Nein, nein! Wiener Neustadt, im Süden Österreichs.*'

'Oh.' Theo picked up the man's pay book. 'What were you doing there?'

'Supervising workers mostly. And having a good time! Easy posting, nice food, willing girls, you know...'

'It is a lovely region.' He flicked pages. The man was a sergeant of artillery. Or was before being demoted. Field postcodes or *Feldpostnummern* stamped in pay books enumerated a man's unit, without naming it. Yale and his team had begun to recognize field postcodes of interest. 'So how did you end up fighting in Tunisia?'

'*Ach.* A fuss about nothing. Maybe I was indiscreet with one of the girls. She blabbed to her foreman – next thing you know I'm up before the plant commandant.'

'Bad luck. What sort of plant? Munitions?'

'*Nein, nein!* Fabrication. Metal casings or something. Steel got shipped in, milled into these big tubes then shipped out again. Other smaller components too. Nothing military, yet totally hush-hush. God knows why.'

Returning to the office he mentioned the matter to Yale, who was soon rummaging through filing cabinets. 'What else did he say?'

'That the finished product was not assembled there, but somewhere on the Baltic. I pressed him for more, but that's all he knew.'

'Ah!' Yale waved a file. 'Here we are, Wiener Neustadt, it's on the list.'

'What list?'

'*The* list. Targets of special interest. So is the milling plant, and look here, a clipping of your old chum Rommel.'

Theo took the clipping. The word 'Crossbow' was handwritten in English on the bottom. Taken from a German newspaper the picture was of a ribbon-cutting ceremony at the newly built factory. Rommel, in uniform, and his wife Lucie, in furs, were performing the honours.

'When was this taken?'

Yale checked the file. 'Last October. Rommel was home on a month's leave.'

'Home?'

'Yes, home. Neustadt. He lives there.'

Two weeks passed, spring turned to summer, days became hot, nights sultry, then in mid-June Theo received a message from Frost. 1st Parachute Brigade was on the move again, to Sousse this time, on the east coast of Tunisia, for advanced jump training. Which could mean but one thing. Invasion. Frost requested Theo return 'as soon as opportune'.

Clare also had news. 'I'm being transferred as well,' she told him that evening.

'Where?'

'Can't say.'

'When?'

'I don't know, but soon.'

'What about our leave?'

They managed three days. Antoine knew of a beach villa along the coast at Ténès. He gave them the key, and they travelled there on the bus. The villa was empty, the beach quiet, windswept and rugged. They swam, strolled, sunbathed, ate grilled fish, and sat up talking until the evening chill moved them inside.

'Tell me about your family,' she asked on the first evening.

'Ah. That's rather, um, complicated.'

'When is it not!' She smiled. 'Who are you closest to?'

He thought briefly. 'My grandmother, Ellie. She raised me in many ways. Always very kind and patient. I think about her often.'

That first night they slept apart, out of decorum, she on the canopied bed, he camping on the couch. On the second night he settled there again, but as he lay watching the moonlight on the wall, she called to him. He crossed the floor; she lifted the sheets, her body lying pale and naked within. 'Come on.' He slipped in beside her, and they made love, repeatedly, lips pressed, limbs tightly entwined, while the moon set and the surf combed the beach beyond the window. Towards dawn he awoke to find her cheek on his chest.

'What is it?'

'It's France,' she whispered.

'What is?'

'Me. Antoine. Vichy France. Liaising with the Resistance. That's the assignment.'

He sat up. 'My God, Clare!'

Her eyes gleamed. 'You did ask what my job is.'

'Yes, but, I mean, France! And for how long? And, well, Antoine...'

'I don't know how long. Months, certainly. We go in as a team, husband and wife. He's a textiles salesman; I'm his secretary, and wife.'

'But... Whereabouts?'

'I can't say. I shouldn't be saying anything. But I wanted you to know. In case.'

'In case? My God, Clare, but...'

'It's what I'm trained for, Theo. I'll be all right.'

'Can you at least tell me your name?'

'No, I can't.'

'For God's sake, I'll go mad with worry, please, you must!'

She hesitated. 'AAB. They're my code letters. Aurélie Anne Bujold.'

In the morning Antoine arrived to collect her. 'You must say nothing,' she murmured as the car pulled up.

'Tadzio!' Arms spread, Antoine leaped out, wearing an open-neck shirt and flannels. 'Fack me, you lose weight or what?'

'Hello, Tony, good to see you.'

He escorted her to the car; they kissed briskly.

'See you soon.'

'Yes, you too. Um, take care. On the road.'

He went to the driver's door, and stooped to the window.

'You too, Tony.' They shook hands. 'Take care of her.'

At sunset on 13 July more than a hundred Dakotas took off from airfields around Sousse, formed up into V-shaped formations like vast skeins of geese, and set off on the 250-mile flight to

Sicily. Aboard them were the three battalions of 1st Parachute Brigade, units of airborne Royal Artillery and Royal Engineers, plus the redoubtable 16th (Parachute) Field Ambulance to provide medical support. Towed gliders carrying heavy equipment were also among them. The evening was calm and warm, morale was high, and the mission – at the very spearhead of the invasion – was exciting, crucial and refreshingly clear-cut. No more crawling about muddy hills, no more hiding in holes, no more infantry slog, this was the kind of *coup de main* task the parachute corps was designed for: drop behind enemy lines; seize and hold a bridge; hand it on to someone else; retire from the scene.

Theo rode in one of the Brigade aircraft. He was there to provide liaison between Brigade HQ and 2nd Battalion, who were in aircraft following behind. His Dakota was commanded by Lathbury's chief of staff, the much-feared Major Hunter, who paced up and down scowling at all the liaison, intelligence, clerical and sundry other supernumeraries on board. 'Bloody JAFOs', he kept calling them disparagingly. One such JAFO was sitting beside Theo, a worried-looking captain who spent much of the flight hunched over a prayer book. A while after they passed Malta he leaned to Theo.

'A little nervous,' he confided. 'First jump, you know.'

'Oh?'

'Operationally, I mean, not counting training. Yours too?'

'Well, no, actually. It's my fourth, I think.' He counted back: Colossus, Bruneval, Depienne; then remembered Gabès, and the terrifying B Type plummet. 'No, it must be my fifth.'

'Fifth! Good heavens, you're a veritable veteran!' His hand appeared. 'I'm Vere Hodge. Of COBU. Delighted to make your acquaintance.'

'Theo Trickey. Yours too. Um, COBU?'

'Combined Ops Bombardment Unit. In case of spotting.'

'Spotting.'

'Artillery spotting. Monty's chaps, for instance, when they come up the road. Or a captured Jerry 88 or something. Or the navy even.'

'The navy.'

'Yes, I know.' Hodge shrugged. 'But Brigade sent me anyway.'

Ten minutes later the navy attacked them. Suddenly and without warning, somewhere between Malta and Sicily, a flash lit the night and the Dakota reared like a startled cow. Seconds more and the sky was ablaze with explosions as a furious anti-aircraft barrage erupted, filling the night with bolts of fire and clouds of exploding steel. Recognition flares popped, signal lamps flashed, desperate radio messages were tapped out to try and stop the onslaught, but to no avail, the ships kept on shooting, and soon aircraft were dropping out of formation in flames, or turning back in panic. Theo looked to his pilots, two ashen-faced Americans hunched fearfully over their controls. Most were ex-civilians, humble cargo crews with no combat training and little night experience. Another flash exploded ahead, the aeroplane bucked, then he felt it banking into a turn. Moments later Hunter was lurching up the fuselage to the cockpit.

'What's happening?'

'We're turning back.'

'Like hell you are!'

'Nobody said nothing about getting shot at.'

'Of course they did. It's war!'

'Sorry, buddy. We're unarmed, no protection and no fighter escort. We ain't sitting here getting blown to bits by your own goddamn navy.'

The Dakota was still banked over, still turning for home. Hunter was braced against the slope, fumbling at his smock.

Then his service pistol was out, and pointing at the co-pilot's head.

'Turn this plane around, or I shoot him!'

'Are you out of your mind!'

'Do it. I mean it.'

Still the pilot hesitated, eyes wide with disbelief. Then came a muffled crack and the shot rang out, piercing the Dakota's roof. The pilot ducked. 'Jesus!'

'Do it, or I will kill him.'

Even as they turned back on course, the barrage began to slacken, as if the navy was belatedly realizing its mistake. But too belatedly, for the damage was done. Quite apart from those shot down, damaged or fleeing, the rest were like startled sheep on a mountainside, a scattering shambles, the neat formations gone, the meticulous drop plans in tatters. Few of the pilots had night-flying skills: they depended on lead navigators to guide them; now they were alone, and lost, and as the Ionian Sea turned to surf, then to a rugged coastline, then to the wild Sicilian interior, most had no idea where they were – or where to go.

Aboard Theo's Dakota, minutes of directionless wandering ensued while the dazed crew searched for clues. Hunter too stayed up front, peering vaguely through the windscreen, pistol at hand. After a while Hodge sighed and stood up.

'Perhaps I can be of help, sir? Landmarks are rather my thing.'

Hunter tossed him the map. 'Be my bloody guest.'

Another half-hour and they were closing in. Scrub fires could be seen glowing up ahead, machine-gun tracer rose to unseen targets, while puffs of flak burst above. Then:

'There!' Hodge pointed. 'That's the river, look. And there's the bridge too. Catania's beyond, and you can see Mount Etna in the distance.'

Hunter followed his arm. 'That's it, all right. OK, stand to, everyone!'

'Well done, Vere,' Theo murmured. Hodge winked, and with that the familiar ritual began. Standing up and shuffling into line, clumsy with packs and weapons. Hooking on, checking the strap, and checking the man's in front. Moving towards the door, nerves tightening as the black void beckons. Red light on, bunching up closer. A glimpse of ground, a blazing haystack and the gleam of a river. Tracer curling up. Hunter at the door: 'Stay close, boys!' Vere behind, muttering prayers. The engines popping as the pilot throttles back. The floor tilting, then green light on and go! The frenzied scuffle, the gaping door, the roar of the slipstream, and the wild leap. Warm wind buffeting, the tumble, the jerk, the swing. The relief. Flames and tracer rising all about, the rushing ground, too soon as always. Shouts, the crackle of small arms and the smell of smoke. The last seconds, knees bent, tuck, roll, and down.

'Well, there it is.' Brigadier Lathbury peered through binoculars.

'Looks quiet,' Hunter murmured.

'Hmm. Question is, who have we got to take it?'

'And who have they got defending it.'

Theo followed their gaze. He was lying in a ditch amid a motley gathering of fifty or so random Paras, which was all Lathbury had managed to assemble since landing. Scattered sounds of gunfire echoed all round the darkened plain, near and distant, suggesting other units were in contact with the enemy. Vineyards and olive groves concealed hundreds more, both friend and foe, while others were still arriving. He heard engines and looked up to see a late Dakota rumble overhead, disgorge its stick, then hurriedly wheel for home. Parachutes fell near and far, many of them unfamiliar in shape and colour. Earlier a glider had whooshed in right beside them, silently like an owl, only to crash into a culvert and explode. Nobody got out, and crackling flames still lit the scene a sickly yellow. Elsewhere scores of other fires burned, glowing across the scrubby plain like beacons: deliberately started by the enemy, or accidentally by the Paras, he couldn't tell. Glancing back, he scanned the ground 2nd Battalion was supposed to occupy, only to see the entire area was ablaze. Hoping Frost and his men weren't there, he turned forward again and focused his binoculars on the target.

Five hundred yards away lay the winding waters of the Simeto River. Spanning it was the Primosole Bridge, a simple box-girder affair standing out criss-cross white in the moonlight like a model. Of modest size, this minor bridge was nevertheless of major importance. Theo knew this, as did everyone, because three days earlier two huge invasion forces had landed on Sicily's southern coast. Their job was to quickly advance across the island, in order to invade Italy itself via the Strait of Messina. One force, the American 7th Army under General Patton, was storming up the west side of Sicily, while the other, Britain's 8th Army under Montgomery, was advancing up the east. This route, more direct than Patton's, would bring 8th Army along the coast road, past Syracuse, Taormina and on to Messina. Halfway along it, at Catania, just south of the smouldering giant Etna, the road crossed Primosole Bridge.

'Right, chaps, here's what's happening,' Lathbury announced. '1st Battalion was to seize the thing from the north side, with 3rd Battalion covering from the east and 2nd from the south. But everything's to cock, men are all scattered, radios are missing, so frankly that plan's gone. What we do know, however, is that the bridge must be taken, and right now it looks pretty quiet. So we're doing it.'

Murmurs circulated, someone choked a laugh, a distant mortar exploded with a crump. As if to comment.

'All right, now there's fifty of us, so we divide into four sections. I'll lead A Section, Major Hunter B Section, Captain Foy C Section, and Captain, er, Hodge D Section. Each section will—'

'Sir?' Hodge raised his hand.

'What is it?'

'Sir, much as I'd like to, I suggest I not lead D Section.'

'Why on earth not?'

'I was only brought in at the last moment, you see. As a JAFO. I've not attended any of the briefings. I don't know a thing about this operation.'

'For goodness' sake!'

'Sorry, sir. Thought I should mention it.'

'Yes, yes. Right, well, in that case then, er, Thickey, you're leading D Section.'

'Um...'

'Right! Here's what we do.'

D Section, he learned, comprising himself, Vere Hodge, and eight others – mostly clerks and signallers – was to crawl along the ditch, away from the bridge and parallel to the river, find a quiet place, and wade or swim across to the north bank. Once there they were to crawl back to the bridge, clamber up and seize it. At the same moment, Lathbury's section would seize the southern end, while the other two sections would provide covering fire.

Before they set out Theo assembled his men. 'What have we got?'

'Just rifles it looks like.'

'Is that all?'

'The weapons containers all got scattered.'

'Stens, anyone? Gammons? Anti-tank rifles?'

'I've got a Very pistol.'

'And I've got a grenade, look!'

'So that's one grenade then. And one flare gun.'

Ten minutes later they were on hands and knees, rifles slung, pushing through dense reed beds towards the river. Then they were elbow-deep in evil-smelling marsh. Finally they reached water.

'Ye Gods.' Hodge peered across. 'Are we really doing this?'

'Speed's the thing, Vere. Go fast and don't stop.'

'Er, sir?' A voice from behind. 'Lieutenant Thickey? I should probably have said earlier. But I can't swim. Sorry.'

'It's all right. You'll wait here and cover our crossing. We're going now, everyone. We move quickly and quietly, we keep on moving, and we all stay together. That's all. Let's go.'

He was the first Allied soldier on to Primosole Bridge.

Having safely attained the north bank, they hurriedly retraced their steps, reaching cover beneath the bridge without incident. Hearing only silence above, he motioned half his force to the other side, and upon an owl-hoot signal, everyone leaped up the bank.

'*Non sparate!*' An anguished Italian shout. Four soldiers, arms raised high, were standing beside a machine gun. One had his overcoat on, and a suitcase at his side, as though late for his train; the others too seemed eager to leave. Other than these four the bridge was deserted. While D Section set up positions, Theo questioned them, learning they were alone, wanted only to surrender and bore no ill will towards Tommies. '*Churchill splendido!*' one man grovelled. Theo corralled them into a corner, checked his men and waited for Lathbury to arrive. But a moment later heavy footsteps were heard running in from behind.

'Who goes there?'

'Pearson, you bloody idiot!'

A score of Paras arrived, sprinting from cover, weapons raised as though for attack. At their head was the unmistakable profile of Colonel Alastair 'Jock' Pearson, officer commanding 1st Battalion.

'Who's in charge here?'

'He is.' Hodge pointed at Theo. 'We just took the bridge.'

'You did? Well... good work. Have you got the charges off?'

'Charges?'

'Yes! This thing's rigged to blow sky high. In fact I'm surprised—'

'Jock! Is that you?' Lathbury arrived from the other end, his section in tow. Behind them followed a smaller party led by a Para leaning on a stick. Meanwhile a third group was approaching along the riverbank. 'Jock, thank goodness. I've got Johnny here, he's hurt.'

'No, he's not.' Frost limped up. 'Hello, Jock. It's nothing. Twisted my blasted knee landing, that's all. Hello, Theo. Well done grabbing the bridge. I say, is that Bill Yeldham coming there?'

Paras were converging from all directions, homing on the bridge like pigeons to a loft. As they assembled, an extraordinary battlefield conference got under way featuring Gerald Lathbury, head of 1st Parachute Brigade, all three of his battalion commanders, Pearson, Frost and Yeldham, and a gaggle of bemused onlookers.

'Well, hello, chaps,' Lathbury began. 'Good of you all to drop in!'

Chuckles of mirth. 'Wouldn't want to miss your birthday, sir,' Yeldham said.

'Is it? Good heavens, so it is!'

'Happy birthday sir, many happy returns, congratulations, top of the morning.'

'How kind, I'd buy you all a drink but forgot my wallet.'

'Typical Scotsman.'

'Soon as we get home, that's a promise. Right, Johnny, what have you got?'

'About a hundred or so men,' Frost replied. 'Some mortar, and Vickers, a few PIATs. Lonsdale's setting up firing positions; we should be able to cover the southern end as planned.'

'Good. Who's Lonsdale?'

'New A Company commander.'

'Right. Bill?'

'Similar sir, more chaps yet to arrive. Heavy stuff's still missing but we'll do our damnedest to hold off anything coming from town.'

'And that's where they'll come from. Jock?'

'About half the battalion accounted for. Light weapons a-plenty, plus a few heavies. Not enough, but we'll hold this bridge, don't you worry.'

'I won't.' Lathbury checked his watch. 'Daylight's in two hours. Jerry won't attack in force before then.'

'Any word from 8th Army?' Yeldham said.

'Nothing. But we're told leading elements should get here by noon, so hopefully we won't have to hold out longer than that. In the meantime I'll set up HQ at the southern end behind those pillboxes. Keep me informed as best you can. Use runners for liaison until the radios turn up. Any questions?'

'What about the charges?'

'No sign of the RE boys, I take it.'

'No, but if we can get underneath we might at least cut—'

A hum, a whistle, then a monstrous explosion right in the centre of the bridge. Debris flew, the whole structure shuddered, clouds of smoke and dust rose and spread out like fog.

'Looks like we've been spotted.'

Lathbury coughed dust. 'Was that the charges?'

'No, sir.' Hodge stepped forward. 'It was an 88. Half a mile south over there.'

Frost straightened. 'I'll take care of him! Permission to rejoin Battalion, sir.'

'Yes, yes, off you go, all of you. And good luck!'

At that the four came to attention, saluted, and hurried off, conference closed.

'Right.' Lathbury rubbed his hands. 'The rest of you come with me.'

'Sir,' Hunter queried. 'The charges?'

'Oh, yes, almost forgot...'

A bomb-disposal company, 25BD, was aboard the Dakotas carrying the Royal Engineers, but nobody knew if they'd even made it to Sicily, let alone the drop zone. Prudence dictated the task wait until they arrive, or at least until daylight, but Lathbury feared the enemy might blow the bridge any time. Thus it was a somewhat reluctant D Section that followed Theo on to the bridge, there to gather in brooding silence around the hole punched in the roadway by the 88 shell. Through it they could see the boxes of explosives, secured beneath by steel cables. Cutting them off was not an option, not without cable-cutters or wire saws. The only other choice was to disable the charges somehow, in the dark, and under increasing threat of enemy fire. A brief discussion ensued, while tracer arced overhead and occasional bullets pinged off girders. In the end it was decided that by equipping a man with torch and penknife, and dangling him through the hole, like fishing through ice, he might sever enough electrical wires to neutralize the charges. Rope was duly found, the smallest man selected, and carefully lowered from view. Half an hour later they hauled him back up.

'Any luck?'

'God knows. Like spaghetti down there. I cut what I could.'

Theo retired to Brigade HQ, which was located behind a captured pillbox on the south side of the river, and settled down to wait for the dawn. After a while he fell asleep.

He was woken by the characteristic rattle of MG42 machine guns. Though subliminally aware of shooting through the night, this new and unwelcome sound shook him swiftly awake. Brigadier Lathbury confirmed it.

'Armoured *Fallschirmjäger*,' he murmured, pointing. 'Battalion strength, arrived before dawn.

'Paratroops? But what are they doing here?'

'Good question. Nobody mentioned *them* at the briefings. But here they are, and well dug in on their side of the river, heavily armed with mortar and MG42s. 2nd Battalion are taking a pasting.'

Theo squinted, and could just make out myriad smoke puffs indicating their positions. *Fallschirmjäger*: theirs must have been the unusually patterned parachutes he'd seen last night. Skilled, aggressive and highly trained, just like their own paratroops, there had been rumours of them in Tunisia, but to his knowledge this was the first head-on confrontation. And as the morning wore on, it was a confrontation the British were losing. With only about a third of their planned force present, no artillery and few heavy weapons to support them, and with enemy reinforcements pouring in by the hour, the situation was soon becoming desperate. 2nd Battalion was forced back to avoid destruction, while at the bridge Pearson's 1st Battalion had to abandon the northern end just to hold on to the south. Furious gunfire from the Catania direction indicated 3rd Battalion was also under pressure. On the credit side a few anti-tank weapons arrived, together with some mortar and machine guns; the Royal Engineers made it to the scene, and also 16th Field Ambulance. Setting up shop south of the bridge, their services were quickly in demand. Vere Hodge managed to locate a container of field radios and was busily trying to get them working; meanwhile Theo, his D Section disbanded, found himself running errands for Lathbury, relaying messages between unit commanders, and shepherding the hundreds of Italian soldiers milling about the scene like lost tourists.

'What the hell are they doing!' Lathbury scowled. 'Apart from getting in the way.'

'Trying to surrender, sir, it seems. And asking when they're going to be fed.'

'I'll give them something to bloody chew on!' They ducked as a mortar shell burst. 'Christ, that one was close. Listen, we've got to get them out the way, so send them back to the road and tell them to wait there. 8th Army can deal with them when they get here. *If* they get here.'

But by late afternoon there was still no sign of 8th Army, and the Paras were losing the bridge. Following another ferocious assault by *Fallschirmjäger* backed by MG42 and artillery fire, Lathbury could see Pearson was overwhelmed.

'He won't like it, but tell him to pull back,' he instructed Theo. 'They can have the blasted bridge for now, but I won't lose the whole brigade.'

Holding his helmet to his head, Theo leaped from behind the pillbox and ran down the slope. Pearson's HQ was in a ditch by the bridge. As he ran, bullets smacked into the earth around him, a shell tore overhead, then he heard a crash behind and turned to see Lathbury's pillbox enveloped in smoke. Figures were emerging from it through the dust. He hesitated and then ran back.

'It's all right!' Lathbury staggered out, his face white with dust, his battledress torn and bloody. 'It's all right, keep going.'

'Sir, let me fetch help.'

'No! Just get Pearson back. Get him back off the bloody bridge, for God's sake.'

By nightfall the scene was largely quiet but for sporadic shots and the bursting of star shells. Drifting smoke from countless fires further obscured movement, allowing both sides to reposition. What remained of 1st Parachute Brigade withdrew to the high ground held by 2nd Battalion; while this was happening Theo was sent to recce the bridge. Crouching among the reeds he could see it was markedly more battle-scarred, with girders dented and smoke-blackened, and the cratered roadway littered with rubble, but it was still intact and looked serviceable. To one side, 16th Field Ambulance stood defiant, now overrun by the enemy but still treating casualties. Then, as he was watching the *Fallschirmjäger* units repositioning about its northern approach, he suddenly glimpsed shadows moving beneath.

'Sappers repairing the charges, one assumes,' Lathbury said.

'Rather looks like it, sir.'

'And we can't allow that. Monty needs that bridge. *If* he ever gets here.'

'The *Fallschirmjäger* seem to have pulled back for the night too.'

'To rest and regroup, lucky bastards.' Lathbury passed a hand over his face. Thirty-seven, tall and gaunt, he had suffered bad lacerations to his legs from the pillbox explosion. The medics treating him insisted he needed surgery, but he refused to relinquish command even for an hour. In any case his battalion commanders were in little better state to take over.

Frost's injured knee was now so swollen he couldn't walk on it. Pearson, unknown to himself, was fighting malaria as well as German paratroops, and Yeldham was nowhere to be found, cut off somewhere near Catania with the remnants of 3rd Battalion.

At dawn the barrage started in earnest. Trapped atop the high ground south of the river, there was little the battered brigade could do but dig in, hold on, and wait for the inevitable ground attack to begin. But it never did, the German paratroops evidently wary of advancing on their British counterparts, knowing the *Roten Teufel* never gave ground without a bloody fight. So the barrage just went on and on, with artillery shells assailing them like Vulcan hammers, giant thunderbolts that blasted the earth to dust, vaporized rock and punched huge smoking craters in the ground as though with a giant fist. And fires were started, upwind in the tinder-dry grass, sending walls of fire and thick choking smoke upon the crouching men, forcing them ever rearward. Finally the dive-bombers came, screaming Stukas, falling like hawks from on high to unleash their bombs and machine guns. And watching it all, looming in and out of the drifting smoke as though circling the scene, the giant steaming cone of Mount Etna looked on like a malevolent god.

'We can't take much more of this, Johnny!' Lathbury shouted. Frost nodded wearily. It was the afternoon, they were slumped in the command post, little more than a dug-out in the hillside. Outside the brigade was burrowed like rats into what little cover it could find, while the mind-numbing pounding continued all round. Pinned down, exposed, with no relief in sight and nowhere to go, complete destruction of the brigade now loomed. Or surrender.

'It's the shelling,' Frost replied. 'If we don't move it'll destroy us completely.'

'What do you propose?'

'There's a lot of smoke. We could fall back under cover of it to the road, try and hold on there for Monty.'

Give up their position, in other words. Surrender the bridge entirely. Admit defeat. Lathbury nodded. 'It may come to that.'

Theo appeared, scrambling breathlessly into the dug-out. Hodge followed, brandishing a radio.

'Sir, Vere has news.'

'8th Army.' Lathbury sat up. 'Hodge, tell me you've got them!'

'Er, well, no, sir. I've got the *Newfoundland*.'

'The what?'

'The *Newfoundland*. She's three miles offshore.'

Another shell crashed in; earth and stones fell; acrid smoke filled the dug-out.

'Hodge,' Lathbury spluttered, 'are you talking about a bloody ship?'

'Yes, sir. A big one too, a cruiser. She's got 6-inch guns. Nine of them, absolute whoppers!'

'And?'

'Would you like me to ask her to shell the enemy?'

Lathbury and Frost exchanged glances. 'Yes, we bloody would!'

The effect was immediate and spectacular. Theo led Hodge to his observation post overlooking the bridge. From there, Hodge, map in hand, read coordinates over the radio and within minutes terrifying tearing shrieks split the air, followed by thunderous explosions erupting among the enemy positions. Vast gouts of rock and earth flew skywards, equipment too, vehicles, artillery, men, tossed through the air like toys. An entire 88 crew plus gun and carriage blasted to fragments before their eyes. Quickly the enemy barrage faltered; five minutes more and they could see men and guns falling hurriedly back. Hodge kept talking on the radio, reporting the movements, fine-tuning the range;

Theo watched, awed by the speed of the turnaround, and the power of the naval shells. 'Keep going,' he encouraged Hodge, 'keep going, it's working!'

He steadied his glasses, watching in amazement. Then a different sound caught his ear, between the shriek and thunder of explosion. Heavy motors. Coming up the coast road. 'Stay here, Vere.'

'Are you going?'

'8th Army's coming.'

'Really?'

'Yes, and I must tell the brigadier.'

'Shall I keep going with *Newfoundland*?'

'Yes, you're doing fine work.' He scrambled up. 'Probably saved the brigade.'

Later that afternoon, safely back in their former positions above the approach road, fed, watered and with their many injured being tended, 1st Para was able to watch while their relief force assaulted the bridge. An entire armoured brigade had arrived, spearheading 8th Army's advance, and from it a battalion of Durham Light Infantry was chosen to do the honours, backed by tanks, mobile artillery, engineers, and 25BD to disarm the charges. As they prepared, Theo was sent to invite their brigadier to join Lathbury, Frost and Pearson at the observation point.

'Ah, good afternoon, Brigadier, good of you to drop in.'

'Delighted. Sorry we were held up rather.'

'Not to worry.'

Pleasantries were exchanged, cigarettes swapped, a little gentle leg-pulling indulged. Then binoculars were collectively raised as the attack got under way.

Everyone went ominously quiet. Theo watched through his German glasses with growing disbelief as the Durhams, like in a Great War advance of old, plodded doggedly towards the river, slowly, fully upright and in broad view of everyone including the enemy. Yes, there were tanks with them, two battered Shermans, and some light artillery pieces were calmly setting up behind, but the men themselves were hopelessly exposed, and making no effort to conceal themselves, or even hurry a little.

'What are they doing?' Frost murmured at his side.

No answer came. Until the Durhams were within fifty yards of the bridge, when suddenly the *Fallschirmjäger* opened up, furiously hosing machine-gun bullets into them from a dozen positions at once. Men fell as though cut down by scythe, others scattered in panic, confused shouts and deathly screams were heard, and the Shermans' guns barked, but with no target to aim at their shots struck nothing, and the Germans replied with anti-tank weapons of their own. Theo saw a Sherman explode into flames, while the second desperately turned to retreat; elsewhere a detachment of sappers scampered towards the bridge to disarm the charges, but not a single man made it. An officer charged forward gesturing heroically, only to be cut down by a hail of bullets. Moments more and the attack was foundering, with men turning back in terror and shock, some still falling as they fled the onslaught, others dragging stricken comrades with them.

Then it was over. Silence fell down on the river as the Germans paused to reload, and also on the vantage point as the spectators looked at the scene. Below, smoke drifted over a vista of blood and desecration; bodies lay everywhere, some still moving, many not. One body, bloody legs gone, was hauling itself stubbornly forward, leaving a darkly stained track behind. No one dared approach it to help. Then it too slumped, while a guttural cheer of derision rose from the northern bank.

The Durham's brigadier cleared his throat. 'Well, that didn't go too badly...'

The Paras could only gape.

'... for a first go, that is, you know. A probing feint.'

Pearson was beside himself. 'What!'

'Yes. We'll have another stab at it in an hour or so.'

'But not like that, for God's sake!'

'Jock,' Lathbury murmured. 'Steady on.' Then he stepped forward. 'What Colonel Pearson is saying, Brigadier, is that perhaps there's another way.'

'Really? How so?'

Quietly. At night. By stealing across the river and seizing the bridge by *coup de main*. Pearson laid out the plan, and even volunteered to lead it, using a mixed force of Durhams, sappers and Paras. 'We've already found crossing points above and below the bridge.' He gestured at the map. 'Two forces cross and seize the northern end; a third takes the southern. Silent order. Surprise is everything.'

'What about Jerry?' the brigadier asked.

'Jerry pulls back after dark: our observers already spotted that. In any case we learned in Tunisia he hates fighting at night. He'll wait till morning when he can call in artillery support. By then we'll have reinforced our position and it'll be too late.'

'Fine.' Lathbury tapped the map. 'Who do you want with you?'

'I'll lead A Force; we'll cross downstream, here. Hunter can lead B Force to take and hold the southern end. And I want *him* to lead C Force across upstream.'

Heads turned. 'Trickey?' Lathbury looked surprised. 'He's only an acting lieutenant, you know.'

'That's as may be.' Pearson winked at Theo. 'But he knows the crossing point – he's already crossed it. Plus he's already taken the bridge once!'

Hodge's hand shot up. 'Permission to accompany him, sir!'

They waited until midnight. By then the Catanian plain was quiet but for the crackle of bushfires and the occasional popping of star shells. Recce units reported the *Fallschirmjäger* had indeed pulled back for the night, leaving only a reduced defence force on the bridge itself, and thus, for the second time in three days, Theo found himself leading a group of men across the Simeto to attack it. This force was much larger than his D Section had been, better armed too, and eager for revenge. And again, once safely across, they stole unobserved along the northern bank until concealed beneath the moonlit shadow of the bridge. A short while later Pearson's team arrived, whereupon, on his signal, both teams scrambled up the bank on to the bridge.

It was all swiftly over. Once again the Germans had left Italians in charge of the bridge for the night, and once again the Italians, suddenly over-run by furious, bayonet-brandishing Tommies, threw down their weapons in surrender. Barely a shot was fired; within twenty minutes the northern end was secure, and soon heavy machine guns, mortars and artillery were moving in to consolidate their defences. Reconnaissance units probed forward too, reporting back that the *Fallschirmjäger* had pulled right back, almost a mile, for reasons known only to themselves.

'Is it all over, Theo?' Vere Hodge asked. They were picking their way back over the rubble-strewn bridge. Beneath them the river slid by, silent and steely, while overhead, stars shone through a veil of drifting smoke. As they progressed, they met more reinforcements crossing over.

'I doubt it. But with 8th Army units arriving every hour, they'll find it hard to win back the bridge.'

'But they'll keep trying?'

'Oh yes. Or trying to destroy it. I don't envy those bomb-disposal men.'

'No. And what about us?'

'Us?' They reached the southern end of the bridge. Off to one side a cluster of luminescent humps, tents glowing with lamplight from within, showed where 16th Field Ambulance worked on, cutting, sawing, stitching, repairing the ravaged victims as best they could. Beyond these the ground rose towards 2nd Battalion's old positions, now pitted with craters and scorched black from fire. 'Brigadier Lathbury says we're being withdrawn.'

'Really? Where to?'

'Heaven knows.'

'Oh. But, Theo, there's something I've been meaning to ask.'

'Yes?'

'What *is* a JAFO?'

'Ah. Um, you probably don't want to know that, Vere.'

'Yes I do.'

'Well... It's "just another fucking observer". And that's certainly not you!'

CHAPTER 9

Following his ignominious recall from Africa before the fall of Tunisia, Erwin Rommel returned home to Neustadt. 'I have fallen into disgrace,' he told Lucie within minutes of landing, 'and can expect no important jobs at present.' Relieved at this news, yet concerned by her husband's poor health and morale, Lucie immediately packed him off to Austria to complete the rest cure prescribed by his doctors the previous October.

A month later he was back and ready for the fray. Expectantly he cleared his desk and sat down to await the summons. But none came. Weeks passed and no telephone rang, no couriers arrived bearing briefing papers, and no instructions came from High Command. Most significantly of all, not one word came from the Führer's office. Still evidently *persona non grata*, all he could do was follow the war via the newspapers – and glean occasional snippets from army friends. 'You're out in the cold, Erwin,' they told him, 'keep your head down and wait for the wind to change.' Resigning himself to a long stay on the sidelines, he sat down to write a memoir of the Africa campaign, failure for which he blamed largely on the Italians. Then late one night in May, two full months after his return, the telephone finally rang.

'It will soon all be over in Tunisia,' Adolf Hitler said quietly. 'It was poorly managed. I should have listened to you. Come back.'

The next day he flew to Berlin. And for the following two months was rarely away from his leader's side. One day they would fly to the 'wolf's lair' in Prussia to check on the Russian campaign, the next they were entertaining dignitaries at his Bavarian mountain retreat, then it was back to headquarters in Berlin to harangue the generals. Rommel fulfilled an uneasy non-role – part strategic adviser, part sounding board, part punchbag. Regarded suspiciously by the Party elite, he held no official portfolio, commanded no forces, nor even had a job title. 'At best I'm a field marshal in waiting,' he wrote plaintively to Lucie. 'But for how long?'

What he gained, however, was a rare and intimate insight into his master's moods and thoughts, something that with the passing weeks caused him increasing concern. Even at this precarious stage of the war, he wrote, with the Russian campaign failing and the Allies about to invade Europe, Hitler was frequently relaxed, charming, witty and irrepressibly optimistic. An hour later by contrast he would be consumed by dark doubts. 'Nobody will ever make peace with me,' he confided one night, and even once adding: 'I'm well aware the war is lost.' More worrying were his delusions, as though his grasp of reality was slipping, convincing himself the war was in fact far from lost, talking expansively of the 'thousand-year Reich' and of magical super-weapons that would snatch victory from defeat. He was dangerously capricious too, staunchly defending a favoured general one day, only to condemn him as a coward the next.

Then there were the rages. One simple, innocent remark could send Hitler into an uncontrollable fury, screaming and frothing like a rabid dog, such that no one dare approach him. These tirades were usually sparked by a perceived weakness in others, or a failure in them to meet his expectations, be it a senior general in Russia, factory workers on the Ruhr, or ordinary civilians grumbling at shortages. At such times the darkest side of his personality would emerge. 'The German people can rot in hell!' he growled chillingly, adding: 'A great race must die heroically, it is historical necessity.' At this time too Rommel first heard mention of the mass killings of Jews and other minorities to the east in Poland. These were never discussed openly, but carried out in secret by the Waffen SS and its sinister leader Heinrich Himmler – a man Rommel greatly disliked. 'Under no circumstances!' he wrote bluntly, when Manfred asked if he could apply for a cadetship to the SS. 'The soldiers have qualities, but they are under the command of a madman.'

Spring turned to summer, the fighting season drew on, Rommel, increasingly restless, chafed for an operational role. Then in June the call finally came, and he was summoned to the chancellery to receive orders. Russia, he assumed straight away, was where he was destined. Hitler was planning a renewed offensive there, a massive pincer movement involving two whole army groups, a full forty-three divisions aimed at halting the Soviet advance once and for all. It was called Operation Citadel; Rommel was familiar with the details, and had already offered suggestions, typically urging his leader to strike hard and fast, and sooner rather than later. But as it turned out his suggestions were irrelevant, for it wasn't Russia he was destined for. It was Greece.

Having won in Africa, Hitler explained, the Allies were now planning their invasion of mainland Europe. This would not be via Sicily and Italy, as many expected, but through Greece. Rommel was incredulous, pointing out that landing an invasion force in Greece and then fighting all the way up through the Balkans would be a logistical nightmare for the Allies, whereas Italy provided the most direct and least complicated route. In his view the Allies would make a three-pronged attack, firstly on the toe of Italy via Sicily, then with simultaneous sea landings on both sides of the peninsula, as far up as they could manage – possibly around the Naples area or even Rome. All the available intelligence, the build-up of troops, the stockpiling of equipment, the radio chatter, everything pointed to this strategy. 'Furthermore,' he went on, 'we should establish a defence line right across northern Italy, place our main forces there, seal off the Alpine routes through South Tyrol, and so be ideally placed to repel the enemy indefinitely.' But Hitler wasn't having it. 'Italy is a ruse,' he insisted, 'a feint aimed at deceiving us and diverting our attention from Greece.' The troop movements in Tunisia were to mask the formation of a new Allied force, the 12th Army, which was secretly assembling in Libya. Greece was the objective, the evidence was indisputable, his agents were certain, and so was he. Rommel could only shake his head. 'And one more thing…' Hitler added. The dead body of a British Intelligence courier had recently washed up on a beach in Spain. Attached to its wrist was a briefcase full of plans – for the invasion of Greece.

Rommel's orders were to assume command of 'Army Group E', which did not yet exist, magically assemble a corps of staff, fly to 'fortress Greece', and start planning for the annihilation of the Allied invasion force. Dumbfounded, he dutifully began his preparations. Meanwhile Operation Citadel finally got under way. Originally planned for April, Hitler had repeatedly pushed back the date, citing equipment shortages, wrongly positioned troops, or the weather. Finally in early July he issued the order and the advance began. At first all went well: movement was swift and the pincers began to close. But it soon became clear the Russians had used the delay to advantage, heavily fortifying their positions, extending their defences, digging tank traps and sowing mines by the tens of thousands, and within a week the

German advance was faltering. Rommel attended the situation conference on 9 July and, although Hitler and his cronies insisted all was well, he instinctively sensed disaster. The very next day he was woken with the news that the Allies had invaded Europe – not in Greece, but in Sicily, exactly as he'd predicted.

Finally he was allowed to prepare plans based on his 'northern Italy defence line' idea. With a provisional headquarters at Salo on Lake Garda, he was even permitted to visit South Tyrol, including Theo's home town of Bolzano, to reconnoitre the geography. But Hitler, hedging as usual, decided also to place a second force in southern Italy to confront the invaders when they came. And he put Rommel's old rival Albert Kesselring in charge of it, deliberately not specifying which man – Rommel or Kesselring – was in overall command. Nor was he finished with his Hellenic obsession.

Rommel, to his fury, was ordered to Greece to assess the situation there. What he found did not impress him. Though defences had been increased, and the Italian navy was theoretically guarding the Adriatic: '... a very great deal is required before Greece can be regarded a fortress!' Wearily he began compiling a report which he knew would be poorly received. But that same night he was woken by an urgent recall to Berlin. Something had occurred to completely eclipse all matters Greek. Hitler's closest foreign friend and ally, Benito Mussolini, had been overthrown and arrested.

I am still keeping a notebook. A minor act of insurrection in an environment where such things are forbidden, it helps offset feelings of impotence – and passes the time. Not strictly a diary per se, it's more a haphazard compilation of notes and recollections, starting with Arnhem and Stalag XIB as Pip Smith suggested, and continuing to the present here in Ulm. Some Rommel insights too. Notepaper is increasingly hard to come by, so I'm currently recycling a child's drawing book left at the drop-in centre. It's full of sketches of castles and princesses and strange animals, which have to be rubbed out before use. Sometimes I leave an illustration in and write round it, adding a natty visual dimension to the narrative. Beside a picture of a particularly vile monster I scrawl: 'Vorst the Vindictive!' A drawing of a huge iced cake gains the caption: 'God, yes!' While a more considered entry beneath a winged fairy describes my second visit to Lucie Rommel.

Which follows a similar pattern to the first: a car, an army officer, a wordless drive, a servant's greeting at the door, then up the stairs to the anteroom. No Manfred this time, but the officer seats himself by the door like a bodyguard, and there's also a young servant woman standing in a corner. Lucie is at the window, sitting at the table with the photographs of her family. Boxes tied with ribbons lie at her feet like presents, the room is bright, the curtains open, a hint of March sunshine lights her profile, she is dressed, composed, and generally looking better.

'Good afternoon, madam,' I begin in my politest German. 'And how do we find you this fine day?'

No response. I pull up a chair. 'Madam?'

'Frau Rommel is endeavouring to comply with the British doctor's instructions.'

'I... Pardon?'

'And wishes to thank him for attending to her.'

This comes from the girl in the corner. Lucie says nothing, while the bodyguard folds his arms. Confused, I plough on, trying to draw her into a response, but after more second-hand pleasantries with the maid, it's clear Lucie either doesn't understand my German, or is still not speaking. A little plate of food sits beside her – tiny squares of black bread and cheese – presumably to show the British doctor that she is eating as instructed. Frankly the British doctor, who missed lunch because the car came early and is perpetually dizzy with hunger anyway, would gladly have wolfed these, but that would be poor form, so I try to ignore them, and, opening my bag, begin a physical examination instead. This finds her anaemic and underweight, but alert, responsive to stimuli and seemingly well enough. Feeling for her pulse, I try a different tack.

'Your son is still here in Herrlingen?'

The pulse skips and she looks away. At the same moment the bodyguard stirs.

'Cadet Rommel has been transferred.'

'Oh?'

'To the Reichsarbeitdienst.'

'What is that?'

'Front-line defence work.'

'But he's just a boy!'

'These are desperate times! Your RAF bombers—'

'That's enough, *Hauptmann*.' This from the maid, whom I'm now thinking is not a maid at all. 'We do not wish to upset the patient, do we?'

No, we don't. Nor get into an argument, something Erik warned me about at the beginning. Never discuss politics or the war with the Germans, he said. Such conversations get nowhere and quickly descend into unpleasantness.

The captain clears his throat. 'My apologies, *Herr Doktor*.'

'Mine also.'

Silence descends. And with my examination complete and the patient not speaking, I'm soon running out of things to do. So I begin packing up. 'Well, the lady is progressing, and I suggest she continue—'

'Wait!' The girl steps forward, while Lucie looks panicked. 'Please wait, there is another matter.'

'Oh?'

'Yes.' She clasps her hands. Early thirties, conservatively dressed in a tweed-like skirt, something of her expression, the lift of the chin perhaps, looks familiar.

'My name is Gertrud Stemmer. I am Frau Rommel's secretary and companion. She asked me to invite you here today for two reasons. No, three. Foremostly to thank you for visiting, especially when she knows how busy you are with other duties.'

'She does? Well, there's no need—'

'Also to offer you assistance. By way of gratitude.'

'Assistance.'

'With your clinic, for the destitute.'

Suddenly it's so quiet I can hear the clock ticking in her bedroom. Nobody knows about the drop-in, *nobody*. We are pilfering Vorst's military hospital supplies and Red Cross medicines meant for POWs, to treat German civilians. Repercussions if discovered don't bear thinking about.

'I'm sorry, there must be a mistake...'

'Don't be alarmed, Doctor, we do not intend exposing you. Do we, Captain?'

A grunt from the *Hauptmann*, then she goes on: 'Frau Rommel greatly appreciates the humanitarian work you are doing and only wishes to assist. Unfortunately cash is short, also she has no medical supplies to donate, but asks if there is some other way to help.'

'Er...'

'Such as providing furniture perhaps, tables and chairs, cabinets and so on. Or blankets, a little coal for heating, or toys for the children.'

All of the above, in fact, would be very welcome, as we're

currently functioning in an abandoned chapel by the railway tracks. But I'm not about to admit anything, not in front of a uniformed Jerry and the widow of one of Hitler's best pals. I close up my bag and make to rise. 'I'm sorry, but I'm late for my next appointment.'

'There is the third matter, *Herr Doktor.*'

Now what. 'Yes?'

'Frau Rommel enquires, how is the patient Trickey progressing?'

And as soon as I get back to the *Revier* I storm upstairs to the patient Trickey – who's progressing reasonably, thank you – to demand some answers.

'Trickey? Where the hell are you?'

He's in his chair facing the window. Beyond it the meagre March sun is setting. He turns and smiles his guileless smile. 'Hello, sir, it's been a better day, hasn't it?'

'Don't give me that! Rommel!'

'I'm sorry?'

'You said he was your mentor.'

'Did I?'

'It was the first bloody thing you said.'

'I don't remember...'

'Yes you do. And you're going to tell me. She's got his letters!'

'I... Who?'

'His widow. Boxes and boxes, one letter for every day he was away apparently. She showed me one – you're in it! Something about an opera in Rome. Back in forty-one.'

'Really?'

'Yes, really. That's four bloody years ago! And she said there are many other references. And she said her family owed you a debt. And she wants to know how you're feeling, for God's sake. So what's it all about?'

'I... It's complicated, and rather confused...'

'Are you a German spy, Trickey?'

'No!'

'Were you his errand boy, and had secret meetings or something?'

'No, nothing like that.'

'Then what, damn it! Tell me. And while you're at it, you can tell me why we're here!'

'Good question, Doc!' someone quips, while another patient chuckles. Several of Theo's ward-mates are now propped on elbows following proceedings. The old *Sanitäter* is also pottering about, although he supposedly speaks no English. I'm talking too loudly, and indiscreetly, because I'm growing exasperated: six months of frustration coming dangerously to the boil. We hear footsteps on the stair; a moment later Erik appears to save the day.

'Hello, Dan, I heard you were back. Do you have a moment?'

I sigh, and follow him to the landing. 'What is it?'

'Everything all right, with the, you know, visit?'

'Yes. No.' I pat my pockets, remembering something else. 'Oh, I don't know, I'll explain later. Why do you ask?'

'You were shouting rather.'

'Was I?'

'Yes. And Vorst wants to see you.'

'Oh, joy.'

Vorst's office is on the ground floor. I descend the stair as though a prisoner to the gallows, straighten my tie, knock and enter. Though he is seated and his head bare, saluting him, copiously, never does any harm, so I stamp loudly to attention and throw up my hand.

'*Herr Oberstabsarzt* wishes to see me.'

More food assaults my senses, an enormous *Wurst* sandwich complete with mustard and pickle sits at his side. He picks it up and takes a leisurely bite, completely ignoring me. The procedure, I have learned, is simply to wait, in silence and at attention, until he is ready.

Still chewing, he eventually looks up. 'The bearings factory at Böfingen.'

'Yes, *Herr Oberstabsarzt*.'

A greasy finger jabs a sheet. 'The *nicht arbeitsfähig* list is over quota.'

'Oh, er, yes, *Herr Oberstabsarzt*, I forgot to mention that. There is a bronchial epidemic, you see, quite serious, it—'

'Silence!' His fist hits the desk. 'I did not ask for excuses!'

'No, *Herr Oberstabsarzt*.'

He waits, glaring. He's breathing heavily; there's spittle on his chin and sweat on his brow, as though he's been building up to this. The danger here is palpable; even I can sense it.

'I've been watching you, *Gar-lant*, with your fancy red beret and insolent attitude. You are disobedient and disrespectful and dishonest.'

I say nothing but stay to attention, absorbing it all, as Erik repeatedly urges.

'You are a lazy and impudent liar. And a disgrace to the name *Doktor*.'

I know what's happening. He's goading me, insulting my professionalism, in the hope I'll lash out. So he can have me removed, like Collinson. And it's working. I can feel the anger rising within, feel my heart racing and fists clenching. Much more and I know I'll lose control.

'You think you're so superior. Yet you are nothing but a trumped-up *Scharlatan*.'

My cheek twitches. My body sways forward.

'Ill trained, ignorant, and above all...'

Yes. Do it.

'*Schlampig.*'

And there's the word. The word that saves me from leaping over his desk and throttling him. *Schlampig.* Slovenly. And I'm transported back to Stalag XIB and the wonderful Bill Alford, confronting the bully Möglich who used the same word. And how Bill dealt with it so magnificently. And I smile within and feel the tension dissipate like water through sand. *Waho Mohammed.*

'I apologize, *Herr Oberstabsarzt.*'

'*Was?*'

'I apologize. Sincerely and with heartfelt shame and regret.'

'I'm not interested in your grovellings.' He waves dismissively, but the apology wrong-foots him.

'Rightly so, *Herr Oberstabsarzt.* Such a thing will not happen again.'

'You're damn right, it won't!' He's lost this round, and knows it. But isn't finished yet. 'So you will return to Böfingen, put the malingerers to work and correct the quota.'

'Yes, sir, first thing tomorrow.'

'No. Now. This very day.'

'But the evening meal! And the curfew...'

'Do as I order!'

I salute and turn.

'And one more thing.'

'Yes, *Herr Oberstabsarzt?*'

'Do not think for one moment that having friends in high places can save you.'

*

It's already dusk when I step outside. And, as I plod wearily towards Münsterplatz, the blacked-out houses seem to encroach with the darkness, enveloping me in shadow like malevolent onlookers. The night is dark and moonless, the first stars pricking a mist-like veil of high cloud. Perfect conditions for bombers, as Ulm's residents know from bitter experience; thus their curtains are tightly drawn and their lights doused early. Few venture on to the streets: queues of hunched silhouettes indicate shops still issuing the day's bread ration, or the week's one egg, or a few rancid meat scraps. Beggars haunt the minster's buttressed crevices, office and factory workers hurry home, labour gangs trudge back to their *Lager*, while patrolling policemen and *Luftschutz* wardens watch for trouble or unguarded lights. All ignore me, which I welcome, hunched angrily into my overcoat as I make for the tram stop. Then it's a long wait, another hour and two changes until finally reaching Böfingen. Drilling, hammering and heavy-machinery noises echo from the plant as I approach, despite the late hour, for work here goes on round the clock. The off-shift labourers are housed in wooden huts outside. I head for them, find my way to the *Krankenhaus*, rouse the bewildered guard and *Sanitäter,* and set about my odious work. Barely pausing to examine them, for there seems little point, I now sign off badly sick men I saw only yesterday as fit to work tomorrow, ruthlessly and arbitrarily. They make little protest. My unscheduled appearance perplexes them, my gloomy mood invites no discussion, and somehow they just sense, and understand, and accept what must be done. Which makes it all the worse.

An hour later, duty done, I step outside and head back to the tram. I walk briskly, putting distance between me and the factory sounds, because my complicity shames me deeply, not just as a doctor but as a human being, and as a man. By submitting to Vorst's demands I am not simply giving in to Nazi oppression, but actively collaborating with it, which is a terrible admission for someone in my uniform. I wonder what Arthur Marrable would say, or Bill Alford, or poor Cliff Poutney. And for the first time since arriving in Ulm, I now seriously consider running away from it.

Quite how is another matter. I have money but only pennies, barely enough for a short tram-ride. But I know where Prien keeps the petty cash. I move freely about the city, because the papers in my pocket permit me to. Yet I am rarely challenged to produce them, and men in odd uniforms are everywhere to be seen in Germany. My German, though improving, is still basic and certainly won't fool a native, but could I pretend to be Dutch or Czech or something? Steal some money, modify my papers, swap my beret for a trilby, and carry my medical bag from one city to the next, like a touring doctor, catching trains and trams until reaching the French border, or the Swiss, or the Italian?

'*Guten Abend*, Daniel.'

'Trudi!' I haven't seen her in a week or more; even though she plies the same routes as me, we seem to keep missing one another. As usual she invites me in off the platform to sit in the warmth. Half full with home-goers, the tram's dimly lit against the blackout, although not dimly enough to mistake the German soldier, complete with rifle and greatcoat, scowling at me from up the carriage.

'How is your mother?' I enquire.

'The tablets you gave are helping her rheumatism. She hopes to resume work at the grocery store soon.'

'Good. And you?'

She manages a smile. 'I work, I wait, I pray, like everyone.'

'For it to end?'

She nods and moves on. Some minutes pass. The tram squeaks and rocks; I feel my head sinking to my chest with the cumulative effects of stress, fatigue and hunger. I try to muster ideas for my escape but find my mind drifting off instead.

'*Aufstehen!*' A boot kicks my shin. '*Aufstehen, Englischer Schläger!*'

Schläger I don't recognize, but suspect is insulting, especially as the speaker is glaring at me with undisguised contempt. Wearily I rise, as bidden, to find my eyeline level with the top of his youthful head. Which surprises us both.

'What?' I enquire sullenly.

'*Heraus!*' He points to the door. 'Out.'

'*Heraus bitte,*' I correct. At which he goes berserk, screaming and gesticulating hysterically while I stand there blinking, and everyone looks on in shock. Flecks of spit hit my cheek, his breath stinks of tobacco and garlic, and his clothes carry that peculiar soapy smell of all German soldiers. Rocking to the tram's motion, he's brandishing his rifle dangerously.

I glimpse Trudi edging towards us. 'He's a doctor!' she protests, but I gesture her back. The driver cranes his neck to the mirror, while the passengers lean away as though from snarling dogs. I wait, emboldened by my cussedness, scarcely caring what happens next, then the youth pauses, momentarily spent, and I glimpse the pain in his eyes behind the rage. Pain and anguish and too much suffering for one so young. And the hardness of my heart thaws to nothing.

'*Sanft, Junge,*' I say quietly. Gently does it.

'You must... leave the carriage!'

'I know. I will. Or, I could stay.'

And in a moment his shoulders slump, tears fill his eyes, and with utter defeat on his face he sinks on to the seat.

'You look unwell. You have been home on sick leave?'

'Three days. It's all they allow.'

'And now you must go back.'

He nods. 'But I can't.'

'The Russians?'

'You British have no idea.'

'Do you want to tell me?'

'No.' He shakes his head, hands tightly gripping the rifle, as though to stop them trembling. Then he begins to speak. 'We were ordered to set up a machine-gun position, at the end of a narrow street. Then the Russkies started sending their men in, and we mowed them down. By the dozen. It was easy at first, but soon became sickening. Inhuman, like slaughter. They kept sending more, and soon their bodies were piling up before us four and five deep, and the street was pouring with blood like a river. Yet still they came, like a tide, like vermin climbing over their own dead, never ending, never stopping until finally the gun jammed with the heat and we had to retreat for our lives. Then we set up once more further back and the whole nightmare began again.'

He props his rifle beside him and buries his head. 'We will never stop them.'

Sometimes there are no words. No point in them, no use for them. I can't think of any, so rest a hand on his back instead. Everyone in the carriage is watching, each confronting the unthinkable future they face. Russians are the collective terror. I glance at Trudi, standing there in her clippie's uniform, her lips pursed, her cap askew; she looks so young and vulnerable. Rumours abound, and she's surely heard them, of what invading Russian soldiers are doing to German women. I try to smile but she only shakes her head.

Then there's a shout from up front: '*Alarm!*' The brakes jam on and we're all thrown forward as the tram lurches to a halt. '*Aussteigen, aussteigen!*' the driver shouts and we pile out through the door. On the street the sirens are already wailing, the passengers scattering, some to their homes, others for the shelters.

'Come on!' Trudi grabs my hand and starts running, I glance back and see the young soldier, rifle in hand, staring up at the sky. I want to go back but Trudi's pulling me on. A shelter sign looms: 'LS12'; beneath it stone steps lead us down, under the pavement, under the building above, to a basement two floors down. It's long and narrow, more a wide corridor than a room, like a wine cellar with curved walls and arched ceiling. It smells damp and musty. Barely have we entered than the first bombs are falling, thumping down on the far side of the city. At the same time we hear the lighter crack of ack-ack guns along the river – token resistance, everyone knows, for anti-aircraft guns are often purloined for the Front. The cellar's quickly filling, women mainly, and children, some very young. They file in without fuss, and take their positions on the floor. Trudi tugs me down; we sit side by side, backs against the wall. Her hand still clasps mine; her eyes are on the overhead bulbs strung along the ceiling, which flicker with each falling bomb.

'Where are we?' I ask.

'Ostplatz,' she replies. 'East side, shops, offices, family homes.'

The explosions are louder now, heavier and more concentrated as the raid gathers momentum. Beneath us the ground trembles with each detonation. I check my watch: ten thirty, which is early for a raid. Something big must be brewing. 'What about your mother?'

Her gaze wavers. 'South of the river. She knows to get under the stairs.'

Suddenly there's a monstrous crash. The whole cellar shudders and the lights go out. Women's voices rise in the darkness, children wail, a male voice calls for calm. Matches flare, candles splutter to life, someone produces a torch, which pierces the fog to show a dust-filled cavern of terrified white faces. A misty vapour floats, the smell close and foetid; more bombs rain, ascending in power like approaching footsteps, the noise rising to a deafening thunder like the banging of a thousand drums. Trudi and I duck our heads together. My teeth are gritted; I've experienced air raids before, but never like this, so intense, so near, so *personal*. I'm taken back to the Schoonoord, cowering in the storeroom with Cliff while shells pound the walls to dust. But my fear there was of exposure, of being caught in the open; here it's about being buried, or crushed like paper beneath falling rubble. It's assault on a scale beyond assimilating, like being endlessly shaken in a mad dog's jaws, or punched senseless in the boxing ring; the bombs never stop, never waver, just keep on coming. Sometimes the explosions retreat, as though resting, circling round for breath, before rushing in again for the kill, stamping towards us like a furious giant. Above the thunder of impact we hear the rumbling drone of the bombers. It's too much to manage; soon the women stop sighing, the children stop whimpering, everyone reduced to shocked immobility by the onslaught. We hunch lower, mothers over their children, old men over their wives, Trudi burrowing into my coat like a terrified mouse. Time stops. An hour passes, perhaps two; still the attack goes on, far longer than any before. But then the sounds begin to fade, receding like a foul tide. Silence grows, and with it an interval of hope, and we dare wonder if the nightmare is ending. But no all-clear sirens sound, no encouraging shouts come from above, and though we exchange expectant glances, none of us dared move. And soon we hear the dread rumbling again, like the relentless march of boots, as the next wave approaches, and we know we're not done yet. A few minutes more and the bombs are falling again like rain.

I'm not asleep, but gradually stir from dream-filled torpor to the realization that the bombing has stopped. It's uncannily quiet; a single overhead bulb lights the cavern, throwing ghostly shadows over the tangle of bodies sprawled over its floor. Someone's snoring, a smoky haze hangs from the ceiling, the air is hot and acrid, an unusual crackling sound comes from the surface, and the distant tinkle of fire engines.

'Come on.' I nudge Trudi and we struggle upright, tiptoeing through the throng to the steps, the crackling noise growing louder as we go. A glow flickers from above, the steps are foggy with smoke, and as we ascend towards the surface we realize Ulm is burning. We stand in the entrance, cowering at the view. For a moment it's too much to take in, too bright and too ferocious. Everything, it seems, in every direction is aflame: shops, houses, cars, even trees and lamp-posts and sections of road. The heat's unbearable, the noise an angry snarl, the light hurtful to the eye. Geysers of flame spurt from gas mains; fire surges skyward through smashed windows, leaps from roof to roof and explodes into clouds of sparks as buildings collapse. And smoke billows everywhere, thick trunks of it coiling upward, or spiralling down to the street in rivers of choking black.

'My mother!' Trudi shouts above the din. 'I must get to her!'
'I'll come with you.'

We set off, stooping, arms raised against the heat. Ahead through the smoke sits the tram, her tram, now nothing but blackened metal. Almost immediately I stumble on something, and looking down see a body, unrecognizable but for shreds of smoking greatcoat, and the rifle gripped in its claw. The face is a skull, black lips twisted back over his teeth. Elsewhere we see more bodies, grotesque mannequins lying as though frozen, stick-like arms raised, legs bent for running.

We hurry on, crouching low, round a corner, and a wave of heat hits us. I'm stunned by the impact, as though from a punch. Both sides of the street are ablaze, two towering cliffs of flame roaring skyward in one giant inferno. We reel back, gasping, I can't breathe. I feel my chest burning, my hair singeing and the skin prickling on my face. 'Not this way!' We turn and run, doubling this way and that, but direction is meaningless, escape impossible, and before we know it we've stumbled back to the tram. The fire's getting worse. Across the street I see two people running from a doorway; their clothes ablaze, they struggle onward, then slow, stumble and fall. Their limbs flail briefly then come to a frozen stop. I too am falling. There's no air to breathe, only suffocating heat; I'm blinded by smoke, dizzy and drowning. Then Trudi grabs my arm and points. And I glimpse it through the billowing clouds, high above the skyline, pointing like a sign. The minster's spire, still up, still erect and defiant, beckoning us to safety. I pull off my coat and throw it over our heads for protection, and we set off one final time. Gradually we navigate the maze of fire, using instinct and the spire as guide, until finally we stagger into calmer waters. Five minutes more and we reach the Danube and safety.

'Electricity's out, water too. Several buildings were hit in the neighbourhood, but nothing like in the east. *Revier* was untouched. We were very lucky.' Erik dabs at my scalded forehead. 'So were you, by the looks of it.'

I respond with a hoarse choke.

'Don't talk, old fellow, you've inhaled a lot of smoke. Here, drink.'

I sip water, nodding gratefully. We're in the bedsit, it's four in the morning. A single candle burns. I stink of fire.

'Your overcoat's somewhat scorched, I'm afraid. Oh, and I found this in a pocket.' He picks up an envelope, singed brown at one corner. The letter from this morning.

'Thanks.'

'Important?'

'I doubt it.' I cough again.

'Trudi got home all right?'

I nod. We'd made it to the old bridge, which was undamaged. Across the river only a few fires burned, with most of the southern city in darkness. I wanted to cross with her but she insisted I get back: 'Before you get into trouble!' Then she kissed me with cracked lips, her cheeks black with smut, her hair smelling of ash.

'Vorst's disappeared.'

'Hmm,' I croak.

'Left Ulm for the night when the first bomb hit, is my guess.'

'Why?'

'Why do you think!'

'No, Erik, why is this happening?'

'Why is what happening?'

'Us. The Allies, bombing whole cities of no importance, like Ulm. Factories, power stations, docks, yes, I get that, but whole cities...'

'Ah.'

'There are no armies here, no factories building tanks or U-boats, no airfields or docks. Just civilians, ordinary women and children and old people. The destruction, the death, I saw, I saw...' But I can't speak, only double over with choking, my poisoned eyes streaming with tears.

Erik walks to the window. Even with the shutters closed and blackouts drawn, the glow of burning buildings can still be seen

221

to the east. From his posture, the folded arms, the pursed lips, I can tell I've touched a nerve.

'Erik?'

'When you were at Arnhem…' he murmurs. 'Oosterbeek, I mean.'

'Yes?'

'How did you find the local people? Their mood, I mean, their attitude.'

I try to think back. The relief and joy as we marched in. The unquestioning support, and faith in our mission. The fervent hopes for deliverance. The disgust and disappointment when we failed.

'They just wanted it over with.'

'Yes. And that's the point. We just want it over with.'

'And this is the way?'

'You've not been invaded, have you? Britain, that is.'

I shake my head. 'And that changes everything?'

'Quite a bit, yes. It certainly hardens hearts.'

'But still…'

He looks round. 'I'm done with it, Dan. This war. I want my life back, my freedom and my future. I want my brother back and I want my country back. I want a career, a wife and children. Life and liberty – that's all anyone wants. And after five years of this, the world's simply had enough of patience and waiting.'

Dear Doctor Garland,

My father was Generalfeldmarschall Erwin Rommel. My mother met him before he was married, whilst still a student at military college. The affair was short-lived, I was the sole product, but since my birth he has always treated me with affection and respect, and as much a part of the family as his wife and son. In honour of this great kindness, and with Frau Rommel's blessing, I am become the guardian of his legacy.

You may wonder how you came to be here in Ulm. You see, much is falsely known about my father, not least questions surrounding his loyalty. Loyalty was everything to him: these false conceptions must be corrected and, with Frau Rommel's help, and that of his many friends and supporters, I will make this my life's work. But not until the war is over, for only then will witnesses speak without fear. Fortunately he kept detailed records, and wrote hundreds of letters which are in our possession. Ultimately I envisage a biography of his life and work. Publication of such a document in a ruined Germany seems an impossible notion; we are seeking therefore to establish contacts abroad, and look to you and others to assist with this.

My father died last October. In the weeks preceding his death, he was here among his loved ones, recovering from injuries sustained in France. At this time he followed with interest your Allied attempt to cross the Rhine in Holland and strike a decisive blow to end the war, something he described as bold, but doomed to failure with Montgomery in charge. Afterwards he went to great lengths to trace survivors from your First Airborne Division, until able to confirm that Theodor Trickey was among them – thanks to you. One of his last acts, via trusted intermediaries, was to arrange to bring you both here. Unfortunately events conspired that he die before you arrived, thus as a family we fulfilled this wish on his behalf.

Frau Rommel's offer to assist with your clinic for Ulm's homeless is genuine and kindly intentioned. It would

mean a great deal to her, in her grief, if you were to allow
her this gesture, as a tribute to her husband. Thank you.
    Sincerely,
    Gertrud Stemmer

A week later it's my turn on duty at the drop-in. A straggly queue of homeless people waits at the door, rather longer than before – on account of the air raid, no doubt. This section of town suffered less devastation than the east, and happily the chapel has escaped unscathed. I lift the hasp of the heavy wooden door and push it open. To find a huge mound of furniture in the centre of the floor.

'Good heavens,' one of the women helpers exclaims. 'What's all this?'

'Donations,' I reply, 'from an anonymous supporter.'

We set to work, me attending the sick, the helpers busy sorting and arranging the furniture. Among it as promised are boxes of toys for the children, and I see one little girl settling down with sketchbook and crayons next to the stove, now glowing with warmth.

'What are you drawing?' I ask her.

She grins. 'An enormous cake!'

CHAPTER 10

Dear Theodorable,

I'm a bit sad to write this letter but know it's the right thing to do and you have the right to know. It's not easy to come out and say these things but here goes anyway. This is to let you know that me and Albert (Fitch remember?) got back together. I was missing you something terrible, and as you know he was going with that Stella Watt (from Woolworth's remember?) but then they parted ways and he got in touch, one thing led to another and we got back together. Things has been going nicely between us, he's a buyer at his Dads greengrocer chain which is a reserved occupation being like farming also his eyesights bad so he won't get called up. Anyway things been going nicely between us then last week guess what! He popped the question and I said yes! We're saving up for the ring and plan to tie the knot next spring probably April or May so I hope you can come!

So I'm writing to let you know that your released from our trough and I hope theres no hard feelings and your happy for us. In the meanwhile I wish you all the best.

Affectionately,

Susanna

PS I popped round to tell your Mum the good news but she was out so I told your landlady who was dead sniffy!

Theo folded the letter, one of several he'd just received, back into its envelope, and discreetly returned the bundle to his pocket. Nobody paid him any heed; around the room the others waited, wilting in the torpid heat. Above their heads a squeaking fan stirred the heavy air, while trapped flies buzzed at the window. Beyond it the Egyptian sun beat down on the yellow sand like burnished brass. Susanna Price, he mused, his auburn-haired Juliet of so long ago, with the laughing eyes and lips tasting of beer, was marrying Albert Fitch. Instead of him. What did he feel about that? he wondered, chewing the notion over like an unusual nut. Nothing, he soon concluded. He could sense no discernible feeling for Susanna at all. Nor had he for months, he realized. Not since the day he'd first met Clare.

Footsteps approached in the corridor, a hurried scraping of chairs followed, and everyone clattered to attention, then the door flew open and a tall officer in freshly pressed fatigues strode in, followed by an adjutant with a clipboard.

'At ease, gentlemen.' The officer flapped his hands. 'Please do sit, it's far too hot to stand on ceremony.'

His name was Colonel Dugdale, he explained, he was their course commandant, and was there to welcome them to 348 OCTU Cairo. His apologies for the spartan conditions were heartfelt. Everything, he explained, had gone somewhat to pot following the invasion of Sicily; he hoped normal order would soon be restored. Then, after a roll call and brief summary of the OCTU curriculum, he perched himself on a desk and began quizzing each student about their previous experiences.

'And you, young man,' he said, turning finally to Theo. 'How long have you been an officer cadet?'

'Well...' Theo thought back. Aldershot. 167 OCTU. Endless PT on a freezing parade ground. 'Um, three and half years, sir. Nearly.'

'Good heavens! What on earth happened?'

'I went to France. Before the course finished. With the BEF.'

Silence fell. The flies buzzed on. Somewhere in the distance a donkey brayed forlornly.

'You were in France with the BEF?'

'Yes, sir. 51st Highland Division. Under General Fortune.'

'Goodness. But how old were you?'

'Seventeen.'

Teo lovely boy!

So you been gone like six months why you not write me letter naughty boy? Your room still here an everything safe tho times hard an so I had let it go to nice man called Brown, paper salesman I think you meet him once no? Anyway he never here but pay rent good an regular, an he don't mind your stuff in his cubbard an say he vacate any time you come back right away. When is that Teo? An what you doing in bloody Africa anyhow? there absolutely no word in newspapers about parachute regimente or nothing! Like you vanish off a cliff or something. Anyway make sure you keep clear African germs like malaria an be sure eat plenty vegetable. If you can get it, we fine here but rationing a bloody nightmare, no fish no meat no fruit no veg hardly a scrap it a disgrace an damn hard make end meet. I get guests pool ration books so we share what we get an make katsarola stew and mutton stifado and something call Woolton pie which bloody disgusting leftover scraps with pastry on top. Still guests eat it so everyone happy. Your mother still here an happy too tho never stop with the bloody politics. she has new boyfriend one of them *thin fellows with strange voice and no chin but I think this one serious. She say she going to write you and tell me say <u>nothing</u> so I say <u>nothing</u> except maybe she leaving here soon. I manage this okay, her room I can rent, my legs an back are not so good but still not bad for old Greek woman! Write me soon bad boy big kisses yours affectionate Popodopoulos Eleni. PS Sorry spellings dictionary bloody useless. PPS strange woman come roun with scruffy little girl erchin age 8 or 9 maybe. She dont say who is but ask I send you letter from little girl. So I inclose for you. Didn't these two come round before Teo? I have suspicions! PPPS I gone right off that Susanna girl from up the road she no good trollup I sure you can do better lovely boy.*

Later the same morning, Theo was in his Cairo classroom, half listening to a lecture on map-reading and compass work, and vaguely thinking he'd heard it somewhere before, when the OCTU adjutant appeared around the door.

'Sorry to disturb you, sir, but Trickey's wanted outside.'

They walked out on to a painfully bright parade ground. All around watery mirages shimmered, dust devils spun skyward, while overhead the sun beat down mercilessly. 'What's this about?'

'No idea, chum. Some major wants to see you. All very hush-hush.'

He was led to a hut with a side-office and ushered in; the door closed behind him and there stood Yale, fanning himself with a file.

'Ah, Trickey, there you are.'

'Major. What are you doing in Cairo?'

'Seeing you, amongst other delights.' He was wearing khaki shorts and a shirt stained dark with sweat. His face was flushed and his brow perspiring. 'How's it all going?'

'All right, sir, so far. Well, apart from the dust and heat and that.'

'Too right, give me Algiers any day.' He mopped his brow with a handkerchief. 'Have a seat, Theodor, something's come up.'

Theodor? His heart lurched. Clare. 'What's come up?'

'Mussolini, of course! I take it you've heard?'

'Oh, um, that he's gone on sick leave or something. Is it true?'

'Not sick leave.' Yale withdrew a sheet. 'Latest gen suggests that he's out.'

'Out?'

'Yes, here we are, apparently his own governing council thing...'

'The Gran Consiglio del Fascismo.'

'That's the one. Apparently they had a secret meeting and voted him out, then voted some chap called Badoglio in.'

'Where is he now?'

'Protective custody, under arrest, on the run – who cares? The point is the bastard's gone!'

Theo shook his head. Mussolini gone. It was scarcely believable. More than twenty years, for all his life, his people had lived under his fist. Now it was over.

'You don't seem overjoyed.'

'I am, sir, it's just a lot to take in.'

'I'd have thought you'd be cock-a-hoop. Good news all round surely, for the Allies *and* the Italians. Your lot up north especially. I mean, no love lost there, eh?'

'No love at all, sir.' He thought at once of Carla, at home in Kingston surrounded by her letters and petitions. How jubilant she'd be at the news. How proud. And of Grandpa

Josef, struggling away in Bolzano for all those years, demonstrating on the streets and secretly printing his posters and pamphlets. His life's work, to free South Tyrol from the tyrant. Accomplished.

'Anyway, the big question now is what happens next. And according to—'

'He should be released!'

'Who?'

'My grandfather. Josef Ladurner, and Gino Lucetti and all the others. They should be freed!'

'Ah. It's funny you should say that.'

'What?'

'Yes, well, you see I have something to discuss with you.'

They were sending him back. Even though it took twenty minutes more for Yale to come out and actually say it, he knew immediately they were sending him back. The situation on the ground was confused, Yale explained, nobody knew who the new authorities were, yet alone what they might do. Or where the myriad political factions fitted in. Or how Germany would react now their staunchest ally was gone. Or what the Italian military would do, or the general public without a functioning government, or the many disparate rebel and partisan groups out in the field.

'It's a right beggar's muddle, Theodor,' he said, using his forename again. 'But also a golden opportunity, and of one thing we can be certain. Now that Sicily's secure, we the Allies are going to invade mainland Italy. Any day. And for that to succeed we need good people on the ground.'

So they were removing him from his OCTU and sending him on a course. A very different course, run by SOE specialists, who would teach him about guerrilla warfare, unarmed combat, signals, radio and Morse code, explosives and demolition, escape and evasion, advanced weapons handling, and many other skills. Once he was trained they were then going to 'insert' him into the hilly interior east of Naples, where he would be met by a local partisan group. And then he would set to work: '... gathering intelligence about German strength and disposition, sabotaging their communications and supply lines, tying up their resources, and generally making their life as unpleasant as possible. Get the idea?'

'Just me?'

'No, we have several operatives going in, but all to different areas. So you'll be on your own. But don't worry, we'll be supporting you every step of the way. You'll be well armed and properly equipped, regularly resupplied by air too, and kept in close contact by radio.'

Theo shook his head. Then managed a wry smile. 'There goes OCTU. Again.'

'Afraid so. For the time being anyway.'

'How much time?'

Yale's gaze flickered. 'Until Italy's secure.'

'Months.'

'Quite possibly.'

'Then I have one condition. Or rather a request.'

'You don't actually. But go on.'

'It's about Clare Taylor.'

'No.' Yale's hand shot up. 'Absolutely not for discussion. Sorry.'

'Tell me she's safe. Or I refuse to go.'

Through the window the crunch of marching feet and barked commands could be heard echoing round the parade ground. Theo folded his arms. The handkerchief reappeared, and Yale mopped sweat.

'Last heard of,' he murmured, 'all well.'

'Thank you. One more question. Why Campania, why Naples? It's not an area I'm familiar with.'

'Naples is seen as crucial to our invasion plans. We need someone well proven and dependable there. I can say no more, you must understand that.'

'Yes, but—'

'Except this. The cell there. Your partisan contacts. They've been keeping in touch, sporadically. Via an intermediary.'

'And?'

'They specifically asked for Horatio.'

Carla's letter was in Italian and written on a typewriter. Composed long before any hint of the turmoil currently engulfing Italy, she wrote at length about the ongoing campaign for South Tyrol's recognition as a free and autonomous state. Progress evidently was slow. On one hand the province was worse off even than in the dark days following the Option Agreement. The programme of compulsory Italianization was now complete and deeply embedded, evidence of cultural or ethnic identity had been suppressed to the point of obliteration, and 95 per cent of all public and official posts were now held by Italian Fascist Party members. To cap it all 'that disgusting criminal Mussolini' had fulfilled his promise to build a wall, a 'Vallo Alpino' isolating the Tyrol from its cultural neighbours in Austria and Switzerland. Little progress could be made on the ground, she acknowledged ruefully, until the war had run its course. On the other hand Partito Popolare Sudtirolese and its London base was thriving, with over a thousand subscribers now signed up as members, a proper office above a Kingston bookmakers, and plenty of cash in the coffers. It also continued to receive recognition from exalted circles, with Carla personally receiving letters of support from various Foreign Secretaries including Britain's nice Mr Eden, Mr Cordell Hull of the United States, Comrade Molotov of Russia and even Germany's von Ribbentrop, who was at least polite enough to answer her letter, acknowledging that the situation was 'uniquely problematic'. Theo read on, impressed yet disheartened by the letter, with its four pages of dense typescript, which enquired little of him, was virtually devoid of endearments, but did at least conclude with the personal news hinted at by Eleni. *I have met someone, Theo dearest,* she wrote towards the end. *His name is Nicholas Abercrombie, he is 42, and an official of the British Foreign Office. He is polite and courteous, careful of his appearance, with excellent manners and diction.* They had been in a respectful *relazione* for some time, she went on, then recently he had proposed marriage, which Carla was of a mind to accept. *So please be happy for me, dearest.*

Towards the end of the meeting with Yale, his tone became reflective.

'File note says you did well in Sicily last month,' he said. 'At that bridge.'

'We took a lot of casualties. The drop didn't go—'

'I mean you personally. Word is you practically took the thing single-handed.'

'Not true, sir, I can assure you.'

'What was it like?'

'I'm sorry?'

Yale was studying the floor. 'What was it like?'

'Well, it was, um, difficult, and very tough. The whole operation, I mean. We only had a third of our intended strength and the German response was very, um, vigorous.'

'Much close-quarters fighting?'

'Some, yes, but not as bad as Tunisia. Mostly it was about surviving the barrage. We had this COBU officer, Vere Hodge his name was, he saved—'

'How do you feel about that? Killing at close quarters, I mean.'

He didn't know. He tried not to think about it. And certainly not 'feel' anything about it. And in the heat and smoke and fury of battle, the kick of the pistol, the flash of the blade, the sickening crack of a rifle butt against a man's head didn't register as real, or calculated, or pre-planned. It was simply an instantaneous reaction. Like a conditioned reflex. 'It's not easy to say.'

'I would imagine.'

'I think it's best not to, you know, dwell on these things.'

'Hmm.' Yale nodded, then tapped the holster on his hip. 'I've never fired this, you know. Not in anger anyway. Probably never will. I'm destined to fight my war in an office, rifling through files and shouting down telephones.'

'Yes, but your work, the work of the SOE, well, it's important, and complicated, and needs to be properly managed...'

'So I'm told.' Yale smiled. 'Nor am I apologizing for it, you understand.'

'No, sir. Sorry.'

'But, you know, this training course.'

'The SOE one.'

'The thing is, Theodor, much of it will cover ground you're already familiar with, from the training you did with 2 Commando, and 11 Special Air Service and the Paras for Colossus and Biting and so on.'

'Yes, sir.'

'But there are other things you'll learn. To do with making difficult decisions, alone and on the spot. Life-or-death decisions even, sometimes. And that's something I do know about. Making life-or-death decisions. Such as sending people to very dangerous places, knowing they might not come back. Knowing they might get caught. And executed, or worse. And you need to be clear about how you'll handle these decisions. Clear in your own mind. Because they tend to be irrevocable.'

'I think I understand.'

'And you have to live with them for ever.'

Hello Anders my boy!

The governor got an address for you at your barracks at Bulford which is down Wiltshire way so I believe. Are you down there now or off gallivanting in France again? Maybe they'll forward mail to wherever you are, like we used to in the mail office at the E. Surreys. A right chore that was too. How have you been, son? I've still got six months left on my ticket, but then home free thank the Lord as this place is driving me mad. Never again I tell you it's the straight and narrow for old Vic from now on. Vi pops in regular and she told me how you brought some biscuits for her and a dolly for Nancy, which is why I'm writing, to thank you for that as it was really most decent of you. Also while you're at it and seeing how you're in regular employ with the King's shilling and that! I wondered could you send me a money order or two, so that I could pass it on to Vi to buy shoes and so on for Nancy. Times are very hard what with my present predicament I'm sure you understand and this would count as a great favour to your old Dad. We're only allowed to accept postal orders here strictly no cash or cheques, but that shouldn't be a problem, just send the postal orders to me, V. Trickey, care of the Governor's

Office, HMP Wandsworth, London SW. Soon as you can, thanks a ton and all the best son.
    Sincerely
    Vic (Dad)

He read through his mail again, sitting on his kitbag in the shade of a tent on the edge of camp. The sun was setting, the sinking air felt cool and calm at last after the day's heat and noise. He wasn't allowed to finish OCTU, not even the lecture on maps, nor was he allowed to speak to the other students or staff. His orders were to pack his belongings, tidy his affairs, make a will, pay his bills, write and post any mail, say nothing to anybody and wait to be picked up.

He didn't mind; the solitude seemed to cloak him like the evening calm. Although apprehensive for the future and fearful of the dangers it held, he felt the thrill of release, of being untied to pursue a purpose, as though falling free from a web of constraint and limit. And he sensed the predestiny of this mission, as though everything else had been preparation. Like a calling. Examining his life, and rereading his mail, he saw that he belonged nowhere and was responsible to no one, except perhaps his destiny, wherever that may lie. And that too was fine. Proper, even. A line of poetry came to him, from a lesson long ago in a secret classroom in Bolzano. '*Fremd bin ich eingezogen, Fremd zieh' ich wieder aus.*' A man called Müller had written it, Nikola had told them, and another called Schubert had set it to music. The story of a lonely man's journey. '*A stranger I arrived, and a stranger I depart...*'

The final letter awaited him. The one enclosed in Eleni's envelope. More a large paper sheet than a letter, it was folded many times until small and tight and thoroughly bound with tape. It took him a while to open without damaging it.

... For my journey I may not choose the time;
I must find my own way in this darkness,
The moon's shadow with me as my companion.

Gradually the page opened and grew. It wasn't a letter, it was a drawing, large and colourful, of a smiling man wearing khaki uniform, holding hands with a smaller figure, a blond-haired girl with a laughing mouth and green-spotted dress. In her free hand was a third figure, much smaller, a little doll with yellow plaits. Two words, in child's writing, were written at the bottom of the page: 'brother sister'.

CHAPTER 11

At dusk on 15 August 1943 the British T-Class submarine HMS *Tribune* slipped her moorings in Valetta's Grand Harbour, passed the defensive boom and torpedo nets guarding its entrance, and nosed out to sea for the four-day journey from Malta to Barletta on Italy's Adriatic coast. On board were her regular crew of fifty-six, plus four passengers. Conditions, in common with most wartime submarines, were cramped and claustrophobic, and the journey, though relatively short, was fraught with danger, requiring her to negotiate anti-submarine patrols, minefields and the narrow gap between Italy's heel and Albania, before creeping 150 miles up the coast to her destination. That first night, with *Tribune* steaming at fourteen knots on the surface, her captain and first officer called the passengers to the wardroom for a briefing.

'Welcome aboard, gents,' the captain began, tugging a little curtain shut around them, 'and sorry about the squash. Thankfully it won't be for long.' He eased himself behind the table. 'I'm Sam Wood, *Tribune*'s captain, and this is my first officer Peter Scrivenor. He'll be looking after you for the duration.' There then followed a grim lecture from Scrivenor, who seemed disapproving of the passengers, during which he listed many procedures and instructions, amounting mainly to keeping out of the way, especially in emergencies, 'when things can get bloody busy'. As guests of the captain, he told them, they would be based in the wardroom, which was little more than a curtained-off cupboard, and must remain there as much as possible, including for meals, so as not to distract from the smooth running of the ship. Social interaction with the crew was not encouraged: 'The men have a job to do and need to stay on their toes.' As for sleeping, two of the passengers would be allocated hammock space in the forward torpedo room, one somewhere aft, and Theo was to camp under the wardroom table. Amid some leg-pulling he stole a rueful glance: below the table the space was restricted and smelled of disinfectant but was clean enough. 'We call it the dog kennel,' Scrivenor joked without smiling. What he said next provoked even less mirth.

'Air consumption, gentlemen, after enemy attack, is our single biggest problem.' His fist was clenched, Theo noted, and lightly thumped the table for emphasis as he spoke. 'In these waters we must stay submerged at all times during daylight. That amounts to sixteen hours at this time of year. T-Class subs are designed to stay under for a maximum twelve hours with a full crew; much more and the air becomes unbreathable. Our lads have learned to cope as needed, up to a point, but even so by the time we finally surface some of the older hands are struggling. And so will you...'

Voices were heard passing beyond the curtain, from further off came the crackle of a radio, while *Tribune*'s hull hummed and vibrated from her diesel motors.

'... especially as we now have four extra bodies aboard consuming our oxygen.' Scrivenor looked round the table. 'So the men would greatly appreciate it if you avoid exerting yourselves, lie down and relax as much as possible, and switch to breathing in slow time during the day.'

'And how the hell do we do that?' Theo's neighbour muttered in Italian.

'I think he's pulling our leg,' replied another.

'He doesn't look like it.'

Later that night they were allowed up to the bridge one at a time to see the view. A strong draught buffeted him as Theo mounted the ladder – air being sucked down for the engines, he was told – then he was clambering past the hatch and up into the open. Narrow and curved with a waist-high coaming, the bridge was cramped and cluttered with tubes and wires and pipes and festooned with radio aerials. Two periscopes rose from a plinth in the middle, steps at the front led to a platform with a deck gun, while a smaller Bofors anti-aircraft gun was mounted at the back. Ahead the pencil-thin hull rose and fell to the swell, piercing the black waves and leaving a long V- shaped wake behind. The wind was moist and tangy, pleasantly refreshing after the stuffy interior. Four men with binoculars stood at each corner keeping watch, with Captain Wood moving among them.

'Biggest risk at night is Jerry aircraft or E-boats,' he said, scouring the horizon. 'That and hitting a mine.' He lowered his voice. 'We've lost a few like that lately.'

'I'm sorry to hear that.'

Wood shrugged. 'Goes with the job.'

Well before dawn a klaxon sounded, the bridge was cleared, the hatch thumped shut, the diesel engines stopped, and the ballast tanks were blown of air with a rumbling sound like far-off thunder. Theo felt the bows tip down and, with only the distant whine of her electric motors for sound, *Tribune* slipped beneath the waves and made for the safety of the deep. Bedding down in his kennel as best he could with blankets and cushions, he closed his eyes and fell asleep.

He awoke five hours later to the murmur of voices above. A watch was changing, officers arriving and departing the wardroom for food and rest. Soft-soled shoes surrounded the kennel; nobody paid him any attention, although someone kicking his leg did mutter an apology. Soon they were gone and he returned to sleeping. The next time he woke his head felt thick and heavy, as though from too much wine. Surfacing from the kennel he rubbed blearily at his neck, noting from the wardroom clock that it was still only noon. Another seven or eight hours remained, he estimated, before the hatch would open and fresh air return. He risked a glance around the curtain. The control room was dimly lit, a thin vapour hung in the air like mist, and men sat quietly at control wheels and switch panels or pored over a navigation table covered in charts. To one side a radio operator in a cubbyhole jotted notes on a pad. Peter Scrivenor looked up from a chart, shook his head at Theo and then went back to his work. Theo dropped the curtain. Curling cheese sandwiches and a water jug stood on the table; he helped himself, munching blearily, and began running through his orders once more, slowly and in detail, partly to refresh his memory, partly to kill more time.

His drop-off point was a stretch of beach to the north of the seaside town of Barletta. He was third in line to go, two operatives leaving before him, one after. He didn't know these men; once ashore from *Tribune* they were expected to go their separate ways and have no contact. All were to be dispatched on the same night, so timing was tight. Somewhere at the front of the submarine were his two suitcases, waterproof clothing, and his 'Folboat', a collapsible canoe small enough to fit through *Tribune*'s hatch yet big enough to carry him and his baggage. Once in position a mile or so offshore, *Tribune* would surface, he would exit through the hatch on to the forward deck, assemble his boat, load and launch it, and paddle off into the night. *Tribune* would then leave, and there would be no coming back. Once ashore he was to hide or bury the canoe and waterproof clothing, change into his civilian attire and lie low until dawn. Then walk ten miles or so inland, carrying his suitcases to the town of Foggia where he would catch a train north to the town of Campobasso, which was situated in Campania's hilly interior, midway between Italy's two coasts, and about fifty miles east of Naples. There at the station he would be met by his partisan contact.

By the time the 6 p.m. watch change came round he felt as though he was drowning. Any breathable air left aboard *Tribune* was all but gone; what remained was stale and poisonous, and like toxic gas to inhale. His chest seemed constrained, as though by belts. He felt flushed and light-headed, a pulse rang in his neck like a warning and, try as he might to breathe in 'slow time', he knew he was gasping like an overworked dog. Two of his colleagues were with him at the table, one had his head lolling in his arms and was groaning through each laboured breath, while the other, panting, was staring round in wide-eyed panic. Their only comfort was that a furtive check past the curtain confirmed the crew were in little better state, the mist in the control room had thickened to a fog, one man was propped on the floor with his head on his knees, and several others looked close to collapse. No one spoke a word. *Tribune* motored on like a ghost ship; everyone kept glancing at the clock.

Yet it was nearly two hours more before Captain Wood rose slowly from his command chair, moved to the men at the trim wheels and nodded. Slowly the wheels turned and *Tribune* tilted nose-up. Minutes more and she was levelling off again. Wood went to the periscope, which slid upwards with a hiss, and with excruciating thoroughness spent minutes walking in slow circles peering through the eyepiece.

Finally he snapped up the handles. 'Surface the boat.'

The relief was like waking from a nightmare, euphoric and instantaneous. Compressed air rumbled, the boat rose, the hatch opened, a trickle of water fell, a clatter of machinery came from aft and the diesels thundered to life, drawing a gale of fresh air down and through the ship. Within minutes men were joking and chatting as though nothing had happened. Lookouts in oilskins clambered up to the bridge, another watch changed below, joshing men came and went past the wardroom, while Theo and his colleagues waited at the table, inhaling deeply. A while later Lieutenant Scrivenor appeared.

'See what I mean?' he said, pouring himself water. 'This is what we have to go through for the likes of you.'

The fourth night was the worst. Nearing the Adriatic coast, Wood waited until dusk before risking the periscope. His plan, he explained, was to surface briefly and replenish the air, before diving once more until midnight, prior to landing Theo and the others. But barely had he raised the periscope than he was snapping it down again.

'Like Piccadilly Circus. Fishing caiques, couple of patrol boats, even some bloody yacht swanning about. Not going to risk it.' Instead he ordered *Tribune* to back away, then vent ballast until she sank, all engines stopped, to settle with a bump on the ocean floor. She then went into a strange limbo state where all but essential stations were left unmanned, unrequired equipment was turned off, the lights were dimmed and everyone was ordered to their bunks to 'silent rest', breathing through special survival masks called rebreathers. Scrivenor distributed the masks to the passengers; Theo sat at the wardroom table trying to fit it to his head. After a while Captain Wood appeared.

'All set in here?' He grinned.

'I'm not quite sure how...'

'Here, let me help you.' Wood began adjusting the straps. 'It's not so much the lack of oxygen that's the killer, you see, it's the increasing levels of carbon dioxide. The mask traps it so we can extract more of the air's oxygen. Clever, no?'

'Yes, I see, sir, thank you.'

'No problem. I expect you'll be glad to get off this tin tube.'

'It's certainly been an experience. I had no idea...'

'How could you? And don't think we don't appreciate the work you chaps do either. Submariners just have a funny way of showing it!'

'I understand. Um, Lieutenant Scrivenor especially.'

'Ah.'

'Have we done something? To offend him, I mean.'

'Not at all.' Wood shook his head. 'It's just, well, his last boat. One of our sister ships. *Triumph*. She was lost on a mission like this. Dropping off special ops bods. Or picking them up, I can't remember. Anyway, Peter should have been aboard, but got appendicitis just before she sailed and had to be replaced. Nobody knows what happened, she just vanished, but the suspicion is she hit a mine nearing the enemy coast. She was lost with all hands. All his friends.'

'I'm very sorry.'

'Not your fault. It's the nature of the beast.'

'I suppose so. What did you say she was called?'

'HMS *Triumph*.'

The sea was rougher than expected, the night pitch-black. Waves sloshed over the deck as *Tribune* rolled sluggishly in the swell. He had some trouble extracting the Folboat through the forward hatch but was helped by sailors pushing from below. Once out, the assembly went smoothly and he spent several minutes securing his baggage in the rear compartment. Launching it by torchlight required him to slither down on to one of the ballast tanks, which was partly submerged, dragging the Folboat behind him, then scramble aboard and shove off with the paddle. When clear he secured himself into the seat, lacing its canvas cover tightly around his waist, and set off into the night.

He heard the breaking surf before he saw it; a few minutes more paddling and a thin line of white was materializing in the distance. No other lights showed. He hoped he was still north of Barletta. Suddenly the Folboat was surging forward, its nose buried in foam. He dug in hard with the paddle, as on canoe expeditions of his youth; the Folboat surged again and then slewed sideways, spilling him into thigh-deep surf. Dragging it up the beach required him to unload it first, only on the second trip, hauling it behind him, did he notice the wire entanglements to his right, and the sign saying 'Mina'. He pressed on, reached scrubby grass and began collapsing the boat. Scouting north and south using his flashlight, he noted cursory attempts at tank traps, two unmanned pillboxes and another area warning of mines. Of gun emplacements, Home Guard, searchlights or watchtowers he saw nothing. Thirty minutes later, wearing his civilian suit, coat and hat, and with the boat buried and camouflaged with driftwood, he gathered his bags and set off inland.

By eight that morning he was entering Foggia and making for the station. The day was already warm and with his coat and baggage he felt hot and conspicuous. Foggia's streets were busy with workers and shoppers; none, he noted, were young men in travelling clothes, and all seemed to be hurrying to their tasks with heads down. To his consternation he also saw long lines of military traffic, including open lorries loaded with German soldiers, streaming through town on the main road south. They paid him no heed, but two cruising Carabinieri saw him watching and crossed the street towards him. Before they could come near he ducked into an alleyway and fled.

By the time he reached the station he knew everything was wrong. The change in attitude from his last visit was shocking and palpable. Then the war barely touched ordinary people; there was a shrugged laissez-faire attitude to it and little sense of urgency or danger. Now people scurried by without looking up; there was fear in their faces, and an atmosphere of impending disaster. Foggia had suffered bomb damage too, with areas of the town reduced to rubble by Allied bombers. He picked up a discarded newspaper but could make little sense of it: the cheap newsprint, the contradictory headlines, the paragraphs of uncertainty and speculation. Posters on walls and lamp-posts proclaimed a multitude of political factions and names, none of which he recognized, while other posters bearing the Nazi eagle listed stringent new regulations, and warned of harsh reprisals against thieves, looters and black marketeers. And warnings about deserters. On the train to Campobasso no one spoke to him, unusually, and one old couple even moved away when he sat near them. The guard punched his ticket with narrowed eyes and without acknowledging his polite *buongiorno*. He sat hunched in a corner watching the arid plains of Apulia gradually give way to the rolling hills of Campania, saw gaggles of Italian troops moving along dusty roads, saw mile upon mile of discarded weapons and equipment, and saw the smoking pyres of wrecked vehicles, and knew the Italy of old was dying. That it was broken and diseased and that worse was probably yet to come. And by the time he stepped off the train at Campobasso, he also knew he was being followed.

He was arrested ten minutes later. No one had met him, as was promised, but waiting aimlessly about the concourse seemed unwise, so having checked the toilets and café he made for the door and walked out into hot sunshine. Barely had he gone ten paces when two large men wearing Sicurezza Civile armbands grabbed him from behind, seized his elbows and frog-marched him to the police station. Helplessly pinioned and with a suitcase in each hand, he could do nothing but comply.

'Got another one,' they told the desk sergeant.

'What do you want me to do about it?'

'Like the others. Lock him up and call the military. We'll be back to collect the *compensazione* in the morning.'

He was led to a cell and locked in. It had an iron bed with no mattress and a tin bucket for a latrine. An hour passed; the temperature climbed. No one came to check on him, or search him, or even question him. His papers were still in his pocket, his suitcases at his side. Craning his neck at the door, he saw the desk sergeant alone reading a newspaper, and noted that the building was old and dilapidated with crumbling brick walls and old-fashioned barred windows. Two of the bars were loose. His cell door was also of iron and secured by an ancient lock. A little later another youth was shown in and sat on the floor without a word; by mid-afternoon, after a meal of watery pasta soup and bread, there were half a dozen. Deserters, he learned from one, a wiry boy with dark beard and round spectacles. Sicurezza Civile was a front, he explained, an excuse for thugs to round up young men of army age and hand them in for the reward – whether they were deserters or not. All would end up in the army, most serving alongside the Germans, or *Tedeschi* as he called them, on the eastern front. Tens of thousands had been rounded up this way, he said, their families despaired of seeing them again.

Theo said nothing and sat tight. Someone said they were unlikely to be collected before dawn next day; his plan was to wait for darkness, loosen the window bars and escape, as he had from Caposele two and a half years before. Failing that, a piece of wire spring from the bed should make short work of the door's ancient lock. Failing *that*, in one suitcase were a selection of pencil fuses – small detonators ideal for blowing locks. Getting out should not be hard, he knew; quite what to do afterwards was less clear. He checked the time. Over thirty hours without sleep, nearly twenty since leaving *Tribune*. Sitting on his suitcases, he folded his arms and tried to doze.

'Don't make any sudden noise.'

He stirred sleepily.

'Horatio.' A hissed whisper. 'Horatio, it's me.'

'What?'

'Me. Nightjar.' The youth with the spectacles was crouching beside him, his face lost in shadow. 'Don't do anything rash, I'm getting you out.'

'Nightjar?' The baker's boy, Armando, the one who drove the van on the Tolomei mission, who blew up the garages and threw grenades so bravely. 'My God, I didn't recognize you! That beard, and those glasses.'

A white grin showed in the darkness. 'The beard is temporary, the glasses sadly not.' He'd been at Campobasso Station that morning, as arranged, he explained, in fact had waited there every morning for a fortnight – at some risk. When he'd finally spotted Theo that day, he was about to approach when he also saw the two militiamen following. 'So I followed you here, waited a while, then got myself arrested too!'

'But that's insanity! Isn't it?'

'Not as long as we're gone before morning. Anyway, I couldn't leave you here alone, could I?'

They wouldn't need to pick the lock, he explained, or wrench out window bars or blow the place up. These days a well-placed bribe was generally all that was needed, that or a mild threat. 'The police sergeant's a local man; he has a son in the army up north. He's on our side.'

Sure enough, about an hour later, they heard a tinkling sound and something metallic and glinting appeared on a string through the window. The key to the door. Five minutes more and the youths were tiptoeing past the deserted front desk and scattering into the moonlight.

He and Nightjar walked out of town, past an ancient fort on a hill and on into open farmland. A strict curfew was in force, but by keeping to paths and tracks their progress went unnoticed. Towards dawn Nightjar began searching the track with a flashlight, then turned into an overgrown olive grove, ducking beneath thick bushes backing on to woodland. 'In here.' Rummaging through the undergrowth he unearthed a knapsack. 'We stay here. Long day today.'

'What of the Cellini cell?' Theo asked as they bedded down. 'And you, you're a long way from home.'

Nightjar produced cheese and wine. 'The Cellinis broke up after you left. After the Tolomei operation. We were amateurs and knew it, and then we had no one to lead us. It was too risky anyway. The authorities made a big fuss about Tolomei, started searching house to house. I was sent south by my father for safety's sake. Stayed in Naples for a while living with an uncle, fell in with some lads there, then moved out into the countryside when Mussolini got ousted.'

'How many are you?'

'Five or six. But more joining all the time.'

Theo nodded. Not the hundreds he'd been led to expect.

'Don't worry.' Nightjar read his thoughts. 'The people's revolution is coming!'

They munched in silence for a while.

250

'What's in the suitcases?'

'Money, supplies, clothing, one Sten, fuses, a couple of handguns.'

'No wonder they're heavy.'

'The second one has a radio.'

'They'll all have to be hidden. So will you.'

'Why, what's happening?'

'Something huge. *Tedeschi* are everywhere, heading south like mad to take on the Allies when they come, and very jumpy, very trigger-happy. Italian army doesn't care any more – everyone thinks they'll throw in the towel. But not the *Tedeschi*: they're fighting it out, and don't care who they take with them. Nor should the Allies underestimate their intent.'

'So why the hiding?'

'Right now they're searching, everywhere, for deserters, partisans, young men to pressgang, arms caches or anything that smells of resistance. And shooting anyone they suspect: ordinary folk, women and pensioners, peasants and villagers, anyone offering help or hiding. But the moment the Allies come their attention will be diverted. And that's the moment we come out and strike.'

'How long, do you think?'

'We're hoping you'd tell us!'

Weeks at most, he'd been told, at his final briefing in Cairo. Sicily had taken longer to secure than anticipated. But now that it was, the main invasion could be expected in a matter of weeks. A month at most.

'It could be a while.'

Nightjar said that moving in open daylight was too risky, so they lay low for most of the day. Throughout it the air grew hot and humid, heavy with pollen and buzzing insects. In the chestnut woods behind the grove a thin stream trickled and they were able to wash and replenish water bottles. No one came near but in the distance they heard the rumble of heavy traffic and twice in the afternoon German fighters passed overhead. At dusk they emerged and made ready. A sultry wind fretted, while to the north lightning flickered within soot-black clouds. Nightjar produced a pistol from the knapsack and tucked it into his wide leather belt. He wore black corduroys and a green collarless shirt with a neckerchief. 'German army,' he said, lacing his boots. 'Took them off a corpse.' He shouldered his knapsack. 'Right, give me a suitcase, we've a long march.'

Half an hour later the rain began.

It went on all night, wind-thrashed downpours that churned roads to rivers, dusty tracks to sucking bog, and drenched them repeatedly as though flung from buckets. The good thing, Nightjar shouted above the din, was that nobody would see them, as nobody would be mad enough to come out searching. Theo nodded, wiped the sodden hair from his face and trudged doggedly on. Mostly upwards it seemed, ever higher and ever deeper into what he guessed were the Apennines' Matese Mountains. As they ascended, the villages became scarcer, smaller and more humble; whenever they came to one Nightjar chose if they would walk straight through it or if they must circle round. He didn't say why and Theo didn't ask, he kept his head down and his legs moving, recalling rain-soaked training marches with 2nd Battalion down in Bulford. How they'd go all night, forty miles or more with full packs, fifty minutes' marching and ten minutes' rest, hour after hour, before arriving back at camp, singing lustily to annoy the other two battalions.

Much later the rain eased and the clouds broke to reveal a thick canopy of stars swirling above steep craggy peaks. A little further and they came to another village, barely a ramshackle cluster of cottages and barns clinging to a hillside. This one they entered, following narrow cobbled alleyways to a tiny piazza with a stone water trough and whitewashed chapel bearing the legend 'San Felice'. Sheep stirred in a pen; somewhere a dog started barking; he thought he glimpsed a curtain twitch.

'Wait here,' Nightjar whispered, and vanished into the shadows.

Theo sat, filling his bottle from the trough and massaging his calves. His feet were sore and blistered, his arms ached from the suitcases, his clothes were sodden and he smelled of mud and sweat. Nearby a rooster crowed the coming dawn. A few minutes more and Nightjar was back. 'Today we stay here, follow me.'

He led them to a cottage in an alley. The door was opened by a middle-aged man in a nightshirt and bearing a candle. His wife, grey hair awry and similarly clothed for night, was already bustling about an iron range. '*Vestiti bagnati*,' she muttered, snapping her fingers, and dutifully they shed their wet clothes. Blankets were found for their shoulders, milky chestnut coffee served, together with *biscotti* and tiny glasses of fiery liquor. Little was said. Theo thanked them politely; they nodded back, eyeing him curiously. Once breakfasted they were shown outside to a hayloft above a chicken pen. Hefting their bags up the rickety wooden ladder, they crawled inside, closed the door and fell into exhausted slumber.

He was roused by the sound of voices outside. Nightjar was gone; sunlight through a chink in the door told him it was afternoon. He listened, breath held, as the talking rose and fell. It was some kind of discussion, or argument, in Italian; Nightjar's voice was among them. Then someone laughed. Wrapping the blanket around his shoulders he descended to the ground.

Five men stood in the yard: Nightjar, three youths and the older man from last night. Theo was introduced, and warmly greeted by the youths who clasped his hand in respectful awe. They were fellow partisans, he gathered, part of Nightjar's cell and eager to meet the famous Horatio. All bore nicknames: Renzo, Lucien and the third boy who was called Guercio or 'one-eyed' after an accident with a carbine. The older man's name was Salvatore. The discussion, it emerged, was about what to do with Horatio now that he was actually among them. Villages in the area were being systematically searched for deserters or partisans, and the hills themselves were regularly combed by patrols. The Carabinieri couldn't be trusted, nor the municipal police; fearful local officials would gladly betray anyone, and even the Corpo Forestale or forest rangers were known to turn in fugitives for cash. Villagers, though sympathetic, were terrified of reprisal, and few anyway could be trusted not to gossip.

'How long are we talking about, boys?' Salvatore asked.

'Just a week or two. Until the Allies come.'

'Then what about the Poeli farm? It's pretty quiet down there.'

'Can't trust old man Poeli, not since the British bombed his sister in Salerno.'

'Oh, yes, I forgot.'

Renzo scratched his chin. 'We could stick him in the caves up on Monte Miletto.'

'And get spotted traipsing up and down with provisions every day?'

'That's right.' Nightjar nodded. 'The caves would do for a day or two, but no longer. We need something better.'

'We could dig him a hole in the ground...' Guercio offered.

'*Idiota.*'

Salvatore's wife appeared, the woman who'd served them

254

the previous night, and began folding stiff white sheets into a laundry basket. 'What about Rosa?' she said.

A pause. 'You mean Pazza Rosa?'

'Didn't she murder her husband?'

'That's just a story,' she scoffed. 'And she's not *pazza*, just a little eccentric. And set in her ways.'

'And old, and deaf!'

'Maybe that's an advantage.'

'Yes, but what about the twins?'

'The twins won't talk.' Salvatore spat in the dirt. 'Rosa's perfect.'

They set off at dusk, the San Felice partisans, comprising Nightjar, Renzo, Lucien, one-eyed Guercio and their reluctant leader Horatio. 'Pazza Rosa', he learned as they ascended steep woodland paths, was a widow of unknown age who lived high above the village on a remote patch of scrubby farmland near dense forests. Few if any visitors ventured there, partly because it was so inaccessible, partly because Rosa was *pazza* and hostile to strangers, and partly because of a bull ox she kept called Bruno who was famously ferocious. She lived with her twin grown-up children, one of whom was a deaf mute called Francesca, the other her brother Vittorio, whose brain had been damaged during their birth.

As the five ascended it grew noticeably colder, and soon began to rain again. Eventually the path levelled, opened on to a narrow plateau and became littered with farmyard jumble: rusting buckets, coils of wire, an ox plough. A painted sign appeared warning 'Keep Away' and then suddenly two hunting dogs on chains leaped up, furiously pulling at their tethers and snarling like wolves. At this point the three younger boys elected to wait, while Theo and Nightjar gingerly continued on. Gradually a cave-like dwelling emerged from the gloom, built of stone and set into the hillside, with tiny windows and a moss-covered roof of thatch. Twenty yards from the threshold the small wooden door flew open and a figure emerged bearing a lantern.

'Who the hell goes there?' it demanded shrilly. 'Halt or I shoot!'

'What with?' Nightjar murmured. '*Mi scusi, signora!* It is Armando, friend of Salvatore, from the village. I, er, bring a traveller. Seeking shelter. For a few days.'

'Well, he can seek it elsewhere!'

The door banged shut. Theo, shivering, lowered his suitcases. His shoes felt soggy once more, and the rain icy at his neck.

Nightjar tried again. 'He has money, *signora*!'

The door creaked. 'How much money?'

'Quite a lot. And he can work.'

'He'll damn well have to. I'm not running a hotel!'

They were shown into a tiny stone parlour featuring a scrubbed wooden table, an ash-filled hearth, a rocking chair, and two split leather armchairs. To one side narrow wooden steps led up to a mezzanine from where two tousled heads poked from a bed. A similar bedroom rose to the other side. Rosa held up the lantern, inspecting Theo from head to toe, her mouth downturned. She was very short, and stooped, with wiry white hair and a pinched face. She wore a heavy cotton nightshift and spoke in an incomprehensible local dialect.

'A bit scrawny, isn't he? And why so pale?'

'He's from the north, *signora*. But strong, I assure you, just look at these muscles. His name's Hor— I mean Theodor. He's come here to—'

'I don't want to know!'

'*Scusi, signora?*'

'His name, why he's here: I don't want to know these things.

All I know is he sleeps in the cowshed, does what he's told, and keeps himself to himself!'

'Yes of course, *signora*.'

'And pays one week in advance. That is all. Goodnight!'

His day began before dawn when he was rudely roused from sleep by someone banging on a tin bath out in the yard. Struggling in panic from his straw palliasse, he threw on clothes and stumbled headlong down the ladder to the cattle shed, which contained four snorting heifers and stank of ammonia and dung.

'Hurry up, northern boy, if you want to eat!'

He lurched into the half-light: '*Buongiorno, signora.*'

She shooed him away. 'Wash, wash! Round the side. Hurry!'

Beside the cottage was a wooden trough filled with rainwater, with a rag for a hand towel. Also available, if required, and set back a safe distance from the main dwelling, was an evil-smelling hut he'd been shown called the *gabinetto*, which consisted of a squatting hole over a black pit seething with flies. Washing his face and teeth with the silky rainwater, he decided the *gabinetto* could wait.

Breakfast was warmed milk with dipped bread. It was taken at the table, together with his two sleepy housemates while Rosa fussed at the stove. The twins, he guessed, were about thirty, Francesca round and dark with powerful shoulders and black hair piled in a bun, while her brother Vittorio was much slighter, shaven-haired and with olive-green eyes which smiled curiously as he slurped his milk. Theo murmured a greeting, but neither spoke back.

Barely had they finished breakfast before Rosa was hurrying them out to work. Vittorio was in charge of the dogs, pigs and chickens, Francesca the oxen, while Theo evidently was to tackle the maize harvest. Equipment for this comprised a huge wooden backpack or hod, which Rosa fastened to his shoulders, tutting and clucking, using leather straps. She then led him up winding paths still shrouded in mist, past a tool shed for drying the cobs, past the pigpen, around a poorly fenced field containing an enormous bull which watched them balefully, until some fifteen minutes later they arrived at the cornfield. Pale dawn light slanted on to a forest of head-high stalks that whispered in the first stirrings of a breeze. Theo surveyed the field, which was large and sloping and bordered by woodland, and wondered how long it would take to harvest the corn from it. With only a box.

'You know what to do,' Rosa barked in her clipped dialect.

'Yes, um, well, no, not exactly, *signora*.'

Her eyes rolled. '*Madre di Dio!*' She bent to a stalk, swept back the leaves to expose the cob, grasped it firmly and then snapped it down and up with a twist to break it off. 'Like that,' she said, tossing it in his hod. 'And don't dawdle!'

He worked all morning. Still wearing his suit trousers and shoes, and with the sleeves of his white shirt rolled, he was soon hot, thirsty and caked in dust from the maize stalks. Small rodents hopped about his feet as he moved and at one point he saw a snake slithering away. His hod soon filled but chafed his back as he worked, so he took it off and used it like a basket. In a short time it was full so he hoisted it on to his shoulders, grunting at the weight, and set off back down the hill to the tool shed, where he emptied it on to the floor. Pausing only to examine rows of ancient tools and a broken toy car on a work bench, he filled his water bottle and set off once more, past the pigs, carefully around the watching bull, and on up to the plain where the maize was. On about the fourth rotation Rosa stopped him at the drying shed to inspect his labours. What she saw did not please her.

'*Maledetto idiota!* What the hell have you done?'

'*Signora?*'

'Can I not leave you this one simple task, for the love of Jesus!' She threw up her hands in exasperation and set off up the hill, Theo following with the hod. This time, possibly because it recognized its mistress, Bruno the bull saw them coming, put his huge head down and came charging straight at them, only to veer away at the last moment when she shooed him with her apron. 'He's a *cucciolo* really,' she said, which meant puppy, but then added: 'Never, ever, go in his field alone.' Up at the maize field it transpired his sin had been to harvest unripe cobs. 'The hair!' she explained, pointing to the silken threads on top of each. 'The hair must be brown and curly, just like in your *pantaloni*, yes?'

'I... What?'

'Only then is it ready. If still green and smooth then is not ready and must wait.'

'*Si, signora*, I see that now. *Mi scusi.*'

'And load the box properly. Like this.' She began stacking the cobs in neat rows. 'This way you will carry twice as much again.'

Some hours later, bent and aching, he heard the distant banging of the tin bath, and began a weary descent. By now his back was stiff and sore, his shoulders raw with chafing, his hands bloody and his clothes spoiled. Unloading his hod he stumbled towards the cottage, sniffing hungrily at delicious baking smells, only to be sent away once more to wash. Having buried his face in the trough, he raised it to the sun and realized it was still barely noon.

Lunch was fresh bread from the oven, a sticky goat's cheese, salami, bitter red wine for Rosa and Theo, and water for the twins. Who were noticeably more animated than earlier, smiling and clucking and nudging each other in amusement at their guest. Francesca prodded his arm, then began tapping her chest and cupping an ear.

'They want to know your name,' Rosa said. 'In sign.'

'Oh? Ah, well, you see, my name is Theo. *Tee-oh*.' He turned to them, tapping his own chest, and making a 'T' with his hands followed by an 'O'. 'T-O, you see?'

Nods and smiles rewarded him, and Vittorio clapped his hands in delight. Then Francesca was signing again, a huge round circle, like a globe, then the finger-pointing, and the cupped ear.

'Um, I think they're asking where I come from.'

A plate clattered on to the table. On it a pear sliced in four.

'Then tell them.'

'Yes, but you said...'

'Tell them.' Rosa's eyes were glinting. 'They haven't met anyone new in years.'

CHAPTER 12

Two weeks went by. With them went high summer in the mountains, the days suddenly becoming shorter and the nights cooler, while the leaves of the chestnut trees turned to rust. Theo became absorbed into the fabric of the farm, an extra component of its patterns and rhythms, like an added voice in its song. His days varied little; he found reassurance in this, and in its natural order and routine. Roused by the tin bath before dawn, thence to the water trough and a drowsy breakfast with the family, it was then straight to the maize field, in fair weather or foul, to bring in the cobs before the first frosts ruined them. Lunch followed before it was back out to work, mending a fence or setting a post, chopping firewood or clearing a ditch, whatever the day required. His labours demanded little thought or decision, just stamina and willingness, and after the chaotic stresses of war, with its waiting and uncertainty, blood, terror and bone-sapping exhaustion, he found the simplicity of bucolic life a welcome tonic. When the day grew dark, the work finished, the family gathered for the evening meal of pasta and salami and fruit and home-cured ham so fine it melted on the tongue, all served with the resinous dark wine of the region. Afterwards he would sit by the fire and do puzzles with the twins, or read from Rosa's small stock of books, or, if she was in the mood, converse a little with her. One night he even tried penning a letter to Carla.

Dearest Mama,

I have received your letter for which I thank you. It is most interesting to catch up on the news of Partito Popolare Sudtirolese and I am of course delighted to hear of your engagement to Nicholas Abercrombie, who sounds a fine gentleman. I am fit and well and currently away from military activity although of course cannot say where. Mama, there is a matter I feel I should bring to your attention which relates to your marriage, namely that your original husband, my father Victor, is not in fact dead but

He balled the page and threw it in the fire. Selecting a second sheet he began again but this time got no further than 'Dearest Mama'. All he could think of were questions. Do you love me, Mama? Did you ever really love me? Am I merely an inconvenience? How can you marry someone when you are already married? Do you want to know about Victor? Do you already know?

'A love note to your *fidanzata*?' Rosa, squinting myopically, was darning a pair of ancient serge trousers pulled from a chest. Francesca, he noted, immediately glanced up at the question.

'I have no fiancée. I am writing to my mother. Or trying to.'

'Up north?'

'I... No. She lives in London.'

'*Madre di Dio*, you're British! I knew it, that accent—'

'No, *signora*, I assure you I was born in Italy.'

'Your papa, then...'

'He... It's complicated.'

'Pah! Show me a family that isn't.' She held up the trousers. 'Here, try these on.'

'Oh, um, I'll just go outside—'

'No, here, *idiota*, where I can see! Just take off yours and put these.'

Hesitantly he began unbuckling his belt, both twins by now staring avidly. The trousers were too large, high at the waist and smelled of old mothballs, but once cinched with a belt looked presentable enough for a farm labourer.

'*Perfetto.*' Rosa's eye was critical. 'My dear Gianluca, how you remind me of him.' She delved into the chest, producing a corduroy waistcoat. 'You should wear this as well. And his boots.'

'I have boots. In my suitcase.'

'Army boots.' Her voice was icy suddenly. 'You will not wear them here.'

'As you prefer, *signora*.' He wondered how she knew. But from that day on, he went to work wearing the clothes of a man called Gianluca.

Some days there were deliveries, although he never saw them as he was banned from venturing down the track. The deliveryman, usually Salvatore or another village tradesman, drove up by mule cart as far as the 'Keep Away' sign, and deposited whatever was ordered under a box. Salvatore would similarly collect goods at the same time: a sack of cobs, boxes of eggs, a ham for the market. Sometimes there was a coded note from Nightjar among the deliveries. 'Eight birds in the coop now!' he wrote one day, meaning new recruits joining the cell. 'The day of release is nearly at hand!' trumpeted another. He also added snippets of political gossip and word of any military activity in the area. Theo replied with 'keep me informed' notes and dutifully passed the information on to his controllers, staying up late in his cowshed loft to laboriously tap out Morse messages on his SOE radio. The equipment took time to set up and operate, and he worried his transmissions might be being monitored. Also, because of the mountain location, the poor range of the radio, and the low power of its batteries, which were steadily fading, he never knew if his messages were received.

Twice during this period he rose early, told Rosa he would not be available for farm work that day, packed a knapsack and set off into the hills. Both times she watched him prepare, purse-lipped as he laced on his army boots, but asked no questions nor made any attempt to stop him. Climbing high into the Matese, he then spent many hours reconnoitring the area, paying particular attention to movements of personnel or equipment. Often he saw formations of aircraft passing high overhead, but couldn't tell whose they were. Once he spotted a dust cloud in the distance, and hurrying up a craggy peak raised his binoculars to glimpse a two-mile-long infantry column plodding steadily south. On another he saw dark smoke rising from a fold in the hills, and, approaching warily, came upon a cluster of burning farm buildings. Outside lay two bodies, a man and woman, both shot through the head. Unable to help them, or even risk disturbing the scene, he could only take note of the location and creep back into the trees. By nightfall on these occasions he was back at Rosa's farm, his return greeted by grins and handclaps from the twins, and disapproving clucks of relief from Rosa. The next day they all went back to work as if nothing had happened.

One morning a heifer in oestrus was brought up to be served by Bruno. This, Theo learned, was a major event requiring much careful planning. As usual the cow's owner approached no nearer than the boundary, leaving it tethered to a tree before departing again. Rosa and Vittorio fetched it, while Francesca, who was in charge of the oxen, readied Bruno for the *consumazione*. Not that he required much readying, Theo saw, for even as they approached his field they could hear him bucking and snorting furiously, as though sensing the heifer, and as they drew nearer the engorged state of his *pene* was embarrassingly obvious, as

Francesca pointed out with a nudge of approval. Her task was to move him into a smaller pen for the mating to take place, and Theo watched with trepidation as she ducked into the field and strode towards him. 'Be careful,' he called, and she turned and nodded. Her pace slowed to a stroll; Bruno turned and glared at her, breath steaming visibly from flared nostrils, one hoof pawing the ground. Then he gave voice to an enormous warning roar, deafening like the blast of trumpets. But just as he was lowering his head to charge, she began to call out in a melodic sing-song tone unlike anything he'd ever heard. Bruno's ears twitched, and his head came up. A few seconds more and she was standing at his side holding his tether. Later, after the mating, he demolished the pen in celebration.

'She can hear, can't she?' he said to Rosa that evening. 'Francesca.' They were in the tool shed, sorting cobs into a box for market. The light was going; they were working by the glow of a lantern.

'I never said she can't.'

'But—'

'You shouldn't listen to village gossip, northern boy.'

'No.'

Tutting, she threw cobs in the box. 'Idiot people. What else did they tell you?'

'Well...'

'About Pazza Rosa the husband-killer? Or about mad Rosa and her idiot twins?'

He went on sorting cobs.

'Of course they did. And everyone wonders why I keep people away!'

'*Mi scusi, signora*. I had no right to mention it.'

She straightened from the box. 'Do you really want to know?'

'It's not necessary.'

'How old do you think I am?'

'Pardon?'

'Go on. How old?'

'Well, I don't know, um, perhaps sixty-something...'

'Seventy-eight! And they're twenty-nine. So do the calculation!'

'I, well...'

'I'm not their mother. I couldn't be.'

'Electricity.'

'What?'

Theo pointed. 'You have electricity. There, I can see a wire hanging, and a fitting for a light.'

'What of it?'

'Does it work?'

That night, over rather more wine than was their custom, they told each other what they needed to. 'I am a soldier of the British army,' he said, 'I have a wireless, and must operate it. Using electricity.' Rosa nodded, crossed herself, and, checking the twins were abed, began her story. Which took rather longer.

Her beloved husband Gianluca, the man whose clothes Theo wore, died of the *tubercolosi* while still a young man. They had one daughter, Maria, who grew up barely remembering him. The farm thrived in those days and they had many workers and visiting tradesmen. When Maria was eighteen the municipality announced that every dwelling was to be connected to the *elettricità*. Rosa was unimpressed. 'I didn't want it, didn't trust it, refused to pay for it and never used it.' But a wire was nevertheless duly extended from the village by a municipal electrician called Rossi who came up to make the connections. Rosa refused to have it in the cottage so told him to terminate it in the tool shed. She never even tested it; in any case, the supply rarely functioned as the project ran out of money. Meanwhile Rossi, who was forty and boastful, had begun to court Maria, and in due course sought her hand. 'They were married on June the twenty-eighth 1914, a Sunday, the same day that archduke was assassinated in Yugoslavia.' Rosa shook her head. 'A bad day for us all.'

Maria died in childbirth a year later. 'Up there, delivering those two.' She nodded at the mezzanine where the twins were sleeping. 'It took four days; she died in my arms. One twin was healthy, but the boy was starved of air in the birth canal and suffered damage to the brain. So I had lost my beloved Gianluca, and my only daughter, and was left with two baby grandchildren, one of them disabled.' She sipped wine. 'And a useless son-in-law who turned to drink.' Rossi by then was out of work, she went on, bitter, angry and increasingly abusive to the children whom he blamed for Maria's death. He spent less and less time at the farm, which was falling into neglect, leaving an overworked Rosa to cope as best she could. More ominously, as the twins grew, he began to take an unhealthy interest in Francesca. 'Several times I caught him, drunk on grappa, trying to touch her where he shouldn't. I warned him off but he just laughed and went back to the *taverna*. I also told Francesca to keep away from him.'

The cottage was silent but for the deep breathing of the twins and the snap of the fire. Rosa leaned forward, poking at the embers.

'*Signora*, don't distress yourself. Not on my account.'

She glanced up. 'If not yours, then who else's?

'One afternoon I had to descend to the village for an appointment with the doctor. Women's matters, you know. The children were about twelve. I didn't like leaving them in his charge but had no choice. I hid the grappa under my bed but he found it and began drinking. When I came back I found Vittorio sitting alone on the dirt in his own soiled clothes. And could hear screams coming from the tool shed. Opening the door I saw he had tied Francesca over the work bench and was rutting her from behind. She was screaming in pain and terror. His back was to the door. I did the first thing I could think of. I picked up a shovel and swung it at his head.'

'*Signora*, you only did—'

She held up her hand. 'He wasn't dead. But on the floor, groaning. So I hit him again. And again, until he *was* dead. Francesca saw it all. That night I buried him in the woods. Later I let it be known he had left in search of work and wouldn't be coming back. The villagers accepted it, as is the way with villagers, and nothing more was said. But over the years the stories began, and grew ever more fanciful, so in a while I stopped going down there and people stopped coming up. It's an arrangement that suits us all.'

'And... Francesca?'

'Has never uttered a word since that day.'

He tried the radio again later that night. Retrieving the suitcase from its hiding place above the cowshed, he carried it down the ladder, pushing past the cud-chewing cattle to the tool shed where he lit the lantern and opened it on to the bench. The batteries, he saw, were by now all but dead. Whenever possible, he had been taught, always use a mains supply, for apart from conserving the batteries, this will greatly improve the performance of the radio. Connecting Rossi's wires to the terminals produced no results, however, and he began to suspect there was no power to the farm. But tracing the wire back through the wall with the lantern, he found a Bakelite box with a switch inside. He turned the switch, and the radio hummed to life. Immediately, tuning the knob, he began hearing faint clicks and hisses of other transmissions. Draping the long copper aerial around the shed's rafters, he took out the Morse key and code book and set to work. An hour later, having transmitted his news into the ether, he packed up the set and went to bed.

The next day Germans came. He would never know if their arrival was connected with his radio transmission, or just part of the ongoing search for partisans and deserters; all he knew was that having harvested the last of the maize, and begun the laborious task of pulling up the stripped stalks ready for the field to be ploughed, he looked up to admire an eagle cruising the ridge above him, and heard the distant rumble of engines. For a moment he froze, unsure if it was road traffic he was hearing or one of the many aircraft that passed each day, then he heard the revving of a motorcycle and knew it was no aeroplane. Deep in the woods above the maize field was an ancient *riparo* – a shepherd's shelter. His instructions from Rosa, should anyone come to the farm, were to go straight there and wait until the coast was clear. But instead he sprinted for the track, one thought burning in his head. If he, or any trace of him, was found, the whole family would be arrested. Like as not Rosa would then be shot for harbouring a fugitive and the twins shipped off to a prison camp. This he could not allow. He ran on, cursing his carelessness. The radio was well hidden, as were the weapons and fuses, but the suitcase containing his clothes was in the hay beside his bedding. He must get to it and remove it along with all signs of his existence. He reached Bruno's field and hesitated. He too had heard the noise and was cantering in furious circles, so Theo ran the long way round. By the time he reached the farm, and crouched down breathlessly behind the pig hut, he realized he was too late.

One motorcycle and a small truck were parked in the yard, six men, all in field grey, one of them an officer, staring curiously about. Heart pumping, he considered his options. Kill them all, was his first instinct, kill them and remove all evidence of their coming. Understandable maybe, but impractical, he knew. Even if he could reach the Sten, load and fire it, he'd be lucky to get two before the rest recovered and overwhelmed him. Perhaps he should simply surrender. Put up his hands, walk out and tell the officer Rosa had no idea he'd been there. Would they believe him? He doubted it. Or might he possibly draw them away? Cause a diversion and lead them into the hills, giving the family a chance to escape. But escape where? On foot, one of them an elderly woman, another a confused youth. Even as he watched, he saw Vittorio hesitantly approaching the motorcycle, fingers outstretched, to the amusement of the soldiers, as though it was some fearful monster. Then Rosa appeared, looking very old and bent, and bearing a tray with one glass on it. Slowly she drew near the officer and offered him the glass, which he took with a slight bow. At the same moment Francesca emerged from the cowshed carrying a pail of milk. Smiling and waving in greeting to the soldiers, she turned briefly to the pigpen, looked straight at Theo and touched her fingers to her forehead. Like horns. Then hurried down to join the soldiers.

He stayed away until dusk, until long after he'd heard the vehicles depart, crouching in the *riparo* as the raindrops plopped on to leaves around him, till certain it was safe. Even then, having crept down to the cottage, he watched it for a full fifteen minutes more before tapping on the door.

Bruno had saved the day, just as Francesca had intended. His field was secured by a gate. Theo had run back there, opened it

270

wide and stood aside waving his neckerchief in provocation. But, already alert to the intruders, Bruno needed no provocation, and with his furious trumpet roar charged the gate, careered straight past him, and disappeared down the track in a cloud of dust.

'You never saw grown men run so fast!' Rosa cackled. 'Like little children, even the *tenente*! I screamed and begged them to save me, but they all cowered like girls.'

It had then taken them a full hour and several attempts to shepherd Bruno into a corner, before Francesca made an elaborate show of approaching him, and finally securing him to a post, amid cheers from the soldiers. Afterwards followed wine, *biscotti* and animated discussion, before, following a perfunctory check of the farm buildings, the party departed, waving merrily.

But it had been a near thing and Theo knew it. 'I cannot stay much longer,' he told Rosa later. 'The risk to you is too great.'

'Nonsense! They have been, they have searched, they have ticked us off the list.'

'But for how long? And what if the *tenente* reconsiders today's events, and wonders about the bull, and the coincidence of his escape? And decides to come back?'

'Pah! You think too much, northern boy.'

'Perhaps.' He nodded ruefully. 'But if anything happened to you, or the twins, because of me, I could never forgive myself.'

Normality returned, and lasted three days more. In the morning the tin bath roused him with its familiar clatter, he dressed, swept the hayloft of his presence and descended through the cowshed for breakfast.

'Today we plough,' Rosa announced. 'Francesca will drive, you will lead. You have done this?'

'Never.'

'She will show you.'

The first task was to yoke two of the oxen together and drag the plough up to the maize field. Once there Francesca fastened it by chains so it was standing upright supported by rickety iron wheels, with two handles protruding at the back for steering. The single ploughshare was of pointed steel and glinted in the autumn sunshine. Theo watched as she adjusted its chains and levers, clucking and tutting self-consciously. The day was warm; she was wearing her usual work clothes: a plain blouse with sleeves rolled high, a black skirt and white apron with bare legs and clog-like shoes. After a while she seemed ready. Handing him a rein attached to the oxen she pointed across the field at a distant tree. He nodded. She returned to the steering handles, flicked a willow twig at the animals' hindquarters and began to plough.

An hour later they paused to rest the beasts and drink water. The sun was high, the tilled earth rich brown and pungent-smelling. Leading the oxen was uncomplicated, he found, but strenuous, as they wanted to veer off-line or duck their heads suddenly, requiring him to pull hard on the rein. Soon his throat was parched and the sweat running down his back. His work boots grew huge with clay, which had to be repeatedly cleaned off with a stick. Francesca's clogs by contrast stayed entirely free of soil, he pointed out, to her amusement. Her cheeks too were flushed with effort, coils of moist hair hung from her bun, and her blouse clung damply to her body. You drive now, she indicated, grabbing his hand. 'No, no!' He laughed. 'I can't.' Yes, she nodded. I will teach you.

Her fingers closed round his on the handles, her body pressing close behind, her breathing heavy in his ear as she switched the willow and the team moved off. At first he struggled with the grips, unnecessarily as it turned out, for though firm hands were needed, heavy ones were not. The plough skittered and dived too, bobbing duck-like on the surface one moment, burying itself deep underground the next. Gently she coached him, her hands on his arms, letting the machine do the work. He nodded, forcing his grip to relax. Gradually his furrows settled and grew straighter.

She made the advance at the next rest stop. He guessed it was coming, and was prepared, but still felt sadness and regret, hoping to the last it might somehow not happen. Settling under a tree beside him, she trickled water on to a handkerchief and dabbed her chest above the blouse. Then without warning she took his hand and placed it on her breast. Before he knew it she was leaning back against the tree, eyes closed, lips pursed, like a little girl expecting a gift.

'Francesca.' He removed his hand. 'Francesca, look at me.'

Her eyes opened, clouded with doubt.

'You are a wonderful young woman.' He smiled. 'Strong and brave and clever, and very beautiful.'

Her head turned away.

'I told your grandmother I didn't have a *fidanzata,* and I know you heard. But I was lying. I do have someone, very special to me, and hope one day she might become my *fidanzata.*'

Tears welled in her eyes and her mouth turned down. From far above came a distant humming, as though of a swarm of bees. He leaned forward and kissed her brow. 'I will always be your friend, Francesca, and hope you will always be mine.'

She sat up, wrapping her arms round him, and pressed her cheek to his chest, like a child seeking comfort. He smelled the warmth of her body, stroked the tousled hair, and looking up saw scores of tiny silver crosses, each trailing a silken thread of white vapour, travelling across the cloudless sky.

The next night when he tuned in his radio, he finally heard the code word everyone was waiting for.

'The Allied invasion of Italy has begun.'

Theo watched as the riotous cheer rang round Salvatore's kitchen. Ten men, his San Felice cell, stood before him, variously attired as brigands and desperados and many brandishing weapons, their expressions ranging from tearful joy to triumphant fury. Nightjar was among them, and the three boys he'd met before: Lucien, Renzo and one-eyed Guercio; the others were new to him and included two South Africans, Vos Smits and Billy, who were escaped POWs from the fall of Tobruk, a runaway Yugoslav conscript inevitably dubbed Tito, and two of Nightjar's Naples contacts: brothers Toni and Gennaro. Excepting Salvatore who was forty, all were in their teens or early twenties, eager, headstrong and impatient for action, but inexperienced. Harnessing their enthusiasm he sensed would be a challenge.

'Tell them the details, Horatio,' Nightjar said.

'I have only my briefing, and the coded radio notification. This confirms, as planned, that landings have been made in Calabria, on the toe of Italy.'

'Who by?' asked one of the South Africans.

Theo smiled. 'Your people, Billy, British 8th Army.'

'Monty!'

'That's right. The plan is to use them to divert the enemy south, before two main landings are made further north.'

'When?'

'I don't know.'

'Where?'

'I don't know that either, but possibly the Naples area on the west coast, maybe the east side too around Foggia.'

'When do we attack!'

'We don't.' He watched as the faces fell like children's. Tito muttered a Slavonic oath, while the two Neapolitans exchanged mutinous glances. 'At least not yet. Our job is to monitor enemy movements and report what we find.'

'Report what?'

'Strength, disposition, composition,' he counted off, suddenly recalling a tent in France and a harassed major briefing a seventeen-year-old boy with a bicycle. 'Weaponry, supplies, communications... We're also to monitor their air strength.'

'Can't we just kill them?'

'That might be difficult. Field Marshal Kesselring is in charge. He has an estimated ten divisions, the Italian army another five or more.'

'Pah!' Toni scoffed. 'Italian army is finished.'

'It's not their fault! Mussolini betrayed them!'

'No, the *Tedeschi* betrayed them. They betrayed us all!'

'Perhaps we should get going.' Theo closed the meeting before he lost control of it. 'Salvatore's brother has kindly agreed to drive us to Isernia in his truck. It is an important road junction. He has also provided maps and directions, and his contacts there will supply us with provisions and a safe place to make camp. We need to be there before daybreak, so I suggest we make a start. Any questions?'

Mutters of assent, then the second Naples boy, Gennaro, spoke. 'One small matter, *Tenente*.'

'Yes?'

'Not being disrespectful or anything, but why do we have to follow you?'

'You don't. Nobody does. It's important you all decide for yourselves, so please give it thought now.' He bent to his backpack, fiddling with the straps to give them time. His civilian suitcase was now gone, and with it his peasant persona. He was wearing crumpled fatigues, and desert boots he'd bought off the LRDG in Gabès. He wore no insignia, but a British officer's Webley was strapped to his thigh, and a yellow lanyard was looped round his shoulder and into his shirt pocket. Straightening up he produced a maroon beret, brushed dust from it and tugged it on to his head. 'Are we ready?'

'*Madre di Dio!*' someone murmured. 'Horatio's a *diavolo rosso*!'

Billy laughed. 'Fuck me, it's the Paras!'

They drove all night. The distance was not great but the main roads were choked with traffic, all military and all heading south, and the back lanes were equally slow and hazardous. Several times they pulled off to avoid confrontation, twice scrambling from the van into ditches as German convoys ground by. On the second occasion Gennaro and Toni had to be restrained from firing their carbines randomly into the convoy.

'Is everyone from Naples so impetuous?' Theo asked.

'Most are worse!' Nightjar replied.

Dawn found them at the rendezvous on the outskirts of Isernia, Salvatore's brother depositing them beside the road on open farmland near a river. Trestle tables had been set up, like a picnic, with women serving olive bread and coffee while their children danced around playing soldiers.

'This is not prudent.' Theo studied the horizon. 'We must get away and into cover as soon as possible.'

After a hurried breakfast, and laden with food, water, stores and assorted weaponry, the eleven set off on foot, following the river upstream into hills laced with olive groves and vineyards. Aircraft flew overhead, all German, but evidently intent on other targets. After three hours, signs of agriculture begin to thin, and soon they were entering a more rugged landscape of craggy hills and low scrub. Their objective was a rocky gorge set high above the river, with commanding views south over the plains of Campania, yet secluded, with caves and crevices for cover. They reached it at sunset and began making camp. Setting up his observation posts, Theo noted dust rising from a distant road. 'That's where they are, so that's where we go,' he instructed. That night he led his first patrol.

It was nearly his last. To their chagrin, he posted Salvatore, Lucien and the two Neapolitans to guard camp, while he and the rest descended a steep wooded path to the valley below. The night was cold and overcast with a stiff breeze stirring the trees. Following the course of the river they soon began to hear faint traffic sounds above the trickle of water and rustling leaves; a mile more and a procession of masked headlights came into view, inching across the skyline like distant ships. Farther off, fingers of white scoured the clouds for bombers. There Theo halted and drew out the map.

'Nightjar. It's this road, yes?'

'Yes, Saccucci, a big junction, east goes to Termoli, west to Cassino.'

'South?'

Nightjar shrugged. 'South goes south. Towards Monty.'

'We must get closer, find out which.'

He split the patrol in two, Nightjar's half to investigate the road west, his half descending to the town to study the junction itself. With him he had Tito the Yugoslav, Renzo and one-eyed Guercio. Creeping through fruit orchards criss-crossed with irrigation ditches, they arrived in a field of roofless Roman ruins, like an ancient villa. Beside it the road ran along a raised embankment. Silently sliding wall to wall among the ruins, and covered by the noise of engines, they were able to close to within twenty yards of the junction.

A pall of diesel fumes hung over the road, which was nose to tail with traffic, mostly unmoving. Troop carriers, half-tracks, low-loaders bearing tanks, towed artillery, lorries of supplies, an entire motorized division or more with staff cars and motorcycle outriders weaving in and out. Rising above the sound of engines were the exasperated shouts of German transport police, trying to keep everything moving.

'Zey don't go south,' Tito whispered in English. 'Zey go east and west.'

'Yes. And why is that? What's Kesselring doing?'

'Don't tell Smits and Billy!' Tito grinned. 'But I think Kesselring don' care a damn about Monty. I think 'e paint line east–west across map, an' reinforce like crazy to stop main invasion.'

'Yes, but where's the line?'

Tito jerked his thumb. 'Looks like here!'

'And we're the wrong side of it.'

Just then a shot rang out, loud and near above the rumble of traffic, like a firecracker. Everyone ducked, except Guercio who was holding his carbine, barrel still smoking, in wide-eyed shock.

'Horatio, I'm sorry, it just went off—'

'*Halt!*' Two figures in grey appeared at the roadside. '*Wer ist da!*'

'GO!'

The ruins saved them. With bullets whining overhead and smacking into the ancient masonry they sprinted away, bent double and madly zigzagging until the shots died away and the traffic noise receded. A little further and they were at the rendezvous with Nightjar's party.

'We heard shooting,' he said.

'Yes you did,' Renzo gasped, collapsing to the ground. 'Guercio will tell you all about it, before I put his other eye out.'

*

Their activities fell into a pattern. Daytimes were for eating, sleeping, staying out of sight and waiting for dusk. Night-time was for patrols. Within a few days, Tito's suspicions were borne out and a sizeable defensive barrier – later known as the Volturno Line – was established all the way from Termoli on the Adriatic to the Volturno River north of Naples. Soon all the central routes south – roads, railways and valleys – were blocked by armoured units equipped with tanks, artillery and heavy machine guns, and covered from the air by roving bands of fighters. Finding ways to reconnoitre the line became progressively more difficult and the San Felices had to make increasingly tortuous detours to get through. Once behind it they found reserve units backing up the forward ones, often Italian, and usually careless about security. From these they were able to raid food, weapons and ammunition. Early skirmishes were hit-and-run affairs on small outposts with poor defences. One night they charged a supply dump and the Italian guard simply threw down their weapons and told them to help themselves.

'Giving up?' Salvatore asked.

'Our officers have fled, our generals gone home, Mussolini's finished and Badoglio has no interest in us. What else should we do?'

In the second week the raids became more ambitious, less about stealing food and more about harassing the enemy. Using pencil fuses attached to explosives and petrol bombs, they blew up a fuel dump, an electricity sub-station and a carriage of supplies parked in a railway siding. Emboldened by their success some were keen to go even further.

'We should be killing Germans!' Toni protested repeatedly. 'Not stealing tinned food and blowing up army stores, but lying

279

in wait, ambushing and killing them!'

'I agree. Show them we really mean business.'

'That would get their attention all right.'

'And bring down a storm of shit on our heads.'

'Not just ours either. The *Tedeschi* have been destroying whole villages, remember.'

'And executing civilians,' Nightjar added. 'You've heard the rumours from Napoli, Toni. Fifty massacred for every German killed.'

'Says who?'

'Says Colonel Schöll, the new bastard in charge. A tough nut, apparently.'

Theo listened as the discussions ebbed and flowed. They were back in their hilltop hideout, a ridge of shallow caves overhung with trees and bushes. Cover was good, but he forbade cooking fires in the open, lookouts were posted at all times and care had to be taken of aircraft. The eleven were sitting in a circle in the dirt, feasting on stolen German sausage and Italian wine. Despite some language difficulties and the arguments, some of them heated, the cell was functioning well, he felt. Factions had developed, inevitably, with the Neapolitans and South Africans more aggressive, and more impulsive than Nightjar and Salvatore, who were the voices of sense and reason. Tito had the most military experience, while the three country boys tended to bend with the breeze. As leader, nominally, it usually fell to him to settle disputes.

'Tonight we take the high route to the rail depot at Miranda. If we're to take on Germans we need better weapons, like a Schmeisser or two and preferably a light mortar. We also need more tools, rifle ammunition, grenades and fresh batteries for my wireless. If all goes well and we get what's needed, then we'll see. Agreed?'

It was the South Africans' turn to stay behind on picket duty; the rest set out with the dusk. The night was moonless, clear and starlit as they followed goat tracks up the ridge to four thousand feet, where an icy wind cut through their flimsy clothing. Winter protection, Theo mused, would be on the shopping list before long. Cresting the ridge they paused to watch flashes illuminating the western horizon.

'Lightning?' Gennaro asked.

'Or anti-aircraft fire.'

'Artillery,' Tito replied. 'From ships.'

'Let's keep going. It's freezing up here.'

An hour later they reached the hilltop village of Miranda, crept through its darkened alleys, then paused to survey the rail depot below. Theo scanned the scene with his binoculars but could see little in the dim light.

'Something looks different,' he murmured.

'It looks the same to me.'

'More freight cars in the sidings maybe?'

'All the more stuff for us!'

'Hmm. Let's everyone go carefully. And we rendezvous back here if separated.'

They skittered down paths of loose rock until reaching the rail track where they split into groups. Theo had Toni and Gennaro with him; scampering over the tracks they approached the nearest trucks and set to work with bolt-cutters. The first few cars were empty, so they switched to another siding. Just as they were breaking into the nearest of these, they heard shouts, a single shot rang out and the whole scene was bathed in floodlight.

'Guard hut!' Toni pointed. 'Over there, look!'

'*Merda!* That's what's new!'

'The lights too. Get under the car! Where are the others?'

'Christ knows!'

Half a dozen guards, some in shirtsleeves, came hurrying from the hut, fumbling with their rifle bolts. Guttural shouts echoed round the siding.

'Shit, they're Germans!'

'They're spreading out, look, heading for the depot.'

'Nightjar's there. And Renzo's boys somewhere.'

'I can see Renzo! Running under those trucks!'

'We must cause a diversion. Grenades, one each, throw them as far as you can. Then try and shoot out the lights. Ready?'

Crouching beneath the car, the three held their grenades, pulled the pins, ran out and threw. At the same moment a burst of gunfire came from the depot and an explosion from behind the guard hut. Chaos ensued with shadowy figures running in all directions and sporadic bursts of shooting and explosions. Two of the four floodlights were quickly shot out, and as Theo was kneeling to disable the third, he saw a body in grey lying on the ground, and figures scurrying for the village.

It was all over in minutes. Scrambling up the path to the rendezvous he arrived to find everyone present except the two Italian boys, Lucien and Renzo. Guercio had been with them but had hidden inside a wagon when the shooting started. 'I didn't see them after that, Horatio! Where are they?'

Theo took out his binoculars. Down below the scene was of figures searching, shouts and the cries of someone injured. All but one of the floodlights was out, leaving the area largely darkened. He could make out a crouched figure beside what looked like a body, apart from that no movement and no sign of the two Italians.

'Should we go back?'

'No. They will have called for reinforcements.' He checked his watch. 'Get back to base, all of you, and prepare to break camp. I'll give them another ten minutes. If they're not back by then we must assume they've been taken. And that we're no longer safe in the caves.'

They didn't come, and after ten minutes he saw a troop truck pull into the siding and soldiers jump out. So he hurried back to the ridge and set out for camp. On the way he noticed the earlier flashes had intensified. Back at camp the others were there, waiting anxiously, surrounded by stores and baggage. They sat in a circle, drinking wine, reliving the incident and discussing options. Theo said they should get some rest, and leave in an hour. Just as they were preparing to bed down, they heard boots on the path above, and rapidly drew their weapons. Heavy breathing and muttered Italian oaths were heard, then an owl hoot of recognition. A moment later a grinning Renzo appeared, closely followed by Lucien. Leading a German prisoner bound with a rope.

'Look what we've got!' he said.

CHAPTER 13

'You stupid bloody idiots! What the hell did you bring him here for?'

'He followed us up to the village. So we lay in wait and jumped him. We thought you'd all be pleased.'

'Pleased? You've just led the enemy to our door!'

'Hardly. He was all alone, nobody saw, and anyway he's just a kid, look.'

The argument raged; the German looked nonplussed; Theo sat on a stump holding his head in his hands. This changed everything, he knew; the implications were enormous and he could imagine no solution. All but Renzo and Lucien saw the folly of their actions, that abducting a German soldier would only provoke ferocious retaliation: manhunts, interrogations, enemy troops flooding the area and the most ruthless of reprisals – whether he was safely found or not. Innocent villagers would be the victims; old men would be dragged off, women terrorized, cottages ransacked, belongings smashed and any younger men – deserters, fugitives or simply innocent bystanders – almost certainly shot on the spot. As for the San Felices, they were finished, he knew, at least in their present form. Maybe, once the hue and cry died down, maybe they might regroup and carry on, but for now they were done. All they could do was disband and scatter.

Once they had dealt with the prisoner.

He stole a look. Standing in the clearing in the half-light, with his wrists tied and an embarrassed smile on his face, his boots muddy and shirt untucked, he was indeed just a kid, perhaps eighteen, with a floppy fringe and pimply cheeks. Small too, by German army standards, his tunic too big for him, his trousers loose at the waist. Which could explain why he was only guarding a railway. A humble reservist most likely, a rear echelon useless mouth, like the boy on the bridge at Caen, marching up and down in the cold and trying to do the right thing by showing some pluck.

'He'll have to go,' one of the South Africans was saying.

'What, you mean be released?' Lucien queried.

'No, I mean go! As in gone.'

'You're not saying...'

'Yes he is,' Gennaro muttered. 'Billy's right. He must go. And then be disappeared. There's no other alternative.'

'Yes, but surely—'

'He's the enemy. And a risk to us all – thanks to you. It's the only thing to do.'

'But—'

'Isn't it, Horatio?'

Suddenly they were all looking at him.

'You agree it's the only thing to do?'

He rose wearily to his feet. 'It'll be dawn soon. I must make the wireless rendezvous before it gets light. I'll be back in a while.'

He set up on a bluff overlooking the plain. Radio traffic was busier than he'd ever heard. Scanning the frequencies was like tuning a domestic wireless – signals at every turn: sudden bursts of Morse, high-pitched whistles, garbled voice transmissions in German, Italian and one which sounded American, an endlessly repeated Italian news broadcast, and even music, including a German jamming signal using Beethoven. Kneeling by the set with his code book and headphones, he struggled to make sense of it all, until finally filtering the noises into a single message to the world.

'The main landings have happened,' he told the others. 'Last night, on the west coast at Salerno.'

'My God, it's really happened?'

'Yes.'

'That must have been the lightning we saw!'

'How big, Horatio?'

'An army, the American 5th. With the British 8th coming up from the south.'

'Salerno. So we'll be in the thick of it!'

'I expect so.' Theo glanced at the German, who appeared not to understand. Lucien had given him a cigarette, which he was smoking inexpertly. 'There's more.'

'More?'

'The Italian government is asking for an armistice with the Allies.'

This news brought only stunned silence. He too could scarcely believe it. Mussolini imprisoned, Fascism dying, years of military rule ended, and in one stroke Italy had gone from deadly foe to new-found friend. Or harmless bystander. And what did it mean for South Tyrol? For Carla working away in London, and Josef in political prison in Rome. And for the whole Italian nation, cast into the unknown like a rock into a well.

'I have to leave. I've to report to Salerno,' Theo continued.

'How long for?'

'I don't know.'

'Are you coming back?' Guercio sounded fearful.

'I can't say. In any case we should split up, and leave here.

You should be near your families at this time. We can stay in contact through Nightjar in Naples.'

'What about him?' Smits nodded at the prisoner.

'I'll take care of it.'

They began packing up. He left them to it, walking along the ridge to the gorge's edge, craving solitude. Dawn was coming, waves of morning mist drifting like a river along the valley below. Far to the west rose the rumble of heavy artillery. He took off his beret, turning it over in his hand and fingering its worn seams. Bruneval, Depienne, Sedjenane, Primosole, from interviewing von Stauffenberg to dinner with Clare at the Café de Paris, it had been his companion and talisman, his badge of honour and his good-luck charm, like the Maori *Hei Tiki* of the LRDG. It was part of who he was, and it had never let him down. Raising his gaze to the horizon, he tossed it out and watched it fall into the mists below.

'What you doing?' Tito approached.

'Leaving.'

'*Horazio*, my friend—'

'I said I'll take care of it.'

'It mus' be done. Billy, Smits, the boys from Naples, even Salvatore. They want it done. An' zey won't go until it is.'

'I understand.'

'No you don't. They will string him up an' do it with hate. They seen too many friends murdered by the Boche, too many family destroyed, an' homes burned. They say is matter of honour. And vengeance.'

'Yes.'

'An' as their leader you—'

'*I said I understand!*'

His name was Emil Köhler. From Dortmund.

'Köhler means charcoal burner, you know, although I don't know much about making charcoal. Do you?'

'Nothing, I'm afraid. My name's Theo. Would you like another cigarette?'

'Not really, it seems I'm not much of a smoker or a charcoal burner!'

'Me neither. How long have you been in the army, Emil?'

'Six months. This is my first posting after basic. I say, your German's very good.'

'Thank you. I learned it as a child. How old are you?'

'Eighteen. My birthday's in June. You?'

'It's odd that you ask.' He managed a wry smile. 'It's my birthday today. My twenty-first, in fact.'

'Well, that's marvellous! Many congratulations, Theo. You should celebrate.'

'We'll see. What do you hope to do after the war?'

'Accountancy. I was about to go to college but then got called up. So I enrolled in a correspondence course but, well, the studying's difficult, in a barracks and so on.'

'I can imagine. Here, let me untie your wrists.'

A flash of panic. 'Why, what's happening?'

'I just thought they must be sore.'

'Oh, yes, they are a bit. Thanks, Theo.'

The sun was coming up, glinting off his eyes, which were round and restless. Theo had led him away from the others, down a slope to a clearing of lichen-covered boulders. Sitting there side by side, before them lay the view of the plain, while behind the path wound down to the river.

'What made you do it, Emil? Chase us up here all on your own.'

Emil looked away, rubbing his wrists. 'When the shooting started, I... I stayed back, in the hut. Because I was afraid. The others all just ran straight outside, but I froze. And found myself in there alone.'

'It happens. Freezing.'

'Yes, well, then I heard shouting, that someone had been hit, so I just grabbed the medical bag and ran out to see. It was Tomas, one of the other new lads. He'd been hit in the stomach. I asked him to show me and do you know what he said? Where were you, Köhler? It's all he said. Where *were* you? And I felt so ashamed I wished it was me that got shot. Anyway, then the shooting stopped and a few minutes later I saw two of your lads running away up the path to the village. I don't know what came over me. I mean, the fighting was over, I didn't even have my rifle, but I just leaped up and ran after them.'

Theo nodded. How detached he felt. How numb.

'What's going to happen, Theo?'

'Well, I'll tell you.' This was the end. The end of any pretence at honour or chivalry. And the end of all innocence. Now he was coming of age. The age of choice. Ahead lay the cliff edge of guilt and damnation, and he must choose to hang back in weakness and vacillation, or step forward and freefall into the abyss. *War is a failure of reason*, von Stauffenberg had said. *In the end there is only conscience*. And Erwin Rommel, who never left him in peace: *Know who you are. And make your decision.*

'You're not going to—'

'You see that path behind you?'

Emil turned to look.

His hand slipped to his thigh. 'The one down there, see?' The leather flap was undone, his hand closed on steel. 'It leads to the river. You then go upstream a short way, and there's a footbridge which brings you to a road. From there you can walk back to the railway. Or maybe thumb a—'

It was the silence after that would forever stay in his memory. Parting from the others, burying the radio, discarding his partisan persona for a civilian one, making his slow way south and west – he had little recollection of these things. He spent a day on the riverbank, not moving, not eating or sleeping, just lying in the reeds listening to the chuckling water and watching the clouds gather like a flock. Other days were more energetic, hiking the valleys and hills of the Matese, fording icy waterfalls, or clinging to craggy limestone peaks, dizzy with vertigo. On one occasion he descended a valley to find himself at a huge lake, lying like quicksilver in the still air, perfectly reflecting the sky as though the world had turned upside down. On another day he hacked his way high into a dense forest of beech and chestnut trees dripping with rain. Breaking suddenly into a clearing he found a primitive dwelling of moss and stone. The clearing was empty, the lodging abandoned; all that remained were wide circles of black ash. *Carbonari*, Rosa had explained, strange woodland peoples who lived only in the forests, spoke their own language, and never settled, but forever wandered as though from a curse. Charcoal burners. Sinking to his knees amid the cinders, he dug deep into the damp with his fingers, then daubed his face and chest with harsh streaks of black, and wept tears of shame into the ashes.

And all the while the sounds of far-off gunfire and a smoky smudge on the horizon spoke of the war he no longer felt part of, yet was drawn to as though by a thread. A week passed. One day he was marching beside a deserted railway when a procession of tramp-like figures appeared in the distance like a mirage. As they neared he realized they weren't tramps but soldiers, Italians, hundreds of them, unfed, unled, disarmed and destitute, many in shabby home clothes, refugees from the conflict they once fought in but which had now disowned them. He stood aside as they drew near. Who are you? What unit? Where are you going? They shook their heads and stumbled on, like a company of ghosts.

Later that same day he was on a road by a river drinking water from his bottle, when without warning an American Jeep roared up and squealed to a halt beside him.

'You speak-a-de English, buddy?' the gum-chewing driver demanded.

'Yes.'

'Great!' He pulled out a map. 'We're looking for some place called Albanella.'

Theo studied the map. The river he was looking at, to his astonishment, was the Sele. He was standing less than five miles from its mouth, and the point where his Colossus mission had ended so long ago. X-Troop. Tag Pritchard, Tony Deane-Drummond, Harry Boulter, poor Fortunato. The freezing drop from the Whitley, moonlight gleaming off icy mountains, the sound of rushing water when the aqueduct blew. The desperate march for freedom.

'Albanella?' The American's thumb jabbed the map.

'What's at Albanella?'

'5th Army headquarters. What else!'

'I'll take you. I'm supposed to report there.'

'Yale? Never heard of him. Was he at Massingham?'

'Yes. Then Cairo.'

'Ah. We were at Oran. Stuck with the Yanks, God help us.'

'You work with 5th Army?'

'That's one way of putting it!' Chuckles circled the room. 'Strictly speaking we're here to provide temporary intelligence support and liaison as required. But the Yanks rarely call on us; quite frankly we might as well not exist. Fancy a cuppa?' The man eyed him doubtfully. 'Looks like you could do with it.'

His name was Lewis and he was a captain of something called 312 FSS, which stood for Field Security Service. As such he was 5th Army's British Intelligence Liaison Officer and the authority to which Theo was to report. His department comprised six men billeted in an abandoned villa in the town of Albanella, where 5th Army was currently based.

'... although we're due to move up to Naples any day.' Lewis poured water into a teapot. 'I say, did you hear about Mussolini?'

'No.'

'Got rescued by Jerry paratroopers. Pinched from right under Badoglio's nose. Hitler's personal orders apparently.'

'Where did they take him?'

'Up north, to Salo on Lake Garda. Hitler's set him up as puppet ruler of something called Reppublica Sociale Italiana. Rommel's there too somewhere, rumour has it. Milk and sugar?'

He was told to wait a few days while Lewis made contact with Yale, checked Theo's bona fides and found out what to do with him. Lewis gave him vouchers for the American canteen, a chit for fresh clothes and told him to relax and enjoy the sights. 'Perhaps get a shave and haircut too? You look like a bloody partisan!'

Albanella was a small hilltop town with an old church tower, a pleasant view of the distant sea, but little else. It was also swarming with Americans who strode about in their hip-hugging uniforms shouting loudly at one another and monopolizing all the spaces at cafés and bars. After two days of enormous meals in the canteen, a swim in the municipal lido, and watching a Betty Grable film in an outdoor cinema, he returned to Lewis's office for news.

'Nothing yet, I'm afraid.' Lewis hefted a box. 'But there's a ton of signals coming and going and we're bottom priority. Airfields – all anyone wants to know about is bloody airfields!'

Theo looked around. Cigarette smoke filled the room. Men were bent over desks, while cardboard boxes of files and stacks of papers were piled on every available surface. It reminded him of Grant's office in Baker Street.

'I should go.'

'Go where, old chap?'

'I don't know. Back to the Volturno. Or south. Try and find 8th Army...'

'You wouldn't get five miles. Anyway, I can't let you, I'm afraid. Not till Massingham gets back to me.'

'I don't know why they ordered me here.'

'Any good at filing?'

Two more days went by. He was given a corner desk, and piles of signals to sort through. All were to do with the Americans, mainly the air force which was setting up bases in Italy from which to launch bombing raids on southern Germany. Abbreviations, acronyms and code words peppered the signals, which rendered them mostly meaningless. In any case his job wasn't to decipher them but merely put them in order and file them. Late on the second afternoon, one did catch his eye.

'"Crossbow"?' he queried with one of the others.

'No idea.' The man waved at a filing cabinet. 'Try in there.'

The next morning he finally heard from Yale.

'Congratulations, Theodor Victor Trickey!' Lewis brandished a page. 'You've been Mentioned in Dispatches – again.'

'What for?'

'Some operation in Sicily. Taking a bridge, er... Primosole, it says.'

'That was hardly, um...'

'*And* your unit's in Taranto!'

'2nd Battalion? In Italy?'

'The whole division, including 2nd Battalion. You're free to join them, assuming we can work out how.'

'What are they doing?'

'Not much, it seems.' Lewis studied the sheet. 'Kicking their heels waiting for a troopship home, lucky beggars.'

Home. A room in a boarding house occupied by someone else. A mother who had no time for him. A father who only wanted money. A country that wasn't his. As for the battalion...

'I'd rather not.'

'Taranto...' Lewis was studying a wall map. 'It won't be easy.'

'I'd rather stay. Keep working.'

'What's that, old thing?'

'If you can find a use for me.'

'What, an experienced SOE operative with fluent languages, an impeccable record *and* a gallantry award?'

Something was happening in Naples, Lewis explained. Monty was closing from the south, his advance units already linking up with 5th Army. The drive now was to smash the Volturno Line: '... but only after we reach Naples and that's going to take time.

'Meanwhile we're getting reports of a revolution there, or popular uprising or something, and also of horrific reprisals. Kesselring's put a hothead called Schöll in charge and apparently he's laying about him like a lunatic. Everything's confused, accurate gen is badly needed, especially by Monty who's likely to get there first.'

'I'll go.'

'Should only be for a few days. Then we'll get you to Taranto.'

'It doesn't matter, I'll go.'

'Thank you. Only problem is how. Roads are blocked, Jerry patrols everywhere, trains and buses at a standstill. We could try for an air drop, I suppose, although cross-country might be safer.'

'Do you have any bicycles?'

He left next morning. Deliberately carrying no identity papers or tags, he wore a shabby Italian suit and plain shirt like the men he'd seen at the railway, and his dirty LRDG boots using string for laces. He asked Lewis to drive him up the coast as far as possible, and somewhere near Gragnano, a dozen miles or so south of Naples, he unloaded his bike and prepared to set off.

'Sure you'll be all right?'

'Yes.'

'Food? Money? A Webley?'

'Nothing. It's best this way.'

'Good luck, then. And take care!'

He pedalled off, soon passing Pompeii on his right with the towering cone of Vesuvius beyond. Thin plumes of smoke had been seen recently, as if a portent, but today the volcano looked quiet. He kept going, battling against a stiff breeze. To his left rain clouds scudded low over the Gulf of Naples, whipping the waters into foaming brown waves. At Portici he met his first roadblock.

'*Documenti*.' The German on the barrier snapped his fingers.

'I have none. Everything was taken when I was demobbed.'

'What unit?'

'11° Alpini. At Foggia. We were told to hand everything in. I was given nothing but these clothes and told to go home.'

'*Napoli?*'

'Yes, sir. I'm to report to the district police. Excuse me, do you have a few lire...'

'Fuck off. Which district?'

'Pendino.'

'Then you'd better get on with it. There's a curfew, you know, and stay away from protesters.'

He arrived at the harbour an hour later. Naples was unfamiliar to him; he knew it only from newspapers and school books as a sprawling giant, Italy's third city, a vital port and a hotbed of political intrigue and unrest. The harbour was strangely deserted, only a few ships lying at anchor, even fewer people out on the streets. Several areas showed bomb damage, with shops abandoned and once-stylish hotels ruined, while checkpoints and roadblocks lay everywhere, many of them unmanned.

'Are you mad?' A woman scurried by. 'Harbour is off limits, unless you want to get shot!'

He pedalled swiftly away, making for the centre and the distant sounds of clamour. On the way he passed barricades of furniture and rubble, a burned-out car with bodies inside, groups of men, many of them young, dashing from alley to alley, carrying weapons and bandoliers of ammunition across their chests. Periodic bursts of gunfire could be heard, the crack of a grenade, and warning notices were posted everywhere. *People of Naples!* proclaimed a poster bearing the swastika. Beneath was a pronouncement from Schöll declaring martial law, instituting a night-long curfew, banning all assemblies, and warning of dire consequences for transgressors. *Anyone acting against German forces will be executed! His home will be destroyed! Every German killed will be avenged a hundred times! Keep calm and act reasonably!*

He rounded a corner to find another barricade, this one

manned entirely by children, all boys. Some as young as seven or eight, and variously armed with knives, clubs and one ancient-looking carbine, they were dirty-faced and poorly dressed and spoke in a coarse city slang.

'Give me that!' In seconds his bicycle had been seized and thrown atop the barricade.

'What's going on?'

'*Tedeschi* weapons store, in that building. We're going to blow it up, and take the weapons.'

'What with?'

'These!' The boy gestured to a basket of petrol bombs.

'Are there Germans in there?'

'I hope so. We'll blow them up too!'

'What if they come out shooting?'

'Piss off, we know what we're doing.'

'As you wish. Which way's Vomero district?'

The youth pointed.

'Thanks. And push in the wicks on your Molotovs. Like the stoppers in wine bottles. It's safer when you throw them.'

The afternoon waned; he continued on his way, picking through the wreckage towards the centre. Buildings stood gutted, vehicles lay on their backs like dead animals, telephone wires drooped, water poured from smashed mains, many streets were blocked by craters, debris and barricades, while choking smoke clogged the air from a hundred fires. No fire pumps attended those fires, no one took charge, nobody attempted to clear up or keep order. To him it was a city in the throes of death, like the torpedoed ship in Algiers harbour, collapsing in on itself before diving for the bottom. Vomero? he enquired as he went. Armando the baker's son? The brothers Toni and Gennaro? No one knew or cared, answering only with shaking heads, too shocked or too frightened for speech. At one crossroads a fever of panic broke out suddenly. Men ducked from sight, old women ran inside, doors and shutters banged, and in seconds he was alone with the drifting smoke and litter. Then with a roar a convoy hove into view: sand-brown vehicles with ominous black crosses, scout cars, lorries carrying troops, machine-gun-toting motorcycles, at its head a staff car with officers in uniform. Their heads turned to him as they passed, he drew himself up and saluted, and the convoy drove on.

'You trying to get yourself killed?' An old man appeared. 'Don't you know they're rounding up every male from eighteen to thirty?'

'No, I didn't. What for?'

'Forced labour. Or the firing squad. They're holding them at the sports stadium.'

'Where's Vomero?'

'You're in it.'

Further on, he was in a shabby alley, still doggedly asking about Nightjar and the others, when a hand grabbed his arm and dragged him into a doorway. 'Horatio!'

'Renzo.'

'Thank God.'

'Are you alone?'

The house was a wreck, the walls cracked, a gaping hole in the ceiling. Broken glass and fallen plaster crunched underfoot as Renzo led him to a kitchen at the back. There were six San Felices in Naples, he explained, Nightjar and the two brothers, who had relatives there, 'and we three country boys who came along for the ride!' Salvatore had gone home, he added, while Tito and the South Africans were trying to get through to British lines further south.

'Where's Nightjar and the others?'

'On patrol. Which means scrounging for weapons, lobbing

a few grenades, taking pot-shots at the *Tedeschi* when we can. Just like everyone.'

'What's happening?'

'Anarchy! All the government officials deserted the city, the Italian army too, leaving tons of guns and ammo. The Germans know the Allies are coming but are ordered to hold the city. They're jumpy as hell. Schöll tried to impose martial law, and ordered the shooting of rioters. Now the whole city's rising up in protest.'

Renzo gave him bread and wine. Later, with the coming of dusk and the curfew, the others began to trickle in. Nightjar embraced him warmly; Toni and Gennaro nodded cautiously. Lucien was last to arrive.

'Where's Guercio?' Renzo asked.

'I thought he was with you.'

'Not me. Last I saw he was heading east.'

'He'll show up, he always does.'

But Guercio didn't show up, and in the morning worrying news came.

'There's to be a public execution. Two lads. At the Palazzo Reale. They've rounded up all the local civilians and are forcing them to watch.'

They hurried for their weapons. Theo was offered a rifle but declined.

'We must approach carefully,' Toni said, 'it could be a trap.'

They set off into the morning. An orange sun pierced the still-drifting smoke and women and children queued forlornly for food while dogs scavenged at rubbish. The former royal palace was a famous landmark, housing the city's library and archive. As they drew near its cobbled piazza, chants and shouting could be heard, drowning the urgent squawk of a loudspeaker.

'Stay back, boys.' They ducked into a shop. '*Tedeschi*, look.'

As they watched, armed figures in grey were seen patrolling the crowd, which was mainly made up of elderly men and women, with small children darting in and out. Then two of the Germans lunged in and dragged out a youth, beating him with clubs, before throwing him into a lorry guarded by a machine gun.

'They're rounding up more for deportation.'

'Or worse.'

Then, as though on a signal, the crowd fell silent. An armed guard marched on to the palace steps, two figures in shirtsleeves and handcuffs in their midst. An officer followed, mounting the steps to stand before the microphone.

'Is the shorter one Guercio?'

'It's too far! I can't tell.'

'I'll go.' Theo darted out, using the colonnade beside the piazza for cover, moving steadily forward until level with the crowd.

'*Citizens of Naples!*' The loudspeaker blared. '*You have been warned repeatedly to respect the forces of law and order...*'

Timing his moment, he sprinted from cover and plunged headlong into the crowd, which enveloped him like a protective blanket. 'This way, *giovane*. Keep your head down. Stay down, we've got you.'

'*... However, these two criminals chose to disregard these forces of law and order and were caught looting German army stores of food.*'

He struggled forward, steered this way and that by thighs and elbows, his head repeatedly pressed down by unseen hands. Eventually he neared the front and gingerly straightened. As he did so someone dropped a cap on his head.

The condemned men had hoods over theirs.

'Is that Schöll talking?' he murmured.

'That's the *bastardo*.'

'*... The penalty for looting is death. Therefore, in accordance with published ordinance and by my authority, they will suffer public execution, as a warning and deterrent to any who transgress the law.*'

It happened very fast. The victims were shoved up against the wall, four Germans with rifles took aim, the hoods came off, Schöll raised his arm, and then dropped it. The volley rang shockingly loud, the two men slumped, a sigh rose from the crowd, and then a single shout came from far back:

'*Viva Napoli! Viva la rivoluzione!*'

'It wasn't Guercio.'

'He must have been rounded up.'

'Then he'll be at the sports stadium.'

'I hear there's tanks and heavy machine guns.'

'We'll need more weapons.'

They set out once more. By mid-morning there were more insurgents on the streets than on any previous day, more skirmishes with the enemy, and more casualties. Gunfire and explosions could be heard everywhere, with bands of rebels springing up in all directions. For their part the Germans set up roadblocks and gun emplacements, mounted motorized patrols and tried to contain each encounter as it arose. But they were fighting bushfires: no sooner was one under control than another broke out. Italian disorder was their enemy; no command structure existed among the rebels, the fighting was uncoordinated and spontaneous. And spreading, with other districts of the city joining by the hour. Rumours abounded of open warfare and mass executions, Allied salvation and even of German surrender, but nothing could be substantiated. The San Felices stayed together, making their way to a disused school used as a makeshift arsenal. The weaponry was Italian and in poor condition, but they restocked with grenades, and loaded their ammunition belts with fresh rounds. 'We need to do better than this,' Gennaro grumbled, checking his rifle. Then they set off for the stadium. Barely had they gone fifty yards when a huge explosion sent them scurrying for cover. 'Tanks!' someone yelled. 'They're shelling the houses!'

The six piled into a doorway. As the dust settled they saw the mottled green turret showing above a shattered wall, its battle-scarred barrel roving from side to side. Infantrymen bearing machine pistols were clambering through the rubble behind it.

'What do we do?'

'Attack!'

'A tank! Are you mad? And those lads are hefting Schmeissers!'

'Horatio?'

'Yes?'

'What do we do?'

'Well, it's your decision. But I'd, um, suggest you fall back.'

'You mean retreat?'

'Getting killed here won't help Guercio.'

They reached the stadium to find it in a state of siege. Surrounded by walls forty feet high, the interior was completely sealed off, although singing and chanting could be heard rising from the stands, as though a football match was going on. Armed Germans ringed the outside, and guarded the gates of the access tunnels. Above them, riflemen roamed the walls like archers on a battlement, while on the piazza below a single tank, squat and menacing, its hatches locked shut for action, stood solitary guard. All round the piazza, women and old men gathered in anxious clusters, the relatives of the young men imprisoned inside. Meanwhile, lurking beyond them in the bars and shops surrounding the stadium were groups of armed rebels.

'It's a stand-off,' Nightjar reported half an hour later. '*Tedeschi* say that if anyone comes near, they'll start shooting the boys inside.'

'So what do we do?'

'General consensus is wait until dark then storm the tunnels.'

'What with?'

'It'll be a massacre.'

'Yes, but we've got to do something. And if we all charge together...'

Food was found and circulated, arguments flared between factions, a priest arrived and held mass among the waiting relatives. And as the afternoon wore on the singing and chanting inside the stadium faded to weary silence. Theo found an empty corner and sat down against the wall, resting his head on his knees.

'Horatio.' A murmur stirred him.

'Hello, Nightjar.'

'How are you doing, old friend?'

'I'll be fine.'

He felt a nudge. 'Remember old Tolomei's place? That was a night, eh!'

'It certainly was. You did very well. You and Francesco, and...'

'Starling?'

'Starling, that's right. It seems a long time ago.'

'It was.' He hesitated. 'Is everything all right with you, Horatio? You seem... not your usual self.'

He raised his head. 'Yes.'

'Ever since—'

'I'm done with it.'

'What do you mean?'

'The war, the fighting and the killing. I can't go on with it. I won't.'

'But you're our leader.'

'Not any more. You're the leader now. And a fine one.'

'But—'

'Armando. Listen to me. Don't storm the stadium.'

'What?'

'Renzo's right. It will be a massacre, and a needless one. Don't do it. Stay back and keep the siege going. Persuade the other groups to do the same. Keep the pressure up but be clever. The Allies are coming; the Germans are losing, and they know it. They won't risk getting caught here. A day or two more and they'll pull out.'

'Yes. All right. I'll try. But what are you going to do?'

'I'll get Guercio.'

At dusk a solitary figure was seen to emerge from a shop on the piazza and, holding a white flag on a stick, walk out to the tank, where it paused, apparently to speak to the occupants. A few minutes passed while an exchange took place on the radio, then two soldiers marched out to the tank and escorted the individual to an open car where an officer was sitting. Another conversation then took place between the officer and the individual, at the end of which the two soldiers were sent inside the stadium. A long interval then passed while nothing happened. Finally the tunnel gates reopened and the two soldiers emerged, with a smaller figure between them. They escorted this youth as far as the tank, he then proceeded alone across the piazza to join his friends outside the shop. The first individual then got into the car beside the officer and was driven off.

CHAPTER 14

A week or so after the air raid that Trudi and I get caught up in, I make my first house call to an Ulm resident. Second, I suppose, if you count Lucie Rommel, but this is different. It's to an old man dying of congestive heart failure, and though unremarkable in itself and ultimately unfortunate, the visit nevertheless heralds a new phase of my Ulm experience, and the beginning of an extraordinary few days.

What happens is an elderly woman comes to the drop-in centre one day and asks me to visit her neighbour. 'Can he not come here?' I say. 'No, he is too ill,' she replies. 'But I have no time,' I plead. 'He only lives two minutes away,' she insists. So without really thinking I agree to stop by on my way back to the *Revier*. His house is a tiny two-roomed affair, undamaged by bombs but without heating or water because the mains are still out. Consequently it is dim and dank, rather unsanitary and freezing cold. She leads me up narrow wooden stairs to the one bedroom where I find the old man on the bed. The room has a grate but the fire is out. 'Nobody has coal,' she explains. I examine the poor fellow, who looks about eighty and exhibits all the signs: pulmonary oedema, respiratory distress, swollen legs, crackling noises down the stethoscope and the rest. The prognosis is poor.

'Does he not have relatives?'

'Not that I know of.'

'He should be in the hospital.'

'The hospital is under military administration.'

'Says who?'

'*Der Direktor.*'

'What's his name?'

'How should I know?'

Back at the *Revier* that evening I discuss the matter with Erik. 'He's completely alone, poor soul. Too sick even to feed himself or make a fire.'

'What about the neighbour?'

'He's not her problem. She made that clear.'

'I too am asked to visit patients at home.' He shakes his head. 'But I always refuse, because we haven't the time. Our movements are so strictly controlled. Also...'

'Yes?'

'Where will it end?'

'True. But what about the hospital being under military control?'

He shrugs. 'I doubt it is Vorst's decision. This comes from higher up.'

'But he could protest or something. Refuse even, if he had any decency. It's a civilian hospital.'

'Not any more, it seems. He's throwing them to the wolves. Hitler is, I mean, like he said he would.'

'Throwing who to the wolves?'

'The German people. That broadcast we hear on Prien's radio, the *totaler Krieg* one Goebbels made. Hitler's finished and knows it, but instead of ending the madness and surrendering, he'll fight to the end, and take the civilian population with him.'

Corporal Prien's wireless is strictly off limits, but he often listens to it, the volume turned high just to annoy us, especially

308

news broadcasts which are nothing but varnished lies and Nazi propaganda. The speech Erik refers to is often played, to our irritation, and we've become familiar with its message, delivered in Goebbels' clipped exhortations. *Do you believe in the final victory of the German people?* he demands. *Are you willing to give everything for victory? Do you want total war? Do you want a war more total and radical than anything ever imagined?* As if they have any choice in the matter.

'And the hospital?'

'Taken over for the war effort, I am guessing, like everything. Fuel, food, clothes, factories, now medical facilities too, and their supplies. Speaking of which...' He hands me a package. 'This was delivered today.'

I examine the parcel. 'Garland & Henning' is handwritten rather grandly on the front: 'Doktoren der Medizin'. With no return address or sender details. 'Sounds impressive,' I joke. 'We should set up in practice!'

'Excellent idea. Open it.'

I duly do, to find bottles and phials of medicines, specifically analgesics, anti-inflammatories, morphine and, most crucially of all, penicillin. Not a large amount, but more than we've seen in ages and hugely welcome.

'These are German.' I study the labels. 'This isn't Red Cross or Allied stuff, but German. See the trademarks? Bayer, look, and Merck.'

'Which suggests...'

The hand of Frau Lucie Rommel and her stepdaughter Gertrud Stemmer.

We're sitting in the bedsit, drinking acorn coffee and puffing on our pipes like two old stagers in a Piccadilly club. Supper was a curious concoction of rabbit leftovers courtesy of Fenton, mixed with Red Cross prunes and stale *Sauerkraut* pinched from the Jerry kitchen. Having completed a final ward round, we have repaired, as has become our custom, to the privacy of our room to write letters and notes, smoke a pipe, read, play chess and chat. Over the weeks, despite differences in character and temperament, we have inevitably grown close, intimate even, rather like two prisoners in a cell.

'What I simply don't understand,' I say, 'is why? I mean, I know nothing about Rommel, but he was a dyed-in-the-wool Nazi, wasn't he? And certainly had no love for the Allies. So why would his widow go to all this trouble to help us? His sworn enemy.'

'Did not the daughter say it is to do with his legacy? And securing the truth.'

Much is falsely known about my father, Gertrud had written in her letter, *not least questions surrounding his loyalty.*

'Yes, I suppose. Oh look, check!'

'*Verdomme*, Garland, you're too good! Anyway, if you ask me, Trickey's the key to all this. If you want answers, you should keep questioning him.'

Which I am. But it's a mind-numbingly frustrating business. Theo is by now physically much improved. He's on his feet and able to walk short distances with the aid of two sticks. He's eating, and putting on weight, his vital organs all seem to be functioning, although he has a hacking cough and sallow pallor due to renal issues caused by months on his back. He gets breathless with the slightest exercise, tires very quickly and sleeps a lot, but in general has come on enormously since the dark days of Stalag XIB. He talks too, commenting on the weather, asking about Ulm, or complaining of itching where I drilled through his skull. And there's an impatience about his conversation, as if he too is searching for answers. Sitting in our room Erik and I often hear him restlessly tap-

tapping across the ceiling to chat with the other patients.

But chat about what, one wonders, because neurologically, *cognitively*, he's a mess. Questioning him is like trying to read pages thrown from a moving train. Everything's jumbled up and a lot is missing. At his bedside I have learned something of his place of birth, his childhood in the Tyrol, the political and ethnic tensions, and of his family which is bewilderingly extended. I know also he and his mother came to England where they lived 'near a racecourse'. But anything more recent than that, of his life in Kingston, for example, or his military service and experiences, I know practically nothing except disjointed fragments. One day he tells me how he and a friend called 'Percy' climbed down from a ship to carry a drum of wire all night. The next day I ask him about it and he remembers nothing. Another time I get very excited when he mentions the name Frost.

'Colonel John Frost?' I repeat. 'So you were in 2nd Battalion. In the Paras?'

'No, the 2/6th Territorials... Wasn't I?'

And by evening he's forgotten that too. Of Arnhem, unsurprisingly, and how he came to be lying among the dead outside the Schoonoord, he has no memory at all.

The next day, to our consternation, Erik and I are summoned to see Vorst. Both together, which is unusual and thus doubly worrying. Descending the stair, we nervously exchange theories. A Vorst summons is invariably bad news, usually involving a telling-off followed by punishments such as stoppage of privileges or confiscation of Red Cross supplies, or threats of transfer or even imprisonment. Lately these castigations have grown worse, probably because of Germany's war situation, which even he knows is dire. The parcel of medicines, I'm thinking, is probably today's bone of contention. 'I hope it's not about the drop-in,' Erik frets.

Neither, as it turns out. We march in, stamp to attention, and wait to be acknowledged. Normally this takes a while, but today Vorst, who is standing at the window, immediately turns at our entry and offers an obsequious smile. Which is even more unnerving.

'Ah, *Herren*, there you are. Thank you for attending at such short notice. Do please come in.'

We shuffle nervously forward.

'I trust you are both in good health and spirits?'

'*Jawohl, Herr Oberstabsarzt!*'

'Good, good.' He returns to his desk, upon which sits a large cardboard box. 'I have asked you here today on a matter of some delicacy.'

'*Herr Oberstabsarzt?*' The box is clearly moving. Or something inside it is.

'To do with an animal.'

Fenton's buck. He's found the bloody rabbit, cottoned on to our scheme and now we're for the chop.

'A very dear friend of mine has recently acquired a dog. *Ein Welpe.*'

A tiny nudge from Erik, who as usual is two steps ahead of me. 'Have they, *Herr Oberstabsarzt?* How delightful. I hope it is not sick.'

It isn't. A *Welpe* is a puppy, the dog is a Dobermann, and what Vorst wants, it transpires, is for a trained surgeon to dock its tail. I don't realize this immediately because he and Erik discuss it in high-speed German, but after a few minutes we are ushered from the office, me holding the box, and Erik holding two bottles of Schnapps, which is to be our payment. Once safely back in the bedsit, he explains the details.

'It's his mistress!' he hisses excitedly. 'The bit on the side he keeps across the river, it's her puppy!'

'I don't care whose puppy it is, I'm not doing it!'

'But, Dan.' He grins, clinking the bottles. 'Lovely Schnapps, look!'

'Yes, but he's the enemy! He's a Nazi bastard, a crook, a tyrant and an appalling human being. Doing him this favour – doing him *any* favour in fact – it's, well, it's tantamount to treason!'

Clink clink. 'But who loses? Not one person. In fact everyone gains.'

'I don't see how!'

'The mistress' – he counts off – 'gets a beautifully docked puppy. Vorst gets a pleased and grateful mistress. We get a pleased and grateful Vorst, *and* two bottles of Schnapps. And because Vorst is happy, everyone in the *Revier* gets an easier time, including the patients.'

'Yes, but—'

'And one more thing.' His tone hardens. 'We will have something to use. On him. Like a lever. If we ever need one.'

'Blackmail, you mean.'

'Because he will be in our debt.'

The arrangements are strictly clandestine. We will perform the procedure in secret tonight, after finishing up for the day. In the meantime the dog stays out of sight in the bedsit, with each of us taking turns to check on it, feed and exercise it and so on. Tomorrow, assuming all is well, it will be returned to its owner, minus tail, and that will be that.

The long day passes; we hold two sick parades which Vorst interestingly does not attend, thus allowing us more time to see patients and also some leeway with the quota. Otherwise the routine is as normal, and eventually evening comes and we

313

repair wearily to our room to make the preparations. Which begin with a glass of Schnapps.

Erik fondles the pup, which is undeniably endearing, licking his hand and wagging its tail in happy ignorance of what's to come. 'You do the honours, Dan,' he says, 'I'll manage the anaesthetic.'

We use ethyl chloride, a well-proven and uncomplicated anaesthetic: you simply apply a few drops to a gauze mask and hold it over the patient's nose and mouth until they sink into unconsciousness. Revival takes place spontaneously a few minutes after removing it. Which makes what follows all the more inexplicable.

Since my reputation's at stake, I decide to do as professional a job of the amputation as possible, beginning with a carefully bevelled incision to disarticulate the selected joint about four inches from the tail bone. I also leave a neatly tailored flap of skin to sew over the stump once completed. All proceeds smoothly and with the Schnapps warming my stomach I soon start to relax.

'Do you know,' I muse, 'the last time I did an amputation was at the Schoonoord with dear old Cliff. We couldn't find a proper saw, so used a blade from an escape—'

'Dan, there's no blood.'

'What's that, old man?'

'Blood. At the stump. There should be. But there is none.'

Quick as a flash he pulls out a stethoscope and begins searching the animal's ribs. An anxious ten seconds passes.

'Erik, don't tell me...'

'Quick, try heart massage!'

I fumble frantically at the pup's chest while Erik, to his credit, seals his mouth over its muzzle and puffs into its lungs. But it's hopeless and after a minute or two the awful truth dawns.

'What could have happened?'

'I don't know! Allergic reaction perhaps, or weak heart, shock, who knows?'

'Jesus! Are you sure?'

'Dan. The dog is dead.'

'What the hell do we tell Vorst?'

'Nothing.' He stares at me over the table. 'We tell him nothing, except the operation has been a complete success.'

'What! But—'

And the escape plan quickly unfolds. But to have the slightest chance of success, we know it needs co-conspirators, so within minutes Fenton and Pugh are forcibly recruited.

'Poor little bugger,' Pugh says, staring down at the corpse.

'Where's Vorst?'

'Home for the night.'

'He'll go stark staring mad!'

'Thank you, Fenton, we're aware of that. But he won't if we keep calm.'

Heavy footsteps are heard on the stair, a moment later Prien walks in looking suspicious. 'You asked to see me?' he says in German. Then spots the dog. '*Mein Gott, was ist das!*'

Erik does the talking; his German is best. He tells Prien in plain terms that he is part of a conspiracy, like it or not, and has two choices. Either he can report the puppy's death to Vorst, whereupon life will become a living hell for everyone at the *Revier* – including him. Or he can do exactly as he's told, and all will be well.

'Don't tell him!' Prien pleads wisely. A few minutes later he's downstairs on the phone, informing Vorst the operation's a complete success and the puppy recovering nicely. The doctors, however, want the dog to rest undisturbed for twenty-four hours, and therefore suggest the *Oberstabsarzt* collect him tomorrow evening. Vorst agrees, we breathe a sigh of relief, I complete the docking operation, we tuck the dog up in its cardboard box, and after another anxious Schnapps or two we all retire to bed.

The next morning passes in a blur of nervous hyperactivity. Vorst drops in for morning sick parade full of bonhomie and we, somehow controlling our stage fright, duly swing into action: me and Erik recounting the successful procedure, Fenton and Pugh laughing about the pup's boisterousness, and Prien earnestly reassuring him all is well. Vorst makes no request to see the animal, tells us how very grateful he is, then slips off to celebrate with his girlfriend.

More collective sighs of relief, and we try to get on with our work. Then halfway through lunch a message comes saying someone is asking for me downstairs. Erik and I exchange wide-eyed stares. By now I'm so paranoid I can only assume it's the police or Gestapo or someone come to drag me off. Consequently, and understandably perhaps, particularly as I have a slight hangover, the significance of the visit eludes me at first. Nor do I recognize the visitor's face.

It is a major of the German army. Looking in a bad way. His uniform is torn and stained, his boots are filthy, dried mud clings to his greatcoat, his face looks pinched and fatigued, with one cheek swollen and peppered with bloody scabs. Finally his left arm hangs in a filthy sling. As I approach I smell the smoke and mud and cordite on him, am immediately transported back to the fighting at Oosterbeek, and know this man has come from the field of battle.

'Herr Doctor Garland,' he says in English.

'You know my name?'

'It is... I am Brandt. Gerhardt Brandt. Husband of Inge Brandt.'

Seconds tick. 'My God, Brandt, yes! From the train.'

'The train, yes.'

'You are injured. You have come for medical attention?'

'No...'

'No? But then, Inge, I mean your wife, I heard she was arrested or something – is she all right?'

'Yes, but she...' He looks warily about. Prien's hovering nearby, and the *Sanitäter* also, slowly mopping the floor. 'Is there somewhere private?'

He follows me up to the treatment room.

'How old is this?' I ask, sniffing at the dressing on his arm.

'Four days. It is from a mortar shell.'

'Then it's high time it was changed. Your face too could do with attention. And I'll give you something for the pain.'

'No morphine. The others have none; I will go without also.'

'Others?'

'At the front. Where I must return.'

I start unwrapping the bandage. 'And where is that?' I ask innocently.

'Everywhere: Italy, Poland, France, the Baltic. But for me, Wiesbaden. British and American forces are at the Rhine. Our orders are to stop them coming across.'

'Wiesbaden? But that's...'

'Not so far from here. Two hundred kilometres maybe. But the Allies over-reach themselves, Doctor, I'm afraid your relief is many weeks away, maybe months.'

The bandage comes off to reveal a dark and suppurating wound above the elbow. He makes no sound but looks away as I gently pull away the dressing, flush the wound clean, debride as best I can, dust with sulphanilamide powder and begin bandaging up again. 'You were saying about your wife.'

'She is in Munich now. She is as well as can be expected.'

'Was she arrested?'

'They didn't use that word. However, she was transferred. She is now medical officer to the women's section of a camp outside Munich.'

'Camp?'

'It is called Dachau. Like the one she showed you near Bergen.'

'But that's a dreadful place! And there are no medical services there. Only what she could smuggle through the wire!'

'The role is merely a title. She also attends to the camp administration staff, and the guards and so on.' He shakes his head. 'The posting is a demotion, her life there is bad, her skills are wasted. It is punishment for her misuse of Wehrmacht supplies.'

'My God. I'm so sorry.'

'It was her choice. She bears no ill will.'

'Please send her my best wishes, if you are able.'

'Yes. I will. Thank you.'

Silence descends. Having finished the arm dressing, I turn to the blast injuries on his cheek. Swabbing with lint, I think back to that day in Bergen, and how she questioned me so closely before taking me to the Belsen camp. *You are a witness.*

'But that is not why I am here.'

I'm inches from his face, tweezers in hand, preparing to pick grit from his flesh. His left eye is badly bloodshot. 'Excuse me?'

'I am here to pay my respects. To a noble family.'

'I don't understand.'

'In Herrlingen.'

'Herrlingen? Do you mean—'

'Yes. An important event will take place tomorrow. I came to attend it.'

And over the next ten minutes another extraordinary facet of the Rommel story gradually unfolds. Gerhardt Brandt, it emerges, served with him in Africa, as an aide on his personal staff. Working closely together for nearly two years, he came to know his master well, both as a strategist and tactician, but also as a man of integrity and compassion, particularly when it came to his men. 'It was this compassion, this concern for their safety and wellbeing, that earned him their complete respect and loyalty, from the most senior officer to the lowest private.'

'Hmm.' I tease a tiny sliver of steel out with the tweezers.

'But he could be overly forthright with his superiors, among whom he made enemies. And this was unfortunate.'

'I can imagine.'

Early on during his Africa posting, he continues, Gerhardt received word from Inge that she had lost the baby they were expecting. Rommel learned of it too, and even though the Tobruk offensive was in full swing, insisted Gerhardt return to Germany to be with her. 'He arranged for flowers, and my transportation, everything.' And Lucie, it transpired, even travelled to Bergen to offer Inge her sympathies and support.

'I never encountered such a thing in twenty years of military service,' he murmurs. 'The German army is founded on order, discipline and... restraint of emotion. Especially compassion, which is seen as a weakness. But he believed it a strength in a leader. Many experienced it, especially those closest to him. I believe you met some?'

The officers in the car on my first visit, I presume. And the captain on my second.

'We are few now, and widely scattered, but glad to come on these important occasions, when we can, and pay our respects one final time.'

'One final... What do you mean?'

'And I am here to invite you to come also.'

Vorst, we are informed, will be arriving this evening at eight to collect his girlfriend's puppy. In the meantime, Erik emphasizes, we must carry on exactly as normal, so as not to arouse suspicion. This means maintaining scheduled visits to outlying clinics during the afternoons, so, having seen Brandt out, I finish lunch, smoke a hurried pipe, don my beret and scorched French greatcoat, collect my tram money from Prien and step outside into the spring-like sunshine.

The smell is of brick dust, ash and mud. Ulm is still Ulm, yet so fundamentally altered from the city I arrived in during January that it might as well be Timbuktu. A sad and battered husk: walking through it is like walking through a bad dream. The worst of the winter has passed, leaving only a few grimy heaps of slush at the roadside; the air feels keen and mild, the trees are budding, and crocuses poke up hopefully in gardens. Where there are still gardens, that is, because for the most part, especially the old quarter around the minster, Ulm is completely obliterated. Barely a single building stands undamaged. Where one does stand, its windows gone, its masonry blackened, you clamber round the back to find only the façade, like the set of a western movie. Or you might come across a chimney poking skyward, complete with chimney pot, fireplace and hearth, but no home around it. Or in some places, whole blocks have been completely flattened, leaving only rubble, with a square of road neatly cleared around it, like the frame of some grotesque artwork.

As has become my habit since the firestorm, I pick my way through to the minster's entrance, and wander inside its dim interior to sit for a few minutes. I'm not a church-goer, nor much given to contemplation, nor do I know the first thing about

Gothic architecture, but I do find this stubborn old pile with its towering columns and vast arched ceilings oddly comforting. It did after all save my life on the night of the inferno. And as I sit, I hope, if not actually pray, that it goes on surviving, like the last man standing, right through to this war's bloody finish. Whenever that might be.

Brandt's visit, there's no denying, was a shock and a wake-up call. We know the war will finish: the evidence is all around us. The silver formations pass overhead almost daily, German infrastructure is collapsing, and the Allies are closing in on all sides. As he says, our relief is a matter of weeks away, a month or two at most. Yet we've been living in a bubble here in Ulm. Yes, the suffering's terrible, the death and the maiming, the shortages and the destruction. A few blocks away Erik sits in a bombed-out chapel handing out aspirin to people with no homes. Nearby an old man lies dying alone in his bedroom. But it's as though we experience these things in isolation, that there is no existence beyond the city walls, no bigger picture. Then one day a warrior comes in from the outside, bloody, wounded and reeking of battle, and reminds us there is a whole world of war out there, and we're living in it together. And this puts everything into proper perspective – including the whole Vorst puppy nonsense. 'The bloody dog died, *Oberstabsfart*,' I shall say. 'So what? Thousands die every day thanks to the lunacy of your master. Good men like Gerhardt Brandt who are not just fighting for their lives, but yours, while you sit at home stuffing your face with *Wurst* and screwing your mistress.'

A while later I rise from my pew, leave the minster and head off for the visits. And I don't say it of course, my fantasy speech to Vorst, no matter how much I yearn to. I dutifully go through with the charade, exactly as rehearsed. And save the speech-making for another day.

Back at the *Revier* later I meet up with Erik, we wolf down supper, complete the final ward round, then hurry to the bedsit to prepare. The dog is still in its box. By now rigor mortis has been and gone, leaving a flaccid cadaver but cold. Using bottles of hot water and blankets we begin warming it up, meanwhile 'dressing the set' by placing a food bowl complete with food scraps, water, and – a nice touch of Erik's – a rolled-up sock as a toy. Soon the 'extras' arrive in the form of Fenton and Pugh. Pugh, who seems to be embracing the role rather too enthusiastically, has even made a little collar for the dog and a nameplate for the box bearing the title 'Monty'.

'Pugh, are you mad?'

'No, Doc! Trust me, it'll work.'

Ten minutes before curtain-up, Prien appears, surveys the set with a sickly nod, then takes up position at the top of the stairs. Then we all wait.

With Teutonic precision the front door opens at eight, and we hear feet marching towards Vorst's office. Prien, whose pallor is sickly white, then charges headlong downstairs.

'*Oberstabsarzt! Oberstabsarzt, komm Sie schnell!*'

'*Was?*'

'Come quickly. The little dog, he is unwell!'

Hurried footsteps on the stair; enter Vorst followed by Prien. The scene that greets him is high melodrama. Centre stage two doctors struggle heroically to save the little dog that has just collapsed. One performs heart massage, the other searches for life signs with his stethoscope. To one side two orderlies, hands wringing, watch in dismay. As the seconds tick, one of them (to my horror) throws his arms around the other and sobs 'Monty!'

'*Mein Gott!*' Vorst looks aghast. 'What happened?'

'We don't know, *Herr Oberstabsarzt*. He was fine, as you know, happily playing and eating all day. Then a few minutes ago, a sudden seizure.'

'His heart perhaps,' I add, 'or maybe a cerebral haemorrhage.'

'But this is terrible.'

We stop resuscitating. 'We're so sorry...'

'*Ist er tot?*'

'I'm afraid so, *Herr Oberstabsarzt*. We have tried everything.'

'A genetic defect possibly,' I offer, knowing this to be a Nazi fixation.

Pugh's hand smacks his brow. 'No, Monty, NO!'

This is too much. Erik swiftly steps in. 'Excuse the orderly, *Herr Oberstabsarzt*. He has become so fond of the little fellow. You know the British and their dogs.'

'Monty?' Vorst stares at the box. 'You named him Monty?'

'Er, well, the orderly, you see...'

Then he sniffs. And his face falls. And a handkerchief appears, and there's loud trumpeting as he blows his nose. '*Monty, lieber Monty.*'

Ten minutes later he's gone, Monty's in the cellar awaiting burial, and we've all collapsed into chairs for post-performance reviews and much-needed Schnapps. Pugh wins best actor hands down, Vorst gets a special mention for realism, and we're all so exhausted and relieved we even give Prien a tot.

The next day is Sunday. Not entirely a day of rest: we must still maintain *Revier* routine, which means ward rounds, treating the bed-bound, writing up case notes, and domestic chores like washing clothes and tidying the bedsit. Normally by noon, however, unless forfeited by punishment, the day is ours and we may venture out. This might involve church for the devout, or a walk beside the river, or even a beer in a tavern – reminiscent of Stalag 357. Today, however, I have a date with Trudi.

How this arose is not entirely straightforward. Two days after the firestorm I felt a strong urge to seek her out. Just to check she was all right, I told myself, but in truth to assess my feelings for her, which were conflicted. That dreadful night in the shelter will be forever seared in memory as the worst of my life – much worse even than the Schoonoord. Yet also one of the most emotionally charged, for enduring it with Trudi clutched in my arms undoubtedly forged something intimate between us, like a bond. But is it an appropriate bond? I worried. Is it even real? The truth is I didn't know, but needed to. So I set off to find her. The tram services were all disrupted following the raid – in some places steel rails had literally buckled in the heat – so I walked out along her route, past the burned-out hulk of the old tram, until eventually her replacement appeared and I jumped aboard. And from the moment I saw her I had my answer. 'Yes, I'm fine,' she said, holding my gaze. 'Would you like to meet my mother?' 'I'd be delighted,' I replied. And that was that.

Which all seemed fine and proper, until I mentioned it to Erik.

'You can't,' he said. 'It wouldn't be right.'

'Why not?'

'Because she's the enemy.'

'No she isn't, she's a civilian clippie on a tram.'

'She is German. You're entering into a relationship with an enemy national.'

'Who said anything about a relationship? We're barely friends.'

'Dan.' He shook his head. 'Let us not pretend.'

'I'm not! And anyway what about the drop-in? They're Germans too.'

'They are not our friends. Our dealings with them are strictly professional.'

'Now who's pretending? I've seen how much you care for them!'

Setting out in my clean uniform and shining boots, I make my way down to the Danube and over the bridge to Neu-Ulm. Trudi and her mother live a short walk from the bridge, near a modern-looking library. Their building too looks recent, comprising several apartments in a four-storey block. In the lobby I look for the name Eichel, climb to the third floor and knock.

It's the first time I've seen her out of uniform. She looks even smaller, trim and elfin in cream lace blouse and wool skirt. Her hair is down, and brushed back into a clasp; her brown shoes are polished; she smells of lavender water.

'Hello, Trudi.'

'Hello, Daniel, please come in.'

Frau Eichel is seated in a small, spotlessly tidy lounge furnished with dark wooden furniture in the Bavarian style. Slight and spare like her daughter, she too has put on her Sunday best, but is obviously uneasy about this meeting. As too am I becoming. Especially when she flinches at the sight of my uniform.

'Good afternoon, madam,' I say in my best German. 'I am Daniel Garland.'

'Thank you for the tablets.'

This she was nagged to say by Trudi, I sense.

'You are most welcome. I hope the rheumatism is improving.'

She inclines her head but says no more.

'Oh, and I have brought... something.' I produce my gifts, a bunch of narcissus picked from the *Revier*'s garden, and a packet of Peak Frean biscuits courtesy of the Red Cross. Even these I agonized over: too much generosity would seem boastful, too little would be an insult. Custard Creams hopefully will strike the right note.

Trudi brings glasses of something dark and sticky which could be sherry, and we sit in a stiff circle sipping politely and trying to make German conversation.

'*Mutti* was asking where you come from in England.'

'Oh, er, London. I live south of the river. Rather like you do here!'

Silence.

'*Mutti* has not been to London.'

'Ah.'

'She has been to Easter-born. On holiday as a child.'

'Easter... oh, yes, Eastbourne.'

'You know it?'

'Not at all.'

'Oh.'

'Although I hear it's nice.'

And so forth. Their third-floor window has rather a pleasant view to the river, and I'm on the point of commenting on it when I glance beyond and see smoke still rising from the ruined old quarter and think better of it. In fact I'm thinking better of the whole visit, which now seems wrong in so many ways. Meanwhile *Mutti* is scrutinizing my uniform and whispering to her daughter again.

'She asks the significance of the patch on your shoulder.'

'This? Well, it's the insignia of the 1st Airborne Division, which is the unit I served with at the battle of, er, never mind. It features the Greek hero Bellerophon riding Pegasus the winged horse to battle. Hence the aerial, er, connotation.'

Aerial connotation comes out as '*Himmel Stelle*' which translates as 'sky thing' or something, but apparently she gets the gist.

Mutti nods and whispers again.

'She asks what battle?'

'Ah, well, it's Homer you see. Bellerophon was sent on an impossible mission to kill a terrible monster called the Chimera. This monster, inhuman in form and rarely seen, held nations in terror and could kill with the power of its roar. Nobody dared confront it for fear of a terrible death, but Bellerophon saw it might be slain if attacked from the air. For that he needed Pegasus, the flying horse, whom he captured while it drank at a spring. In time and after many adventures, he and Pegasus tracked the monster to its mountain lair and killed it by thrusting a capsule of lead into its throat. It suffocated to death. *Und das was das!*'

Silence descends. The women blink. I swig sherry, exhausted by the effort of translating the longest and most technically difficult tract I have ever attempted. Eventually *Mutti* leans once more to her daughter.

'She doesn't mean *that* battle,' Trudi says. 'She means the battle *you* were in.'

The Rommel family car picks me up from the *Revier* that evening at six. Strictly speaking I'm not allowed out after sunset, but Vorst as usual is absent on Sundays, and when I tell Prien I'm attending the lady patient in Herrlingen, he just nods and waves in dismissal.

Arriving at the house ten minutes later I see quite a gathering of cars parked outside. A servant in gloves opens the front door for me, and I enter the hallway, which is dimly lit only with candles. As my eyes adjust to the gloom I see perhaps thirty people standing about, many of them in uniform. They're talking in unusually subdued voices, and their expressions are unvaryingly solemn. I recognize one of the two majors from my first visit, and the captain from my second, and also Brandt, who comes over.

'Hello, Doctor, it is good that you are here.'

I nod at all the uniforms. 'If a little odd perhaps, for a lone British officer. I feel like a lamb among wolves.'

'Foxes perhaps would be a better analogy, as many of us served in the desert. And I can assure you British paratroops are never thought of as lambs.'

'Glad to hear it. How's the arm?'

'Improving, thank you.' He lifts it to show me. Indeed overall he looks much better than yesterday, with the unblemished side of his face clean and shaven, the uniform spotless once more, and the bloody eye clearer.

'When do you go back?' I ask.

'Tonight. After.'

'After?'

'Yes. We are expecting renewed assaults in the morning.'

'Ah. I'd wish you luck, but that would seem...'

'*Heuchlerisch?*'

'Hypocritical, yes. No offence.'

'None taken. Oh, and I have a message from Inge.'

'For me?'

'Yes, we managed to speak earlier. I told her about you; she said she is managing well and not to worry. Also that Aurelia is there.'

'Who's Aurelia?'

'She said you would know.'

'Gut h'evening, Herr Doctor Garland.'

A boy's halting English. I turn; it's Manfred, smiling sheepishly in his Luftwaffe cadet's uniform. It is only weeks since last I saw him, but there is a maturity now: he seems taller and more assured. Beside him stands his half-sister Gertrud, soberly dressed in black. As are all the women, I now note.

'Manfred, hello, young man, I trust you are well?'

'Very well thank you, Doctor.'

'And your mother?'

'A little stronger every time. Thanks to your offices.' He points across the hall to a slight figure surrounded by others. 'She asks me to thank you also for your judgement here tonight.'

'My judgement...'

'Hello again, Doctor.' Gertrud steps forward, one hand extended. Behind her a younger bespectacled man in a suit is hovering, clutching a briefcase. 'May I introduce another of your profession? Doctor Garland, this is Doctor Friedrich Breiderhoff of the reserve military hospital in Ulm.'

Breiderhoff bows, we shake hands, and I'm seriously now wondering what's going on.

I'm about to find out.

'Ladies and gentlemen, may I have your attention!' A senior officer, a colonel at least, has mounted the stairs to address the gathering, now numbering fifty or more, and falling to a respectful hush.

'We have come here tonight to honour our great friend, leader and comrade in arms Generalfeldmarschall Erwin Rommel. And to accompany him on the final part of his journey, to his resting place at the church of Saint Andreas here in Herrlingen...'

A hand grips my arm. 'This way, Doctor,' and before I know it I'm being steered through the throng. Nobody bats an eye; the eulogy goes on. My escorts are the two majors from my first visit. Breiderhoff, I note in my confusion, briefcase in hand, is following behind.

'What the...' I tug at my arm, but the grip just tightens.

'Come with us. Do not be alarmed.'

329

Across the hall we arrive at double doors, which they open to reveal a panelled office or study. Once again the drapes are tightly drawn and the lighting dim. A curious smell – a musty mix of soil and damp, chemicals and wood polish – assaults my senses. Despite this odour, and even with the poor lighting, I realize that we are standing in Erwin Rommel's private study.

Because his coffin is in the middle of the floor.

'Lights, please.' Breiderhoff steps forward and peels off his jacket. One major guards the door while the other throws a switch and suddenly the floor is bathed in white light from a ring of lamps on stands. The coffin, resting on trestles at about thigh height, is draped in the ancient flag of the German army. The second major whips it off to reveal stained and mottled joinery. The lid, I notice immediately, has been loosened.

'Stop!' I raise my hands. 'Stop this, whatever it is. I want no part, and demand to be returned to the *Revier* immediately.'

'In good time, Doctor, I assure you.'

'No, now! I am a British officer and prisoner of war. I have rights and expect to be treated in accordance with proper convention.'

Silence. Then Breiderhoff speaks. 'Will you please just hear me out?'

'No. Return me to the *Revier*.'

Another silence. Then a click, and I find myself gazing into the barrel of a Luger.

'You will hear him out, or by God I will drag you outside and shoot you dead.'

Something about this officer's gaze convinces me. This is no spotty youth hefting a rifle in a POW camp. This man, like

Brandt, is a hardened warrior. He's seen killing and maiming and dying close up, he's lost friends and colleagues, and killed enemies. Killing one more won't daunt him.

'Yes, well.' I clear my throat. 'I'll hear him out, if you insist. Then you will return me to the *Revier*.'

'Thank you, Doctor.' The Luger is lowered; Breiderhoff mops his brow.

The main purpose of tonight's gathering, he then explains, is to move Rommel's coffin from its temporary place of burial in the cemetery at Ulm's military hospital, to its final resting place at Saint Andreas's church, just a short walk from the house here in Herrlingen.

'Why has this taken so long?' I ask.

'A proper and fitting plot had to be found and prepared,' he says. 'Also the necessary authorizations had to be obtained, following the state funeral.'

'Fine. I understand. Is that all?'

It's not, of course. And I can see now he's struggling with his emotions.

'When the Generalfeldmarschall died in October, you see, I was sent from the hospital in Ulm to certify his death. I am not the senior doctor there, in fact I'm rather a junior one. But I was ordered by the director.'

'Wilhelm Vorst.'

'Yes. Anyway, when I arrived here, I was shown to a car parked in the driveway, where I found the Generalfeldmarschall slumped dead in the back seat. Two men, one in plain clothes, the other an officer of the SS, were also in the car. They told me the Generalfeldmarschall had suffered a heart attack whilst out driving with them, and I was to issue a death certificate to that effect. I was not permitted to examine him, nor request an autopsy, which would have been normal in such circumstances.

331

They said the Generalfeldmarschall had been in poor health since being injured in a strafing attack a few months previously, and his death was therefore not unexpected. I was extremely unhappy about this, but it was made clear to me that I must comply or face dire consequences, and so, I'm ashamed to say, I did as ordered.'

'And that is the official version of his death as announced to the German people?'

'Heart attack, yes.'

'What is your version?'

'That he was murdered, or forced to take his own life, by those two men.'

'Really.'

'Yes. And at the request of Frau Rommel and her family, I propose to prove it now, with the senior Allied medical officer for the district present as witness.'

'The what?'

'Doctor. A great injustice has been done. And must be made right. For the sake of the German people. And of history. Germany will soon fall to the Allies. You are their senior medical representative for this district. It is essential that you witness what I am about to do. Which is prove my theory. *Post mortem.*'

'But it's been five months!'

'It won't matter, I assure you. And will take only two or three minutes.'

And before I know it, he turns to his briefcase and begins withdrawing instruments. At the same moment the two majors step forward, slide the coffin lid off and lower it to the floor *'Beeile dich,'* one murmurs. Hurry up. Then the door opens behind me, I glance round and to my horror see Manfred and Gertrud taking up position against the wall. They are holding hands, their faces set. Breiderhoff turns to the coffin. He's wearing a surgeon's light strapped to his head, and holding a large scalpel in one hand and forceps in the other. 'Come, Doctor,' he says and I'm led firmly forward.

The rest proceeds as though in a dream. I've seen enough dead bodies not to be shocked by one more. And after professional embalming and only five months in a good-quality coffin, the human form degrades very little. The eyes and cheeks have sunk, the pallor is a waxy grey, the lips are dark and slightly pulled back, but that's all. And from the set of the nose and chin it is still unmistakably the Erwin Rommel of so many newspaper photos. But degradation aside, trying to establish cause of death on a body five months dead is extremely difficult in any circumstances – assuming death is natural.

'His collar please,' Breiderhoff murmurs and a major steps forward, lifts the Iron Cross from his throat and unbuttons the shirt to expose the neck and chest. With no further ado Breiderhoff, who I sense has been preparing for this moment for months, leans forward and makes a deep incision from the base of the chin vertically down eight inches or more to expose the trachea. He then cuts straight into the oesophagus, opening it over a length of four inches. '*So*,' he says, and despite everything I lean down to look. 'Unnaturally dark, the mucosa, is it not, Doctor?'

'Well...'

'Come closer! What do you smell?'

Embalming fluid, mainly, that overpowering reek of formaldehyde. But then a hint of something else, coming from the open throat. I get even closer, and there it is again. Bitter almonds. Breiderhoff is bent low too, our heads are practically touching; he focuses the light, and reaches down into the oesophagus with the forceps, closes on something, tugs it out with a little

333

difficulty, and lays it on Rommel's chest. Something small and crumpled and metallic.

'Potassium cyanide, Doctor. Also known as the suicide capsule.'

CHAPTER 15

The final part of a journey that began on a beach in Apulia many weeks before got under way for Theo two days after his arrest in Naples. Walter Schöll's headquarters were in Chiaia, an administrative district of the city adjoining Volmero, and it was to there he was driven from the sports stadium, pulling up outside a municipal court building, escorted to the basement and thrown into a crowded cell alongside twenty others. The basement held several cells, in all containing at least a hundred young Italian men arrested during the rioting. All that night they were ignored, denied food or water, while throughout the building were heard shouts, hurrying feet, ringing telephones and the moving of furniture and equipment. Rather than deliberate maltreatment, one rebel speculated, it was almost as though they'd been forgotten, and next morning the ignoring went on, although bread and soup were hurriedly issued and they were allowed to use the bathroom. As the day wore on, through gratings in the walls they could hear the uprising itself reaching a climax, near and far all round the city, with continuous gun and grenade fire, the occasional crump of artillery, rumbling military traffic, and the excited cheers of insurgents running through the streets, mingled with the confused shouts of the Germans. 'The *Tedeschi* are fleeing!' The rumour spread through the basement. 'The Allies have arrived!' went another. 'Schöll's been arrested!' ran a third.

But at dusk the shouts and shooting died out and a tense silence descended on the city. The prisoners waited, fearing the worst; eventually marching feet were heard in the corridor and armed guards appeared, led by an officer.

'What now?' murmured one youth.

'They're going to shoot us all,' replied another.

'Silence!' Keys were produced; the guards began unlocking doors. 'Right, listen, all of you! There's a ceasefire, and an amnesty. You're free to fuck off. But there's still a curfew, so go straight home and don't make any trouble.'

The prisoners hurried to leave the cells, jostling each other excitedly. The guards stood by the doors counting heads; Theo joined the queue leaving his cell, yet already sensing what would happen.

'Not you.' The guard pulled him aside, waited for the cell to empty, then thrust him back inside and locked the door. Within two minutes he was alone in the silent basement. He remained there the rest of the night.

He was roused at dawn, handcuffed, dragged roughly up into the daylight and pushed into the back of a staff car. Two guards sat either side of him. In front was a driver, and the officer he'd surrendered to the day before last.

'What's happening?'

'We're leaving.'

'The Germans are?'

'Too right. Our job is done, the city secure, so we're rejoining the main defence force. Oh, and by the way, *Ho-ratz-io*' – he enunciated the word distastefully – 'you surrendered yourself needlessly! Everyone at the stadium was released this morning as a gesture of goodwill to the citizens of Naples.'

And a bargaining chip to ensure the Germans safe passage, Theo guessed. Soon they joined a slow-moving military convoy snaking its way northward out of the city. The streets were eerily quiet and deserted, with barely a handful of flag-waving demonstrators leaning from windows to cheer the aggressor on his way. Incredibly, he realized, the uprising had succeeded, Schöll and the Germans driven from the city by the will of the Neapolitan people.

'Where are we going?'

'Well, I'm going to Cassino to kill Yanks, wherever that is. You're going to Rome, you lucky fellow.'

'Rome.'

'Apparently we've agreed to let the Blackshirts have first go at you. Damned cheek, I say, but good news for you, no?'

'I doubt it.'

'But yes! It means you'll still be alive when they finish with you. So our boys can have their turn.'

The journey was long and tedious, the roads chaotic and frequently blocked. For a while he dozed, waking later to find the officer and one guard disembarking to another vehicle, leaving him with only the driver and second guard. At the next traffic jam he slid nearer the door and discreetly tried the handle, but it was disconnected from the inside. The guard winked, grinning at him knowingly, and tapped the Schmeisser resting on his knee. Another hour went by; the guard produced a bag containing black bread and stale sausage, which Theo forced down with water from a canteen – the first food he'd eaten since his arrest. Afterwards he was ejected at gunpoint, still handcuffed, and told to relieve himself at the roadside. In the afternoon rain began to fall and his view of the world shrank to blurred streaks on a grimy window, and black sky beyond the hypnotic rocking of the windscreen wipers. Finally they arrived at Rome's southern outskirts, crawled their way to the centre and pulled up, to his astonishment, outside Regina Coeli prison.

The entrance was as he remembered, but once inside he was led to a holding cell where he was stripped, his clothes taken, his body searched, and he was issued with pyjama-type prison garb and espadrille sandals. He was then escorted to the basement and a long corridor of steel-doored cells. Halfway along, one door was opened and he was thrust inside.

His cell was small and windowless, about eight feet square with a low ceiling, a single overhead bulb, a palliasse and a bucket. The door was heavy steel, locked and bolted with only a small peephole and sliding hatch for food. Nobody came to him that evening except an elderly *custode* who shoved bread and watery pasta through the hatch. '*Grazie, mi amico*,' he tried, but received only a grunt in reply. An hour or so later the overhead light went off, plunging him into smothering darkness.

The next morning the *custode* was back with ersatz coffee and dried biscuit, but before Theo could consume it, boots were heard outside, the bolt drawn and two guards dragged him out. A vicious beating then occurred right there in the corridor, so sudden and forceful several seconds elapsed before he realized what was happening. Kicked to the floor, a hail of blows fell on his head and back from baton-like sticks, while their boots went for his ribs. Numb with shock and pain, he could only hunch forward, protect himself as best he could, and wait for it to end.

Which it did as abruptly as it began. He was then hauled to his feet and frog-marched along the corridor to a smoke-filled office. There he was pushed into a chair before two officers of the Guardia Nazionale Repubblicana, the new name for the Blackshirt militia. Both men – middle-aged, overweight, cigarette-smoking – were dressed according to their unit, complete with new insignia. But shabbily so, as though they and their uniforms had seen better times.

'The *confessione* is drawn up,' one said, pushing a paper across the desk. 'You just sign it, here and here, and we're all done.'

Theo rubbed his bruised neck. 'Done?'

'Yes, done! Do you want another beating?'

'No.'

'Then sign. And we can all be on our way.'

'What is it?'

'I told you: it's a confession. You sign, and our work's finished. In due course you get sentenced to death and that's that.'

'The Germans won't be happy. They want to question me.'

'Fuck the Germans.'

'But the GNR's part of the new regime, isn't it? In support of Germany.'

'I know what it bloody is! Now will you sign the damn confession!'

'What am I confessing to?'

'Oh, for God's sake!' Stubbing out his cigarette, the second man opened a file. 'Have you not already told the Germans you are the Campanian partisan leader known as Horatio?'

'Yes.'

'Are you not also the same Horatio more properly known as Andreas Ladurner, who led an assassination attempt on Senator Ettore Tolomei in forty-one?'

'Forty-one... That's a while ago.'

'Were you?'

He looked them both in the eye. 'Not necessarily.'

The second beating was much worse. It took place there in the office, the two Blackshirts watching and smoking in bored silence as the guards set about with sticks and boots once more. This time there was less haste, and more thoroughness. While he tried to retain a foetal position to protect himself, one guard

339

would prise him straight to kick his stomach and ribs while the other assaulted his head and back with the stick. Delay, defend, disconnect, his SOE instructor had lectured back in Cairo. Delay the attack by any means you can, argue with them, keep them talking, keep them guessing. Meanwhile get ready to defend yourself, prepare and compose your mind for what's coming. Then when it starts, disconnect from it, think about something else, a special memory perhaps, or the view through the window, or simply a smudge on the wall. Seize on it and focus on nothing else until the business ends. Theo tried. From his curled position on the floor he could see the officers' boots; he tried to focus on these, the worn tread, the hanging lace, the splitting sole, but the beating went on too long, his mind kept wondering at the unreality of it, and the harm being done to him, and all the while he could feel his resilience faltering, and his will to resist ebbing like a tide. Then suddenly a boot hit his temple and he reeled into unconsciousness.

When he came to he was back in his cell, his face sticky with blood, ears ringing and heart pounding. Dizzy and gasping he crawled to the palliasse and collapsed on to his back, gazing up at the overhead bulb through a tear-filled blur.

A pattern evolved. Twice a day, usually once in the morning and again late in the afternoon, the door-bolt banged and the two heavies fetched him from his cell, dragged him along the corridor to the smoky office and presented him before the Blackshirts to sign his confession. He delayed this by trying to engage them in discussion, asking them about the new regime, about the changing role of the Blackshirts, or about the war in general. Sometimes they obliged, cheerfully complaining about their working conditions or unfair treatment by superiors, and he soon learned they were uninterested in their work and disgruntled with their lot. They didn't even want information from him, never once asking about the San Felices, or the Naples uprising, or even the Tolomei operation of 1941. They had an open dossier on their desk, all that mattered was closing it, and to do this they must get him to sign the confession.

And beating him was their one tool for achieving this. So at some point during the session, perhaps after a few minutes, usually much less, the talking stopped and the heavies went to work. They liked to surprise him, dragging him suddenly from the chair and felling him with punches before commencing the main assault. Then, working together or taking turns, they set to, methodically beating, kicking and punching, sometimes concentrating on his lower body and legs, at others the head or back. Mostly they used the stave-like sticks but sometimes other weapons appeared. Once they brought lengths of insulated cable, another time chair legs, one day it was bamboo canes which raised bloody welts on his back and thighs. They broke his teeth, and his ribs; he sensed damage to his internal organs, and he frequently lost consciousness, spiralling into the welcome oblivion, only to be wrenched back to awareness by a bucket of water, drenched in his own sweat and blood.

Gradually his strength faded. Between bouts he rested, drank water, ate what appeared through the hatch, and tended his injuries as best he could. But as his body weakened, so too did his resolve. He could feel it, slipping like sand through his fingers. One day soon, he knew he would sign the confession. And the beatings would stop. An option which became ever more logical. To counter the temptation he lay on the palliasse reliving adventures from his childhood, or imagining one of Eleni's special meals in Kingston. Or recalling an evening with Clare in Algiers. Anything to take his mind off the misery, and fend off the dreaded sliding of the bolt. And he listened at the door, for hours, trying to catch sounds from the outside, to learn

341

something of his surroundings, his neighbours, or of news from beyond the corridor. For which his one source was the elderly *custode*, whom he never saw but only heard.

'Still here, then.' A cackling laugh would come through the hatch.

Theo shuffled over. 'Yes, still here. Thanks for the soup.'

'It's slop but what do you expect?'

'Nothing.'

'Hardly anyone left here, that's why.'

'Left?'

'Since the new bosses. Word is they might close the place.'

'What about upstairs? The political prisoners. Like Lucetti?'

'Lucetti long gone, son. All the politicos have.'

'Gone where?'

'Christ knows. Up north, I suppose. Some got released, I heard.'

'Is that why it's so quiet here?'

But the *custode* had already gone.

One evening a week later, he awoke to the harsh sliding of the bolt, and in an instant of clarity knew he was finished with the beatings. Tonight he would sign the confession. But when the door opened, it wasn't the heavies waiting in the corridor as usual, but one of the Blackshirts.

So much the better. 'I've made a decision,' he mumbled groggily.

'Too late, shit-head. The Gestapo are here.'

He was taken upstairs to the holding area. Two men waited, wearing suits and raincoats.

'Clean him up, for Christ's sake!' one of them scolded in German.

The handcuffs were removed, he was shown to a washroom, doused under a cold shower, and given a face cloth, soap and a razor to shave. When he emerged his old clothes were waiting on a chair, and a packet of sandwiches, which he guessed was from the *custode*.

They led him outside. Night had fallen. The sudden chill made him dizzy; overhead the stars shone brightly above the blacked-out city. A car waited.

'In the back.'

'Where are we going?'

'A long way.'

'Where?'

'No talking.'

They set off into the night, a driver, one passenger in front, the other in the back beside him. The shock of the cold, and the shower, and the suddenness of the departure disoriented him; for a long time he stared sightlessly into the night, hugging himself, his battered body rocking to the unaccustomed motion. On his knee lay the *custode*'s packet of food. He smelled cheese and garlic, and felt hunger, so took a sandwich from the bag, opened his split and bloody lips and took a cautious bite.

Then he slept, lulled by the motion, the mesmeric rumble of the engine and the sweeping beam of the headlights. Checkpoints came and went. At one stage they refuelled at a floodlit depot, at another they pulled in for the driver to sleep for an hour. Nobody spoke to Theo; they conversed with each other, murmuring the unfamiliar German vowels in low tones. Grateful for the respite, he dozed, or stared through the window and said nothing. From the stars he knew they were travelling north. Early in the pre-dawn mist they traversed a mountain pass with snow-capped peaks to either side, which he sensed was Tuscan, before descending again to a broad plain of olive groves, woodland

and corn stubble. Then the sun began to rise to their right, and something primal stirred within him.

'*Entschuldigen Sie?*' he asked. 'Excuse me. But where are we?'

The man in front turned and nodded to the second, who produced a folded cloth from a pocket. A moment later the orange ball of the sun was abruptly cut off as the hood was pulled over his head.

'We said no talking. This is your last warning.'

An hour later the car pulled up. From the sounds he guessed they were in a town or city – he heard traffic, talking voices and a dog barking – then he was led up steps and into a building. Echoing footsteps suggested a stone or marble hallway. He heard a telephone and typing, then was pushed through a door and down stairs to a cellar or basement. Here it was very quiet, their footsteps muffled by carpet. He was pulled to a halt, keys were inserted in a door, he was pushed two steps in, and the door banged shut behind.

Gingerly he removed the hood. His new cell was bigger than the last, more resembling a washroom or storeroom than a prison, windowless as before, but harshly lit by a caged bulb, with bright yellow walls, a handbasin, cot-bed with blanket, table and one chair. A picture hung incongruously above the bed, of a camel train plodding across a desert. There was even a square of threadbare carpet on the floor.

He spent all morning waiting. He wasn't shackled, he was wearing his own clothes, he had a chair to sit on or a bed for lying. He tried the washbasin but the tap was disconnected. No one came and no sounds were heard, even when he pressed his ear to the door. It was as though nothing existed beyond the walls of the room. With no wristwatch and no outside cues, marking the passage of time was a matter of guesswork. Eventually, hours later, he lay down on the cot and closed his eyes.

Whereupon a voice was heard.

'*Augenbinde auf.*'

He sat up. The voice sounded electrified, as though through a loudspeaker, but he couldn't tell from where. A moment later it came again.

'*Augenbinde auf!*'

Blindfold on. Hastily he gathered the hood and pulled it over his head. Seconds later the door opened.

'Keep it on,' a voice instructed in German. 'It is the one rule. If you break it, punishment will be severe. Do you understand?'

'Yes.'

'Food will be brought in due course. Afterwards there will be questioning. You should stay alert and prepare yourself.'

And with that the door clicked shut. He waited, heart pounding, then removed the hood. Everything was as before, as though the visit had been an illusion. He rose from the bed, massaging his bruised ribs. Delay, defend, disconnect. Somehow, he felt this would not be as straightforward as in Rome.

The day dragged on; as it did he grew tenser and more restive. Food did come, potato soup with black bread, brought by hands unseen through the blindfold. But he was too keyed-up to eat. He tried lying down, but was nervous and restless, and the bulb in its wire cage shone too brightly, pulsating against the lurid yellow walls. So he took to pacing, measuring ten steps across the floor and ten steps back, counting them like the seconds of a ticking clock until he lost track. Finally, hours later, sitting in the chair with his head drooping, the voice came again.

'*Augenbinde auf.*'

Relieved to be active at last, he swiftly donned the hood and waited at the door. For a long time. Nothing happened, for perhaps an hour, then suddenly it squeaked open, an arm took

345

his, leading him a short distance into another room, where he was lowered on to a chair.

'Wait here, take the hood off,' his escort said, closing the door.

The room was office-like, windowless again but with metal desk and chairs, a filing cabinet and large wooden cupboard. Paper and pens lay ready on the desk; a 1943 calendar hung on the wall. He tried to remember the date, then realized he had no idea. Late autumn, possibly early November, was the best he could imagine.

Thirty minutes passed, an hour. The door opened a crack: 'There is some delay, you are to wait here,' then closed again. Delay, defend, disconnect: it seemed they were managing the 'delay' for him, which was almost amusing. But then not. Another hour dragged by, his body oscillating from nervous tension to drooping fatigue. And it seemed every time his eyes fluttered, the door would open behind and the voice tell him to stay alert as the questioning would begin soon. 'Then do it!' he wanted to shout. 'Come and do it, I'm ready!'

'*Augenbinde auf.*'

'What? But—'

'No talking! Put the hood on. There has been a delay. You are to return to your room. The questioning will begin in a short while.'

Only gradually did he realize what was happening. But by then it was already too late. There was no day and no night in his cell. Meals appeared randomly; their content gave no clue to time. The room was noise-proofed, and specially designed to unsettle him, with its harsh electric light, fluorescent walls and bizarre picture of camels. At some stage he wrenched it from the wall and threw it under the bed. Behind it was a steel grille housing the loudspeaker, but the grille was solid, and he couldn't get at the speaker. Sometimes music blared from it, sometimes a high-pitched whistling, or a hissing noise like breaking surf. Sometimes it was silent for hours and he would stare at it from the bed, daring it to crackle to life. Often it voiced its two-word command, 'Blindfold on', and he would stand by the door, waiting to be taken for questioning that never happened.

Then one day it did happen. By now almost incoherent with sleeplessness, and plagued by fantasies and hallucinations, the command came through the loudspeaker, he fumbled for the hood, and when he took it off he was seated before a slender man in jacket and tie, with spectacles, swept-back hair and a business-like demeanour. He didn't look up, he said nothing, but jotted notes into a file.

Several minutes passed. Then at last the questioning began. 'Full name.'

He opened his mouth, but no words came. He tried again, clearing his throat gruffly. 'Lad-ur-ner. Andreas.'

'Not that name. British-registered name. Hurry up.'

'Oh. Trickey. Theodor Victor.'

'Rank and service number.'

'Private. 71076.'

'Wrong. You are a second lieutenant. Don't make this worse for yourself.'

'Yes. That's true. But, only acting second...'

'Unit.'

The pen was poised, waiting. The fingers holding it were slender and white. He was left-handed, Theo noted. 'Ah... I don't have to—'

'Tell me your unit or there will be suffering.'

'I don't care.'

'Guard!'

The door flew open, the hood went on, he was dragged to his feet, hauled along the corridor, and into another room. The hood came off, he was staring at a man, more a youth, eighteen or nineteen, with dark dishevelled hair, poor clothes, bare feet with grime-stained toes. His eyes were wide and terrified. He was strapped into a chair, arms and legs bound. Another man, broad and bald with rolled-up shirtsleeves and braces, was crouched beside him, grasping one of the youth's fingernails with pliers.

'Unit!'

Theo's head reeled. To one side stood a bed-like bench with manacles for wrists and ankles. Beneath it were lorry batteries with wires leading to a box and electrodes. Buckets of water and lengths of hose lined the wall; steel hooks hung from the ceiling. The room reeked of sweat and urine.

'But...'

The officer nodded.

'Wait! The... the 2/6th Territorials East Surreys!'

The nail tore from the finger with a rasping sound, the youth's scream, head back, mouth agape, was an animal shriek. Theo closed his eyes and the room swam, his legs buckling. Rough hands pulled him up, when he looked once more, the youth was staring at him, sobbing pitifully, his tear-filled eyes round and pleading, while blood dripped from his finger to the floor.

'Unit. In full.'

'2nd Battalion, 1st Parachute Brigade, 1st Airborne Division.'

Back in the first room the questioning went on.

'Where are they now? Your unit.'

'I don't know.'

'Guard!'

'I don't! I... I think they were in Taranto.'

'Who is divisional commander.'

'General Browning. No, General Down, I think.'

'So who is Massingham?'

'What?'

'You heard. Who or what is Massingham!'

'I don't know.'

'Guard!'

'I don't! For God's sake...'

Entering the second room the youth in the chair immediately broke into whimpers, rolling his head from side to side and muttering in Italian.

'*Perdonami*,' Theo pleaded. '*Perdonami, per favore.*'

But the youth only shook his head.

'Massingham?'

'I don't know.'

And the pliers tore, and the youth screamed, and the blood flowed to the floor once more.

Days and nights fused into one, all existence contracting to a single moment that never ended, a waking nightmare of eternally repeating scenes, like a loop of film, running on and on, never changing and never stopping. A revolving drama on three stages: his room, the interview room, the torture room; with three characters: himself, his interrogator and the Italian youth. To stop the torture he must answer the questions; to stop the questions he must endure the pain. He tried with the questions, sometimes truthfully, sometimes not, inventing and dissembling as best he could, but no sooner was one answered than the next immediately followed. And he tried with the pain, sinking to the ground, sobbing and screaming with the youth, as though the torture was his own. Once the hood came off and he was lying on the bench writhing from electric shocks to his hands and feet; another time the wires were fastened to his temples, blasting white bolts through his head until his hair singed and his tongue was bitten through. And in time his mind, distorted by shock and sleeplessness, began to break down and trick him. Was this reality or was it a dream? Was there a boy in the chair or were they different people? And who was lying in the yellow room with the hood over his head? And he began to hear voices. Not just the endlessly repeated questions – tell me about the submarine, who was your handler in Algiers, what weapons do paratroops carry; and not just the voices hiding amid the white noise in the loudspeaker – *Augenbinde auf, Augenbinde aus*, get up, wake up, stay alert, no sleeping – but other voices, coming through the door, as though in argument.

'He is an officer of the British army. He should be treated accordingly.'

'Sorry, Major, he's a spy and saboteur and will get what's coming.'

'Nevertheless the Generalfeldmarschall insists he question the prisoner himself.'

'About what?'

'Classified military matters, nothing to do with the Geheime Staatspolizei.'

'We'll need to see some paperwork.'

'I'll arrange it.'

Then the music was blaring from the speaker again, and his arms clamped over his ears, and he rolled on his side with his knees drawn to his chin like a child.

A long period of darkness followed. Darkness and silence except for the roaring in his head. He was on a different bed, in a different room, with no yellow walls or bright lights in cages, and no loudspeaker. But with a pillow, plump and warm, that cradled his head like soft hands. That was all he knew, except that from time to time a figure in white appeared, speaking in low tones, and tended his wounds, or tipped a mug to his lips, or led him to the bathroom and back. Was it another dream? He was not asleep, he felt, nor was he awake. He simply *was*. Suspended between states like a chrysalis on a thread.

He heard a tinkling sound, and opened his eyes. No soft figure in white this time, but a man in a grey uniform, sitting beside him in a high-backed chair. One leg resting comfortably over the other, he was drinking from a china cup and saucer, delicately, with the finger crooked as though at a tea party. He looked about fifty.

'Ah. There you are, *Junge*. And feeling a little better, I trust.'

'I...'

'Don't speak. Rest for now.'

He closed his eyes, nodding, and sank back into the pillow. When he awoke later, night had fallen, and the man was there once more.

'Back again?' The man smiled. 'How do you feel now?'

A single sob rose from deep in his chest. He buried his face in the pillow.

'It's all right, *Junge*.' A hand rested on his shoulder. '*Alles ist in Ordnung.*'

Silence for a while. The click of a cigarette case, then the rasp of a lighter.

'Do you know, the first time I saw you, I said to myself, now here's a young fellow with potential.'

That voice. *You must decide, Theodor.*

'All that is needed is a guiding hand, and he'll go far.'

I can't decide.

'The Hitlerjugend games in Mittenwald it was, nineteen thirty-six. I remember it like it was yesterday.'

Who the hell was that?

Rommel, you idiot.

'I was sacked shortly after those games, did you know? From my job as military attaché to the Hitlerjugend. I felt greater emphasis should be placed on fitness and education than on political indoctrination.'

A sigh of exhaling smoke.

'But my superiors didn't agree.'

Bolts of lightning exploding between his temples. Inexpressible pain at the tips of his fingers. All because of some *thing* he knows.

'Which has unfortunately become a recurring theme of late.'

Something urgent, something imperative.

'But enough of that. Here we are again, we two, in Salo this time, which is presently our headquarters, yet in your part of the world, ironically. And a few days ago it came to my attention that a young British South Tyrolean was being held here for questioning.'

A word. A message. Like a weapon.

'Using the code name Horatio, and I thought to myself, surely it cannot be the same boy whom I last saw outside the opera in Rome. And before that beside the harbour at Saint-Valery-en-Caux. And before that at the games in Mittenwald. And so I made enquiries and—'

'Move them!' He sat up, seizing the man's arm, his eyes wide with panic. 'You must move them now!'

'Move who?'

'Wife. Family. You must get them away from Neustadt. Now! Today!'

'But why?

'Because it's to be destroyed. Because of Crossbow!'

*

Two days later Rommel was back, albeit briefly. He arrived in a state of high agitation, pacing the floor, smoking and shaking his head, and barely acknowledging Theo who remained on his bed unspeaking.

'Mussolini's here, did you know, *verdammt*! Right here in Salo, living in a mansion! Supposedly he heads the new Italian government of the north, but he does nothing! Never lifts a finger, just stuffs his face and whispers in the Führer's ear! I went to see him, you know – oh yes, we had words about Africa, let me tell you! Deceiving bastard, do you know why we lost there? Because of that pig's treachery!'

He stopped pacing suddenly, and wheeled on Theo.

'Loyalty, *Junge*! Loyalty to your country, your people, your leader, your *allies*, these are vitally important matters – especially in war, do you understand?'

Theo said nothing.

'But you know what's most important of all? Loyalty to yourself! Loyalty to your beliefs and convictions, and to what you know is right. Without it you are nothing, I tell you, nothing! Never forget that!'

Their final meeting took place three days later. It was late evening; Theo was in the chair in his bedroom, which was the attic of an imposing town house in the centre of Salo. From the room's shuttered window he could see Lake Garda stretching away to the north, with the snow-capped peaks of the Alps beyond. Trento lay barely forty miles away, his home town of Bolzano less than eighty. Yet he felt no longing, no pull, no desire to be there, and no urge at all to escape. He felt only numbness. He ate, he walked up and down, he lay on the bed and stared at the ceiling. The injuries to his body were beginning to heal, and the bruises to fade. But his mind was a stopped clock, irreparably broken, damaged beyond what mere rest could restore.

'I have better news, *Junge*!' Rommel said, walking through the door. He wore a long leather coat, with gloves and scarf, which he peeled off and flung over a chair. '*Mein Gott*, winter is coming!' He rubbed his hands. 'How you Tyroleans put up with this endless ice I shall never understand!'

He took out the cigarette case and lighter, and seated himself opposite.

'So, anyway, we made some enquiries, arranged a few things, and the long and short of it is you are to be moved.'

Theo's gaze remained on the window.

'Well away from Salo and our Gestapo colleagues, you'll be relieved to hear.'

Though the blackout was strictly in force, tiny pinpricks of light could always be sought out at night, he'd noticed, like fireflies in a forest.

'Your status is changing too, to that of political prisoner, which is somewhat ironic, don't you think! Furthermore, and this is the really good news, you have a place in the political wing of the prison at Trento – a relatively comfortable billet, so I hear, and right in your homeland...'

And on still nights, and clear ones, like this one, he could see the stars reflected in the waters of the lake.

'... where I believe you will find one Josef Ladurner is currently enjoying rather better conditions than he was in Rome.'

The same lake that someone took him to play at once as a child.

'Your grandfather, see? So you will be reunited with family!'

I have no family. '*Ich bin der Welt abhanden gekommen*.'

Rommel drew on his cigarette, studying the young man hunched wordlessly before him. Twenty-one, the file said, but he looked ten years older. And broken, like an abused animal. He leaned forward confidentially.

'I learned of your meeting with von Stauffenberg.'

We fight for a cause, not an ideology.

'At first I thought him a madman. Over-privileged aristocrat with a grudge to bear. But what he says begins to make sense. This war. It has been atrociously mismanaged, you know. Many fine soldiers slaughtered needlessly, and much futile suffering by the German people.'

We fight for our beliefs, not someone's dogma.

'And worse. I told the Führer himself, this business with the Jews has to stop.'

For a people. Not one person.

'Which went down well, as you can imagine.'

Until we are left with just one thing.

'So much so that I'm being demoted – yet again! Can you believe it, that toadying dolt Kesselring is to get the whole of Italy, it seems, which doesn't bode well for the Tyrol. While I'm to be put to work digging trenches in France.'

'*Gewissen.*'

'Defence work, would you believe? Me! Barbed wire, tank traps and pillboxes!' He hesitated. '*Junge*? What did you say?'

Theo's eyes were filling. 'Conscience.'

Silence fell in the room; far out in the lake a ferry sounded its horn. Rommel nodded, stubbing his cigarette. Then leaned forward again.

'I know what it is to reach the end, *Junge*. To be so spent you have nothing left to give. Can't think, or act, or reason, or even get up in the morning. So beaten you no longer care. But this place you go, the Trento prison, it has medical facilities, I hear. With help, and rest, and with your grandfather nearby, remember, in time, you know...'

'I can't see him.'

'Then don't. Until you feel ready.' He rose, and began gathering his coat and gloves. 'And now I must leave. Berlin calls, and it's sure to be bad news. So tomorrow you may go to Trento. Transport is arranged. Your future is in your hands. Good luck, *Junge*, I wish you well.'

'Thank...'

'Thanks are not necessary.' He pulled on his gloves. 'I... ah, I have been in touch with my wife, Lucie, and my children. She has heard of a house, near Ulm in the south. She is going to see it this weekend.'

'Oh.'

He grasped Theo's hand suddenly. 'Goodbye, Horatio. Perhaps we shall meet once more.'

CHAPTER 16

His escorts were not prison guards, nor Gestapo, nor military police, but two regular army corporals – one of them wearing Afrika Korps insignia. Having roused him from sleep with real coffee and *biscotti*, they waited outside his door, chatting and joking, while he rose slowly from bed, ate, washed and dressed. Fresh clothes had been left out for him: a worn but serviceable suit, collarless shirt, sleeveless woollen pullover, and an old overcoat and cap against the cold. Finally beneath the chair he found his LRDG boots, filthy and worn too, but still in sound condition.

Down in the street the air was crisp and cold, and Salo busy with shoppers and office workers hurrying to work. He gave them barely a glance, sliding quickly on to the seat of the German staff car parked at the kerb. Nor did his sightless gaze notice Salo's bustling streets as they set off through the city, the flags of the new *repubblica* flying on municipal buildings, the heavy military presence, or even the azure blue of the sky above the mountains. Instead he sat hunched in the corner, enveloped in the overcoat, with the cloth cap on his head, recalling images at random: a red beret floating down into a mist-filled valley, rings of black ash on the ground, and a train of camels plodding through the desert. He didn't even notice they were travelling east rather than north.

An hour later they entered the suburbs of a city.

'Is this Verona, then?' one German asked the other.

'Sure is. Best flesh-pots in the north, so the sergeant says. Great food too.'

'Christ, look at all the tramps on the streets.'

'Not tramps. Ex-Italian army, come looking for work at the factories.'

'Hundreds, look. A man could just disappear among them if he wanted.'

'Like a flea on a dog.'

They pulled up outside a grocery store. The corporal with the Afrika Korps patch turned to Theo.

'Right.' He grinned. 'We've shopping to do for the mess, if you know what I mean. We'll be gone about an hour. After that it's on to Trento. I take it we can trust you to be sensible while we're away?'

A twitch seemed to have developed in the man's eye, Theo saw, nodding back blankly. Seconds later the doors slammed and he was alone in the car.

He wandered into the old part of the city, pausing here and there to stare at a Roman amphitheatre, a fort on a bridge, and a statue of the poet Dante. As he walked, one battered leg limping, his body still weak, his head numb and dizzy, his hands found the pockets of his overcoat, and pulled out grubby lire notes, and an Italian army pay book belonging to a stranger named Corlotta. Then for a long time he sat on a bench in a piazza beneath a tall clock tower.

'Why are you weeping?' a little girl asked him. 'Are you lost?'

His reply was a nod.

'Then you should go home.'

At the railway station all trains south ended at Rome, so he bought a third-class ticket and sat in a crowded carriage among the old women, itinerant labourers and destitute ex-soldiers. The journey was long and slow. Somewhere in Umbria they stopped for an hour, 'because of partisans', and an old woman gave him a boiled egg to eat, before the train lurched into motion once more, grinding on through a series of tunnels and bridges. Later he fell into fitful sleep but woke to find his neighbours staring at him in alarm. '*Scusi*,' he muttered and went to stand by the door. Long after nightfall the train snaked into dark and oppressive suburbs, he smelled smoke and slums, watched the limestone gate of Porta Maggiore creep pass, and the ruined temple of Minerva, and finally Termini station, where it squealed to a weary halt.

Rione XVI district was a short walk from the station. Dawn found him there, camped beneath a leafless plane tree across the road from his uncle Rodolfo's house. The property was closed up, the door locked, the windows shuttered, and his knocks went unanswered. All morning he waited, shivering in the December wind, while hunger gnawed at his stomach and cats scavenged in the gutter. Eventually a woman pedalled up on a bicycle, produced keys from her belt and let herself in. He rose stiffly to his feet, crossed the road and knocked once more.

'Signor and Signora Zambon have moved away,' she said, eyeing him suspiciously. 'Since all the trouble.'

'Trouble.'

'The overthrow. Rioting and that.'

'Where?'

'North somewhere. Milan. The new government. Who are you?'

'Nobody. The daughter – Renata?'

'Gone all radical. Lives in some Communist doss house in the Tenth. Works for one of the new parties. I forget which; there are so many.'

'You... you're the housekeeper.'

'That's right. I look in on the place, pick up the mail, keep an eye out for trouble. Talking of which, do I know you?'

'I... came to see, the *patrona*. The grandmother. Ellie, I mean Eleanora.'

'Signora Ladurner?' The eyes narrowed. 'She died months ago.'

He flinched. 'What?'

'In the summer. At the *infermeria*. Her mind went. Then she caught the *polmonite* and that was that. Listen, I'm sure I know you from somewhere...'

He turned and walked away, cast adrift with the severing of the last mooring. He wandered, without purpose or direction, for hours, and then days, criss-crossing the city like a leaf in the breeze. Time and place ceased to have meaning. The streets were either in light or darkness, the weather cold, or colder: none of it mattered. If he needed food he scavenged scraps or joined vagrants at the soup kitchen; if he wanted sleep he found a shop doorway or lay on a bench wrapped in newspaper. When the police stopped him he pulled Corlotta's pay book from his pocket and they waved him on. Occasionally people gave him food, or pressed coins into his hands. One woman gave him her dead son's mittens; a priest gave him a scarf and invited him into his church for a night. Others were hostile, scolding him for his laziness or cursing the army's ineptitude. At one point, standing in line at a soup kitchen, a voice started shouting angrily and he found himself corralled into a street-clearing party amid other former *soldati*. He remained with them a few days, toiling with picks and shovels to clear the debris caused by the Allied bombs. Then, picking through the rubble of a ruined house one morning, he lifted masonry to see a child's hand reaching to him from below. Cold, dusty and lifeless, he could only kneel amid the wreckage tightly holding it and weeping uncontrollably until the others pulled him off.

After that he began moving again. Away from Rome, slowly, randomly but always vaguely south, as though pulled on a slender thread. He walked the quieter routes, avoiding main roads in favour of farm tracks and hill passes. By now winter was upon the Apennines and the war in suspension as both sides dug in to wait for spring. Occasionally he saw signs of a patrol, or came across discarded equipment, or heard aircraft passing, but the weather was his main threat now, and repeatedly he found himself struggling through wind-ravaged valleys, fording icy rivers or wading through snow up to his thighs. Progress was slow, his ebbing strength made it slower, and when the storms struck, it stopped altogether and he was forced to shelter in shepherds' huts or farm buildings. Sometimes he knocked on doors and begged food or a roof; mostly he chose to proceed alone, safely cloaked in his solitude.

Driven by demons, steered by instinct, his journey went on. Then one evening, two weeks after leaving Rome, and following a day-long mountain slog through heavy weather, a worsening storm forced him to descend in search of shelter. Exhausted and starving, he staggered down to the treeline and entered thick woodland. There, slithering and stumbling blindly, he looked for crags or crevices to shelter in, or a boulder to burrow behind, while the wind shrieked in torment all round and jostling trees crowded him, swaying and twisting like crazed dancers. And as the darkness gathered and his fatigue overcame him, he knew his journey was done, and the struggle over, and he sank to the ground in grateful release, to await the end.

Then he heard a noise. Like a trumpet calling, or a distant ship, or a horn blown in warning, floating to him faintly on the storm, like a raft on the ocean.

A bull.

He struggled to his feet, and set off down through the woods one final time. After a while the ground began to level beneath his boots, and then he broke out of the trees and into the open and blasts of icy wind stung his face and eyes. Bowing his head, he pushed on towards the roaring sound. He came to flat pasture, thick white with snow, and skirted round to an empty field bounded by posts. This led to a buried track, where shapes began emerging through the drifting white. Chicken huts and pig shelters, then a ramshackle shed and another pen. And within this, tethered to a post, its coat long and shaggy, its broad back blanketed with snow, its huge hooves caked in mud and ice, stood the bull. It eyed him idly for a moment, jaws chewing slowly, before tilting its head back and releasing its trumpet roar once more. A crack of light appeared further on, framing a hunched figure holding a lantern. *'Chi va là?'* it demanded shrilly. Who goes there? He stumbled towards it.

'God's holy name be praised,' Rosa said, seizing his arm. 'Our prayers are answered.'

Keep reading for a preview of

THE BRIDGE

BOOK III

in the

AIRBORNE TRILOGY

CHAPTER 1

A little further and he came to another village, barely a ramshackle cluster of cottages and barns clinging to a hillside. He mopped his brow, squinting up at a brassy noon sun, then entered, following narrow cobbled alleyways to a tiny piazza with a stone water trough and a whitewashed chapel bearing the legend *San Felice*. He sat, filling his water bottle from the trough and massaging his ankle. A rooster crowed, nearby sheep stirred in a pen, and somewhere a dog started barking, but the piazza was empty of human life. Fled the area, he guessed, gazing around, or simply hiding indoors fearful of strangers, as in every village he visited. Pulling the crumpled photo from his pocket, he rose wearily from the trough and approached the nearest door.

Twenty minutes later and having gained nothing but hostile stares and head shakes, he knocked on a door in a narrow alleyway to have it opened by a grey-haired woman of about forty.

'*Scusi Signora*,' he began in his accented Italian, but after the merest hesitation she swung the door in his face. Instinctively his boot jerked forward, wedging the door ajar, for in that moment's hesitation, that fractional hiatus he glimpsed something he'd not seen all day. Recognition. Of the face in the photo. And the fact that she was now cursing him furiously and shouldering the door and kicking at his foot like a madwoman told him for certain she knew who it was.

1

'*Stop!*' he pleaded, '*Cessare! Finire!*'

'*Tedeschi* murderer!'

'*Tedeschi*? Me? No! I'm—'

'You're Gestapo, I can smell it!'

'No, *Signora*, you're wrong. I'm, ow! That's my bad foot!'

'Then get it out of my door!'

'No, but listen . . .'

A gun barrel appeared in the gap, a British one, he noted, Lee Enfield, old but well oiled. Then the wooden stock, gripped firmly in two large and hairy hands.

'Step back,' a gruff voice ordered. 'Right now, or I shoot you dead.'

He wrenched his boot free and stood obediently back, hands raised. Mad kicking women was one thing, menacing husbands with rifles quite another. The door opened wider and a middle-aged man appeared from the shadows, dark and swarthy, hefting the gun in the crook of his arm.

'Who are you?'

'Not what you think, *Signore*, I assure you!'

'Then what?'

'I'm . . . Well, I'm a friend.'

It took another ten tense minutes to convince them, and in that time the rifle never left his chest for a second. Using his pigeon Italian and the photo, and the other documents he'd been given as *bona fides*, and electing wisely not to inflame the situation further by offering the bribe money he'd also been issued with, he recited his story, answered their questions and explained his mission, repeatedly and unwaveringly, until finally they looked at one another and exchanged a dubious nod.

'Very well,' the man warned grimly. 'But if you're lying, and the slightest harm comes to anyone up there . . .'

'I'm not, and it won't, I assure you.'

'But if it does, I will hunt you down and kill you like a dog.'

They gave him water to drink, an onion to chew on, vague

pointing directions, and sent him on his way. The path was long, steeply uphill and in the warm spring sunshine he was soon breathless and sweating once more. His foot too became troublesome and he paused frequently to rest it, gazing up towards the distant hills for signs of human habitation. None appeared until after nearly an hour the path began to level onto a narrow plateau, and became pockmarked with farmyard jumble; rusting buckets, coils of wire, an ox plough. Then a badly painted sign appeared warning strangers to keep away, then suddenly two hunting dogs on chains leapt up from the grass, furiously pulling on their tethers and snarling like wolves. He gave them a wide berth, left the path and struck out in a wide arc that took him into dank chestnut woods smelling of leaf mould and humming with flies. At one point he moved to the forest's edge to glimpse a huge bull penned in a field. It tossed its head and stamped and snorted, and he knew he must be drawing near. Sure enough, ascending further, the trees began to thin at last onto a higher plain, and bordering a sloping field of freshly sown maize. To one side, a second field had been newly marked out, and the coarse soil roughly turned, ready for working. In it a man laboured, bent over, painstakingly clearing stones into piles by hand. Dressed in simple farmer's garb of serge trousers cinched with string, a collarless white shirt, corduroy waistcoat and cap, he moved slowly and looked much slighter and older than he should. Then he stood up to stretch his back, and doffing the cap to dab his brow, tilted his face to the sky, head cocked, as though listening.

And then there was no doubt at all.

THE BRIDGE

will be published in 2019
To keep in touch, sign up for our newsletter at
www.headofzeus.com